In the Days of My Youth

Amelia Ann Blandford Edwards

Contents

IN THE DAYS OF MY YOUTH

BY

Amelia Ann Blandford Edwards

CHAPTER I.
MY BIRTHPLACE AND PARENTAGE.

Dolce sentier,
Colle, che mi piacesti,
Ov'ancor per usanza amor mi mena!
PETRARCH.

Sweet, secluded, shady Saxonholme! I doubt if our whole England contains another hamlet so quaint, so picturesquely irregular, so thoroughly national in all its rustic characteristics. It lies in a warm hollow environed by hills. Woods, parks and young plantations clothe every height and slope for miles around, whilst here and there, peeping down through green vistas, or towering above undulating seas of summer foliage, stands many a fine old country mansion, turreted and gabled, and built of that warm red brick that seems to hold the light of the sunset long after it has faded from the rest of the landscape. A silver thread of streamlet, swift but shallow, runs noisily through the meadows beside the town and loses itself in the Chad, about a mile and a half farther eastward. Many a picturesque old wooden bridge, many a foaming weir and ruinous water-mill with weedy wheel, may be found scattered up and down the wooded banks of this little river Chad; while to the brook, which we call the Gipstream, attaches a vague tradition of trout.

The hamlet itself is clean and old-fashioned, consisting of one long, straggling street, and a few tributary lanes and passages. The houses some few years back were mostly long and low-fronted, with projecting upper stories, and diamond-paned bay-windows bowered in with myrtle and clematis; but modern improvements have done much of late to sweep away these antique tenements, and a fine new suburb of Italian and Gothic villas has sprung up, between the town and the railway station. Besides this, we have a new church in the mediaeval style, rich in gilding and colors and thirteenth-century brass-work; and a new cemetery, laid out like a pleasure-garden; and a new school-house, where the children are taught upon a system with a foreign name; and a Mechanics' Institute, where London professors come down at long intervals to expound popular science, and where agriculturists meet to discuss popular grievances.

At the other extremity of the town, down by Girdlestone Grange, an old moated residence where the squire's family have resided these four centuries past, we are full fifty years behind our modern neighbors. Here stands our famous old "King's-head Inn," a well-known place of resort so early as the reign of Elizabeth. The great oak beside the porch is as old as the house itself; and on the windows of a little disused parlor overlooking the garden may still be seen the names of Sedley, Rochester and other wits of the Restoration. They scrawled those autographs after dinner, most likely, with their diamond rings, and went reeling afterwards, arm-in-arm, along the village street, singing and swearing, and eager for adventures--as gentlemen were wont to be in those famous old times when they drank the king's health more freely than was good for their own.

Not far from the "King's Head," and almost hidden by the trees which divide it from the road, stands an ancient charitable institution called the College--quadrangular, mullion-windowed, many-gabled, and colonized by some twenty aged people of both sexes. At the back of the college, adjoining a space of waste ground and some ruined cloisters, lies the churchyard, in the midst of which, surrounded by solemn yews and mouldering tombs, stands the Priory Church. It is a rare old church, founded, according to the county history, in the reign of Edward the Confessor, and entered with a full description in Domesday Book. Its sculptured monuments and precious brasses, its Norman crypt, carved stalls and tattered banners drooping over faded scutcheons, tell all of generations long gone by, of noble families extinct, of gallant deeds forgotten, of knights and ladies remembered only by the names above their graves. Amongst these, some two or three modest tablets record the passing away of several generations of my own predecessors--obscure professional men for the most part, of whom some few became soldiers and died abroad.

In close proximity to the church stands the vicarage, once the Priory; a quaint old rambling building, surrounded by magnificent old trees. Here for long centuries, a tribe of rooks have held undisputed possession, filling the boughs with their nests and the air with their voices, and, like genuine lords of the soil, descending at their own grave will and pleasure upon the adjacent lands.

Picturesque and mediaeval as all these old buildings and old associations help to make us, we of Saxonholme pretend to something more. We claim to be, not only picturesque but historic. Nay, more than this--we are classical. WE WERE FOUNDED BY THE ROMANS. A great Roman road, well known to antiquaries, passed transversely through the old churchyard. Roman coins and relics, and fragments of tesselated pavement, have been found in and about the town. Roman camps may be traced on most of the heights around. Above all, we are said to be indebted to the Romans for that inestimable breed of poultry in right of which we have for years carried off the leading prizes at every poultry-show in the county, and have even been enabled to make head against the exaggerated pretensions of modern Cochin-China interlopers.

Such, briefly sketched, is my native Saxonholme. Born beneath the shade of its towering trees and overhanging eaves, brought up to reverence its antiquities, and educated in the love of its natural beauties, what wonder that I cling to it with every fibre of my heart, and even when affecting to smile at my own fond prejudice, continue to believe it the loveliest peacefulest nook in rural England?

My father's name was John Arbuthnot. Sprung from the Arbuthnots of Montrose, we claim to derive from a common ancestor with the celebrated author of "Martinus Scriblerus." Indeed, the first of our name who settled at Saxonholme was one James Arbuthnot, son to a certain nonjuring parson Arbuthnot, who lived and died abroad, and was own brother to that famous wit, physician and courtier whose genius, my father was wont to say, conferred a higher distinction upon our branch of the family than did those Royal Letters-Patent whereby the elder stock was ennobled by His most Gracious Majesty King George the Fourth, on the occasion of his visit to Edinburgh in 1823. From this James Arbuthnot (who, being born and bred at St. Omer, and married, moreover, to a French wife, was himself half a Frenchman) we Saxonholme Arbuthnots were the direct descendants.

Our French ancestress, according to the family tradition, was of no very exalted origin, being in fact the only daughter and heiress of one Monsieur Tartine,

Perruquier in chief at the Court of Versailles. But what this lady wanted in birth, she made up in fortune, and the modest estate which her husband purchased with her dowry came down to us unimpaired through five generations. In the substantial and somewhat foreign-looking red-brick house which he built (also, doubtless, with Madame's Louis d'ors) we, his successors, had lived and died ever since. His portrait, together with the portraits of his wife, son, and grandson, hung on the dining-room walls; and of the quaint old spindle-legged chairs and tables that had adorned our best rooms from time immemorial, some were supposed to date as far back as the first founding and furnishing of the house.

It is almost needless to say that the son of the non-juror and his immediate posterity were staunch Jacobites, one and all. I am not aware that they ever risked or suffered anything for the cause; but they were not therefore the less vehement. Many were the signs and tokens of that dead-and-gone political faith which these loyal Arbuthnots left behind them. In the bed-rooms there hung prints of King James the Second at the Battle of the Boyne; of the Royal Martyr with his plumed hat, lace collar, and melancholy fatal face; of the Old and Young Pretenders; of the Princess Louisa Teresia, and of the Cardinal York. In the library were to be found all kinds of books relating to the career of that unhappy family: "Ye Tragicall History of ye Stuarts, 1697;" "Memoirs of King James II., writ by his own hand;" "La Stuartide," an unfinished epic in the French language by one Jean de Schelandre; "The Fate of Majesty exemplified in the barbarous and disloyal treatment (by traitorous and undutiful subjects) of the Kings and Queens of the Royal House of Stuart," genealogies of the Stuarts in English, French and Latin; a fine copy of "Eikon Basilike," bound in old red morocco, with the royal arms stamped upon the cover; and many other volumes on the same subject, the names of which (although as a boy I was wont to pore over their contents with profound awe and sympathy) I have now for the most part forgotten.

Most persons, I suppose, have observed how the example of a successful ancestor is apt to determine the pursuits of his descendants down to the third and fourth generations, inclining the lads of this house to the sea, and of that to the bar, according as the great man of the family achieved his honors on shipboard, or climbed his way to the woolsack. The Arbuthnots offered no exception to this very natural law of selection. They could not help remembering how the famous doctor had excelled in literature as in medicine; how he had been not only Physician in Ordinary to Queen Anne and Prince George of Denmark, but a satirist and pamphleteer, a wit and the friend of wits--of such wits as Pope and Swift, Harley and Bolingbroke. Hence they took, as it were instinctively, to physic and the **belles lettres**, and were never without a doctor or an author in the family.

My father, however, like the great Martinus Scriblerus, was both doctor and author. And he was a John Arbuthnot. And to carry the resemblance still further, he was gifted with a vein of rough epigrammatic humor, in which it pleased his independence to indulge without much respect of persons, times, or places. His tongue, indeed, cost him some friends and gained him some enemies; but I am not sure that it diminished his popularity as a physician. People compared him to Abernethy, whereby he was secretly flattered. Some even went so far as to argue that only a very clever man could afford to be a bear; and I must say that he pushed this conclusion to its farthest limit, showing his temper alike to rich and poor upon no provocation whatever. He cared little, to be sure, for his connection. He loved the profession theoretically, and from a scientific point of view; but he disliked the drudgery of country practice, and stood in no need of its hardly-earned profits. Yet he was a man who so loved to indulge his humor, no matter at what cost, that I doubt whether he would have been more courteous had his bread depended on it. As it was, he practised and grumbled, snarled at his patients, quarrelled with the rich, bestowed his time and money liberally upon the poor, and amused his leisure by writing for a variety of scientific periodicals, both English and foreign.

Our home stood at the corner of a lane towards the eastern extremity of the town, commanding a view of the Squire's Park, and a glimpse of the mill-pool and meadows in the valley beyond. This lane led up to Barnard's Green, a breezy space of high, uneven ground dedicated to fairs, cricket matches, and travelling circuses, whence the noisy music of brass bands, and the echoes of alternate laughter and applause, were wafted past our windows in the summer evenings. We had a large garden at the back, and a stable up the lane; and though the house was but one story in height, it covered a considerable space of ground, and contained more rooms than we ever had occasion to use. Thus it happened that since my mother's death, which took place when I was a very little boy, many doors on the upper floor were kept locked, to the undue development of my natural inquisitiveness by day, and my mortal terror when sent to bed at night. In one of these her portrait still hung above the mantelpiece, and her harp stood in its accustomed corner. In another, which was once her bedroom, everything was left as in her lifetime, her clothes yet hanging in the wardrobe, her dressing-case standing upon the toilet, her favorite book upon the table beside the bed. These things, told to me by the servants with much mystery, took a powerful hold upon my childish imagination. I trembled as I passed the closed doors at dusk, and listened fearfully outside when daylight gave me courage to linger near them. Something of my mother's presence, I fancied, must yet dwell within--something in her shape still wander from room to room in the dim moonlight, and echo back the sighing of the night winds. Alas! I could not remember her. Now and then, as if recalled by a dream, some broken and shadowy images of a pale face and a slender hand floated vaguely through my mind; but faded even as I strove to realize them. Sometimes, too, when I was falling off to sleep in my little bed, or making out pictures in the fire on a winter evening, strange fragments of old rhymes seemed to come back upon me, mingled with the tones of a soft voice and the haunting of a long-forgotten melody. But these, after all, were yearnings more of the heart than the memory:--

> "I felt a mother-want about the world.
> And still went seeking."

To return to my description of my early home:--the two rooms on either side of the hall, facing the road, were appropriated by my father for his surgery and consulting-room; while the two corresponding rooms at the back were fitted up as our general reception-room, and my father's bed-room. In the former of these, and in the weedy old garden upon which it opened, were passed all the days of my boyhood.

It was my father's good-will and pleasure to undertake the sole charge of my education. Fain would I have gone like other lads of my age to public school and college; but on this point, as on most others, he was inflexible. Himself an obscure physician in a remote country town, he brought me up with no other view than to be his own successor. The profession was not to my liking. Somewhat contemplative and nervous by nature, there were few pursuits for which I was less fitted. I knew this, but dared not oppose him. Loving study for its own sake, and trusting to the future for some lucky turn of destiny, I yielded to that which seemed inevitable, and strove to make the best of it.

Thus it came to pass that I lived a quiet, hard-working home life, while other boys of my age were going through the joyous experience of school, and chose my companions from the dusty shelves of some three or four gigantic book-cases, instead of from the class and the playground. Not that I regret it. I believe, on the contrary, that a boy may have worse companions than books and busts, employments less healthy than the study of anatomy, and amusements more pernicious than Shakespeare and Horace. Thank Heaven! I escaped all such; and if, as I have been told, my boyhood was unboyish, and my youth prematurely cultivated, I am content to have been spared the dangers in exchange for the pleasures of a public school.

I do not, however, pretend to say that I did not sometimes pine for the recreations common to my age. Well do I remember the manifold attractions of Barnard's Green. What longing glances I used to steal towards the boisterous cricketers, when going gravely forth upon a botanical walk with my father! With what eager curiosity have I not lingered many a time before the entrance to a forbidden booth, and scanned the scenic advertisement of a travelling show! Alas! how the charms of study paled before those intervals of brief but bitter temptation! What, then, was pathology compared to the pig-faced lady, or the Materia Medica to Smith's Mexican Circus, patronized by all the sovereigns of Europe? But my father was inexorable. He held that such places were, to use his own words, "opened by swindlers for the ruin of fools," and from one never-to-be-forgotten hour, when he caught me in the very act of taking out my penny-worth at a portable peep-show, he bound me over by a solemn promise (sealed by a whipping) never to repeat the offence under any provocation or pretext whatsoever. I was a tiny fellow in pinafores when this happened, but having once pledged my word, I kept it faithfully through all the studious years that lay between six and sixteen.

At sixteen an immense crisis occurred in my life. I fell in love. I had been in love several times before--chiefly with the elder pupils at the Miss Andrews' establishment; and once (but that was when I was very young indeed) with the cook. This, however, was a much more romantic and desperate affair. The lady was a Columbine by profession, and as beautiful as an angel. She came down to our neighbor-hood with a strolling company, and performed every evening, in a temporary the-atre on the green, for nearly three weeks. I used to steal out after dinner when my father was taking his nap, and run the whole way, that I might be in time to see the object of my adoration walking up and down the platform outside the booth before the performances commenced. This incomparable creature wore a blue petticoat spangled with tinfoil, and a wreath of faded poppies. Her age might have been about forty. I thought her the loveliest of created beings. I wrote sonnets to her--dozens of them--intending to leave them at the theatre door, but never finding the courage to do it. I made up bouquets for her, over and over again, chosen from the best flowers in our neglected garden; but invariably with the same result. I hated the harlequin who presumed to put his arm about her waist. I envied the clown, whom she con-descended to address as Mr. Merriman. In short, I was so desperately in love that I even tried to lie awake at night and lose my appetite; but, I am ashamed to own, failed signally in both endeavors.

At length I wrote to her. I can even now recall passages out of that passion-ate epistle. I well remember how it took me a whole morning to write it; how I crammed it with quotations from Horace; and how I fondly compared her to most of the mythological divinities. I then copied it out on pale pink paper, folded it in the form of a heart, and directed it to Miss Angelina Lascelles, and left it, about dusk, with the money-taker at the pit door. I signed myself, if I remember rightly, Pyramus. What would I not have given that evening to pay my sixpence like the rest of the audience, and feast my eyes upon her from some obscure corner! What would I not have given to add my quota to the applause!

I could hardly sleep that night; I could hardly read or write, or eat my breakfast the next morning, for thinking of my letter and its probable effect. It never once occurred to me that my Angelina might possibly find it difficult to construe Horace. Towards evening, I escaped again, and flew to Barnard's Green. It wanted nearly an hour to the time of performance; but the tuning of a violin was audible from within, and the money-taker was already there with his pipe in his mouth and his hands in his pockets. I had no courage to address that functionary; but I lingered in his sight and sighed audibly, and wandered round and round the canvas walls that hedged my divinity. Presently he took his pipe out of, his mouth and his hands out of his pockets; surveyed me deliberately from head to foot, and said:--

"Hollo there! aint you the party that brought a three-cornered letter here last evening!"

I owned it, falteringly.

He lifted a fold in the canvas, and gave me a gentle shove between the shoulders.

"Then you're to go in," said he, shortly. "She's there, somewhere. You're sure to find her."

The canvas dropped behind me, and I found myself inside. My heart beat so fast that I could scarcely breathe. The booth was almost dark; the curtain was down; and a gentleman with striped legs was lighting the footlamps. On the front pit bench next the orchestra, discussing a plate of bread and meat and the contents of a brown jug, sat a stout man in shirt-sleeves and a woman in a cotton gown. The woman rose as I made my appearance, and asked, civilly enough, whom I pleased to want.

I stammered the name of Miss Angelina Lascelles.

"Miss Lascelles!" she repeated. "I am Miss Lascelles," Then, looking at me more narrowly, "I suppose," she added, "you are the little boy that brought the letter?"

The little boy that brought the letter! Gracious heavens! And this middle-aged woman in a cotton gown--was she the Angelina of my dreams! The booth went round with me, and the lights danced before my eyes.

"If you have come for an answer," she continued, "you may just say to your Mr. Pyramid that I am a respectable married woman, and he ought to be ashamed of himself--and, as for his letter, I never read such a heap of nonsense in my life! There, you can go out by the way you came in, and if you take my advice, you won't come back again!"

How I looked, what I said, how I made my exit, whether the doorkeeper spoke to me as I passed, I have no idea to this day. I only know that I flung myself on the dewy grass under a great tree in the first field I came to, and shed tears of such shame, disappointment, and wounded pride, as my eyes had never known before. She had called me a little boy, and my letter a heap of nonsense! She was elderly-- she was ignorant--she was married! I had been a fool; but that knowledge came too late, and was not consolatory.

By-and-by, while I was yet sobbing and disconsolate, I heard the drumming and fifing which heralded the appearance of the ***Corps Dramatique*** on the outer platform. I resolved to see her for the last time. I pulled my hat over my eyes, went back to the Green, and mingled with the crowd outside the booth. It was growing dusk. I made my way to the foot of the ladder, and observed her narrowly. I saw that her ankles were thick, and her elbows red. The illusion was all over. The spangles had lost their lustre, and the poppies their glow. I no longer hated the harlequin, or envied the clown, or felt anything but mortification at my own folly.

"Miss Angelina Lascelles, indeed!" I said to myself, as I sauntered moodily home. "Pshaw! I shouldn't wonder if her name was Snooks!"

CHAPTER II.
THE LITTLE CHEVALIER.

A mere anatomy, a mountebank,
A threadbare juggler.
Comedy of Errors.

Nay, then, he is a conjuror.
Henry VI.

My adventure with Miss Lascelles did me good service, and cured me for some time, at least, of my leaning towards the tender passion. I consequently devoted myself more closely than ever to my studies--indulged in a passing mania for genealogy and heraldry--began a collection of local geological specimens, all of which I threw away at the end of the first fortnight--and took to rearing rabbits in an old tumble-down summer-house at the end of the garden. I believe that from somewhere about this time I may also date the commencement of a great epic poem in blank verse, and Heaven knows how many cantos, which was to be called the Columbiad. It began, I remember, with a description of the Court of Ferdinand and Isabella, and the departure of Columbus, and was intended to celebrate the discovery, colonization, and subsequent history of America. I never got beyond ten or a dozen pages of the first canto, however, and that Transatlantic epic remains unfinished to this day.

The great event which I have recorded in the preceding chapter took place in the early summer. It must, therefore, have been towards the close of autumn in the same year when my next important adventure befell. This time the temptation assumed a different shape.

Coming briskly homewards one fine frosty morning after having left a note at the Vicarage, I saw a bill-sticker at work upon a line of dead wall which at that time reached from the Red Lion Inn to the corner of Pitcairn's Lane. His posters were printed in enormous type, and decorated with a florid bordering in which the signs of the zodiac conspicuously figured Being somewhat idly disposed, I followed the example of other passers-by, and lingered to watch the process and read the advertisement. It ran as follows:----

MAGIC AND MYSTERY! MAGIC AND MYSTERY!

*   *   *   *   *

M. LE CHEVALIER ARMAND PROUDHINE, (of Paris) surnamed
THE WIZARD OF THE CAUCASUS,
Has the honor to announce to the Nobility and Gentry of Saxonholme and its vicinity, that he will, to-morrow evening (October--, 18--), hold his First
SOIREE FANTASTIQUE
IN
THE LARGE ROOM OF THE RED LION HOTEL.

*   *   *   *   *

ADMISSION 1s. RESERVED SEATS 2s. 6d.
To commence at Seven.
N.B.--*The performance will include a variety of new and surprising feats of Legerdemain never before exhibited*.

A soiree fantastique! what would I not give to be present at a ***soiree fantastique***! I had read of the Rosicrucians, of Count Cagliostro, and of Doctor Dee. I had peeped into more than one curious treatise on Demonology, and I fancied there could be nothing in the world half so marvellous as that last surviving branch of the Black Art entitled the Science of Legerdemain.

What if, for this once, I were to ask leave to be present at the performance? Should I do so with even the remotest chance of success? It was easier to propound this momentous question than to answer it. My father, as I have already said, disapproved of public entertainments, and his prejudices were tolerably inveterate. But then, what could be more genteel than the programme, or more select than the prices? How different was an entertainment given in the large room of the Red Lion Hotel to a three-penny wax-work, or a strolling circus on Barnard's Green! I had made one of the audience in that very room over and over again when the Vicar read his celebrated "Discourses to Youth," or Dr. Dunks came down from Grinstead to deliver an explosive lecture on chemistry; and I had always seen the reserved seats filled by the best families in the neighborhood. Fully persuaded of the force of my own arguments, I made up my mind to prefer this tremendous request on the first favorable opportunity, and so hurried home, with my head full of quite other thoughts than usual.

My father was sitting at the table with a mountain of books and papers before him. He looked up sharply as I entered, jerked his chair round so as to get the light at his back, put on his spectacles, and ejaculated:--

"Well, sir!"

This was a bad sign, and one with which I was only too familiar. Nature had intended my father for a barrister. He was an adept in all the arts of intimidation, and would have conducted a cross-examination to perfection. As it was, he indulged in a good deal of amateur practice, and from the moment when he turned his back to the light and donned the inexorable spectacles, there was not a soul in the house, from myself down to the errand-boy, who was not perfectly aware of something unpleasant to follow.

"Well, sir!" he repeated, rapping impatiently upon the table with his knuckles.

Having nothing to reply to this greeting, I looked out of the window and remained silent; whereby, unfortunately. I irritated him still more.

"Confound you, sir!" he exclaimed, "have you nothing to say?"

"Nothing," I replied, doggedly.

"Stand there!" he said, pointing to a particular square in the pattern of the carpet. "Stand there!"

I obeyed.

"And now, perhaps, you will have the goodness to explain what you have been about this morning; and why it should have taken you just thirty-seven minutes by the clock to accomplish a journey which a tortoise--yes, sir, a tortoise,--might have done in less than ten?"

I gravely compared my watch with the clock before replying.

"Upon my word, sir," I said, "your tortoise would have the advantage of me."

"The advantage of you! What do you mean by the advantage of you, you affected puppy?"

"I had no idea," said I, provokingly, "that you were in unusual haste this morning."

"Haste!" shouted my father. "I never said I was in haste. I never choose to be in haste. I hate haste!"

"Then why..."

"Because you have been wasting your time and mine, sir," interrupted he. "Because I will not permit you to go idling and vagabondizing about the village."

My *sang froid* was gone directly.

"Idling and vagabondizing!" I repeated angrily. "I have done nothing of the kind. I defy you to prove it. When have you known me forget that I am a gentleman?"

"Humph!" growled my father, mollified but sarcastic; "a pretty gentleman--a gentleman of sixteen!"

"It is true,"' I continued, without heeding the interruption, "that I lingered for a moment to read a placard by the way; but if you will take the trouble, sir, to inquire at the Rectory, you will find that I waited a quarter of an hour before I could send up your letter."

My father grinned and rubbed his hands. If there was one thing in the world that aggravated him more than another, it was to find his fire opposed to ice. Let him, however, succeed in igniting his adversary, and he was in a good humor directly.

"Come, come, Basil," said he, taking off his spectacles, "I never said you were not a good lad. Go to your books, boy--go to your books; and this evening I will examine you in vegetable physiology."

Silently, but not sullenly, I drew a chair to the table, and resumed my work. We were both satisfied, because each in his heart considered himself the victor. My father was amused at having irritated me, whereas I was content because he had, in some sort, withdrawn the expressions that annoyed me. Hence we both became good-tempered, and, according to our own tacit fashion, continued during the rest of that morning to be rather more than usually sociable.

Hours passed thus--hours of quiet study, during which the quick travelling of a pen or the occasional turning of a page alone disturbed the silence. The warm sunlight which shone in so greenly through the vine leaves, stole, inch by inch, round the broken vases in the garden beyond, and touched their brown mosses with a golden bloom. The patient shadow on the antique sundial wound its way imperceptibly from left to right, and long slanting threads of light and shadow pierced in time between the branches of the poplars. Our mornings were long, for we rose early and dined late; and while my father paid professional visits, I devoted my hours to study. It rarely happened that he could thus spend a whole day among his books. Just as the clock struck four, however, there came a ring at the bell.

My father settled himself obstinately in his chair.

"If that's a gratis patient," said he, between his teeth, "I'll not stir. From eight to ten are their hours, confound them!"

"If you please, sir," said Mary, peeping in, "if you please, sir, it's a gentleman."

"A stranger?" asked my father.

Mary nodded, put her hand to her mouth, and burst into an irrepressible giggle.

"If you please, sir," she began--but could get no farther.

My father was in a towering passion directly.

"Is the girl mad?" he shouted. "What is the meaning of this buffoonery?"

"Oh, sir--if you please, sir," ejaculated Mary, struggling with terror and laughter together, "it's the gentleman, sir. He--he says, if you please, sir, that his name is Almond Pudding!"

"Your pardon, Mademoiselle," said a plaintive voice. "Armand Proudhine--le Chevalier Armand Proudhine, at your service."

Mary disappeared with her apron to her mouth, and subsided into distant peals of laughter, leaving the Chevalier standing in the doorway.

He was a very little man, with a pinched and melancholy countenance, and an eye as wistful as a dog's. His threadbare clothes, made in the fashion of a dozen years before, had been decently mended in many places. A paste pin in a faded cravat, and a jaunty cane with a pinchbeck top, betrayed that he was still somewhat of a beau. His scant gray hair was tied behind with a piece of black ribbon, and he carried his hat under his arm, after the fashion of Elliston and the Prince Regent, as one sees them in the colored prints of fifty years ago.

He advanced a step, bowed, and laid his card upon the table.

"I believe," he said in his plaintive voice, and imperfect English, "that I have the honor to introduce myself to Monsieur Arbuthnot."

"If you want me, sir," said my father, gruffly, "I am Doctor Arbuthnot."

"And I, Monsieur," said the little Frenchman, laying his hand upon his heart, and bowing again--"I am the Wizard of the Caucasus."

"The what?" exclaimed my father.

"The Wizard of the Caucasus," replied our visitor, impressively.

There was an awkward pause, during which my father looked at me and touched his forehead significantly with his forefinger; while the Chevalier, embarrassed between his natural timidity and his desire to appear of importance, glanced from one face to the other, and waited for a reply. I hastened to disentangle the situation.

"I think I can explain this gentleman's meaning," I said. "Monsieur le Chevalier will perform to-morrow evening in the large room of the Red Lion Hotel. He is a professor of legerdemain."

"Of the marvellous art of legerdemain, Monsieur Arbuthnot," interrupted the Chevalier eagerly. "Prestidigitateur to the Court of Sachsenhausen, and successor to Al Hakim, the wise. It is I, Monsieur, that have invent the famous *tour du pistolet;* it is I, that have originate the great and surprising deception of the bottle; it is I whom the world does surname the Wizard of the Caucasus. *Me voici!*"

Carried away by the force of his own eloquence, the Chevalier fell into an attitude at the conclusion of his little speech; but remembering where he was, blushed, and bowed again.

"Pshaw," said my father impatiently, "the man's a conjuror."

The little Frenchman did not hear him. He was at that moment untying a packet which he carried in his hat, the contents whereof appeared to consist of a number of very small pink and yellow cards. Selecting a couple of each color, he deposited his hat carefully upon the floor and came a few steps nearer to the table.

"Monsieur will give me the hope to see him, with Monsieur *son fils*, at my

Soiree Fantastique, *n'est-ce pas?*" he asked, timidly.

"Sir," said my father shortly, "I never encourage peripatetic mendicity."

The little Frenchman looked puzzled.

"*Comment?*" said he, and glanced to me for an explanation.

"I am very sorry, Monsieur," I interposed hastily; "but my father objects to public entertainments."

"*Ah, mon Dieu!* but not to this," cried the Chevalier, raising his hands and eyes in deprecating astonishment. "Not to my Soiree Fantastique! The art of legerdemain, Monsieur, is not immoral. He is graceful--he is surprising--he is innocent; and, Monsieur, he is patronized by the Church; he is patronized by your amiable *Cure*, Monsieur le Docteur Brand."

"Oh, father," I exclaimed, "Dr. Brand has taken tickets!"

"And pray, sir, what's that to me?" growled my father, without looking up from the book which he had ungraciously resumed. "Let Dr. Brand make a fool of himself, if he pleases. I'm not bound to do the same."

The Chevalier blushed crimson--not with humility this time, but with pride. He gathered the cards into his pocket, took up his hat, and saying stiffly--"*Monsieur, je vous demande pardon.*"--moved towards the door.

On the threshold he paused, and turning towards me with an air of faded dignity:--"Young gentleman," he said, "*you* I thank for your politeness."

He seemed as if he would have said more--hesitated--became suddenly livid--put his hand to his head, and leaned for support against the wall.

My father was up and beside him in an instant. We carried rather than led him to the sofa, untied his cravat, and administered the necessary restoratives. He was all but insensible for some moments. Then the color came back to his lips, and he sighed heavily.

"An attack of the nerves," he said, shaking his head feebly. "An attack of the nerves, Messieurs."

My father looked doubtful.

"Are you often taken in this way?" he asked, with unusual gentleness.

"*Mais oui*, Monsieur," admitted the Frenchman, reluctantly. "He does often arrive to me. Not--not that he is dangerous. Ah, bah! *Pas du tout!*"

"Humph!" ejaculated my father, more doubtfully than before. "Let me feel your pulse."

The Chevalier bowed and submitted, watching the countenance of the operator all the time with an anxiety that was not lost upon me.

"Do you sleep well?" asked my father, holding the fragile little wrist between his finger and thumb.

"Passably, Monsieur."

"Dream much?"

"Ye--es, I dream."

"Are you subject to giddiness?"

The Chevalier shrugged his shoulders and looked uneasy.

"*C'est vrai*" he acknowledged, more unwillingly than ever, "*J'ai des vertiges*."

My father relinquished his hold and scribbled a rapid prescription.

"There, sir," said he, "get that preparation made up, and when you next feel as you felt just now, drink a wine-glassful. I should recommend you to keep some always at hand, in case of emergency. You will find further directions on the other side."

The little Frenchman attempted to get up with his usual vivacity; but was obliged to balance himself against the back of a chair.

"Monsieur," said he, with another of his profound bows, "I thank you infinitely. You make me too much attention; but I am grateful. And, Monsieur, my little girl--my child that is far away across the sea--she thanks you also. *Elle m'aime, Monsieur--elle m'aime, cette pauvre petite*! What shall she do if I die?"

Again he raised his hand to his brow. He was unconscious of anything theatrical in the gesture. He was in sad earnest, and his eyes were wet with tears, which he made no effort to conceal.

My father shuffled restlessly in his chair.

"No obligation--no obligation at all," he muttered, with a touch of impatience in his voice. "And now, what about those tickets? I suppose, Basil, you're dying to see all this tomfoolery?"

"That I am, sir," said I, joyfully. "I should like it above all things!"

The Chevalier glided forward, and laid a couple of little pink cards upon my father's desk.

"If," said he, timidly, "if Monsieur will make me the honor to accept...."

"Not for the world, sir--not for the world!" interposed my father. "The boy shan't go, unless I pay for the tickets."

"But, Monsieur...."

"Nothing of the kind, sir. I cannot hear of it. What are the prices of the seats?"

Our little visitor looked down and was silent; but I replied for him.

"The reserved seats," I whispered, "are half-a-crown each."

"Then I will take eight reserved," said my father, opening a drawer in his desk and bringing out a bright, new sovereign.

The little Frenchman started. He could hardly believe in such munificence.

"When? How much?" stammered he, with a pleasant confusion of adverbs.

"Eight," growled my father, scarcely able to repress a smile.

"Eight? **mon Dieu**, Monsieur, how you are generous! I shall keep for you all the first row."

"Oblige me by doing nothing of the kind," said my father, very decisively. "It would displease me extremely."

The Chevalier counted out the eight little pink cards, and ranged them in a row beside my father's desk.

"Count them, Monsieur, if you please," said he, his eyes wandering involuntarily towards the sovereign.

My father did so with much gravity, and handed over the money.

The Chevalier consigned it, with trembling fingers, to a small canvas bag, which looked very empty, and which came from the deepest recesses of his pocket.

"Monsieur," said he, "my thanks are in my heart. I will not fatigue you with them. Good-morning."

He bowed again, for perhaps the twentieth time; lingered a moment at the threshold; and then retired, closing the door softly after him.

My father rubbbed his head all over, and gave a great yawn of satisfaction.

"I am so much obliged to you, sir," I said, eagerly.

"What for?"

"For having bought those tickets. It was very kind of you."

"Hold your tongue. I hate to be thanked," snarled he, and plunged back again into his books and papers.

Once more the studious silence in the room--once more the rustling leaf and scratching pen, which only made the stillness seem more still, within and without.

"I beg your pardons," murmured the voice of the little Chevalier.

I turned, and saw him peeping through the half-open door. He looked more wistful than ever, and twisted the handle nervously between his fingers.

My father frowned, and muttered something between his teeth. I fear it was not very complimentary to the Chevalier.

"One word, Monsieur," pleaded the little man, edging himself round the door, "one small word!"

"Say it, sir, and have done with it," said my father, savagely.

The Chevalier hesitated.

"I--I--Monsieur le Docteur--that is, I wish...."

"Confound it, sir, what do you wish?"

The Chevalier brushed away a tear.

"***Dites-moi,***" he said with suppressed agitation. "One word--yes or no--is he dangerous?"

My father's countenance softened.

"My good friend," he said, gently, "we are none of us safe for even a day, or an hour; but after all, that which we call danger is merely a relative position. I have known men in a state more precarious than yours who lived to a long old age, and I see no reason to doubt that with good living, good spirits, and precaution, you stand as fair a chance as another."

The little Frenchman pressed his hands together in token of gratitude, whispered a broken word or two of thanks, and bowed himself out of the room.

When he was fairly gone, my father flung a book at my head, and said, with more brevity than politeness:--

"Boy, bolt the door."

CHAPTER III.
THE EVENTS OF AN EVENING.

Basil, my boy, if you are going to that place, you must take Collins with you."

"Won't you go yourself, father?"

"I! Is the boy mad!"

"I hope not, sir; only as you took eight reserved seats, I thought...."

"You've no business to think, sir! Seven of those tickets are in the fire."

"For fear, then, you should fancy to burn the eighth, I'll wish you good-evening!"

So away I darted, called to Collins to follow me, and set off at a brisk pace towards the Red Lion Hotel. Collins was our indoor servant; a sharp, merry fellow, some ten years older than myself, who desired no better employment than to escort me upon such an occasion as the present. The audience had begun to assemble when we arrived. Collins went into the shilling places, while I ensconced myself in the second row of reserved seats. I had an excellent view of the stage. There, in the middle of the platform, stood the conjuror's table--a quaint, cabalistic-looking piece of furniture with carved black legs and a deep bordering of green cloth all round the top. A gay pagoda-shaped canopy of many hues was erected overhead. A long white wand leaned up against the wall. To the right stood a bench laden with mysterious jars, glittering bowls, gilded cones, mystical globes, colored glass boxes, and other properties. To the left stood a large arm-chair covered with crimson cloth. All this was very exciting, and I waited breathlessly till the Wizard should appear.

He came at last; but not, surely, our dapper little visitor of yesterday! A majestic beard of ashen gray fell in patriarchal locks almost to his knees. Upon his head he wore a high cap of some dark fur; upon his feet embroidered slippers; and round his waist a glittering belt patterned with hieroglyphics. A long woollen robe of chocolate and orange fell about him in heavy folds, and swept behind him, like a train. I could scarcely believe, at first, that it was the same person; but, when he spoke, despite the pomp and obscurity of his language. I recognised the plaintive voice of the little Chevalier.

"*Messieurs et Mesdames*," he began, and took up the wand to emphasize his discourse; "to read in the stars the events of the future--to transform into gold the metals inferior--to discover the composition of that Elixir who, by himself, would perpetuate life, was in past ages the aim and aspiration of the natural philosopher. But they are gone, those days--they are displaced, those sciences. The Alchemist and the Rosicrucian are no more, and of all their race, the professor of Legerdemain alone survives. Ladies and gentlemen, my magic he is simple. I retain not familiars. I employ not crucible, nor furnace, nor retort. I but amuse you with my agility of hand, and for commencement I tell you that you shall be deceived as well as the Wizard of the Caucasus can deceive you."

His voice trembled, and the slender wand shivered in his hand. Was this nervousness? Or was he, in accordance with the quaintness of his costume and the amplitude of his beard, enacting the feebleness of age?

He advanced to the front of the platform. "Three things I require," he said. "A watch, a pocket-handkerchief and a hat. Is there here among my visitors any person so gracious as to lend me these trifles? I will not injure them, ladies and gentlemen. I will only pound the watch in my mortar--burn the *mouchoir* in my lamp, and make a pudding in the *chapeau*. And, with all this, I engage to return them to their proprietors, better as new."

There was a pause, and a laugh. Presently a gentleman volunteered his hat, and a lady her embroidered handkerchief; but no person seemed willing to submit his watch to the pounding process.

"Shall nobody lend me the watch?" asked the Chevalier; but in a voice so hoarse that I scarcely recognised it.

A sudden thought struck me, and I rose in my place.

"I shall be happy to do so," I said aloud, and made my way round to the front of the platform.

At the moment when he took it from me, I spoke to him.

"Monsieur Proudhine," I whispered, "you are ill! What can I do for you?"

"Nothing, *mon enfant*," he answered, in the same low tone. "I suffer; *mais il faut se resigner*."

"Break off the performance--retire for half an hour."

"Impossible. See, they already observe us!"

And he drew back abruptly. There was a seat vacant in the front row. I took it, resolved at all events to watch him narrowly.

Not to detail too minutely the events of a performance which since that time has become sufficiently familiar, I may say that he carried out his programme with dreadful exactness, and, after appearing to burn the handkerchief to ashes and mix up a quantity of eggs and flour in the hat, proceeded very coolly to smash the works of my watch beneath his ponderous pestle. Notwithstanding my faith, I began to feel seriously uncomfortable. It was a neat little silver watch of foreign workmanship-- not very valuable, to be sure, but precious to me as the most precious of repeaters.

"He is very tough, your watch, Monsieur," said the Wizard, pounding away vigorously. "He--he takes a long time ... *Ah! mon Dieu!*"

He raised his hand to his head, uttered a faint cry, and snatched at the back of the chair for support.

My first thought was that he had destroyed my watch by mistake--my second, that he was very ill indeed. Scarcely knowing what I did, and quite forgetting the audience, I jumped on the platform to his aid.

He shook his head, waved me away with one trembling hand, made a last effort to articulate, and fell heavily to the ground.

All was confusion in an instant. Everybody crowded to the stage; whilst I, with a presence of mind which afterwards surprised myself, made my way out by a side-door and ran to fetch my father. He was fortunately at home, and in less than ten minutes the Chevalier was under his care. We found him laid upon a sofa in one of the sitting-rooms of the inn, pale, rigid, insensible, and surrounded by an idle crowd of lookers-on. They had taken off his cap and beard, and the landlady was endeavoring to pour some brandy down his throat; but his teeth were fast set, and his lips were blue and cold.

"Oh, Doctor Arbuthnot! Doctor Arbuthnot!" cried a dozen voices at once, "the Conjuror is dying!"

"For which reason, I suppose, you are all trying to smother him!" said my father angrily. "Mistress Cobbe, I beg you will not trouble yourself to pour that brandy down the man's throat. He has no more power to swallow it than my stick. Basil, open the window, and help me to loosen these things about his throat. Good people, all, I must request you to leave the room. This man's life is in peril, and I can do nothing while you remain. Go home--go home. You will see no more conjuring to-night."

My father was peremptory, and the crowd unwillingly dispersed. One by one they left the room and gathered discontentedly in the passage. When it came to the last two or three, he took them by the shoulders, closed the door upon them, and turned the key.

Only the landlady, and elderly woman-servant, and myself remained.

The first thing my father did was to examine the pupil of the patient's eye, and lay his hand upon his heart. It still fluttered feebly, but the action of the lungs was suspended, and his hands and feet were cold as death.

My father shook his head.

"This man must be bled," said he, "but I have little hope of saving him."

He was bled, and, though still unconscious, became less rigid They then poured a little wine down his throat, and he fell into a passive but painless condition, more inanimate than sleep, but less positive than a state of trance.

A fire was then lighted, a mattress brought down, and the patient laid upon it, wrapped in many blankets. My father announced his intention of sitting up with him all night. In vain I begged for leave to share his vigil. He would hear of no such thing, but turned me out as he had turned out the others, bade me a brief "Good-night," and desired me to run home as quickly as I could.

At that stage of my history, to hear was to obey; so I took my way quietly through the bar of the hotel, and had just reached the door when a touch on my sleeve arrested me. It was Mr. Cobbe, the landlord--a portly, red-whiskered Boniface of the old English type.

"Good-evening, Mr. Basil," said he. "Going home, sir?"

"Yes, Mr. Cobbe," I replied. "I can be of no further use here."

"Well, sir, you've been of more use this evening than anybody--let alone the Doctor--that I must say for you," observed Mr. Cobbe, approvingly. "I never see such presence o' mind in so young a gen'leman before. Never, sir. Have a glass of grog and a cigar, sir, before you turn out."

Much as I felt flattered by the supposition that I smoked (which was more than I could have done to save my life), I declined Mr. Cobbe's obliging offer and wished him good-night. But the landlord of the Red Lion was in a gossiping humor, and would not let me go.

"If you won't take spirits, Mr. Basil," said he, "you must have a glass of negus. I couldn't let you go out without something warm--particular after the excitement you've gone through. Why, bless you, sir, when they ran out and told me, I shook like a leaf--and I don't look like a very nervous subject, do I? And so sudden as it was, too, poor little gentleman!"

"Very sudden, indeed," I replied, mechanically.

"Does Doctor Arbuthnot think he'll get the better of it, Mr. Basil?"

"I fear he has little hope."

Mr. Cobbe sighed, and shook his head, and smoked in silence.

"To be struck down just when he was playing such tricks as them conjuring dodges, do seem uncommon awful," said he, after a time. "What was he after at the minute?--making a pudding, wasn't he, in some gentleman's hat?"

I uttered a sudden ejaculation, and set down my glass of negus untasted. Till that moment I had not once thought of my watch.

"Oh, Mr. Cobbe!" I cried, "he was pounding my watch in the mortar!"

"*Your* watch, Mr. Basil?"

"Yes, mine--and I have not seen it since. What can have become of it? What shall I do?"

"Do!" echoed the landlord, seizing a candle; "why, go and look for it, to be sure, Mr. Basil. That's safe enough, you may be sure!"

I followed him to the room where the performance had taken place. It showed darkly and drearily by the light of one feeble candle. The benches and chairs were all in disorder. The wand lay where it had fallen from the hand of the Wizard. The mortar still stood on the table, with the pestle beside it. It contained only some fragments of broken glass.

Mr. Cobbe laughed triumphantly.

"Come, sir," said he, "the watch is safe enough, anyhow. Mounseer only made believe to pound it up, and now all that concerns us is to find it."

That was indeed all--not only all, but too much. We searched everything. We looked in all the jars and under all the moveables. We took the cover off the chair; we cleared the table; but without success. My watch had totally disappeared, and we at length decided that it must be concealed about the conjuror's person. Mr. Cobbe was my consoling angel.

"Bless you, sir," said he, "don't never be cast down. My wife shall look for the watch to-morrow morning, and I'll promise you we'll find out every pocket he has about him."

"And my father--you won't tell my father?" I said, dolefully.

Mr. Cobbe replied by a mute but expressive piece of pantomime and took me back to the bar, where the good landlady ratified all that her husband had promised in her name.

The stars shone brightly as I went home, and there was no moon. The town was intensely silent, and the road intensely solitary. I met no one on my way; let myself quietly in, and stole up to my bed-room in the dark.

It was already late; but I was restless and weary--too restless to sleep, and too weary to read. I could not detach myself from the impressions of the day; and I longed for the morning, that I might learn the fate of my watch, and the condition of the Chevalier.

At length, after some hours of wakefulness, I dropped into a profound and dreamless sleep.

CHAPTER IV.
THE CHEVALIER MAKES HIS LAST EXIT.

All the world's a stage,
And all the men and women merely players:
They have their exits and their entrances.
As You Like It.

I was waked by my father's voice calling to me from the garden, and so started up with that strange and sudden sense of trouble which most of us have experienced at some time or other in our lives.

"Nine o'clock, Basil," cried my father. "Nine o'clock--come down directly, sir!"

I sprang out of bed, and for some seconds could remember nothing of what had happened; but when I looked out of the window and saw my father in his dressing-gown and slippers walking up and down the sunny path with his hands behind his back and his eyes fixed on the ground, it all flashed suddenly upon me. To plunge into my bath, dress, run down, and join him in the garden, was the work of but a few minutes.

"Good-morning, sir," I said, breathlessly.

He stopped short in his walk, and looked at me from head to foot.

"Humph!" said he, "you have dressed quickly...."

"Yes, sir; I was startled to find myself so late."

"So quickly," he continued, "that you have forgotten your watch."

I felt my face burn. I had not a word to answer.

"I suppose," said he, "you thought I should not find it out?"

"I had hoped to recover it first," I replied, falteringly; "but...."

"But you may make up your mind to the loss of it, sir; and serve you rightly, too," interposed my father. "I can tell you, for your satisfaction, that the man's clothes have been thoroughly examined, and that your watch has not been found. No doubt it lay somewhere on the table, and was stolen in the confusion."

I hung my head. I could have wept for vexation.

My father laughed sardonically.

"Well, Master Basil," he said, "the loss is yours, and yours only. You won't get another watch from me, I promise you."

I retorted angrily, whereat he only laughed the more; and then we went in to breakfast.

Our morning meal was more unsociable than usual. I was too much annoyed to speak, and my father too preoccupied. I longed to inquire after the Chevalier, but not choosing to break the silence, hurried through my breakfast that I might run round to the Red Lion immediately after. Before we had left the table, a messenger came to say that "the conjuror was taken worse," and so my father and I hastened away together.

He had passed from his trance-like sleep into a state of delirium, and when we entered the room was sitting up, pale and ghost-like, muttering to himself, and gesticulating as if in the presence of an audience.

"*Pas du tout*," said he fantastically, "*pas du tout, Messieurs*--here is no deception. You shall see him pass from my hand to the *coffre*, and yet you shall not find how he does travel."

My father smiled bitterly.

"Conjurer to the last!" said he. "In the face of death, what a mockery is his trade!"

Wandering as were his wits, he caught the last word and turned fiercely round; but there was no recognition in his eye.

"Trade, Monsieur!" he echoed. "Trade!--you shall not call him trade! Do you know who I am, that you dare call him trade? *Dieu des Dieux! N'est-ce pas que je suis noble, moi?* Trade!--when did one of my race embrace a trade? *Canaille!* I do condescend for my reasons to take your money, but you shall not call him a trade!"

Exhausted by this sudden burst of passion, he fell back upon his pillow, muttering and flushed. I bent over him, and caught a scattered phrase from time to time.

He was dreaming of wealth, fancying himself rich and powerful, poor wretch! and all unconscious of his condition.

"You shall see my Chateaux," he said, "my horses--my carriages. Listen--it is the ringing of the bells. Aha! *le jour viendra--le jour viendra*! Conjuror! who speaks of a conjuror? I never was a conjuror! I deny it: and he lies who says it! *Attendons*! Is the curtain up? Ah! my table--where is my table? I cannot play till I have my table. *Scelerats! je suis vole! je l'ai perdu! je l'ai perdu*! Ah, what shall I do? What shall I do? They have taken my table--they have taken...."

He burst into tears, moaned twice or thrice, closed his eyes, and fell into a troubled sleep.

The landlady sobbed. Hers was a kind heart, and the little Frenchman's simple courtesy had won her good-will from the first.

"He had real quality manners," she said, disconsolately. "I do believe, gentlemen, that he had seen better days. Poor as he was, he never disputed the price of anything; and he never spoke to me without taking off his hat."

"Upon my soul, Mistress Cobbe," said my father, "I incline to your opinion. I do think he is not what he seems."

"And if I only knew where to find his friends, I shouldn't care half so much!" exclaimed the landlady. "It do seem so hard that he should die here, and not one of his own blood follow him to the grave! Surely he has some one who loves him!"

"There was something said the other day about a child," mused my father. "Have no papers or letters been found about his person?"

"None at all. Why, Doctor, you were here last night when we searched for Master Basil's watch, and you are witness that he had nothing of the kind in his possession. As to his luggage, that's only a carpet-bag and his conjuring things, and we looked through them as carefully as possible."

The Chevalier moaned again, and tossed his arms feebly in his sleep. "The proofs," said he. "The proofs! I can do nothing without the proofs."

My father listened. The landlady shook her head.

"He has been going on like that ever since you left, sir," she said pitifully; "fancying he's been robbed, and calling out about the proofs--only ten times more violent. Then, again, he thinks he is going to act, and asks for his table. It's wonderful how he takes on about that trumpery table!"

Scarcely had she spoken the words when the Chevalier opened his eyes, and, by a supreme effort, sat upright in his bed. The cold dew rose upon his brow; his lips quivered; he strove to speak, and only an inarticulate cry found utterance. My father flew to his support.

"If you have anything to say," he urged earnestly, "try to say it now!"

The dying man trembled convulsively, and a terrible look of despair came into his wan face.

"Tell--tell" ... he gasped; but his voice failed him, and he could get no further.

My father laid him gently down. There came an interval of terrible suspense--a moment of sharp agony--a deep, deep sigh--and then silence.

My father laid his hand gently upon my shoulder.

"It is all over," he said; "and his secret, if he had one, is in closer keeping than ours. Come away, boy; this is no place for you."

CHAPTER V.
IN MEMORIAM.

The poor little Chevalier! He died and became famous.

Births, deaths and marriages are the great events of a country town; the prime novelties of a country newspaper; the salt of conversation, and the soul of gossip. An individual who furnishes the community with one or other of these topics, is a benefactor to his species. To be born is much; to marry is more; to die is to confer a favor on all the old ladies of the neighborhood. They love a christening and caudle--they rejoice in a wedding and cake--but they prefer a funeral and black kid gloves. It is a tragedy played off at the expense of the few for the gratification of the many--a costly luxury, of which it is pleasanter to be the spectator than the entertainer.

Occurring, therefore, at a season when the supply of news was particularly scanty, the death of the little Chevalier was a boon to Saxonholme. The wildest reports were bandied about, and the most extraordinary fictions set on foot respecting his origin and station. He was a Russian spy. He was the unfortunate son of Louis XIV and Marie Antoinette. He was a pupil of Cagliostro, and the husband of Mlle. Lenormand. Customers flocked to the tap of the Red Lion as they had never flocked before, unless in election-time; and good Mrs. Cobbe had to repeat the story of the conjuror's illness and death till, like many other reciters, she had told it so often that she began to forget it. As for her husband, he had enough to do to serve the customers and take the money, to say nothing of showing the room, which proved a vast attraction, and remained for more than a week just as it was left on the evening of the performance, with the table, canopy and paraphernalia of wizardom still set out upon the platform.

In the midst of these things arose a momentous question--what was the religion of the deceased, and where should he be buried? As in the old miracle plays we find good and bad angels contending for the souls of the dead, so on this occasion did the heads of all the Saxonholme churches, chapels and meeting-houses contend for the body of the little Chevalier. He was a Roman Catholic. He was a Dissenter. He was a member of the Established Church. He must be buried in the new Protestant Cemetery. He must lie in the churchyard of the Ebenezer Tabernacle. He must sleep in the far-away "God's Acre" of Father Daly's Chapel, and have a cross at his head, and masses said for the repose of his soul. The controversy ran high. The reverend gentlemen convoked a meeting, quarrelled outrageously, and separated in high dudgeon without having arrived at any conclusion.

Whereupon arose another question, melancholy, ludicrous, perplexing, and, withal, as momentous as the first--Would the little Chevalier get buried at all? Or was he destined to remain, like Mahomet's coffin, for ever in a state of suspense?

At the last, when Mr. and Mrs. Cobbe despairingly believed that they were never to be relieved of their troublesome guest, a vestry was called, and the church-wardens brought the matter to a conclusion. When he went round with his tickets, the conjuror called first at the Rectory, and solicited the patronage of Doctor Brand. Would he have paid that compliment to the cloth had he been other than a member of that religion "by law established?" Certainly not. The point was clear--could not be clearer; so orthodoxy and the new Protestant Cemetery carried the day.

The funeral was a great event--not so far as mutes, feathers and carriages were concerned, for the Chevalier left but little worldly gear, and without hard cash even the most deserving must forego "the trappings and the suits of woe;" but it was a great event, inasmuch as it celebrated the victory of the Church, and the defeat of all schismatics. The rector himself, complacent and dignified, preached the funeral sermon to a crowded congregation, the following Sunday. We almost forgot, in fact, that the little Chevalier had any concern in the matter, and regarded it only as the triumph of orthodoxy.

All was not ended, even here. For some weeks our conjuror continued to be the hero of every pulpit round about. He was cited as a shining light, denounced as a vessel of wrath, praised, pitied and calumniated according to the creed and temper of each declaimer. At length the controversy languished, died a natural death, and became "alms for oblivion."

Laid to rest under a young willow, in a quiet corner, with a plain stone at his head, the little Frenchman was himself in course of time forgotten:--

"Alas! Poor Yorick!"

CHAPTER VI.
POLONIUS TO LAERTES.

Years went by. I studied; outgrew my jackets; became a young man. It was time, in short, that I walked the hospitals, and passed my examination. I had spoken to my father more than once upon the subject--spoken earnestly and urgently, as one who felt the necessity and justice of his appeal. But he put me off from time to time; persisted in looking upon me as a boy long after I had become acquainted with the penalties of the razor; and counselled me to be patient, till patience was well-nigh exhausted. The result of this treatment was that I became miserable and discontented; spent whole days wandering about the woods; and degenerated into a creature half idler and half misanthrope. I had never loved the profession of medicine. I should never have chosen it had I been free to follow my own inclinations: but having diligently fitted myself to enter it with credit, I felt that my father wronged me in this delay; and I felt it perhaps all the more bitterly because my labor had been none of love. Happily for me, however, he saw his error before it was too late, and repaired it generously.

"Basil," said he, beckoning me one morning into the consulting-room, "I want to speak to you."

I obeyed sullenly, and stood leaning up against the window, with my hands in my pockets.

"You've been worrying me, Basil, more than enough these last few months," he said, rummaging among his papers, and speaking in a low, constrained voice. "I don't choose to be worried any longer. It is time you walked the hospitals, and--you may go."

"To London, sir?"

"No. I don't intend you to go to London."

"To Edinburgh, then, I suppose," said I, in a tone of disappointment.

"Nor to Edinburgh. You shall go to Paris."

"To Paris!"

"Yes--the French surgeons are the most skilful in the world, and Cheron will do everything for you. I know no eminent man in London from whom I should choose to ask a favor; and Cheron is one of my oldest friends--nay, the oldest friend I have in the world. If you have but two ounces of brains, he will make a clever man of you. Under him you will study French practice; walk the hospitals of Paris; acquire the language and, I hope, some of the polish of the French people. Are you satisfied?"

"More than satisfied, sir," I replied, eagerly.

"You shall not want for money, boy; and you may start as soon as you please. Is the thing settled?"

"Quite, as far as I am concerned."

My father rubbed his head all over with both hands, took off his spectacles, and walked up and down the room. By these signs he expressed any unusual degree of satisfaction. All at once he stopped, looked me full in the face, and said:--

"Understand me, Basil. I require one thing in return."

"If that thing be industry, sir, I think I may promise that you shall not have cause to complain,"

My father shook his head.

"Not industry," he said; "not industry alone. Keep good company, my boy. Keep good hours. Never forget that a gentleman must look like a gentleman, dress like a gentleman, frequent the society of gentlemen. To be a mere bookworm is to be a drone in the great hive. I hate a drone--as I hate a sloven."

"I understand you, father," I faltered, blushing. "I know that of late I--I have not...."

My father laid his hand suddenly over my mouth.

"No confessions--no apologies," he said hastily. "We have both been to blame in more respects than one, and we shall both know how to be wiser in the future. Now go, and consider all that you may require for your journey."

Agitated, delighted, full of hope, I ran up to my own room, locked the door, and indulged in a delightful reverie. What a prospect had suddenly opened before me! What novelty! what adventure! To have visited London would have been to fulfil all my desires; but to be sent to Paris was to receive a passport for Fairyland!

That day, for the first time in many months, I dressed myself carefully, and went down to dinner with a light heart, a cheerful face, and an unexceptionable neckcloth.

As I took my place at the table, my father looked up cheerily and gave me a pleased nod of recognition.

Our meal passed off very silently. It was my father's maxim that no man could do more than one thing well at a time--especially at table; so we had contracted a habit which to strangers would have seemed even more unsociable than it really was, and gave to all our meals an air more penitential than convivial. But this day was, in reality, a festive occasion, and my father was disposed to be more than usually agreeable. When the cloth was removed, he flung the cellar-key at my head, and exclaimed, in a burst of unexampled good-humor:--

"Basil, you dog, fetch up a bottle of the particular port!"

Now it is one of my theories that a man's after-dinner talk takes much of its weight, color, and variety from the quality of his wines. A generous vintage brings out generous sentiments. Good fellowship, hospitality, liberal politics, and the milk of human kindness, may be uncorked simultaneously with a bottle of old Madeira; while a pint of thin Sauterne is productive only of envy, hatred, malice, and all uncharitableness. We grow sententious on Burgundy--logical on Bordeaux--sentimental on Cyprus--maudlin on Lagrima Christi--and witty on Champagne.

Port was my father's favorite wine. It warmed his heart, cooled his temper, and made him not only conversational, but expansive. Leaning back complacently in his easy-chair, with the glass upheld between his eye and the window, he discoursed to me of my journey, of my prospects in life, and of all that I should do and avoid, professionally and morally.

"Work," he said, "is the panacea for every sorrow--the plaster for every pain--your only universal remedy. Industry, air, and exercise are our best physicians. Trust to them, boy; but beware how you publish the prescription, lest you find your occupation gone. Remember, if you wish to be rich, you must never seem to be poor; and as soon as you stand in need of your friends, you will find yourself with none left. Be discreet of speech, and cultivate the art of silence. Above all things, be truthful. Hold your tongue as long as you please, but never open your lips to a lie. Show no man the contents of your purse--he would either despise you for having so little, or try to relieve you of the burden of carrying so much. Above all, never get into debt, and never fall in love. The first is disgrace, and the last is the devil! Respect yourself, if you wish others to respect you; and bear in mind that the world takes you at your own estimate. To dress well is a duty one owes to society. The man who neglects his own appearance not only degrades himself to the level of his inferiors, but puts an affront upon his friends and acquaintances."

"I trust, sir," I said in some confusion, "that I shall never incur the last reproach again."

"I hope not, Basil," replied my father, with a smile. "I hope not. Keep your conscience clean and your boots blacked, and I have no fear of you. You are no hero, my boy, but it depends upon yourself whether you become a man of honor or a scamp; a gentleman or a clown. You have, I see, registered a good resolution to-day. Keep it; and remember that Pandemonium will get paved without your help. There would be no industry, boy, if there was no idleness, and all true progress begins with--Reform."

CHAPTER VII.
AT THE CHEVAL BLANC

My journey, even at this distance of time, appears to me like an enchanted dream. I observed, yet scarcely remembered, the scenes through which I passed, so divided was I between the novelty of travelling and the eagerness of anticipation. Provided with my letters of introduction, the sum of one hundred guineas, English, and the enthusiasm of twenty years of age, I fancied myself endowed with an immortality of wealth and happiness.

The Brighton coach passed through our town once a week; so I started for Paris without having ever visited London, and took the route by Newhaven and Dieppe. Having left home on Tuesday morning, I reached Rouen in the course of the next day but one. At Rouen I stayed to dine and sleep, and so made my way to the *Cheval Blanc*, a grand hotel on the quay, where I was received by an aristocratic elderly waiter who sauntered out from a side office, surveyed me patronizingly, entered my name upon a card for a seat at the *table d'hote*, and, having rung a feeble little bell, sank exhausted upon a seat in the hall.

"To number seventeen, Marie," said this majestic personage, handing me over to a pretty little chambermaid who attended the summons. "And, Marie, on thy return, my child, bring me an absinthe."

We left this gentleman in a condition of ostentatious languor, and Marie deposited me in a pretty room overlooking an exquisite little garden set round with beds of verbena and scarlet geranium, with a fountain sparkling in the midst. This garden was planted in what had once been the courtyard, of the building. The trees nodded and whispered, and the windows at the opposite side of the quadrangle glittered like burnished gold in the sunlight. I threw open the jalousies, plucked one of the white roses that clustered outside, and drank in with delight the sunny perfumed air that played among the leaves, and scattered the waters of the fountain. I could not long rest thus, however. I longed to be out and about; so, as it was now no more than half-past three o'clock, and two good hours of the glorious midsummer afternoon yet remained to me before the hotel dinner-hour, I took my hat, and went out along the quays and streets of this beautiful and ancient Norman city.

Under the crumbling archways; through narrow alleys where the upper stories nearly met overhead, leaving only a bright strip of dazzling sky between; past quaint old mansions, and sculptured fountains, and stately churches hidden away in all kinds of strange forgotten nooks and corners, I wandered, wondering and unwearied. I saw the statue of Jeanne d'Arc; the chateau of Diane de Poitiers; the archway carved in oak where the founder of the city still, in rude effigy, presides; the museum rich in mediaeval relics; the market-place crowded with fruit-sellers and flower-girls in their high Norman caps. Above all, I saw the rare old Gothic Cathedral, with its wondrous wealth of antique sculpture; its iron spire, destined, despite its traceried beauty, to everlasting incompleteness; its grass-grown buttresses, and crumbling pinnacles, and portals crowded with images of saints and kings. I went in. All was gray, shadowy, vast; dusk with the rich gloom of painted windows; and so silent that I scarcely dared disturb the echoes by my footsteps. There stood in a corner near the door a triangular iron stand stuck full of votive tapers that flickered and sputtered and guttered dismally, shedding showers of penitential grease-drops on the paved floor below; and there was a very old peasant woman on her knees before the altar. I sat down on a stone bench and fell into a long study of the stained oriel, the light o'erarching roof, and the long perspective of the pillared aisles. Presently the verger came out of the vestry-room, followed by two gentlemen. He was short and plump, with a loose black gown, slender black legs, and a pointed nose-- like a larger species of raven.

"***Bon jour, M'sieur***" croaked he, laying his head a little on one side, and surveying me with one glittering eye. "Will M'sieur be pleased to see the treasury?"

"The treasury!" I repeated. "What is there to be seen in the treasury?"

"Nothing, sir, worth one son of an Englishman's money," said the taller of the gentlemen. "Tinsel, paste, and dusty bones--all humbug and extortion."

Something in the scornful accent and the deep voice aroused the suspicions of the verger, though the words were spoken in English.

"Our treasury, M'sieur," croaked he, more ravenly than ever, "is rich--rich in episcopal jewels; in relics--inestimable relics. Tickets two francs each."

Grateful, however, for the timely caution, I acknowledged my countryman's courtesy by a bow, declined the proffered investment, and went out again into the sunny streets.

At five o'clock I found myself installed near the head of an immensely long dinner-table in the *salle a manger* of the Cheval Blanc. The *salle a manger* was a magnificent temple radiant with mirrors, and lustres, and panels painted in fresco. The dinner was an imposing rite, served with solemn ceremonies by ministering waiters. There were about thirty guests seated round, in august silence, most of them very smartly dressed, and nearly all English. A stout gentleman, with a little knob on the top of his bald head, a buff waistcoat, and a shirt amply frilled, sat opposite to me, flanked on either side by an elderly daughter in green silk. On my left I was supported by a thin young gentleman with fair hair, and blue glasses. To my right stood a vacant chair, the occupant of which had not yet arrived; and at the head of the table sat a spare pale man dressed all in black, who spoke to no one, kept his eyes fixed upon his plate, and was served by the waiters with especial servility. The soup came and went in profound silence. Faint whispers passed to and fro with the fish. It was not till the roast made its appearance that anything like conversation broke the sacred silence of the meal. At this point the owner of the vacant chair arrived, and took his place beside me. I recognised him immediately. It was the Englishman whom I had met in the Cathedral. We bowed, and presently he spoke to me. In the meantime, he had every forgone item of the dinner served to him as exactly as if he had not been late at table, and sipped his soup with perfect deliberation while others were busy with the sweets. Our conversation began, of course, with the weather and the place.

"Your first visit to Rouen, I suppose?" said he. "Beautiful old city, is it not? *Garcon*, a pint of Bordeaux-Leoville."

I modestly admitted that it was not only my first visit to Rouen, but my first to the Continent.

"Ah, you may go farther than Rouen, and fare worse," said he. "Do you sketch? No? That's a pity, for it's deliciously picturesque--though, for my own part, I am not enthusiastic about gutters and gables, and I object to a population composed exclusively of old women. I'm glad, by the way, that I preserved you from wasting your time among the atrocious lumber of that so-called treasury."

"The treasury!" exclaimed my slim neighbor with the blue glasses. "Beg your p--p--pardon, sir, but are you speaking of the Cathedral treasury? Is it worth v--v--visiting?"

"Singularly so," replied he to my right. "One of the rarest collections of authentic curiosities in France. They have the snuff-box of Clovis, the great toe of Saint Helena, and the tongs with which St. Dunstan took the devil by the nose."

"Up--p--pon my word, now, that's curious," ejaculated the thin tourist, who had an impediment in his speech. "I must p--p--put that down. Dear me! the snuff-box of King Clovis! I must see these relics to-morrow."

"Be sure you ask for the great toe of St. Helena," said my right hand companion, proceeding imperturbably with his dinner. "The saint had but one leg at the period of her martyrdom, and that great toe is unique."

"G--g--good gracious!" exclaimed the tourist, pulling out a gigantic note-book, and entering the fact upon the spot. "A saint with one leg--and a lady, too! Wouldn't m--m--miss that for the world!"

I looked round, puzzled by the gravity of my new acquaintance.

"Is this all true?" I whispered. "You told me the treasury was a humbug."

"And so it is."

"But the snuff-box of Clovis, and...."

"Pure inventions! The man's a muff, and on muffs I have no mercy. Do you stay long in Rouen?"

"No, I go on to Paris to-morrow. I wish I could remain longer."

"I am not sure that you would gain more from a long visit than from a short one. Some places are like some women, charming, *en passant*, but intolerable upon close acquaintance. It is just so with Rouen. The place contains no fine galleries, and no places of public entertainment; and though exquisitely picturesque, is nothing more. One cannot always be looking at old houses, and admiring old churches. You will be delighted with Paris."

"B--b--beautiful city," interposed the stammerer, eager to join our conversation, whenever he could catch a word of it. "I'm going to P--P--Paris myself."

"Then, sir, I don't doubt you will do ample justice to its attractions," observed my right-hand neighbor. "From the size of your note-book, and the industry with which you accumulate useful information, I should presume that you are a conscientious observer of all that is recondite and curious."

"I as--p--pire to be so," replied the other, with a blush and a bow. "I m--m--mean to exhaust P--P--Paris. I'm going to write a b--b--book about it, when I get home.'"

My friend to the right flashed one glance of silent scorn upon the future author, drained the last glass of his Bordeaux-Leoville, pushed his chair impatiently back, and said:--"This place smells like a kitchen. Will you come out, and have a cigar?"

So we rose, took our hats, and in a few moments were strolling under the lindens on the Quai de Corneille.

I, of course, had never smoked in my life; and, humiliating though it was, found myself obliged to decline a "prime Havana," proffered in the daintiest of embroidered cigar-cases. My companion looked as if he pitied me. "You'll soon learn," said he. "A man can't live in Paris without tobacco. Do you stay there many weeks?"

"Two years, at least," I replied, registering an inward resolution to conquer the difficulties of tobacco without delay. "I am going to study medicine under an eminent French surgeon."

"Indeed! Well, you could not go to a better school, or embrace a nobler profession. I used to think a soldier's life the grandest under heaven; but curing is a finer thing than killing, after all! What a delicious evening, is it not? If one were only in Paris, now, or Vienna,...."

"What, Oscar Dalrymple!" exclaimed a voice close beside us. "I should as soon have expected to meet the great Panjandrum himself!"

"--With the little round button at top," added my companion, tossing away the end of his cigar, and shaking hands heartily with the new-comer. "By Jove, Frank, I'm glad to see you! What brings you here?"

"Business--confound it! And not pleasant business either. *A proces* which my father has instituted against a great manufacturing firm here at Rouen, and of which I have to bear the brunt. And you?"

"And I, my dear fellow? Pshaw! what should I be but an idler in search of amusement?"

"Is it true that you have sold out of the Enniskillens?"

"Unquestionably. Liberty is sweet; and who cares to carry a sword in time of peace? Not I, at all events."

While this brief greeting was going forward, I hung somewhat in the rear, and amused myself by comparing the speakers. The new-comer was rather below than above the middle height, fair-haired and boyish, with a smile full of mirth and an eye full of mischief. He looked about two years my senior. The other was much older--two or three and thirty, at the least--dark, tall, powerful, finely built; his wavy hair clipped close about his sun-burnt neck; a thick moustache of unusual length; and a chest that looked as if it would have withstood the shock of a battering-ram. Without being at all handsome, there was a look of brightness, and boldness, and gallantry about him that arrested one's attention at first sight. I think I should have taken him for a soldier, had I not already gathered it from the last words of their conversation.

"Who is your friend?" I heard the new-comer whisper.

To which the other replied:--"Haven't the ghost of an idea."

Presently he took out his pocket-book, and handing me a card, said:--

"We are under the mutual disadvantage of all chance acquaintances. My name is Dalrymple--Oscar Dalrymple, late of the Enniskillen Dragoons. My friend here is unknown to fame as Mr. Frank Sullivan; a young gentleman who has the good fortune to be younger partner in a firm of merchant princes, and the bad taste to dislike his occupation."

How I blushed as I took Captain Dalrymple's card, and stammered out my own name in return! I had never possessed a card in my life, nor needed one, till this moment. I rather think that Captain Dalrymple guessed these facts, for he shook hands with me at once, and put an end to my embarrassment by proposing that we should take a boat, and pull a mile or two up the river. The thing was no sooner said than done. There were plenty of boats below the iron bridge; so we chose one of the cleanest, and jumped into it without any kind of reference to the owner, whoever he might be.

"*Batelier, Messieurs? Batelier?*" cried a dozen men at once, rushing down to the water's edge.

But Dalrymple had already thrown off his coat, and seized the oars.

"*Batelier*, indeed!" laughed he, as with two or three powerful strokes he carried us right into the middle, of the stream. "Trust an Oxford man for employing any arms but his own, when a pair of sculls are in question!"

CHAPTER VIII.
THE ISLAND IN THE RIVER.

It was just eight o'clock when we started, with the twilight coming on. Our course lay up the river, with a strong current setting against us; so we made but little way, and enjoyed the tranquil beauty of the evening. The sky was pale and clear, somewhat greenish overhead and deepening along the line of the horizon into amber and rose. Behind us lay the town with every brown spire articulated against the sky and every vane glittering in the last glow that streamed up from the west. To our left rose a line of steep chalk cliffs, and before us lay the river, winding away through meadow lands fringed with willows and poplars, and interspersed with green islands wooded to the water's edge. Presently the last flush faded, and one large planet, splendid and solitary, like the first poet of a dark century, emerged from the deepening gray.

My companions were in high spirits. They jested; they laughed; they hummed scraps of songs; they had a greeting for every boat that passed. By-and-by, we came to an island with a little landing-place where a score or two of boats were moored against the alders by the water's edge. A tall flag-staff gay with streamers peeped above the tree-tops, and a cheerful sound of piping and fiddling, mingled with the hum of many voices, came and went with the passing breeze. As Dalrymple rested on his oars to listen, a boat which we had outstripped some minutes before, shot past us to the landing-place, and its occupants, five in number, alighted.

"Bet you ten to one that's a bridal party," said Mr. Sullivan.

"Say you so? Then suppose we follow, and have a look at the bride!" exclaimed his friend. "The place is a public garden."

The proposition was carried unanimously, and we landed, having first tied the boat to a willow. We found the island laid out very prettily; intersected by numbers of little paths, with rustic seats here and there among the trees, and variegated lamps gleaming out amid the grass, like parti-colored glow-worms. Following one of these paths, we came presently to an open space, brilliantly lighted and crowded by holiday-makers. Here were refreshment stalls, and Russian swings, and queer-looking merry-go-rounds, where each individual sat on a wooden horse and went gravely round and round with a stick in his hand, trying to knock off a ring from the top of a pole in the middle. Here, also, was a band in a gaily decorated orchestra; a circular area roped off for dancers; a mysterious tent with a fortune-teller inside; a lottery-stall resplendent with vases and knick-knacks, which nobody was ever known to win; in short, all kinds of attractions, stale enough, no doubt, to my companions, but sufficiently novel and amusing to me.

We strolled about for some time among the stalls and promenaders and amused ourselves by criticising the company, which was composed almost entirely of peasants, soldiers, artisans in blue blouses and humble tradespeople. The younger women were mostly handsome, with high Norman caps, white kerchiefs and massive gold ear-rings. Many, in addition to the ear-rings, wore a gold cross suspended round the neck by a piece of black velvet; and some had a brooch to match. Here, sitting round a table under a tree, we came upon a family group, consisting of a little plump, bald-headed *bourgeois* with his wife and two children--the wife stout and rosy; the children noisy and authoritative. They were discussing a dish of poached eggs and a bottle of red wine, to the music of a polka close by.

"I should like to dance," said the little girl, drumming with her feet against the leg of the table, and eating an egg with her fingers. "I may dance presently with Phillippe, may I not, papa?"

"I won't dance," said Phillippe sulkily. "I want some oysters."

"Oysters, *mon enfant*! I have told you twice already that no one eats oysters in July," observed his mother.

"I don't care for that," said Phillippe. "It's my *fete* day, and Uncle Jacques said I was to have whatever I fancied; I want some oysters."

"Your Uncle Jacques did not know what an unreasonable boy you are," replied the father angrily. "If you say another word about oysters, you shall not ride in the *manege* to-night."

Phillippe thrust his fists into his eyes and began to roar--so we walked away.

In an arbor, a little further on, we saw two young people whispering earnestly, and conscious of no eyes but each other's.

"A pair of lovers," said Sullivan.

"And a pair that seldom get the chance of meeting, if we may judge by their untasted omelette," replied Dalrymple. "But where's the bridal party?"

"Oh, we shall find them presently. You seem interested."

"I am. I mean to dance with the bride and make the bridegroom jealous."

We laughed and passed on, peeping into every arbor, observing every group, and turning to stare at every pretty girl we met. My own aptitude in the acquisition of these arts of gallantry astonished myself. Now, we passed a couple of soldiers playing at dominoes; now a noisy party round a table in the open air covered with bottles; now an arbor where half a dozen young men and three or four girls were assembled round a bowl of blazing punch. The girls were protesting they dare not drink it, but were drinking it, nevertheless, with exceeding gusto.

"Grisettes and ***commis voyageurs!***" said Dalrymple, contemptuously. "Let us go and look at the dancers."

We went on, and stood in the shelter of some trees near the orchestra. The players consisted of three violins, a clarionette and a big drum. The big drum was an enthusiastic performer. He belabored his instrument as heartily as if it had been his worst enemy, but with so much independence of character that he never kept the same time as his fellow-players for two minutes together. They were playing a polka for the benefit of some twelve or fifteen couples, who were dancing with all their might in the space before the orchestra. On they came, round and round and never weary, two at a time--a mechanic and a grisette, a rustic and a Normandy girl, a tall soldier and a short widow, a fat tradesman and his wife, a couple of milliners assistants who preferred dancing together to not dancing at all, and so forth.

"How I wish somebody would ask me, ***ma mere***!" said a coquettish brunette, close by, with a sidelong glance at ourselves."

"You shall dance with your brother Paul, my dear, as soon as he comes," replied her mother, a stout ***bourgeoise*** with a green fan.

"But it is such dull work to dance with one's brother!" pouted the brunette. "If it were one's cousin, even, it would be different."

Mr. Frank Sullivan flung away his cigar, and began buttoning up his gloves.

"I'll take that damsel out immediately," said he. "A girl who objects to dance with her brother deserves encouragement."

So away he went with his hat inclining jauntily on one side, and, having obtained the mother's permission, whirled away with the pretty brunette into the very thickest of the throng.

"There they are!" said Dalrymple, suddenly. "There's the wedding party. **Per Bacco**! but our little bride is charming!"

"And the bridegroom is a handsome specimen of rusticity."

"Yes--a genuine pastoral pair, like a Dresden china shepherd and shepherdess. See, the girl is looking up in his face--he shakes his head. She is urging him to dance, and he refuses! Never mind, **ma belle**--you shall have your valse, and Corydon may be as cross as he pleases!"

"Don't flatter yourself that she will displease Corydon to dance with your lordship!" I said, laughingly.

"Pshaw! she would displease fifty Corydons if I chose to make her do so," said Dalrymple, with a smile of conscious power.

"True; but not on her wedding-day."

"Wedding-day or not, I beg to observe that in less than half an hour you will see me whirling along with my arm round little Phillis's dainty waist. Now come and see how I do it."

He made his way through the crowd, and I, half curious, half abashed, went with him. The party was five in number, consisting of the bride and bridegroom, a rosy, middle-aged peasant woman, evidently the mother of the bride, and an elderly couple who looked like humble townsfolk, and were probably related to one or other of the newly-married pair. Dalrymple opened the attack by stumbling against the mother, and then overwhelming her with elaborate apologies.

"In these crowded places, Madame," said he, in his fluent French, "one is scarcely responsible for an impoliteness. I beg ten thousand pardons, however. I hope I have not hurt you?"

"**Ma foi!** no, M'sieur. It would take more than that to hurt me!"

"Nor injured your dress, I trust, Madame?"

"**Ah, par exemple**! do I wear muslins or gauzes that they should not bear touching? No, no, no, M'sieur--thanking you all the same."

"You are very amiable, Madame, to say so."

"You are very polite, M'sieur, to think so much of a trifle."

"Nothing is a trifle, Madame, where a lady is concerned. At least, so we Englishmen consider."

"Bah! M'sieur is not English?"

"Indeed, Madame, I am."

"***Mais, mon Dieu! c'est incroyable***. Suzette--brother Jacques--Andre, do you hear this? M'sieur, here, swears that he is English, and yet he speaks French like one of ourselves! Ah, what a fine thing learning is!"

"I may say with truth, Madame, that I never appreciate the advantages of education so highly, as when they enable me to converse with ladies who are not my own countrywomen," said Dalrymple, carrying on the conversation with as much studied politeness as if his interlocutor had been a duchess. "But--excuse the observation--you are here, I imagine, upon a happy occasion?"

The mother laughed, and rubbed her hands.

"***Dame***! one may see that," replied she, "with one's eyes shut! Yes, M'sieur,--yes--their wedding-day, the dear children--their wedding-day! They've been betrothed these two years."

"The bride is very like you, Madame," said Dalrymple, gravely. "Your younger sister, I presume?"

"***Ah, quel farceur***! He takes my daughter for my sister! Suzette, do you hear this? M'sieur is killing me with laughter!"

And the good lady chuckled, and gasped, and wiped her eyes, and dealt Dalrymple a playful push between the shoulders, which would have upset the balance of any less heavy dragoon.

"Your daughter, Madame!" said he. "Allow me to congratulate you. May I also be permitted to congratulate the bride?" And with this he took off his hat to Suzette and shook hands with Andre, who looked not overpleased, and proceeded to introduce me as his friend Monsieur Basil Arbuthnot, "a young English gentleman, ***tres distingue***"

The old lady then said her name was Madame Roquet, and that she rented a small farm about a mile and a half from Rouen; that Suzette was her only child; and that she had lost her "blessed man" about eight years ago. She next introduced the

elderly couple as her brother Jacques Robineau and his wife, and informed us that
Jacques was a tailor, and had a shop opposite the church of St. Maclou, "*la bas*."

To judge of Monsieur Robineau's skill by his outward appearance, I should
have said that he was professionally unsuccessful, and supplied his own wardrobe
from the misfits returned by his customers. He wore a waistcoat which was considerably too long for him, trousers which were considerably too short, and a green
cloth coat with a high velvet collar which came up nearly to the tops of his ears. In
respect of personal characteristics, Monsieur Robineau and his wife were the most
admirable contrast imaginable. Monsieur Robineau was short; Madame Robineau
was tall. Monsieur Robineau was as plump and rosy as a robin; Madame Robineau
was pale and bony to behold. Monsieur Robineau looked the soul of good nature,
ready to chirrup over his *grog-au-vin,* to smoke a pipe with his neighbor, to cut a
harmless joke or enjoy a harmless frolic, as cheerfully as any little tailor that ever
lived; Madame Robineau, on the contrary, preserved a dreadful dignity, and looked
as if she could laugh at nothing on this side of the grave. Not to consider the question too curiously, I should have said, at first sight, that Monsieur Robineau stood
in no little awe of his wife, and that Madame Robineau was the very head and front
of their domestic establishment.

It was wonderful and delightful to see how Captain Dalrymple placed himself on the best of terms with all these good people--how he patted Robineau on
the back and complimented Madame, banished the cloud from Andre's brow, and
summoned a smile to the pretty cheek of Suzette. One would have thought he had
known them for years already, so thoroughly was he at home with every member
of the wedding party.

Presently, he asked Suzette to dance. She blushed scarlet, and cast a pretty ap-
pealing look at her husband and her mother. I could almost guess what she whispered to the former by the motion of her lips.

"Monsieur Andre will, I am sure, spare Madame for one gallop," said Dalrymple, with that kind of courtesy which accepts no denial. It was quite another tone,
quite another manner. It was no longer the persuasive suavity of one who is desir-
ous only to please, but the politeness of a gentleman to au inferior.

The cloud came back upon Andre's brow, and he hesitated; but Madame Roquet
interposed.

"Spare her!" she exclaimed. "*Dame*! I should think so! She has never left his arm all day. Here, my child, give me your shawl while you dance, and bake care not to get too warm, for the evening air is dangerous."

And so Suzette took off her shawl, and Andre was silenced, and Dalrymple, in less than the half hour, was actually whirling away with his arm round little Phillis's dainty waist.

I am afraid that I proved a very indifferent *locum tenens* for my brilliant friend, and that the good people thought me exceedingly stupid. I tried to talk to them, but the language tripped me up at every turn, and the right words never would come when they were wanted. Besides, I felt uneasy without knowing exactly why. I could not keep from watching Dalrymple and Suzette. I could not help noticing how closely he held her; how he never ceased talking to her; and how the smiles and blushes chased each other over her pretty face. That I should have wit enough to observe these things proved that my education was progressing rapidly; but then, to be sure, I was studying under an accomplished teacher.

They danced for a long time. So long, that Andre became uneasy, and my available French was quite exhausted. I was heartily glad when Dalrymple brought back the little bride at last, flushed and panting, and (himself as cool as a diplomatist) assisted her with her shawl and resigned her to the protection of her husband.

"Why hast thou danced so long with that big Englishman?" murmured Andre, discontentedly. "When *I* asked thee, thou wast too tired, and now...."

"And now I am so happy to be near thee again," whispered Suzette.

Andre softened directly.

"But to dance for twenty minutes...." began he.

"Ah, but he danced so well, and I am so fond of waltzing, Andre!"

The cloud gathered again, and an impatient reply was coming, when Dalrymple opportunely invited the whole party to a bowl of punch in an adjoining arbor, and himself led the way with Madame Roquet. The arbor was vacant, a waiter was placing the chairs, and the punch was blazing in the bowl. It had evidently been ordered during one of the pauses in the dance, that it might be ready to the moment--a little attention which called forth exclamations of pleasure from both Madame Roquet and Monsieur Robineau, and touched with something like a gleam of satisfaction even the grim visage of Monsieur Robineau's wife.

Dalrymple took the head of the table, and stirred the punch into leaping tongues of blue flame till it looked like a miniature Vesuvius.

"What diabolical-looking stuff!" I exclaimed. "You might, to all appearance, be Lucifer's own cupbearer."

"A proof that it ought to be devilish good," replied Dalrymple, ladling it out into the glasses. "Allow me, ladies and gentlemen, to propose the health, happiness, and prosperity of the bride and bridegroom. May they never die, and may they be remembered for ever after!"

We all laughed as if this was the best joke we had heard in our lives, and Dalrymple filled the glasses up again.

"What, in the name of all that's mischievous, can have become of Sullivan?" said he to me. "I have not caught so much as a glimpse of him for the last hour."

"When I last saw him, he was dancing."

"Yes, with a pretty little dark-eyed girl in a blue dress. By Jove! that fellow will be getting into trouble if left to himself!"

"But the girl has her mother with her!"

"All the stronger probability of a scrimmage," replied Dalrymple, sipping his punch with a covert glance of salutation at Suzette.

"Shall I see if they are among the dancers?"

"Do--but make haste; for the punch is disappearing fast."

I left them, and went back to the platform where the indefatigable public was now engaged in the performance of quadrilles. Never, surely, were people so industrious in the pursuit of pleasure! They poussetted, bowed, curtsied, joined hands, and threaded the mysteries of every figure, as if their very lives depended on their agility.

"Look at Jean Thomas," said a young girl to her still younger companion. "He dances like an angel!"

The one thus called upon to admire, looked at Jean Thomas, and sighed.

"He never asks me, by any chance," said she, sadly, "although his mother and mine are good neighbors. I suppose I don't dance well enough--or dress well enough," she added, glancing at her friend's gay shawl and coquettish cap.

"He has danced with me twice this evening," said the first speaker triumphantly; "and he danced with me twice last Sunday at the Jardin d'Armide. Elise says...."

Her voice dropped to a whisper, and I heard no more. It was a passing glimpse behind the curtain--a peep at one of the many dramas of real life that are being played for ever around us. Here were all the elements of romance--love, admiration, vanity, envy. Here was a hero in humble life--a lady-killer in his own little sphere. He dances with one, neglects another, and multiplies his conquests with all the heartlessness of a gentleman.

I wandered round the platform once or twice, scrutinizing the dancers, but without success. There was no sign of Sullivan, or of his partner, or of his partner's mother, the *bourgeoise* with the green fan. I then went to the grotto of the fortune-teller, but it was full of noisy rustics; and thence to the lottery hall, where there were plenty of players, but not those of whom I was in search.

"Wheel of fortune, Messieurs et Mesdames," said the young lady behind the counter. "Only fifty centimes each. All prizes, and no blanks--try your fortune, *monsieur le capitaine!* Put it once, *monsieur le capitaine*; once for yourself, and once for madame. Only fifty centimes each, and the certainty of winning!"

Monsieur le capitaine was a great, rawboned corporal, with a pretty little maid-servant on his arm. The flattery was not very delicate; but it succeeded. He threw down a franc. The wheel flew round, the papers were drawn, and the corporal won a needle-case, and the maid-servant a cigar-holder. In the midst of the laugh to which this distribution gave rise, I walked away in the direction of the refreshment stalls. Here were parties supping substantially, dancers drinking orgeat and lemonade, and little knots of tradesmen and mechanics sipping beer ridiculously out of wine-glasses to an accompaniment of cakes and sweet-biscuits. Still I could see no trace of Mr. Frank Sullivan.

At length I gave up the search in despair, and on my way back encountered Master Philippe leaning against a tree, and looking exceedingly helpless and unwell.

"You ate too many eggs, Philippe," said his mother. "I told you so at the time."

"It--it wasn't the eggs," faltered the wretched Philippe. "It was the Russian swing."

"And serve you rightly, too," said his father angrily. "I wish with all my heart that you had had your favorite oysters as well!"

When I came back to the arbor, I found the little party immensely happy, and a fresh bowl of punch just placed upon the table. Andre was sitting next to Suzette, as proud as a king. Madame Roquet, volubly convivial, was talking to every one. Madame Robineau was silently disposing of all the biscuits and punch that came in her way. Monsieur Robineau, with his hat a little pushed back and his thumb in the arm-hole of his waistcoat, was telling a long story to which nobody listened; while Dalrymple, sitting on the other side of the bride, was gallantly doing the duties of entertainer.

He looked up--I shook my head, slipped back into my place, and listened to the tangled threads of conversation going on around me.

"And so," said Monsieur Robineau, proceeding with his story, and staring down into the bottom of his empty glass, "and so I said to myself, 'Robineau, *mon ami*, take care. One honest man is better than two rogues; and if thou keepest thine eyes open, the devil himself stands small chance of cheating thee!' So I buttoned up my coat--this very coat I have on now, only that I have re-lined and re-cuffed it since then, and changed the buttons for brass ones; and brass buttons for one's holiday coat, you know, look so much more *comme il faut*--and said to the landlord...."

"Another glass of punch, Monsieur Robineau," interrupted Dalrymple.

"Thank you, M'sieur, you are very good; well, as I was saying...."

"Ah, bah, brother Jacques!" exclaimed Madame Roquet, impatiently, "don't give us that old story of the miller and the gray colt, this evening! We've all heard it a hundred times already. Sing us a song instead, *mon ami*!"

"I shall be happy to sing, sister Marie," replied Monsieur Robineau, with somewhat husky dignity, "when I have finished my story. You may have heard the story before. So may Andre--so may Suzette--so may my wife. I admit it. But these gentlemen--these gentlemen who have never heard it, and who have done me the honor...."

"Not to listen to a word of it," said Madame Robineau, sharply. "There, you are answered, husband. Drink your punch, and hold your tongue."

Monsieur Robineau waved his hand majestically, and assumed a Parliamentary air.

"Madame Robineau," he said, getting more and more husky, "be so obliging as to wait till I ask for your advice. With regard to drinking my punch, I have drunk it--" and here he again stared down into the bottom of his glass, which was again empty--"and with regard to holding my tongue, that is my business, and--and...."

"Monsieur Robineau," said Dalrymple, "allow me to offer you some more punch."

"Not another drop, Jacques," said Madame, sternly. "You have had too much already."

Poor Monsieur Robineau, who had put out his glass to be refilled, paused and looked helplessly at his wife.

"***Mon cher ange***,...." he began; but she shook her head inflexibly, and Monsieur Robineau submitted with the air of a man who knows that from the sentence of the supreme court there is no appeal.

"***Dame***!" whispered Madame Roquet, with a confidential attack upon my ribs that gave me a pain in my side for half an hour after, "my brother has the heart of a rabbit. He gives way to her in everything--so much the worse for him. My blessed man, who was a saint of a husband, would have broken the bowl over my ears if I had dared to interfere between his glass and his mouth!"

Whereupon Madame Roquet filled her own glass and mine, and Madame Robineau, less indulgent to her husband than herself, followed our example.

Just at this moment, a confused hubbub of voices, and other sounds expressive of a *fracas*, broke out in the direction of the trees behind the orchestra. The dancers deserted their polka, the musicians stopped fiddling, the noisy supper-party in the next arbor abandoned their cold chicken and salad, and everybody ran to the scene of action. Dalrymple was on his feet in a moment; but Suzette held Andre back with both hands and implored him to stay.

"Some *mauvais sujets*, no doubt, who refuse to pay the score," suggested Madame Roquet.

"Or Sullivan, who has got into one of his infernal scrapes," muttered Dalrymple, with a determined wrench at his moustache. "Come on, anyhow, and let us see what is the matter!"

So we snatched up our hats and ran out, just as Monsieur Robineau seized the opportunity to drink another tumbler of punch when his wife was not looking.

Following in the direction of the rest, we took one of the paths behind the orchestra, and came upon a noisy crowd gathered round a wooden summer-house.

"It's a fight," said one.

"It's a pickpocket," said another.

"Bah! it's only a young fellow who has been making love to a girl," exclaimed a third.

We forced our way through, and there we saw Mr. Frank Sullivan with his hat off, his arms crossed, and his back against the wall, presenting a dauntless front to the gesticulations and threats of an exceedingly enraged young man with red hair, who was abusing him furiously. The amount of temper displayed by this young man was something unparalleled. He was angry in every one of his limbs. He stamped, he shook his fist, he shook his head. The very tips of his ears looked scarlet with rage. Every now and then he faced round to the spectators, and appealed to them-- or to a stout woman with a green fan, who was almost as red and angry as himself, and who always rushed forward when addressed, and shook the green fan in Sullivan's face.

"You are an aristocrat!" stormed the young man. "A pampered, insolent aristocrat! A dog of an Englishman! A *scelerat*! Don't suppose you are to trample upon us for nothing! We are Frenchmen, you beggarly islander--Frenchmen, do you hear?"

A growl of sympathetic indignation ran through the crowd, and "*a bas les aristocrats--a bas les Anglais*!" broke out here and there.

"In the devil's name, Sullivan," said Dalrymple, shouldering his way up to the object of these agreeable menaces, "what have you been after, to bring this storm about your ears?"

"Pshaw! nothing at all," replied he with a mocking laugh, and a contemptuous gesture. "I danced with a pretty girl, and treated her to champagne afterwards. Her mother and brother hunted us out, and spoiled our flirtation. That's the whole story."

Something in the laugh and gesture--something, too, perhaps in the language which they could not understand, appeared to give the last aggravation to both of Sullivan's assailants. I saw the young man raise his arm to strike--I saw Dalrymple fell him with a blow that would have stunned an ox--I saw the crowd close in, heard the storm break out on every side, and, above it all, the deep, strong tones of Dalrymple's voice, saying:--

"To the boat, boys! Follow me."

In another moment he had flung himself into the crowd, dealt one or two sounding blows to left and right, cleared a passage for himself and us, and sped away down one of the narrow walks leading to the river. Presently, having taken one or two turnings, none of which seemed to lead to the spot we sought, we came upon an open space full of piled-up benches, pyramids of empty bottles, boxes, baskets, and all kinds of lumber. Here we paused to listen and take breath.

We had left the crowd behind us, but they were still within hearing.

"By Jove!" said Dalrymple, "I don't know which way to go. I believe we are on the wrong side of the island."

"And I believe they are after us," added Sullivan, peering into the baskets. "By all that's fortunate, here are the fireworks! Has anybody got a match? We'll take these with us, and go off in a blaze of triumph!"

The suggestion was no sooner made than adopted. We filled our hats and pockets with crackers and Catherine-wheels, piled the rest into one great heap, threw a dozen or so of lighted fusees into the midst of them, and just as the voices of our pursuers were growing momentarily louder and nearer, darted away again down a fresh turning, and saw the river gleaming at the end of it.

"Hurrah! here's a boat," shouted Sullivan, leaping into it, and we after him.

It was not our boat, but we did not care for that. Ours was at the other side of the island, far enough away, down by the landing-place. Just as Dalrymple seized the oars, there burst forth a tremendous explosion. A column of rockets shot up into the air, and instantly the place was as light as day. Then a yell of discovery broke forth, and we were seen almost as soon as we were fairly out of reach. We had secured the only boat on that side of the island, and three or four of Dalrymple's powerful strokes had already carried us well into the middle of the stream. To let off our own store of fireworks--to pitch tokens of our regard to our friends on the island in the shape of blazing crackers, which fell sputtering and fizzing into the water half-way between the boat and the shore--to stand up in the stern and bow politely--finally, to row away singing "God save the Queen" with all our might, were feats upon which we prided ourselves very considerably at the time, and the recollection of which afforded us infinite amusement all the way home.

That evening we all supped together at the Chaval Blane, and of what we did or said after supper I have but a confused remembrance. I believe that I tried to smoke a cigar; and it is my impression that I made a speech, in which I swore eternal friendship to both of my new friends; but the only circumstance about which I cannot be mistaken is that I awoke next morning with the worst specimen of headache that had yet come within the limits of my experience.

CHAPTER IX.
DAMON AND PYTHIAS.

I left Rouen the day after my great adventure on the river, and Captain Dalrymple went with me to the station.

"You have my Paris address upon my card," he said, as we walked to and fro upon the platform. "It's just a bachelor's den, you know--and I shall be there in about a fortnight or three weeks. Come and look me up."

To which I replied that I was glad to be allowed to do so, and that I should "look him up" as soon as he came home. And so, with words of cordial good-will and a hearty shake of the hand, we parted.

Having started late in the evening, I arrived in Paris between four and five o'clock on a bright midsummer Sunday morning. I was not long delayed by the customs officers, for I carried but a scant supply of luggage. Having left this at an hotel, I wandered about till it should be time for breakfast. After breakfast I meant to dress and call upon Dr. Cheron.

The morning air was clear and cool. The sun shone brilliantly, and was reflected back with dazzling vividness from long vistas of high white houses, innumerable windows, and gilded balconies. Theatres, shops, cafes, and hotels not yet opened, lined the great thoroughfares. Triumphal arches, columns, parks, palaces, and churches succeeded one another in apparently endless succession. I passed a lofty pillar crowned with a conqueror's statue--a palace tragic in history--a modern Parthenon surrounded by columns, peopled with sculptured friezes, and approached by a flight of steps extending the whole width of the building. I went in, for the doors had just been opened, and a white-haired Sacristan was preparing the seats for matin service. There were acolytes decorating the altar with fresh flowers, and early devotees on their knees before the shrine of the Madonna. The gilded ornaments, the tapers winking in the morning light, the statues, the paintings, the faint clinging odors of incense, the hushed atmosphere, the devotional silence, the marble angels kneeling round the altar, all united to increase my dream of delight. I gazed and gazed again; wandered round and round; and at last, worn out with excitement and fatigue, sank into a chair in a distant corner of the Church, and fell into a heavy sleep. How long it lasted I know not; but the voices of the choristers and the deep tones of the organ mingled with my dreams. When I awoke the last worshippers were departing, the music had died into silence, the wax-lights were being extinguished, and the service was ended.

Again I went out into the streets; but all was changed. Where there had been the silence of early morning there was now the confusion of a great city. Where there had been closed shutters and deserted thoroughfares, there was the bustle of life, gayety, business, and pleasure. The shops blazed with jewels and merchandise; the stonemasons were at work on the new buildings; the lemonade venders, with their gay reservoirs upon their backs, were plying a noisy trade; the bill-stickers were papering boardings and lamp-posts with variegated advertisements; the charlatan, in his gaudy chariot, was selling pencils and penknives to the accompaniment of a hand-organ; soldiers were marching to the clangor of military music; the merchant was in his counting-house, the stock-broker at the Bourse, and the lounger, whose name is Legion, was sitting in the open air outside his favorite cafe, drinking chocolate, and yawning over the *Charivari*.

I thought I must be dreaming. I scarcely believed the evidence of my eyes. Was this Sunday? Was it possible that in our own little church at home--in our own little church, where we could hear the birds twittering outside in every interval of the quiet service--the old familiar faces, row beyond row, were even now upturned in reverent attention to the words of the preacher? Prince Bedreddin, transported in his sleep to the gates of Damascus, could scarcely have opened his eyes upon a foreign city and a strange people with more incredulous amazement.

I can now scarcely remember how that day of wonders went by. I only know that I rambled about as in a dream, and am vaguely conscious of having wandered through the gardens of the Tuilleries; of having found the Louvre open, and of losing myself among some of the upper galleries; of lying exhausted upon a bench in the Champs Elysees; of returning by quays lined with palaces and spanned by noble bridges; of pacing round and round the enchanted arcades of the Palais Royal; of wondering how and where I should find my hotel, and of deciding at last that I could go no farther without dining somehow. Wearied and half stupefied, I ventured, at length, into one of the large **restaurants** upon the Boulevards. Here I found spacious rooms lighted by superb chandeliers which were again reflected in mirrors that extended from floor to ceiling. Rows of small tables ran round the rooms, and a double line down the centre, each laid with its snowy cloth and glittering silver.

It was early when I arrived; so I passed up to the top of the room and appropriated a small table commanding a view of the great thoroughfare below. The waiters were slow to serve me; the place filled speedily; and by the time I had finished my soup, nearly all the tables were occupied. Here sat a party of officers, bronzed and mustachioed; yonder a group of laughing girls; a pair of provincials; a family party, children, governess and all; a stout capitalist, solitary and self content; a quatuor of rollicking **commis-voyageurs**; an English couple, perplexed and curious. Amused by the sight of so many faces, listening to the hum of voices, and watching the flying waiters bearing all kinds of mysterious dishes, I loitered over my lonely meal, and wished that this delightful whirl of novelty might last for ever. By and by a gentleman entered, walked up the whole length of the room in search of a seat, found my table occupied by only a single person, bowed politely, and drew his chair opposite mine.

He was a portly man of about forty-five or fifty years of age, with a broad, calm brow; curling light hair, somewhat worn upon the temples; and large blue eyes, more keen than tender. His dress was scrupulously simple, and his hands were immaculately white. He carried an umbrella little thicker than a walking-stick, and wrote out his list of dishes with a massive gold pencil. The waiter bowed down before him as if he were an habitue of the place.

It was not long before we fell into conversation. I do not remember which spoke first; but we talked of Paris--or rather, I talked and he listened; for, what with the excitement and fatigue of the day, and what with the half bottle of champagne which I had magnificently ordered, I found myself gifted with a sudden flood of words, and ran on, I fear, not very discreetly.

A few civil rejoinders, a smile, a bow, an assent, a question implied rather than spoken, sufficed to draw from me the particulars of my journey. I told everything, from my birthplace and education to my future plans and prospects; and the stranger, with a frosty humor twinkling about his eyes, listened politely. He was himself particularly silent; but he had the art of provoking conversation while quietly enjoying his own dinner. When this was finished, however, he leaned back in his chair, sipped his claret, and talked a little more freely.

"And so," said he, in very excellent English, "you have come to Paris to finish your studies. But have you no fear, young gentleman, that the attractions of so gay a city may divert your mind from graver subjects? Do you think that, when every pleasure may be had for the seeking, you will be content to devote yourself to the dry details of an uninteresting profession?"

"It is not an uninteresting profession," I replied. "I might perhaps have preferred the church or the law; but having embarked in the study of medicine, I shall do my best to succeed in it."

The stranger smiled.

"I am glad," he said, "to see you so ambitious. I do not doubt that you will become a shining light in the brotherhood of Esculapius."

"I hope so," I replied, boldly. "I have studied closer than most men of my age, already."

He smiled again, coughed doubtfully, and insisted on filling my glass from his own bottle.

"I only fear," he said, "that you will be too diffident of your own merits. Now, when you call upon this Doctor....what did you say was his name?"

"Cheron," I replied, huskily.

"True, Cheron. Well, when you meet him for the first time you will, perhaps, be timid, hesitating, and silent. But, believe me, a young man of your remarkable abilities should be self-possessed. You ought to inspire him from the beginning with a suitable respect for your talents."

"That's precisely the line I mean to take," said I, boastfully. "I'll--I'll astonish him. I'm afraid of nobody--not I!"

The stranger filled my glass again. His claret must have been very strong or my head very weak, for it seemed to me, as he did so, that all the chandeliers were in motion.

"Upon my word," observed he, "you are a young man of infinite spirit."

"And you," I replied, making an effort to bring the glass steadily to my lips, "you are a capital fellow--a clear-sighted, sensible, capital fellow. We'll be friends."

He bowed, and said, somewhat coldly,

"I have no doubt that we shall become better acquainted."

"Better acquainted, indeed!--we'll be intimate!" I ejaculated, affectionately. "I'll introduce you to Dalrymple--you'll like him excessively. Just the fellow to delight you."

"So I should say," observed the stranger, drily.

"And as for you and myself, we'll--we'll be Damon and ... what's the other one's name?"

"Pythias," replied my new acquaintance, leaning back in his chair, and surveying me with a peculiar and very deliberate stare. "Exactly so--Damon and Pythias! A charming arrangement."

"Bravo! Famous! And now we'll have another bottle of wine."

"Not on my account, I beg," said the gentleman firmly. "My head is not so cool as yours."

Cool, indeed, and the room whirling round and round, like a teetotum!

"Oh, if you won't, I won't," said I confusedly; "but I--I could--drink my share of another bottle, I assure you, and not--feel the slightest...."

"I have no doubt on that point," said my neighbor, gravely; "but our French wines are deceptive, Mr. Arbuthnot, and you might possibly suffer some inconvenience to-morrow. You, as a medical man, should understand the evils of dyspepsia."

"Dy--dy--dyspepsia be hanged," I muttered, dreamily. "Tell me, friend--by the by, I forget your name. Friend what?"

"Friend Pythias," returned the stranger, drily. "You gave me the name yourself."

"Ay, but your real name?"

He shrugged his shoulders.

"One name is as good as another," said he, lightly. "Let it be Pythias, for the present. But you were about to ask me some question?"

"About old Cheron," I said, leaning both elbows on the table, and speaking very confidentially. "Now tell me, have you--have you any notion of what he is like? Do you--know--know anything about him?"

"I have heard of him," he replied, intent for the moment on the pattern of his wine-glass.

"Clever?"

"That is a point upon which I could not venture an opinion. You must ask some more competent judge."

"Come, now," said I, shaking my head, and trying to look knowing; "you--you know what I mean, well enough. Is he a grim old fellow? A--a--griffin, you know! Come, is he a gr--r--r--riffin?"

My words had by this time acquired a distressing, self-propelling tendency, and linked themselves into compounds of twenty and thirty syllables.

My *vis-a-vis* smiled, bit his lip, then laughed a dry, short laugh.

"Really," he said, "I am not in a position to reply to your question; but upon the whole, I should say that Dr. Cheron was not quite a griffin. The species, you see, is extinct."

I roared with laughter; vowed I had never heard a better joke in my life; and repeated his last words over and over, like a degraded idiot as I was. All at once a sense of deadly faintness came upon me. I turned hot and cold by turns, and lifting my hand to my head, said, or tried to say:--

"Room's--'bominably--close!"

"We had better go," he replied promptly. "The air will do you good. Leave me to settle for our dinners, and you shall make it right with me by-and-by."

He did so, and we left the room. Once out in the open air I found myself unable to stand. He called a *fiacre*; almost lifted me in; took his place beside me, and asked the name of my hotel.

I had forgotten it; but I knew that it was opposite the railway station, and that was enough. When we arrived, I was on the verge of insensibility. I remember that I was led up-stairs by two waiters, and that the stranger saw me to my room. Then all was darkness and stupor.

CHAPTER X.
THE NEXT MORNING.

"Oh, my Christian ducats!" *Merchant of Venice*.

Gone!--gone!--both gone!--my new gold watch and my purse full of notes and Napoleons!

I rang the bell furiously. It was answered by a demure-looking waiter, with a face like a parroquet.

"Does Monsieur please to require anything?"

"Require anything!" I exclaimed, in the best French I could muster. "I have been robbed!"

"Robbed, Monsieur?"

"Yes, of my watch and purse!"

"*Tiens*! Of a watch and purse?" repeated the parroquet, lifting his eyebrows with an air of well-bred surprise. "*C'est drole.*"

"Droll!" I cried, furiously. "Droll, you scoundrel! I'll let you know whether I think it droll! I'll complain to the authorities! I'll have the house searched! I'll--I'll...."

I rang the bell again. Two or three more waiters came, and the master of the hotel. They all treated my communication in the same manner--coolly; incredulously; but with unruffled politeness.

"Monsieur forgets," urged the master, "that he came back to the hotel last night in a state of absolute intoxication. Monsieur was accompanied by a stranger, who was gentlemanly, it it true; but since Monsieur acknowledges that that stranger was personally unknown to him, Monsieur may well perceive it would be more reasonable if his suspicions first pointed in that direction."

Struck by the force of this observation, I flung myself into a chair and remained silent.

"Has Monsieur no acquaintances in Paris to whom he may apply for advice?" inquired the landlord.

"None," said I, moodily; "except that I have a letter of introduction to one Dr. Cheron."

The landlord and his waiters exchanged glances.

"I would respectfully recommend Monsieur to present his letter immediately," said the former. "Monsieur le Docteur Cheron is a man of the world--a man of high reputation and sagacity. Monsieur could not do better than advise with him."

"Call a cab for me," said I, after a long pause. "I will go."

The determination cost me something. Dismayed by the extent of my loss, racked with headache, languid, pale, and full of remorse for last night's folly, it needed but this humiliation to complete my misery. What! appear before my instructor for the first time with such a tale! I could have bitten my lips through with vexation.

The cab was called. I saw, but would not see, the winks and nods exchanged behind my back by the grinning waiters. I flung myself into the vehicle, and soon was once more rattling through the noisy streets. But those brilliant streets had now lost all their charm for me. I admired nothing, saw nothing, heard nothing, on the way. I could think only of my father's anger and the contempt of Dr. Cheron.

Presently the cab stopped before a large wooden gate with two enormous knockers. One half of this gate was opened by a servant in a sad-colored livery. I was shown across a broad courtyard, up a flight of lofty steps, and into a spacious *salon* plainly furnished.

"Monsieur le Docteur is at present engaged," said the servant, with an air of profound respect. "Will Monsieur have the goodness to be seated for a few moments."

I sat down. I rose up. I examined the books upon the table, and the pictures on the walls. I wished myself "anywhere, anywhere out of the world," and more than once was on the point of stealing out of the house, jumping into my cab, and making off without seeing the doctor at all. One consideration alone prevented me. I had lost all my money, and had not even a franc left to pay the driver. Presently the door again opened, the grave footman reappeared, and I heard the dreaded announcement:--"Monsieur le Docteur will be happy to receive Monsieur in his consulting-room."

I followed mechanically. We passed through a passage thickly carpeted, and paused before a green baize door. This door opened noiselessly, and I found myself in the great man's presence.

"It gives me pleasure to welcome the son of my old friend John Arbuthnot," said a clear, and not unfamiliar voice.

I started, looked up, grew red and white, hot and cold, and had not a syllable to utter in reply.

In Doctor Cheron, I recognised--
PYTHIAS!

CHAPTER XI.
MYSTERIOUS PROCEEDINGS.

The doctor pointed to a chair, looked at his watch, and said:--

"I hope you have had a pleasant journey. Arrived this morning?"

There was not the faintest gleam of recognition on his face. Not a smile; not a glance; nothing but the easy politeness of a stranger to a stranger.

"N--not exactly," I faltered. "Yesterday morning, sir."

"Ah, indeed! Spent the day in sight-seeing, I dare say. Admire Paris?"

Too much astonished to speak, I took refuge in a bow.

"Not found any lodgings yet, I presume?" asked the doctor, mending a pen very deliberately.

"N--not yet, sir."

"I concluded so The English do not seek apartments on Sunday. You observe the day very strictly, no doubt?"

Blushing and confused, I stammered some incoherent words and sat twirling my hat, the very picture of remorse.

"At what hotel have you put up?" he next inquired, without appearing to observe my agitation.

"The--the Hotel des Messageries."

"Good, but expensive. You must find a lodging to-day."

I bowed again.

"And, as your father's representative, I must take care that you procure something suitable, and are not imposed upon. My valet shall go with you."

He rang the bell, and the sad-colored footman appeared on the threshold.

"Desire Brunet to be in readiness to walk out with this gentleman," he said, briefly, and the servant retired.

"Brunet," he continued, addressing me again, "is faithful and sagacious. He will instruct you on certain points indispensable to a resident in Paris, and will see that you are not ill-accommodated or overcharged. A young man has few wants, and I should infer that a couple of rooms in some quiet street will be all that you require?"

"I--I am very grateful."

He waved down my thanks with an air of cold but polite authority; took out his note-book and pencil; (I could have sworn to that massive gold pencil!) and proceeded to question me.

"Your age, I think," said he, "is twenty-one?"

"Twenty, sir."

"Ah--twenty. You desire to be entered upon the list of visiting students at the Hotel Dieu, to be free of the library and lecture-rooms, and to be admitted into my public classes?"

"Yes, sir."

"Also, to attend here in my house for private instruction."

"Yes, sir."

He filled in a few words upon a printed form, and handed it to me with his visiting card.

"You will present these, and your passport, to the secretary at the hospital," said he, "and will receive in return the requisite tickets of admission. Your fees have already been paid in, and your name has been entered. You must see to this matter at once, for the *bureau* closes at two o'clock. You will then require the rest of the day for lodging-seeking, moving, and so forth. To-morrow morning, at nine o'clock, I shall expect you here."

"Indeed, sir," I murmured, "I am more obliged than...."

"Not in the least," he interrupted, decisively; "your father's son has every claim upon me. I object to thanks. All that I require from you are habits of industry, punctuality, and respect. Your father speaks well of you, and I have no doubt I shall find you all that he represents. Can I do anything more for you this morning?"

I hesitated; could not bring myself to utter one word of that which I had come to say; and murmured--

"Nothing more, I thank you, sir."

He looked at me piercingly, paused an instant, and then rang the bell.

"I am about to order my carriage," he said; "and, as I am going in that direction, I will take you as far as the Hotel Dieu."

"But--but I have a cab at the door," I faltered, remembering, with a sinking heart, that I had not a sou to pay the driver.

The servant appeared again.

"Let the carriage be brought round immediately, and dismiss this gentleman's cab."

The man retired, and I heaved a sigh of relief. The doctor bent low over the papers on his desk, and I fancied for the moment that a faint smile flitted over his face. Then he took up his hat, and pointed to the door.

"Now, my young friend," he said authoritatively, "we must be gone. Time is gold. After you."

I bowed and preceded him. His very courtesy was sterner than the displeasure of another, and I already felt towards him a greater degree of awe than I should have quite cared to confess. The carriage was waiting in the courtyard. I placed myself with my back to the horses; Dr. Cheron flung himself upon the opposite seat; a servant out of livery sprang up beside the coachman; the great gates were flung open; and we glided away on the easiest of springs and the softest of cushions.

Dr. Cheron took a newspaper from his pocket, and began to read; so leaving me to my own uncomfortable reflections.

And, indeed, when I came to consider my position I was almost in despair. Moneyless, what was to become of me? Watchless and moneyless, with a bill awaiting me at my hotel, and not a stiver in my pocket wherewith to pay it.... Miserable pupil of a stern master! luckless son of a savage father! to whom could I turn for help? Not certainly to Dr. Cheron, whom I had been ready to accuse, half an hour ago, of having stolen my watch and purse. Petty larceny and Dr. Cheron! how ludicrously incongruous! And yet, where was my property? Was the Hotel des Messageries a den of thieves? And again, how was it that this same Dr. Cheron looked, and spoke, and acted, as if he had never seen me in his life till this morning? Was I mad, or dreaming, or both?

The carriage stopped and the door opened.

"Hotel Dieu, M'sieur," said the servant, touching his hat.

Dr. Cheron just raised his eyes from the paper.

"This is your first destination," he said. "I would advise you, on leaving here, to return to your hotel. There may be letters awaiting you. Good-morning."

With this he resumed his paper, the carriage rolled away, and I found myself at the Hotel Dieu, with the servant out of livery standing respectfully behind me.

Go back to my hotel! Why should I go back? Letters there could be none, unless at the Poste Restante. I thought this a very unnecessary piece of advice, rejected it in my own mind, and so went into the hospital *bureau*, and transacted my business. When I came out again, Brunet took the lead.

He was an elderly man with a solemn countenance and a mysterious voice. His manner was oppressively respectful; his address diplomatic; his step stealthy as a courtier's. When we came to a crossing he bowed, stood aside, and followed me; then took the lead again; and so on, during a brisk walk of about half an hour. All at once, I found myself at the Hotel des Messageries.

"Monsieur's hotel," said the doctor's valet, touching his hat.

"You are mistaken," said I, rather impatiently. "I did not ask to be brought here. My object this morning is to look for apartments."

"Post in at mid-day, Monsieur," he observed, gravely. "Monsieur's letters may have arrived."

"I expect none, thank you."

"Monsieur will, nevertheless, permit me to inquire," said the persevering valet, and glided in before my eyes.

The thing was absurd! Both master and servant insisted that I must have letters, whether I would, or no! To my amazement, however, Brunet came back with a small sealed box in his hands.

"No letters have arrived for Monsieur," he said; "but this box was left with the porter about an hour ago."

I weighed it, shook it, examined the seals, and, going into the public room, desired Brunet to follow me. There I opened it. It contained a folded paper, a quantity of wadding, my purse, my roll of bank-notes, and my watch! On the paper, I read the following words:--

"Learn from the events of last night the value of temperance, the wisdom of silence, and the danger of chance acquaintanceships. Accept the lesson, and he by whom it is administered will forget the error."

The paper dropped from my hands and fell upon the floor. The impenetrable Brunet picked it up, and returned it to me.

"Brunet!" I ejaculated.

"Monsieur?" said he, interrogatively, raising his hand to his forehead by force of habit, although his hat stood beside him on the floor.

There was not a shadow of meaning in his face--not a quiver to denote that he knew anything of what had passed. To judge by the stolid indifference of his manner, one might have supposed that the delivery of caskets full of watches and valuables was an event of daily occurrence in the house of Dr. Cheron. His coolness silenced me. I drew a long breath; hastened to put my watch in my pocket, and lock up my money in my room; and then went to the master of the hotel, and informed him of the recovery of my property. He smiled and congratulated me; but he did not seem to be in the least surprised. I fancied, some how, that matters were not quite so mysterious to him as they had been to me.

I also fancied that I heard a suspicious roar of laughter as I passed out into the street.

It was not long before I found such apartments as I required, Piloted by Brunet through some broad thoroughfares and along part of the Boulevards, I came upon a cluster of narrow streets branching off through a massive stone gateway from the Rue du Faubourg Montmartre. This little nook was called the Cite Bergere. The houses were white and lofty. Some had courtyards, and all were decorated with pretty iron balconies and delicately-tinted Venetian shutters. Most of them bore the announcement--"***Apartements a louer***"--suspended above the door. Outside one of these houses sat two men with a little table between them. They were playing at dominoes, and wore the common blue blouse of the mechanic class. A woman stood by, paring celery, with an infant playing on the mat inside the door and a cat purring at her feet. It was a pleasant group. The men looked honest, the woman good-tempered, and the house exquisitely clean; so the diplomatic Brunet went forward to negotiate, while I walked up and down outside. There were rooms to be let on the second, third and fifth floors. The fifth was too high, and the second too expensive; but the third seemed likely to suit me. The ***suite*** consisted of a bed-room, dressing-room, and tiny ***salon***, and was furnished with the elegant uncomfortableness characteristic of our French neighbors. Here were floors shiny and carpetless; windows that objected to open, and drawers that refused to shut; mirrors all round the walls a set of hanging shelves; an ormolu time piece that struck all kinds of miscellaneous hours at unexpected times; an abundance of vases filled with faded artificial flowers; insecure chairs of white and gold; and a round table that had a way of turning over suddenly like a table in a pantomime, if you ventured to place anything on any part but the inlaid star in the centre. Above all, there was a balcony big enough for a couple of chairs, and some flower-pots, overlooking the street.

I was delighted with everything. In imagination I beheld my balcony already blooming with roses, and my shelves laden with books. I admired the white and gold chairs with all my heart, and saw myself reflected in half a dozen mirrors at once with an innocent pride of ownership which can only be appreciated by those who have tasted the supreme luxury of going into chambers for the first time.

"Shall I conclude for Monsieur at twenty francs a week?" murmured the sagacious Brunet.

"Of course," said I, laying the first week's rent upon the table.

And so the thing was done, and, brimful of satisfaction, I went off to the hotel for my luggage, and moved in immediately.

CHAPTER XII.
BROADCLOTH AND CIVILIZATION.

Allowing for my inexperience in the use of the language, I prospered better than I had expected, and found, to my satisfaction, that I was by no means behind my French fellow-students in medical knowledge. I passed through my preliminary examination with credit, and although Dr. Cheron was careful not to praise me too soon, I had reason to believe that he was satisfied with my progress. My life, indeed, was now wholly given up to my work. My country-breeding had made me timid, and the necessity for speaking a foreign tongue served only to increase my natural reserve; so that although I lived and studied day after day in the society of some two or three hundred young men, I yet lived as solitary a life as Robinson Crusoe in his island. No one sought to know me. No one took a liking for me. Gay, noisy, chattering fellows that they were, they passed me by for a "dull and muddy-pated rogue;" voted me uncompanionable when I was only shy; and, doubtless, quoted me to each other as a rare specimen of the silent Englishman. I lived, too, quite out of the students' colony. To me the *Quartier Latin* (except as I went to and fro between the Hotel Dieu and the Ecole de Medicine) was a land unknown; and the student's life--that wonderful *Vie de Boheme* which furnishes forth half the fiction of the Paris press--a condition of being, about which I had never even heard. What wonder, then, that I never arrived at Dr. Cheron's door five minutes behind time, never missed a lecture, never forgot an appointment? What wonder that, after dropping moodily into one or two of the theatres, I settled down quite quietly in my lodgings; gave up my days to study; sauntered about the lighted alleys of the Champs Elysees in the sweet spring evenings, and, going home betimes, spent an hour or two with my books, and kept almost as early hours as in my father's house at Saxonholme?

After I had been living thus for rather longer than three weeks, I made up my mind one Sunday morning to call at Dalrymple's rooms, and inquire if he had yet arrived in Paris. It was about eleven o'clock when I reached the Chaussee d'Antin, and there learned that he was not only arrived, but at home. Being by this time in possession of the luxury of a card, I sent one up, and was immediately admitted. I found breakfast still upon the table; Dalrymple sitting with an open desk and cash-box before him; and, standing somewhat back, with his elbow resting on the chimney-piece, a gentleman smoking a cigar. They both looked up as I was announced, and Dalrymple, welcoming me with a hearty grasp, introduced this gentleman as Monsieur de Simoncourt.

M. de Simoncourt bowed, knocked the ash from his cigar, and looked as if he wished me at the Antipodes. Dalrymple was really glad to see me.

"I have been expecting you, Arbuthnot," said he, "for the last week. If you had not soon beaten up my quarters, I should have tried, somehow, to find out yours. What have you been about all this time? Where are you located? What mischief have you been perpetrating since our expedition to the *guingette* on the river? Come, you have a thousand things to tell me!"

M. de Simoncourt looked at his watch--a magnificent affair, decorated with a costly chain, and a profusion of pendant trifles--and threw the last-half of his cigar into the fireplace.

"You must excuse me, *mon cher*" said he. "I have at least a dozen calls to make before dinner."

Dalrymple rose, readily enough, and took a roll of bank-notes from the cash-box.

"If you are going," he said, "I may as well hand over the price of that Tilbury. When will they send it home?"

"To-morrow, undoubtedly."

"And I am to pay fifteen hundred franks for it!"

"Just half its value!" observed M. de Simoncourt, with a shrug of his shoulders.

Dalrymple smiled, counted the notes, and handed them to his friend.

"Fifteen hundred may be half its cost," said he; "but I doubt if I am paying much less than its full value. Just see that these are right."

M. de Simoncourt ruffled the papers daintily over, and consigned them to his pocket-book. As he did so, I could not help observing the whiteness of his hands and the sparkle of a huge brilliant on his little finger. He was a pale, slender, olive-hued man, with very dark eyes, and glittering teeth, and a black moustache inclining superciliously upwards at each corner; somewhat too ***nonchalant***, perhaps, in his manner, and somewhat too profuse in the article of jewellery; but a very elegant gentleman, nevertheless.

"***Bon***!" said he. "I am glad you have bought it. I would have taken it myself, had the thing happened a week or two earlier. Poor Duchesne! To think that he should have come to this, after all!"

"I am sorry for him," said Dalrymple; "but it is a case of wilful ruin. He made up his mind to go to the devil, and went accordingly. I am only surprised that the crash came no sooner."

M. de Simoneourt twitched at the supercilious moustache.

"And you think you would not care to take the black mare with the Tilbury?" said he, negligently.

"No--I have a capital horse, already."

"Hah I--well--'tis almost a pity. The mare is a dead bargain. Shouldn't wonder if I buy her, after all."

"And yet you don't want her," said Dalrymple.

"Quite true; but one must have a favorite sin, and horseflesh is mine. I shall ruin myself by it some day--***mort de ma vie!*** By the way, have you seen my chestnut in harness? No? Then you will be really pleased. Goes delightfully with the gray, and manages tandem to perfection. ***Parbleu!*** I was forgetting--do we meet to-night?"

"Where?"

"At Chardonnier's."

Dalrymple shook his head, and turned the key in his cash box.

"Not this evening," he replied. I have other engagements."

"Bah! and I promised to go, believing you were sure to be of the party. St. Pol, I know, will be there, and De Brezy also."

"Chardonnier's parties are charming things in their way," said Dalrymple, somewhat coldly, "and no man enjoys Burgundy and lansquenet more heartily than myself; but one might grow to care for nothing else, and I have no desire to fall into worse habits than those I have contracted already."

M. de Simoneourt laughed a dry, short laugh, and twitched again at the supercilious moustache.

"I had no idea you were a philosopher," said he.

"Nor am I. I am a *mauvais sujet--mauvais* enough, already, without seeking to become worse."

"Well, adieu--I will see to this affair of the Tilbury, and desire them to let you have it by noon to-morrow."

"A thousand thanks. I am ashamed that you have so much trouble in the matter. *Au revoir*."

"*Au revoir*."

Whereupon M. de Simoncourt honored me with a passing bow, and took his departure. Being near the window, I saw him spring into an elegant cabriolet, and drive off with the showiest of high horses and the tiniest of tigers.

He was no sooner gone than Dalrymple took me by the shoulders, placed me in an easy chair, poured out a couple of glasses of hock, and said:--

"Now, then, my young friend, your news or your life! Out with it, every word, as you hope to be forgiven!"

I had but little to tell, and for that little, found myself, as I had anticipated, heartily laughed at. My adventure at the restaurant, my unlucky meeting with Dr. Cheron, and the history of my interview with him next morning, delighted Dalrymple beyond measure.

Nothing would satisfy him, after this, but to call me Damon, to tease me continually about Doctor Pythias, and to remind me at every turn of the desirableness of Arcadian friendships.

"And so, Damon," said he, "you go nowhere, see nothing, and know nobody. This sort of life will never do for you! I must take you out--introduce you--get you an *entree* into society, before I leave Paris."

"I should be heartily glad to visit at one or two private houses," I replied. "To spend the winter in this place without knowing a soul, would be something frightful."

Dalrymple looked at me half laughingly, half compassionately.

"Before I do it, however," said he, "you must look a little less like a savage, and more like a tame Christian. You must have your hair cut, and learn to tie your cravat properly. Do you possess an evening suit?"

Blushing to the tips of my ears, I not only confessed that I was destitute of that desirable outfit, but also that I had never yet in all my life had occasion to wear it.

"I am glad of it; for now you are sure to be well fitted. Your tailor, depend on it, is your great civilizer, and a well-made suit of clothes is in itself a liberal education. I'll take you to Michaud--my own especial purveyor. He is a great artist. With so many yards of superfine black cloth, he will give you the tone of good society and the exterior of a gentleman. In short, he will do for you in eight or ten hours more than I could do in as many years."

"Pray introduce me at once to this illustrious man," I exclaimed laughingly, "and let me do him homage!"

"You will have to pay heavily for the honor," said Dalrymple. "Of that I give you notice."

"No matter. I am willing to pay heavily for the tone of good society and the exterior of a gentleman."

"Very good. Take a book, then, or a cigar, and amuse yourself for five minutes while I write a note. That done, you may command me for as long as you please."

I took the first book that came, and finding it to be a history of the horse, amused myself, instead, by observing the aspect of Dalrymple's apartment.

Rooms are eloquent biographies. They betray at once if the owner be careless or orderly, studious or idle, vulgar or refined. Flowers on the table, engravings on the walls, indicate refinement and taste; while a well-filled book-case says more in favor of its possessor than the most elaborate letter of recommendation. Dalrymple's room was a monograph of himself. Careless, luxurious, disorderly, crammed with all sorts of costly things, and characterized by a sort of reckless elegance, it expressed, as I interpreted it, the very history of the man. Rich hangings; luxurious carpets; walls covered with paintings; cabinets of bronze and rare porcelain; a statuette of Rachel beside a bust of Homer; a book-case full of French novels with a sprinkling of Shakespeare and Horace; a stand of foreign arms; a lamp from Pompeii; a silver casket full of cigars; tables piled up with newspapers, letters, pipes, riding-whips, faded bouquets, and all kinds of miscellaneous rubbish--such were my friend's surroundings; and such, had I speculated upon them beforehand, I should have expected to find them. Dalrymple, in the meanwhile, despatched his letter with characteristic rapidity. His pen rushed over the paper like a dragoon charge, nor was once laid aside till both letter and address were finished. Just as he was sealing it, a note was brought to him by his servant--a slender, narrow, perfumed note, written on creamy paper, and adorned on the envelope with an elaborate cypher in gold and colors. Had I lived in the world of society for the last hundred seasons, I could not have interpreted the appearance of that note more sagaciously.

"It is from a lady," said I to myself. Then seeing Dalrymple tear up his own letter immediately after reading it, and begin another, I added, still in my own mind--"And it is from the lady to whom he was writing."

Presently he paused, laid his pen aside, and said:--

"Arbuthnot, would you like to go with me to-morrow evening to one or two **soirees**?"

"Can your Civilizer provide me with my evening suit in time?"

"He? The great Michaud? Why, he would equip you for this evening, if it were necessary!"

"In that case, I shall be very glad."

"**Bon!** I will call for you at ten o'clock; so do not forget to leave me your address."

Whereupon he resumed his letter. When it was written, he returned to the subject.

"Then I will take you to-morrow night," said he, "to a reception at Madame Rachel's. Hers is the most beautiful house in Paris. I know fifty men who would give their ears to be admitted to her **salons**."

Even in the wilds of Saxonholme I had heard and read of the great **tragedienne** whose wealth vied with the Rothschilds, and whose diamonds might have graced a crown. I had looked forward to the probability of beholding her from afar off, if she was ever to be seen on the boards of the Theatre Francais; but to be admitted to her presence--received in her house--introduced to her in person ... it seemed ever so much too good to be true!

Dalrymple smiled good-naturedly, and put my thanks aside.

"It is a great sight," said he, "and nothing more. She will bow to you--she may not even speak; and she would pass you the next morning without remembering that she had ever seen you in her life. Actresses are a race apart, my dear fellow, and care for no one who is neither rich nor famous."

"I never imagined," said I, half annoyed, "that she would take any notice of me at all. Even a bow from such a woman is an event to be remembered."

"Having received that bow, then," continued Dalrymple, "and having enjoyed the ineffable satisfaction of returning it, you can go on with me to the house of a lady close by, who receives every Monday evening. At her ***soirees*** you will meet pleasant and refined people, and having been once introduced by me, you will, I have no doubt, find the house open to you for the future."

"That would, indeed, be a privilege. Who is this lady?"

"Her name," said Dalrymple, with an involuntary glance at the little note upon his desk, "is Madame de Courcelles. She is a very charming and accomplished lady."

I decided in my own mind that Madame de Courcelles was the writer of that note.

"Is she married?" was my next question.

"She is a widow," replied Dalrymple. "Monsieur de Courcelles was many years older than his wife, and held office as a cabinet minister during the greater part of the reign of Louis Phillippe. He has been dead these four or five years."

"Then she is rich?"

"No--not rich; but sufficiently independent."

"And handsome?"

"Not handsome, either; but graceful, and very fascinating."

Graceful, fascinating, independent, and a widow! Coupling these facts with the correspondence which I believed I had detected, I grouped them into a little romance, and laid out my friend's future career as confidently as if it had depended only on myself to marry him out of hand, and make all parties happy.

Dalrymple sat musing for a moment, with his chin resting on his hands and his eyes fixed on the desk. Then shaking back his hair as if he would shake back his thoughts with it, he started suddenly to his feet and said, laughingly:--

"Now, young Damon, to Michaud's--to Michaud's, with what speed we may! Farewell to 'Tempe and the vales of Arcady,' and hey for civilization, and a swallow-tailed coat!" I noticed, however, that before we left the room, he put the little note tenderly away in a drawer of his desk, and locked it with a tiny gold key that hung upon his watch-chain.

CHAPTER XIII.
I MAKE MY DEBUT IN SOCIETY.

At ten o'clock on Monday evening, Dalrymple called for me, and by ten o'clock, thanks to the great Michaud and other men of genius, I presented a faultless exterior. My friend walked round me with a candle, and then sat down and examined me critically.

"By Jove!" said he, "I don't believe I should have known you! You are a living testimony to the science of tailoring. I shall call on Michaud, to-morrow, and pay my tribute of admiration."

"I am very uncomfortable," said I, ruefully.

"Uncomfortable! nonsense--Michaud's customers don't know the meaning of the word."

"But he has not made me a single pocket!"

"And what of that? Do you suppose the great Michaud would spoil the fit of a masterpiece for your convenience?"

"What am I to do with my pocket-handkerchief?"

"Michaud's customers never need pocket-handkerchiefs."

"And then my trousers..."

"Unreasonable Juvenile, what of the trousers?"

"They are so tight that I dare not sit down in them."

"Barbarian! Michaud's customers never sit down in society."

"And my boots are so small that I can hardly endure them."

"Very becoming to the foot," said Dalyrmple, with exasperating indifference.

"And my collar is so stiff that it almost cuts my throat."

"Makes you hold your head up," said Dalrymple, "and leaves you no inducement to commit suicide."

I could not help laughing, despite my discomfort.

"Job himself never had such a comforter!" I exclaimed.

"It would be a downright pleasure to quarrel with you."

"Put on your hat instead, and let us delay no longer," replied my friend. "My cab is waiting."

So we went down, and in another moment were driving through the lighted streets. I should hardly have chosen to confess how my heart beat when, on turning an angle of the Rue Trudon, our cab fell into the rear of three or four other carriages, passed into a courtyard crowded with arriving and departing vehicles, and drew up before an open door, whence a broad stream of light flowed out to meet us. A couple of footmen received us in a hall lighted by torches and decorated with stands of antique armor. From the centre of this hall sprang a Gothic staircase, so light, so richly sculptured, so full of niches and statues, slender columns, foliated capitals, and delicate ornamentation of every kind, that it looked a very blossoming of the stone. Following Dalrymple up this superb staircase and through a vestibule of carved oak, I next found myself in a room that might have been the scene of Plato's symposium. Here were walls painted in classic fresco; windows curtained with draperies of chocolate and amber; chairs and couches of ebony, carved in antique fashion; Etruscan amphorae; vases and paterae of terracotta; exquisite lamps, statuettes and candelabra in rare green bronze; and curious parti-colored busts of philosophers and heroes, in all kinds of variegated marbles. Powdered footmen serving modern coffee seemed here like anachronisms in livery. In such a room one should have been waited on by boys crowned with roses, and have partaken only of classic dishes--of Venafran olives or oysters from the Lucrine lake, washed down with Massic, or Chian, or honeyed Falernian.

Some half-dozen gentlemen, chatting over their coffee, bowed to Dalrymple when we came in. They were talking of the war in Algiers, and especially of the gallantry of a certain Vicomte de Caylus, in whose deeds they seemed to take a more than ordinary interest.

"Rode single-handed right through the enemy's camp," said a bronzed, elderly man, with a short, gray beard.

"And escaped without a scratch," added another, with a tiny red ribbon at his button-hole.

"He comes of a gallant stock," said a third. "I remember his father at Austerlitz--literally cut to pieces at the head of his squadron."

"You are speaking of de Caylus," said Dalrymple. "What news of him from Algiers?"

"This--that having volunteered to carry some important despatches to head-quarters, he preferred riding by night through Abd-el-Kader's camp, to taking a *detour* by the mountains," replied the first speaker.

"A wild piece of boyish daring," said Dalrymple, somewhat drily. "I presume he did not return by the same road?"

"I should think not. It would have been certain death a second time!"

"And this happened how long since?"

"About a fortnight ago. But we shall soon know all particulars from himself."

"From himself?"

"Yes, he has obtained leave of absence--is, perhaps, by this time in Paris."

Dalrymple set down his cup untasted, and turned away.

"Come, Arbuthnot," he said, hastily, "I must introduce you to Madame Rachel."

We passed through a small antechamber, and into a brilliant *salon*, the very reverse of antique. Here all was light and color. Here were hangings of flowered chintz; fantastic divans; lounge-chairs of every conceivable shape and hue; great Indian jars; richly framed drawings; stands of exotic plants; Chinese cages, filled with valuable birds from distant climes; folios of engravings; and, above all, a large cabinet in marqueterie, crowded with bronzes, Chinese carvings, pastille burners, fans, medals, Dresden groups, Sevres vases, Venetian glass, Asiatic idols, and all kinds of precious trifles in tortoise-shall, mother o'-pearl, malachite, onyx, lapis lazuli, jasper, ivory, and mosaic. In this room, sitting, standing, turning over engravings, or grouped here and there on sofas and divans, were some twenty-five or thirty gentlemen, all busily engaged in conversation. Saluting some of these by a passing bow, my friend led the way straight through this *salon* and into a larger one immediately beyond it.

"This," he said, "is one of the most beautiful rooms in Paris. Look round and tell me if you recognise, among all her votaries, the divinity herself."

I looked round, bewildered.

"Recognise!" I echoed. "I should not recognise my own father at this moment.

I feel like Abou Hassan in the palace of the Caliph."

"Or like Christopher Sly, when he wakes in the nobleman's bedchamber," said Dalrymple; "though I should ask your pardon for the comparison. But see what it is to be an actress with forty-two thousand francs of salary per week. See these panels painted by Muller--this chandelier by Deniere, of which no copy exists--this bust of Napoleon by Canova--these hangings of purple and gold--this ceiling all carved and gilded, than which Versailles contains nothing more elaborate. ***Allons donc***! have you nothing to say in admiration of so much splendor?"

I shook my head.

"What can I say? Is this the house of an actress, or the palace of a prince? But stay--that pale woman yonder, all in white, with a plain gold circlet on her head--who is she?"

"Phedre herself," replied Dalrymple. "Follow me, and be introduced."

She was sitting in a large fauteuil of purple velvet. One foot rested on a stool richly carved and gilt; one arm rested negligently on a table covered with curious foreign weapons. In her right hand she held a singular poignard, the blade of which was damascened with gold, while the handle, made of bronze and exquisitely modelled, represented a tiny human skeleton. With this ghastly toy she kept playing as she spoke, apparently unconscious of its grim significance. She was surrounded by some ten or a dozen distinguished-looking men, most of whom were profusely ***decore***. They made way courteously at our approach. Dalrymple then presented me. I made my bow, was graciously received, and dropped modestly into the rear.

"I began to think that Captain Dalrymple had forsworn Paris," said Rachel, still toying with the skeleton dagger. "It is surely a year since I last had this pleasure?"

"Nay, Madame, you flatter me," said Dalrymple. "I have been absent only five months."

"Then, you see, I have measured your absence by my loss."

Dalrymple bowed profoundly.

Rachel turned to a young man behind her chair.

"Monsieur le Prince," said she, "do you know what is rumored in the ***foyer*** of the Francais? That you have offered me your hand!"

"I offer you both my hands, in applause, Madame, every night of your performance," replied the gentleman so addressed.

She smiled and made a feint at him with the dagger.

"Excellent!" said she. "One is not enough for a tragedian But where is Alphonse Karr?"

"I have been looking for him all the evening," said a tall man, with an iron-gray beard. "He told me he was coming; but authors are capricious beings--the slaves of the pen."

"True; he lives by his pen--others die by it," said Rachel bitterly. "By the way, has any one seen Scribe's new Vaudeville?"

"I have," replied a bald little gentleman with a red and green ribbon in his button-hole.

"And your verdict?"

"The plot is not ill-conceived; but Scribe is only godfather to the piece. It is almost entirely written by Duverger, his *collaborateur*."

"The life of a *collaborateur*," said Rachel, "is one long act of self-abnegation. Another takes all the honor--he all the labor. Thus soldiers fall, and their generals reap the glory."

"A *collaborateur*," said a cynical-looking man who had not yet spoken, "is a hackney vehicle which one hires on the road to fame, and dismisses at the end of the journey."

"Sometimes without paying the fare," added a gentleman who had till now been examining, weapon by weapon, all the curious poignards and pistols on the table. "But what is this singular ornament?"

And he held up what appeared to be a large bone, perforated in several places.

The bald little man with the red and green ribbon uttered an exclamation of surprise.

"It is a tibia!" said he, examining it through his double eye-glass.

"And what of that?" laughed Rachel. "Is it so wonderful to find one leg in a collection of arms? However, not to puzzle you, I may as well acknowledge that it was brought to me from Rome by a learned Italian, and is a curious antique. The Romans made flutes of the leg-bones of their enemies, and this is one of them."

"A melodious barbarism!" exclaimed one.

"Puts a 'stop,' at all events, to the enemy's flight!" said another.

"Almost as good as drinking out of his skull," added a third.

"Or as eating him, ***tout de bon***," said Rachel.

"There must be a certain satisfaction in cannibalism," observed the cynic who had spoken before. "There are people upon whom one would sup willingly."

"As, for instance, critics, who are our natural enemies," said Rachel. "***C'est a dire***, if critics were not too sour to be eaten."

"Nay, with the sweet sauce of vengeance!"

"You speak feelingly, Monsieur de Musset. I am almost sorry, for your sake, that cannibalism is out of fashion!"

"It is one of the penalties of civilization," replied de Musset, with a shrug. "Besides, one would not wish to be an epicure."

Dalrymple, who had been listening somewhat disdainfully to this skirmish of words, here touched me on the arm and turned away.

"Don't you hate this sort of high-pressure talk?" he said, impatiently.

"I was just thinking it so brilliant."

"Pshaw!--conversational fireworks--every speaker bent on eclipsing every other speaker. It's an artificial atmosphere, my dear Damon--a sort of forcing-house for good things; and I hate forced witticisms, as I hate forced peas. But have you had enough of it? Or has this feast of reason taken away your appetite for simpler fare?"

"If you mean, am I ready to go with you to Madame de Courcelles'--yes."

"***A la bonne heure***!"

"But you are not going away without taking leave of Madame Rachel?"

"Unquestionably. Leave-taking is a custom more honored in the breach than the observance."

"But isn't that very impolite?"

"***Ingenu!*** Do you know that society ignores everything disagreeable? A leave-taker sets an unpleasant example, disturbs the harmony of things, and reminds others of their watches. Besides, he suggests unwelcome possibilities. Perhaps he finds the party dull; or, worse still, he may be going to one that is pleasanter."

By this time we were again rattling along the Boulevard. The theatres were ablaze with lights. The road was full of carriages. The ***trottoir*** was almost as populous as at noon. The idlers outside the ***cafes*** were still eating their ices and sipping their ***eau-sucre*** as though, instead of being past eleven at night, it was scarcely eleven in the morning. In a few minutes, we had once more turned aside out of the great thoroughfare, and stopped at a private house in a quiet street. A carriage driving off, a cab drawing up behind our own, open windows with drawn blinds, upon which were profiled passing shadows of the guests within, and the ringing tones of a soprano voice, accompanied by a piano, gave sufficient indication of a party, and had served to attract a little crowd of soldiers and ***gamins*** about the doorway.

Having left our over-coats with a servant, we were ushered upstairs, and, as the song was not yet ended, slipped in unannounced and stationed ourselves just between two crowded drawing-rooms, where, sheltered by the folds of a muslin curtain, we could see all that was going on in both. I observed, at a glance, that I was now in a society altogether unlike that which I had just left.

At Rachel's there were present only two ladies besides herself, and those were members of her own family. Here I found at least an equal proportion of both sexes. At Rachel's a princely magnificence reigned. Here the rooms were elegant, but simple; the paintings choice but few; the ornaments costly, but in no unnecessary profusion.

"It is just the difference between taste and display," said Dalrymple. "Rachel is an actress, and Madame de Courcelles is a lady. Rachel exhibits her riches as an Indian chief exhibits the scalps of his victims--Madame de Courcelles adorns her house with no other view than to make it attractive to her friends."

"As a Greek girl covers her head with sequins to show the amount of her fortune, and an English girl puts a rose in her hair for grace and beauty only," said I, fancying that I had made rather a clever observation. I was therefore considerably disappointed when Dalrymple merely said, "just so."

The lady in the larger room here finished her song and returned to her seat, amid a shower of ***bravas***.

"She sings exquisitely," said I, following her with my eyes.

"And so she ought," replied my friend. "She is the Countess Rossi, whom you may have heard of as Mademoiselle Sontag."

"What! the celebrated Sontag?" I exclaimed.

"The same. And the gentleman to whom she is now speaking is no less famous a person than the author of ***Pelham***."

I was as much delighted as a rustic at a menagerie, and Dalrymple, seeing this, continued to point out one celebrity after another till I began no longer to remember which was which. Thus Lamartine, Horace Vernet, Scribe, Baron Humboldt, Miss Bremer, Arago, Auber, and Sir Edwin Landseer, were successively indicated, and I thought myself one of the most fortunate fellows in Paris, only to be allowed to look upon them.

"I suppose the spirit of lion-hunting is an original instinct," I said, presently. "Call it vulgar excitement, if you will; but I must confess that to see these people, and to be able to write about them to my father, is just the most delightful thing that has happened to me since I left home."

"Call things by their right names, Damon," said Dalrymple, good-naturedly. "If you were a *parvenu* giving a party, and wanted all these fine folks to be seen at your house, that would be lion-hunting; but being whom and what you are, it is hero-worship--a disease peculiar to the young; wholesome and inevitable, like the measles."

"What have I done," said a charming voice close by, "that Captain Dalrymple will not even deign to look upon me?"

The charming voice proceeded from the still more charming lips of an exceedingly pretty brunette in a dress of light green silk, fastened here and there with bouquets of rosebuds. Plump, rosy, black-haired, bright-eyed, bewilderingly coquettish, this lady might have been about thirty years of age, and seemed by no means unconscious of her powers of fascination.

"I implore a thousand pardons, Madame...." began my friend.

"*Comment*! A thousand pardons for a single offence!" exclaimed the lady. "What an unreasonable culprit!"

To which she added, quite audibly, though behind the temporary shelter of her fan:--

"Who is this *beau garcon* whom you seem to have brought with you?"

I turned aside, affecting not to hear the question; but could not help listening, nevertheless. Of Dalrymple's reply, however, I caught but my own name.

"So much the better," observed the lady. "I delight in civilizing handsome boys. Introduce him."

Dalrymple tapped me on the arm.

"Madame de Marignan permits me to introduce you, *mon ami*," said he. "Mr. Basil Arbuthnot--Madame de Marignan."

I bowed profoundly--all the more profoundly because I felt myself blushing to the eyes, and would not for the universe have been suspected of overhearing the preceding conversation; nor was my timidity alleviated when Dalrymple announced his intention of going in search of Madame de Courcelles, and of leaving me in the care of Madame de Marignan.

"Now, Damon, make the most of your opportunities," whispered he, as he passed by. "*Vogue la galere*!"

Vogue la galere, indeed! As if I had anything to do with the *galere*, except to sit down in it, the most helpless of galley-slaves, and blindly submit to the gyves and chains of Madame de Marignan, who, regarding me as the lawful captive of her bow and spear, carried me off at once to a vacant *causeuse* in a distant corner.

To send me in search of a footstool, to make me hold her fan, to overwhelm me with questions and bewilder me with a thousand coquetries, were the immediate proceedings of Madame de Marignan. A consummate tactician, she succeeded, before a quarter of an hour had gone by, in putting me at my ease, and in drawing from me everything that I had to tell--all my past; all my prospects for the future; the name and condition of my father; a description of Saxonholme, and the very date of my birth. Then she criticized all the ladies in the room, which only drew my attention more admiringly upon herself; and she quizzed all the young men, whereby I felt indirectly flattered, without exactly knowing why; and she praised Dalrymple in terms for which I could have embraced her on the spot had she been ten times less pretty, and ten times less fascinating.

I was an easy victim, after all, and scarcely worth the powder and shot of an experienced *franc-tireur;* but Madame de Marignan, according to her own confession, had a taste for civilizing "handsome boys," and as I may, perhaps, have come under that category a good many years ago, the little victory amused her! By the time, at all events, that Dalrymple returned to tell me it was past one o'clock in the morning, and I must be introduced to the mistress of the house before leaving, my head was as completely turned as that of old Time himself.

"Past one!" I exclaimed. "Impossible! We cannot have been here half-an hour."

At which neither Dalrymple nor Madame de Marignan could forbear smiling.

"I hope our acquaintance is not to end here, monsieur," said Madame de Marignan. "I live in the Rue Castellane, and am at home to my friends every Wednesday evening."

I bowed almost to my boots.

"And to my intimates, every morning from twelve to two," she added very softly, with a dimpled smile that went straight to my heart, and set it beating like the paddle-wheels of a steamer.

I stammered some incoherent thanks, bowed again, nearly upset a servant with a tray of ices, and, covered with confusion, followed Dalrymple into the farther room. Here I was introduced to Madame de Courcelles, a pale, aristocratic woman some few years younger than Madame de Marignan, and received a gracious invitation to all her Monday receptions. But I was much less interested in Madame de Courcelles than I should have been a couple of hours before. I scarcely looked at her, and five minutes after I was out of her presence, could not have told whether she was fair or dark, if my life had depended on it!

"What say you to walking home?" said Dalrymple, as we went down stairs. "It is a superb night, and the fresh air would be delightful after these hot rooms."

I assented gladly; so we dismissed the cab, and went out, arm-in-arm, along a labyrinth of quiet streets lighted by gas-lamps few and far between, and traversed only by a few homeward-bound pedestrians. Emerging presently at the back of the Madeleine, we paused for a moment to admire the noble building by moonlight; then struck across the Marche aux Fleurs and took our way along the Boulevard.

"Are you tired, Damon?" said Dalrymple presently.

"Not in the least," I replied, with my head full of Madame de Marignan.

"Would you like to look in at an artists' club close by here, where I have the *entree?*--queer place enough, but amusing to a stranger."

"Yes, very much."

"Come along, then; but first button up your overcoat to the throat, and tie this colored scarf round your neck. See, I do the same. Now take off your gloves--that's it. And give your hat the least possible inclination to the left ear. You may turn up the bottoms of your trousers, if you like--anything to look a little slangy."

"Is that necessary?"

"Indispensable--at all events in the honorable society of *Les Chicards.*"

"*Les Chicards!*" I repeated. "What are they?"

"It is the name of the club, and means--Heaven only knows what! for Greek or

Latin root it has none, and record of it there exists not, unless in the dictionary of Argot. And yet if you were an old Parisian and had matriculated for the last dozen years at the Bal de l'Opera, you would know the illustrious Chicard by sight as familiarly as Punch, or Paul Pry, or Pierrot. He is a gravely comic personage with a bandage over one eye, a battered hat considerably inclining to the back of his head, a coat with a high collar and long tails, and a ***tout ensemble*** indescribably seedy-- something between a street preacher and a travelling showman. But here we are. Take care how you come down, and mind your head."

Having turned aside some few minutes before into the Rue St. Honore, we had thence diverged down a narrow street with a gutter running along the middle and no foot-pavements on either side. The houses seemed to be nearly all shops, some few of which, for the retailing of ***charbonnerie***, stale vegetables, uninviting cooked meats, and so forth, were still open; but that before which we halted was closely shuttered up, with only a private door open at the side, lighted by a single oil-lamp. Following my friend for a couple of yards along the dim passage within, I became aware of strange sounds, proceeding apparently from the bowels of the earth, and found myself at the head of a steep staircase, down which it was necessary to proceed with my body bent almost double, in consequence of the close proximity of the ceiling and the steps. At the foot of this staircase came another dim passage and another oil-lamp over a low door, at which Dalrymple paused a moment before entering. The sounds which I had heard above now resolved themselves into their component parts, consisting of roars of laughter, snatches of songs, clinkings of glasses, and thumpings of bottles upon tables, to the accompaniment of a deep bass hum of conversation, all of which prepared me to find a very merry company within.

CHAPTER XIV.
THE HONORABLE SOCIETY OF LES CHICARDS.

"When a set of men find themselves agree in any particular,
though never so trivial, they establish themselves into a
kind of fraternity, and meet once or twice a
week."--***Spectator***.

It was a long, low room lighted by gas, with a table reaching from end to end. Round about this table, in various stages of conviviality and conversation, were seated some thirty or forty men, capped, bearded, and eccentric-looking, with all kinds of queer blouses and wonderful heads of hair. Dropping into a couple of vacant chairs at the lower end of this table, we called for a bottle of Chablis, lit our cigars, and fell in with the general business of the evening. At the top, dimly visible through a dense fog of tobacco smoke, sat a stout man in a green coat fastened by a belt round the waist. He was evidently the President, and, instead of a hammer, had a small bugle lying by his side, which he blew from time to time to enforce silence.

Somewhat perplexed by the general aspect of the club, I turned to my companion for an explanation.

"Is it possible," I asked, "that these amazing individuals are all artists and gentlemen?"

"Artists, every one," replied Dalrymple; "but as to their claim to be gentlemen, I won't undertake to establish it. After all, the ***Chicards*** are not first-rate men."

"What are they, then?"

"Oh, the Helots of the profession--hewers of wood engravings, and drawers of water-colors, with a sprinkling of daguerreotypists, and academy students. But hush--somebody is going to sing!"

And now, heralded by a convulsive flourish from the President's bugle, a young **Chicard**, whose dilapidated outer man sufficiently contradicted the burthen of his song, shouted with better will than skill, a **chanson** of Beranger's, every verse of which ended with:--

"J'ai cinquante ecus,
J'ai cinquante ecus,
J'ai cinquante ecus de rente!"

Having brought this performance to a satisfactory conclusion, the singer sat down amid great clapping of hands and clattering of glasses, and the President, with another flourish on the bugle, called upon one Monsieur Tourterelle. Monsieur Tourterelle was a tall, gaunt, swarthy personage, who appeared to have cultivated his beard at the expense of his head, since the former reached nearly to his waist, while the latter was as bare as a billiard-ball. Preparing himself for the effort with a wine-glass full of raw cognac, this gentleman leaned back in his chair, stuck his thumbs into the armholes of his waistcoat, fixed his eyes on the ceiling, and plunged at once into a doleful ballad about one Mademoiselle Rosine, and a certain village **aupres de la mer**, which seemed to be in an indefinite number of verses, and amused no one but himself. In the midst of this ditty, just as the audience had begun to testify their impatience by much whispering and shuffling of feet, an elderly **Chicard**, with a very bald and shiny head, was discovered to have fallen asleep in the seat next but one to my own; whereupon my nearest neighbor, a merry-looking young fellow with a profusion of rough light hair surmounted by a cap of scarlet cloth, forthwith charred a cork in one of the candles, and decorated the bald head of the sleeper with a comic countenance and a pair of huge mustachios. An uproarious burst of laughter was the immediate result, and the singer, interrupted somewhere about his 18th verse, subsided into offended silence.

"Monsieur Mueller is requested to favor the honorable society with a song," cried the President, as soon as the tumult had somewhat subsided.

My red-capped neighbor, answering to that name, begged to be excused, on the score of having pledged his **ut de poitrine** a week since at the Mont de Piete, without yet having been able to redeem it. This apology was received with laughter, hisses, and general incredulity.

"But," he added, "I am willing to relate an adventure that happened to myself in Rome two winters ago, if my honorable brother *Chicards* will be pleased to hear it."

An immense burst of approbation from all but Monsieur Tourterelle and the bald sleeper, followed this announcement; and so, after a preliminary *grog au vin*, and another explosive demonstration on the part of the chairman, Monsieur Mueller thus began:--

THE STUDENT'S STORY.

"When I was in Rome, I lodged in the Via Margutta, which, for the benefit of those who have not been there, may be described as a street of studios and stables, crossed at one end by a little roofed gallery with a single window, like a shabby 'Bridge of Sighs,' A gutter runs down the middle, interrupted occasionally by heaps of stable-litter; and the perspective is damaged by rows of linen suspended across the street at uncertain intervals. The houses in this agreeable thoroughfare are dingy, dilapidated, and comfortless, and all which are not in use as stables, are occupied by artists. However, it was a very jolly place, and I never was happier anywhere in my life. I had but just touched my little patrimony, and I was acquainted with plenty of pleasant fellows who used to come down to my rooms at night from the French Academy where they had been studying all day. Ah, what evenings those were! What suppers we used to have in from the *Lepre*! What lots of Orvieto we drank! And what a mountain of empty wicker bottles had to be cleared away from the little square yard with the solitary lemon-tree at the back of the house!"

"Come, Mueller--no fond memories!" cried a student in a holland blouse. "Get on with the story."

"Ay, get on with the story!" echoed several voices.

To which Mueller, who took advantage of the interruption to finish his *grog au vin*, deigned no reply.

"Well," he continued, "like a good many other fellows who, having everything to learn and nothing to do, fancy themselves great geniuses only because they are in Rome, I put a grand brass plate on the door, testifying to all passers-by that mine was the STUDIO DI HERR FRANZ MULLER; and, having done this, I believed, of course, that my fortune was to be made out of hand. Nothing came of it, however. People in search of Dessoulavy's rooms knocked occasionally to ask their way, and a few English and Americans dropped in from time to time to stare about them, after the free-and-easy fashion of foreigners in Rome; but, for all this, I found no patrons. Thus several months went by, during which I studied from the life, worked hard at the antique, and relieved the monotony of study with occasional trips to Frascati, or supper parties at the Cafe Greco."

"The story! the story!" interrupted a dozen impatient voices.

"All in good time," said Mueller, with provoking indifference. "We are now coming to it."

And assuming an attitude expressive of mystery, he dropped his voice, looked round the table, and proceeded:--

"It was on the last evening of the Carnival. It had been raining at intervals during the day, but held up for a good hour just at dusk, as if on purpose for the *moc-coli*. Scarcely, however, had the guns of St. Angelo thundered an end to the frolic, when the rain came down again in torrents, and put out the last tapers that yet lingered along the Corso. Wet, weary, and splashed from head to foot with mud and tallow, I came home about seven o'clock, having to dine and dress before going to a masked-ball in the evening. To light my stove, change my wet clothes, and make the best of a half-cold *trattore* dinner, were my first proceedings; after which, I laid out my costume ready to put on, wrapped myself in a huge cloak, swallowed a tumbler full of hot cognac and water, and lay down in front of the fire, determined to have a sound nap and a thorough warming, before venturing out again that night. I fell asleep, of course, and never woke till roused by a tremendous peal upon the studio-bell, about two hours and a half afterwards. More dead than alive, I started to my feet. The fire had gone out in the stove; the room was in utter darkness; and the bell still pealed loud enough to raise the neighborhood.

"'Who's there?' I said, half-opening the door, through which the wind and rain came rushing. 'And what, in the name of ten thousand devils, do you want?'

"'I want an artist,' said my visitor, in Italian. 'Are you one?'

"'I flatter myself that I am,' replied I, still holding the door tolerably close.

"'Can you paint heads?'

"'Heads, figures, landscapes--anything,' said I, with my teeth chattering like castanets.

"The stranger pushed the door open, walked in without further ceremony, closed it behind him, and said, in a low, distinct voice:--

"'Could you take the portrait of a dead man?'

"'Of a dead man?' I stammered. 'I--I ... Suppose I strike a light?'

"The stranger laid his hand upon my arm.

"'Not till you have given me an answer,' said he. 'Yes or no? Remember, you will be paid well for your work.'

"'Well, then--yes,' I replied.

"'And can you do it at once?'

"'At once?'

"'Ay, Signore, will you bring your colors, and come with me this instant--or must I seek some other painter?'

"I thought of the masked-ball, and sighed; but the promise of good payment, and, above all, the peculiarity of the adventure determined me.

"'Nay, if it is to be done,' said I, 'one time is as good as another. Let me strike a light, and I will at once pack up my colors and come with you.'

"'***Bene***!' said the stranger. 'But be as quick as you can, Signore, for time presses.'

"I was quick, you may be sure, and yet not so quick but that I found time to look at my strange visitor. He was a dark, elderly man, dressed in a suit of plain black, and might have been a clerk, or a tradesman, or a confidential servant. As soon as I was ready, he took the lead; conducted me to a carriage which was waiting at the corner of a neighboring street; took his place respectfully on the opposite seat; pulled down both the blinds, and gave the word to drive on. I never knew by what streets we went, or to what part of Rome he took me; but the way seemed long and intricate. At length, we stopped and alighted. The night was pitch-dark, and still stormy. I saw before me only the outline of a large building, indistinct and gloomy, and a small open door dimly lighted-from within. Hurried across the strip of narrow pavement, and shut in immediately, I had no time to identify localities--no choice, except to follow my conductor and blindly pursue the adventure to its close. Having entered by a back door, we went up and down a labyrinth of stair-cases and passages, for the mere purpose, as it seemed, of bewildering me as much as possible--then paused before an oaken door at the end of the corridor. Here my conductor signified by a gesture that I was to precede him.

"It was a large, panelled chamber, richly furnished. A wood fire smouldered on the hearth--a curtained alcove to the left partly concealed a bed--a corresponding alcove to the right, fitted with altar and crucifix, served as an oratory. In the centre of the room stood a table covered with a cloth. It needed no second glance to tell me what object lay beneath that cloth, uplifting it in ghastly outline! My conductor pointed to the table, and asked if there was anything I needed. To this I replied that I must have more light and more fire, and so proceeded to disembarrass myself of my cloak, and prepare my palette. In the meantime, he threw on a log and some pine-cones, and went to fetch an additional lamp.

"Left alone with the body and impelled by an irresistible impulse, I rolled back the cloth and saw before me the corpse of a young man in fancy dress--a magnifi-cent fellow cast in the very mould of strength and grace, and measuring his six feet, if an inch. The features were singularly handsome; the brow open and resolute; the hair dark, and crisp with curls. Looking more closely, I saw that a lock had been lately cut from the right temple, and found one of the severed hairs upon the cheek, where it had fallen. The dress was that of a jester of the middle ages, half scarlet and half white, with a rich belt round the waist. In this belt, as if in hor-rible mockery of the dead, was stuck a tiny baton surmounted by a fool's cap, and hung with silver bells. Looking down thus upon the body--so young, so beautiful, so evidently unprepared for death--a conviction of foul play flashed upon me with all the suddenness and certainty of revelation. Here were no appearances of disease and no signs of strife. The expression was not that of a man who had fallen weapon in hand. Neither, however, was it that of one who had died in the agony of poison. The longer I looked, the more mysterious it seemed; yet the more I felt assured that there was guilt at the bottom of the mystery.

"While I was yet under the first confused and shuddering impression of this doubt, my guide came back with a powerful solar lamp, and, seeing me stand beside the body, said sharply:--

"'Well, Signore, you look as if you had never seen a dead man before in all your life!'

"'I have seen plenty,' I replied, 'but never one so young, and so handsome.'

"'He dropped down quite suddenly,' said he, volunteering the information, 'and died in a few minutes. 'Then finding that I remained silent, added:--

"'But I am told that it is always so in cases of heart-disease.'

"'I turned away without replying, and, having placed the lamp to my satisfaction, began rapidly sketching in my subject. My instructions were simple. I was to give the head only; to produce as rapid an effect with as little labor as possible; to alter nothing; to add nothing; and, above all, to be ready to leave the house before daybreak. So I set steadily to work, and my conductor, establishing himself in an easy-chair by the fire, watched my progress for some time, and then, as the night advanced, fell profoundly asleep. Thus, hour after hour went by, and, absorbed in my work, I painted on, unconscious of fatigue-- might almost say with something of a morbid pleasure in the task before me. The silence within; the raving of the wind and rain without; the solemn mystery of death, and the still more solemn mystery of crime which, as I followed out train after train of wild conjectures, grew to still deeper conviction, had each and all their own gloomy fascination. Was it not possible, I asked myself, by mere force of will to penetrate the secret? Was it not possible to study that dead face till the springs of thought so lately stilled within the stricken brain should vibrate once more, if only for an instant, as wire vibrates to wire, and sound to sound! Could I not, by long studying of the passive mouth, compel some sympathetic revelation of the last word that it uttered, though that revelation took no outward form, and were communicable to the apprehension only? Pondering thus, I lost myself in a labyrinth of fantastic reveries, till the hand and the brain worked independently of each other--the one swiftly reproducing upon canvas the outer lineaments of the dead; the other laboring to retrace foregone facts of which no palpable evidence remained. Thus my work progressed; thus the night waned; thus the sleeper by the fireside stirred from time to time, or moaned at intervals in his dreams.

"At length, when many hours had gone by, and I began to be conscious of the first languor of sleeplessness, I heard, or fancied I heard, a light sound in the corridor without. I held my breath, and listened. As I listened, it ceased--was renewed--drew nearer--paused outside the door. Involuntarily, I rose and looked round for some means of defence, in case of need. Was I brought here to perpetuate the record of a crime, and was I, when my task was done, to be silenced in a dungeon, or a grave? This thought flashed upon me almost before I was conscious of the horror it involved. At the same moment, I saw the handle of the door turned slowly and cautiously--then held back--and then, after a brief pause, the door itself gradually opening."

Here the student paused as if overcome by the recollection of that moment, and passed his hand nervously across his brow. I took the liberty of pushing our bottle of Chablis towards him, for which he thanked me with a nod and a smile, and filled his glass to the brim.

"Well?" cried two or three voices eagerly; my own being one of them. "The door opened--what then?"

"And a lady entered," he continued. "A lady dressed in black from head to foot, with a small lamp in her hand. Seeing me, she laid her finger significantly on her lip, closed the door as cautiously as she had opened it, and, with the faltering, uncertain steps of one just risen from a sick-bed, came over to where I had been sitting, and leaned for support against my chair. She was very pale, very calm, very young and beautiful, with just that look of passive despair in her face that one sees in Guido's portrait of Beatrice Cenci. Standing thus, I observed that she kept her eyes turned from the corpse, and her attention concentrated on the portrait. So several minutes passed, and neither of us spoke nor stirred. Then, slowly, shudderingly, she turned, grasped me by the arm, pointed to the dead form stretched upon the table, and less with her breath than by the motion of her lips, shaped out the one word:--'*Murdered*!'

"Stunned by this confirmation of my doubts, I could only clasp my hands in mute horror, and stare helplessly from the lady to the corpse, from the corpse to the sleeper. Wildly, feverishly, with all her calmness turned to eager haste, she then bent over the body, tore open the rich doublet, turned back the shirt, and, without uttering one syllable, pointed to a tiny puncture just above the region of the heart--a spot so small, so insignificant, such a mere speck upon the marble, that but for the pale violet discoloration which spread round it like a halo, I could scarcely have believed it to be the cause of death. The wound had evidently bled inwardly, and, being inflicted with some singularly slender weapon, had closed again so completely as to leave an aperture no larger than might have been caused by the prick of a needle. While I was yet examining it, the fire fell together, and my conductor stirred uneasily in his sleep. To cover the body hastily with the cloth and resume my seat, was, with me, the instinctive work of a moment; but he was quiet again the next instant, and breathing heavily. With trembling hands, my visitor next re-closed the shirt and doublet, replaced the outer covering, and bending down till her lips almost touched my ear, whispered:--

"'You have seen it. If called upon to do so, will you swear it?'

"I promised.

"'You will not let yourself be intimidated by threats? nor bribed by gold? nor lured by promises?

"'Never, so help me Heaven!'

"She looked into my eyes, as if she would read my very soul; then, before I knew what she was about to do, seized my hand, and pressed it to her lip.

"'I believe you,' she said. 'I believe, and I thank you. Not a word to him that you have seen me'--here she pointed to the sleeper by the fire. 'He is faithful; but not to my interests alone. I dare tell you no more--at all events, not now. Heaven bless and reward you. In this portrait you give me the only treasure--the only consolation of my future life!'

"So saying, she took a ring from her finger, pressed it, without another word, into my unwilling hand; and, with the same passive dreary look that her face had worn on first entering took up her lamp again, and glided from the room.

"How the next hour, or half hour, went by, I know not--except that I sat before the canvas like one dreaming. Now and then I added a few touches; but mechanically, and, as it were, in a trance of wonder and dismay. I had, however, made such good progress before being interrupted, that when my companion woke and told me it would soon be day and I must make haste to be gone, the portrait was even more finished than I had myself hoped to make it in the time. So I packed up my colors and palette again, and, while I was doing so, observed that he not only drew the cloth once more over the features of the dead, but concealed the likeness behind the altar in the oratory, and even restored the chairs to their old positions against the wall. This done, he extinguished the solar lamp; put it out of sight; desired me once more to follow him; and led the way back along the same labyrinth of stair-cases and corridors by which he brought me. It was gray dawn as he hurried me into the coach. The blinds were already down--the door was instantly closed--again we seemed to be going through an infinite number of streets--again we stopped, and I found myself at the corner of the Via Margutta.

"'Alight, Signore,' said the stranger, speaking for the first time since we started. 'Alight--you are but a few yards from your own door. Here are a hundred scudi; and all that you have now to do, is to forget your night's work, as if it had never been.'

"With this he closed the carriage-door, the horses dashed on again, and, before I had time even to see if any arms were blazoned on the panels, the whole equipage had disappeared.

"And here, strange to say, the adventure ended. I never was called upon for evidence. I never saw anything more of the stranger, or the lady. I never heard of any sudden death, or accident, or disappearance having taken place about that time; and I never even obtained any clue to the neighborhood of the house in which these things took place. Often and often afterwards, when I was strolling by night along the streets of Rome, I lingered before some old palazzo, and fancied that I recognised the gloomy outline that caught my eye in that hurried transit from the carriage to the house. Often and often I paused and started, thinking that I had found at last the very side-door by which I entered. But these were mere guesses after all. Perhaps that house stood in some remote quarter of the city where my footsteps never went again--perhaps in some neighboring street or piazza, where I passed it every day! At all events, the whole thing vanished like a dream, and, but for the ring and the hundred scudi, a dream I should by this time believe it to have been. The scudi, I am sorry to say, were spent within a month--the ring I have never parted from, and here it is."

Hereupon the student took from his finger a superb ruby set between two brilliants of inferior size, and allowed it to pass from hand to hand, all round the table. Exclamations of surprise and admiration, accompanied by all sorts of conjectures and comments, broke from every lip.

"The dead man was the lady's lover," said one. "That is why she wanted his portrait."

"Of course, and her husband had murdered him," said another.

"Who, then, was the man in black?" asked a third.

"A servant, to be sure. She said, if you remember, that he was faithful; but not devoted to her interests alone. That meant that he would obey to the extent of procuring for her the portrait of her lover; but that he did not choose to betray his master, even though his master was a murderer."

"But if so, where was the master?" said the first speaker. "Is it likely that he would have neglected to conceal the body during all these hours?"

"Certainly. Nothing more likely, if he were a man of the world, and knew how to play his game out boldly to the end. Have we not been told that it was the last night of the Carnival, and what better could he do, to avert suspicion, than show himself at as many balls as he could visit in the course of the evening? But really, this ring is magnificent!"

"Superb. The ruby alone must be worth a thousand francs."

"To say nothing of the diamonds, and the setting," observed the next to whom it was handed.

At length, after having gone nearly the round of the table, the ring came to a little dark, sagacious-looking man, just one seat beyond Dalrymple's, who peered at it suspiciously on every side, breathed upon it, rubbed it bright again upon his coat-sleeve, and, finally, held the stones up sideways between his eyes and the light.

"Bah!" said he, sending it on with a contemptuous fillip of the forefinger and thumb. "Glass and paste, *mon ami*. Not worth five francs of anybody's money."

Mueller, who had been eyeing him all the time with an odd smile lurking about the corners of his mouth, emptied his last drop of Chablis, turned the glass over on the table, bottom upwards, and said very coolly:--

"Well, I'm sorry for that; because I gave seven francs for it myself this morning, in the Palais Royal."

"You!"

"Seven francs!"

"Bought in the Palais Royal!"

"What does he mean?"

"Mean?" echoed the student, in reply to this chorus of exclamations. "I mean that I bought it this morning, and gave seven francs for it. It is not every morning of my life, let me tell you, that I have seven francs to throw away on my personal appearance."

"But then the ring that the lady took from her finger?"

"And the murder?"

"And the servant in black?"

"And the hundred scudi?"

"One great invention from beginning to end, Messieurs les Chicards, and being got up expressly for your amusement, I hope you liked it. *Garcon?*--another *grog au vin*, and sweeter than the last!"

It would be difficult to say whether the Chicards were most disappointed or delighted at this *denoument*--disappointed at its want of fact, or delighted with the story-weaving power of Herr Franz Mueller. They expressed themselves, at all events, with a tumultuous burst of applause, in the midst of which we rose and left the room. When we once more came out into the open air, the stars had disappeared and the air was heavy with the damps of approaching daybreak. Fortunately, we caught an empty *fiacre* in the next street and, as we were nearer the Rue du Faubourg Montmartre than the Chaussee d' Antin, Dalrymple set me down first.

"Adieu, Damon," he said, laughingly, as we shook hands through the window. "If we don't meet before, come and dine with me next Sunday at seven o'clock--and don't dream of dreadful murders, if you can help it!"

I did not dream of dreadful murders. I dreamt, instead, of Madame de Marignan, and never woke the next morning till eleven o'clock, just two hours later than the time at which I should have presented myself at Dr. Cheron's.

CHAPTER XV.
WHAT IT IS TO BE A CAVALIERE SERVENTE.

"Everye white will have its blacke,
And everye sweet its sowere."
Old Ballad.

Neither the example of Oscar Dalrymple nor the broadcloth of the great Michaud, achieved half so much for my education as did the apprenticeship I was destined to serve to Madame de Marignan. Having once made up her mind to civilize me, she spared no pains for the accomplishment of that end, cost what it might to herself--or me. Before I had been for one week her subject, she taught me how to bow; how to pick up a pocket-handkerchief; how to present a bouquet; how to hold a fan; how to pay a compliment; how to turn over the leaves of a music-book--in short, how to obey and anticipate every imperious wish; and how to fetch and carry, like a dog. My vassalage began from the very day when I first ventured to call upon her. Her house was small, but very elegant, and she received me in a delicious little room overlooking the Champs Elysees--a very nest of flowers, books, and birds. Before I had breathed the air of that fatal boudoir for one quarter of an hour, I was as abjectly her slave as the poodle with the rose-colored collar which lay curled upon a velvet cushion at her feet.

"I shall elect you my ***cavaliere servente***," said she, after I had twice nervously risen to take my leave within the first half hour, and twice been desired to remain a little longer. "Will you accept the office?"

I thought it the greatest privilege under heaven. Perhaps I said so.

"The duties of the situation are onerous," added she, "and I ought not to accept your allegiance without setting them before you. In the first place, you will have to bring me every new novel of George Sand, Flaubert, or About, on the day of publication."

"I will move heaven and earth to get them the day before, if that be all!" I exclaimed.

Madame de Marignan nodded approvingly, and went on telling off my duties, one by one, upon her pretty fingers.

"You will have to accompany me to the Opera at least twice a week, on which occasions you will bring me a bouquet--camellias being my favorite flowers."

"Were they the flowers that bloom but once in a century," said I, with more enthusiasm than sense, "they should be yours!"

Madame de Marignan smiled and nodded again.

"When I drive in the Bois, you will sometimes take a seat in my carriage, and sometimes ride beside it, like an attentive cavalier."

I was just about to avow that I had no horse, when I remembered that I could borrow Dalrymple's, or hire one, if necessary; so I checked myself, and bowed.

"When I go to an exhibition," said Madame de Marignan, "it will be your business to look out the pictures in the catalogue--when I walk, you will carry my parasol--when I go into a shop, you will take care of my dog--when I embroider, you will wind off my silks, and look for my scissors--when I want amusement, you must make me laugh--and when I am sleepy, you must read to me. In short, my *cavaliere servente* must be my shadow."

"Then, like your shadow, Madame," said I, "his place is ever at your feet, and that is all I desire!"

Madame de Marignan laughed outright, and showed the loveliest little double row of pearls in all the world.

"Admirable!" said she. "Quite an elegant compliment, and worthy of an accomplished lady-killer! *Allons*! you are a promising scholar."

"In all that I have dared to say, Madame, I am, at least, sincere," I added, abashed by the kind of praise.

"Sincere? Of course you are sincere. Who ever doubted it? Nay, to blush like that is enough to spoil the finest compliment in the world. There--it is three o'clock, and at half-past I have an engagement, for which I must now make my *toilette*. Come to-morrow evening to my box at the *Italiens*, and so adieu. Stay--being my *cavaliere*, I permit you, at parting, to kiss my hand."

Trembling, breathless, scarcely daring to touch it with mine, I lifted the soft little hand to my lips, stammered something which was, no doubt, sufficiently foolish, and hurried away, as if I were treading on air and breathing sunshine.

All the rest of that day went by in a kind of agreeable delirium. I walked about, almost without knowledge where I went. I talked, without exactly knowing what I said. I have some recollection of marching to and fro among the side-alleys of the Bois de Boulogne, which at that time was really a woody park, and not a pleasure-garden--of lying under a tree, and listening to the birds overhead, and indulging myself in some idiotic romance about love, and solitude, and Madame de Marignan--of wandering into a *restaurant* somewhere about seven o'clock, and sitting down to a dinner for which I had no appetite--of going back, sometime during the evening, to the Rue Castellane, and walking to and fro on the opposite side of the way, looking up for ever so long at the darkened windows where my divinity did not show herself--of coming back to my lodgings, weary, dusty, and not a bit more sober, somewhere about eleven o'clock at night, driven to-bed by sheer fatigue, and, even then, too much in love to go to sleep!

The next day I went through my duties at Dr. Cheron's, and attended an afternoon lecture at the hospital; but mechanically, like one dreaming. In the evening I presented myself at the Opera, where Madame de Marignan received me very graciously, and deigned to accept a superb bouquet for which I had paid sixteen francs. I found her surrounded by elegant men, who looked upon me as nobody, and treated me accordingly. Driven to the back of the box where I could neither speak to her, nor see the stage, nor achieve even a glimpse of the house, I spent an evening which certainly fell short of my anticipations. I had, however, the gratification of seeing my bouquet thrown to Grisi at the end of the second act, and was permitted the privilege of going in search of Madame de Marignan's carriage, while somebody else handed her downstairs, and assisted her with her cloak. A whispered word of thanks, a tiny pressure of the hand, and the words "come early to-morrow," compensated me, nevertheless, for every disappointment, and sent me home as blindly happy as ever.

The next day I called upon her, according to command, and was transported to the seventh heaven by receiving permission to accompany her to a morning concert, whereby I missed two lectures, and spent ten francs.

On the Sunday, having hired a good horse for the occasion, I had the honor of riding beside her carriage till some better-mounted acquaintance came to usurp my place and her attention; after which I was forced to drop behind and bear the eclipse of my glory as philosophically as I could.

Thus day after day went by, and, for the delusive sake of Madame de Marignan's bright eyes, I neglected my studies, spent my money, wasted my time, and incurred the displeasure of Dr. Cheron. Led on from folly to folly, I was perpetually buoyed up by coquetries which meant nothing, and as perpetually mortified, disappointed, and neglected. I hoped; I feared; I fretted; I lost my sleep and my appetite; I felt dissatisfied with all the world, sometimes blaming myself, and sometimes her--yet ready to excuse and forgive her at a moment's notice. A boy in experience even more than in years, I loved with a boy's headlong passion, and suffered with all a boy's acute susceptibility. I was intensely sensitive--abashed by a slight, humbled by a glance, and so easily wounded that there were often times when, seeing myself forgotten, I could with difficulty drive back the tears that kept rising to my eyes. On the other hand, I was as easily elated. A kind word, an encouraging smile, a lingering touch upon my sleeve, was enough at any time to make me forget all my foregone troubles. How often the mere gift of a flower sent me home rejoicing! How the tiniest show of preference set my heart beating! How proud I was if mine was the arm chosen to lead her to her carriage! How more than happy, if allowed for even one half-hour in the whole evening to occupy the seat beside her own! To dangle after her the whole day long--to traverse all Paris on her errands--to wait upon her pleasure like a slave, and this, too, without even expecting to be thanked for my devotion, seemed the most natural thing in the world. She was capricious; but caprice became her. She was exacting; but her exactions were so coquettish and attractive, that one would not have wished her more reasonable. She was, at least, ten or twelve years my senior; but boys proverbially fall in love with women older than themselves, and this one was in all respects so charming, that I do not, even now, wonder at my infatuation.

After all, there are few things under heaven more beautiful, or more touching, than a boy's first love.

Passionate is it as a man's--pure as a woman's--trusting as a child's--timid, through the very excess of its unselfishness--chivalrous, as though handed down direct from the days of old romance--poetical beyond the utterances of the poet. To the boy-lover, his mistress is only something less than a divinity. He believes in her truth as in his own; in her purity, as in the sun at noon. Her practised arts of voice and manner are, in his eyes, the unstudied graces that spring as naturally from her beauty as the scent from the flower. Single-hearted himself, it seems impossible that she whom he adores should trifle with the most sacred sentiment he has ever known. Conscious of his own devotion, he cannot conceive that his wealth is poured forth in vain, and that he is but the plaything of her idle hours. Yet it is so. The boy's first love is almost always misplaced; seldom rated at its true value; hardly ever productive of anything but disappointment. Aspirant of the highest mysteries of the soul, he passes through the ordeal of fire and tears, happy if he keep his faith unshaken and his heart pure, for the wiser worship hereafter. We all know this; and few know it better than myself. Yet, with all its suffering, which of us would choose to obliterate all record of his first romance? Which of us would be without the memory of its smiles and tears, its sunshine and its clouds? Not I for one.

CHAPTER XVI.
A CONTRETEMPS IN A CARRIAGE.

My slavery lasted somewhat longer than three weeks, and less than a month; and was brought, oddly enough, to an abrupt conclusion. This was how it happened.

I had, as usual, attended Madame de Marignan one evening to the Opera, and found myself, also as usual, neglected for a host of others. There was one man in particular whom I hated, and whom (perhaps because I hated him) she distinguished rather more than the rest. His name was Delaroche, and he called himself Monsieur le Comte Delaroche. Most likely he was a Count---I have no reason to doubt his title; but I chose to doubt it for mere spite, and because he was loud and conceited, and wore a little red and green ribbon in his button-hole. He had, besides, an offensive sense of my youth and his own superiority, which I have never forgiven to this day. On the particular occasion of which I am now speaking, this person had made his appearance in Madame de Marignan's box at the close of the first act, established himself in the seat behind hers, and there held the lists against all comers during the remainder of the evening. Everything he said, everything he did, aggravated me. When he looked through her lorgnette, I loathed him. When he admired her fan, I longed to thrust it down his throat. When he held her bouquet to his odious nose (the bouquet that I had given her!) I felt it would have been justifiable manslaughter to take him up bodily, and pitch him over into the pit.

At length the performance came to a close, and M. Delaroche, having taken upon himself to arrange Madame de Marignan's cloak, carry Madame de Marignan's fan, and put Madame de Marignan's opera-glass into its morocco case, completed his officiousness by offering his arm and conducting her into the lobby, whilst I, outwardly indifferent but inwardly boiling, dropped behind, and consigned him silently to all the torments of the seven circles.

It was an oppressive autumnal night without a star in the sky, and so still that one might have carried a lighted taper through the streets. Finding it thus warm, Madame de Marignan proposed walking down the line of carriages, instead of waiting till her own came up; and so she and M. Delaroche led the way and I followed. Having found the carriage, he assisted her in, placed her fan and bouquet on the opposite seat, lingered a moment at the open door, and had the unparalleled audacity to raise her hand to his lips at parting. As for me, I stood proudly back, and lifted my hat.

"*Comment*!" she said, holding out her hand--the pretty, ungloved hand that had just been kissed--"is that your good night?"

I bowed over the hand, I would not have touched it with my lips at that moment for all the wealth of Paris.

"You are coming to me to-morrow morning at twelve?" she murmured tenderly.

"If Madame desires it."

"Of course I desire it. I am going to Auteuil, to look at a house for a friend--and to Pignot's for some flowers--and to Lubin's for some scent--and to a host of places. What should I do without you? Nay, why that grave face? Have I done anything to offend you?"

"Madame, I--I confess that--"

"That you are jealous of that absurd Delaroche, who is so much in love with himself that he has no place in his heart for any one else! *Fi donc!* I am ashamed of you. There--adieu, twelve to-morrow!"

And with this she laughed, waved her hand, gave the signal to drive on, and left me looking after the carriage, still irritated but already half consoled.

I then sauntered moodily on, thinking of my tyrant, and her caprices, and her beauty. Her smile, for instance; surely it was the sweetest smile in the world--if only she were less lavish of it! Then, what a delicious little hand--if mine were the only lips permitted to kiss it! Why was she so charming?--or why, being so charming, need she prize the attentions of every *flaneur* who had only enough wit to admire her? Was I not a fool to believe that she cared more for my devotion than for another's! Did I believe it? Yes ... no ... sometimes. But then that "sometimes" was only when under the immediate influence of her presence. She fascinated me; but she would fascinate a hundred others in precisely the same way. It was true that she accepted from me more devotion, more worship, more time, more outward and visible homage than from any other. Was I not her *Cavaliere servente?* Did she not accept my bouquets? Did she not say the other day, when I gave her that volume of Tennyson, that she loved all that was English for my sake? Surely, I was worse than ungrateful, when, having so much, I was still dissatisfied! Why was I not the happiest fellow in Paris? Why .....

My meditations were here interrupted by a sudden flash of very vivid lightning, followed by a low muttering of distant thunder. I paused, and looked round. The sky was darker than ever, and though the air was singularly stagnant, I could hear among the uppermost leaves of the tall trees that stealthy rustling that generally precedes a storm. Unfortunately for myself, I had not felt disposed to go home at once on leaving the theatre; but, being restless alike in mind and body, had struck down through the Place Vendome and up the Rue de Rivoli, intending to come home by a circuitous route. At this precise moment I found myself in the middle of the Place de la Concorde, with Cleopatra's needle towering above my head, the lamps in the Champs Elysees twinkling in long chains of light through the blank darkness before me, and no vehicle anywhere in sight. To be caught in a heavy shower, was not, certainly, an agreeable prospect for one who had just emerged from the opera in the thinnest of boots and the lightest of folding hats, with neither umbrella nor paletot of proof; so, having given a hasty glance in every direction from which a cab might be expected, I took valiantly to my heels, and made straight for the Madeleine.

Long before I had accomplished half the distance, however, another flash announced the quick coming of the tempest, and the first premonitory drops began to plash down heavily upon the pavement. Still I ran on, thinking that I should find a cab in the Place de la Madeleine; but the Place de la Madeleine was empty. Even the cafe at the corner was closed. Even the omnibus office was shut up, and the red lamp above the door extinguished.

What was I to do now? Panting and breathless, I leaned up against a doorway, and resigned myself to fate. Stay, what was that file of carriages, dimly seen through the rain which was now coming down in earnest? It was in a private street opening off at the back of the Madeleine--a street in which I could remember no public stand. Perhaps there was an evening party at one of the large houses lower down, and, if so, I might surely find a not wholly incorruptible cabman, who would consent for a liberal *pourboire* to drive me home and keep his fare waiting, if need were, for one little half-hour! At all events it was worth trying for; so away I darted again, with the wind whistling about my ears, and the rain driving in my face.

But my troubles were not to be so speedily ended. Among the ten or fifteen equipages which I found drawn up in file, there was not one hackney vehicle. They were private carriages, and all, therefore, inaccessible.

Did I say inaccessible?

A bold idea occurred to me. The rain was so heavy that it could scarcely be expected to last many minutes. The carriage at the very end of the line was not likely to be the first called; and, even if it were, one could spring out in a moment, if necessary. In short, the very daring of the deed was as attractive as the shelter! I made my way swiftly down the line. The last carriage was a neat little brougham, and the coachman, with his hat pulled down over his eyes, and his collar drawn up about his ears, was too much absorbed in taking care of himself and his horses to pay much attention to a foot-passenger. I passed boldly by--doubled back stealthily on my own steps--looked round cautiously--opened the door, and glided in.

It was a delightfully comfortable little vehicle--cushioned, soft, yielding, and pervaded by a delicate perfume of eglantine. Wondering who the owner might be--if she was young--if she was pretty--if she was married, or single, or a widow--I settled myself in the darkest corner of the carriage, intending only to remain there till the rain had abated. Thus I fell, as fate would have it--first into a profound reverie, and then into a still profounder sleep. How long this sleep may have lasted I know not. I only remember becoming slowly conscious of a gentle movement, which, without awaking, partly roused me; of a check to that movement, which brought my thoughts suddenly to the surface; of a stream of light--of an open door--a crowded hall--a lady waiting to come out, and a little crowd of attentive beaux surrounding her!

I comprehended my position in an instant, and the impossibility of extricating myself from it. To get out next the house was to brave detection; whilst at the other side I found myself blocked in by carriages. Escape was now hopeless! I turned hot and cold; I shrank back; I would have gone through the bottom of the carriage, if I could. At this moment, to my horror, the footman opened the door. I gave my-self up for lost, and, in a sudden access of desperation, was on the point of rushing out ***coute que coute***, when the lady ran forward; sprang lightly in; recoiled; and uttered a little breathless cry of surprise and apprehension!

"***Mon Dieu***, Madame! what is it? Are you hurt?" cried two or three of the gentlemen, running out, bareheaded, to her assistance.

But, to my amazement, she unfastened her cloak, and threw it over me in such a manner as to leave me completely hidden beneath the folds.

"Oh, nothing, thank you!--I only caught my foot in my cloak. I am really quite ashamed to have alarmed you! A thousand thanks--good-night."

And so, with something of a slight tremor in her voice, the lady drew up the window. The next instant the carriage moved on.

And now, what was to be done? I blessed the accident which rendered me in-visible; but, at the same time, asked myself how it was to end.

Should I wait till she reached her own door, and then, still feigning sleep, allow myself to be discovered? Or should I take the bull by the horns, and reveal myself? If the latter, would she scream, or faint, or go into hysterics? Then, again, suppos-ing she resumed her cloak ... a cold damp broke out upon my forehead at the mere thought! All at once, just as these questions flashed across my mind, the lady drew the mantle aside, and said:--

"How imprudent of you to hide in my carriage?"

I could not believe my ears.

"Suppose any of those people had caught sight of you ... why, it would have been all over Paris to-morrow! Happily, I had the presence of mind to cover you with my cloak; otherwise ... but there, Monsieur, I have a great mind to be very angry with you!"

It was now clear that I was mistaken for some one else. Fortunately the car-riage-lamps were unlit, the windows still blurred with rain, and the night intensely dark; so, feeling like a wretch reprieved on the scaffold, I shrank farther and farther into the corner, glad to favor a mistake which promised some hope of escape.

"***Eh bien***!" said the lady, half tenderly, half reproachfully; "have you nothing to say to me?"

Say to her, indeed! What could I say to her? Would not my voice betray me directly?

"Ah," she continued, without waiting for a reply; "you are ashamed of the cruel scene of this morning! Well, since you have not allowed the night to pass without seeking a reconciliation, I suppose I must forgive you!"

I thought, at this point, that I could not do better than press her hand, which was exquisitely soft and small--softer and smaller than even Madame de Marignan's.

"Naughty Hippolyte!" murmured my companion. "Confess, now, that you were unreasonable."

I sighed heavily, and caressed the little hand with both of mine.

"And are you very penitent?"

I expressed my penitence by another prodigious sigh, and ventured, this time, to kiss the tips of the dainty fingers.

"*Ciel*!" exclaimed the lady. "You have shaved off your beard! What can have induced you to do such a thing?"

My beard, indeed! Alas! I would have given any money for even a moustache! However, the fatal moment was come when I must speak.

"*Mon cher ange*," I began, trying a hoarse whisper, "I--I--the fact is--a bet--"

"A bet indeed! The idea of sacrificing such a handsome beard for a mere bet! I never heard of anything so foolish. But how hoarse you are, Hippolyte!"

"All within the last hour," whispered I. "I was caught in the storm, just now, and ..."

"And have taken cold, for my sake! Alas! my poor, dear friend, why did you wait to speak to me? Why did you not go home at once, and change your clothes? Your sleeve, I declare, is still quite damp! Hippolyte, if you fall ill, I shall never forgive myself!"

I kissed her hand again. It was much pleasanter than whispering, and expressed all that was necessary.

"But you have not once asked after poor Bibi!" exclaimed my companion, after a momentary silence. "Poor, dear Bibi, who has been suffering from a martyrdom with her cough all the afternoon!"

Now, who the deuce was Bibi? She might be a baby. Or--who could tell?--she might be a poodle? On this point, however, I was left uninformed; for my unknown friend, who, luckily, seemed fond of talking and had a great deal to say, launched off into another topic immediately.

"After all," said she, "I should have been wrong not to go to the party! My uncle was evidently pleased with my compliance; and it is not wise to vex one's rich uncles, if one can help it--is it, Hippolyte!"

I pressed her hand again.

"Besides, Monsieur Delaroche was not there. He was not even invited; so you see how far they were from laying matchmaking plots, and how groundless were all your fears and reproaches!"

Monsieur Delaroche! Could this be the Delaroche of my special aversion? I pressed her hand again, more closely, more tenderly, and listened for what might come next.

"Well, it is all over now! And will you promise **never, never, never** to be jealous again? Then, to be jealous of such a creature as that ridiculous Delaroche--a man who knows nothing--who can think and talk only of his own absurd self!--a man who has not even wit enough to see that every one laughs at him!"

I was delighted. I longed to embrace her on the spot! Was there ever such a charming, sensible, lively creature?

"Besides, the coxcomb is just now devoting himself, body and soul (such as they are!) to that insufferable little **intriguante**, Madame de Marignan. He is to be seen with her in every drawing-room and theatre throughout Paris. For my part, I am amazed that a woman of the world should suffer herself to be compromised to that extent--especially one so experienced in these **affaires du coeur**."

Madame de Marignan! Compromised--experienced--**intriguante**! I felt as if I were choking.

"To be sure, there is that poor English lad whom she drags about with her, to play propriety," continued she; "but do you suppose the world is blinded by so shallow an artifice?"

"What English lad?" I asked, startled out of all sense of precaution, and desperately resolved to know the worst.

"What English lad? Why, Hippolyte, you are more stupid than ever! I pointed him out to you the other night at the Comedie Francaise--a pale, handsome boy, of about nineteen or twenty, with brown curling hair, and very fine eyes, which were riveted on Madame de Marignan the whole evening. Poor fellow! I cannot help pitying him."

"Then--then, you think she really does not love him?" I said. And this time my voice was hoarse enough, without any need of feigning.

"Love him! Ridiculous! What does such a woman understand by love? Certainly neither the sentiment nor the poetry of it! Tush, Hippolyte! I do not wish to be censorious; but every one knows that ever since M. de Marignan has been away in Algiers, that woman has had, not one devoted admirer, but a dozen; and now that her husband is coming back...."

"Coming back! ... her husband!" I echoed, half rising in my place, and falling back again, as if stunned. "Good heavens! is she not a widow?"

It was now the lady's turn to be startled.

"A widow!" she repeated. "Why, you know as well as I that--***Dieu***! To whom I am speaking?"

"Madame," I said, as steadily as my agitation would let me, "I beg you not to be alarmed. I am not, it is true, the person whom you have supposed; but--Nay, I implore you...."

She here uttered a quick cry, and darted forward for the check-string. Arresting her hand half way, respectfully but firmly, I went on:--

"How I came here, I will explain presently. I am a gentleman; and upon the word of a gentleman, Madame, am innocent of any desire to offend or alarm you. Can you--will you--hear me for one moment?"

"I appear, sir, to have no alternative," replied she, trembling like a caged bird.

"I might have left you undeceived, Madame. I might have extricated myself from, this painful position undiscovered--but for some words which just escaped your lips; some words so nearly concerning the--the honor and happiness of--of.... in short, I lost my presence of mind. I now implore you to tell me if all that you have just been saying of Madame de Marignan is strictly true."

"Who are you, sir, that you should dare to surprise confidences intended for another, and by what right do you question me?" said the lady, haughtily.

"By no right, Madame," I replied, fairly breaking into sobs, and burying my face in my hands. "I can only appeal to your compassion. I am that Englishman whom--whom...."

For a moment there was silence. My companion was the first to speak.

"Poor boy!" she said; and her voice, now, was gentle and compassionate. "You have been rudely undeceived. Did Madame de Marignan pass herself off upon you for a widow?"

"She never named her husband to me--I believed that she was free. I fancied he had been dead for years. She knew that was my impression."

"And you would have married her--actually married her?"

"I--I--hardly dared to hope...."

"*Ciel*! it is almost beyond belief. And you never inquired into her past history?"

"Never. Why should I?"

"Monsieur de Marignan holds a government appointment in Algiers, and has been absent more than four years. He is, I understand, expected back shortly, on leave of absence."

I conquered my agitation by a supreme effort.

"Madame," I said, "I thank you. It now only remains for me to explain my intrusion. I can do so in half a dozen words. Caught in the storm and unable to find a conveyance, I sought shelter in this carriage, which being the last on the file, offered the only refuge of which I could avail myself unobserved. While waiting for the tempest to abate, I fell asleep; and but for the chance which led you to mistake me for another, I must have been discovered when you entered the carriage."

"Then, finding yourself so mistaken, Monsieur, would it not have been more honorable to undeceive me than to usurp a conversation which...."

"Madame, I dared not. I feared to alarm you--I hoped to find some means of escape, and...."

"*Mon Dieu*! what means? How are you to escape as it is? How leave the carriage without being seen by my servants?"

I had not thought of this, nor of the dilemma in which my presence must place her.

"I can open the door softly," said I, "and jump out unperceived."

"Impossible, at the pace we are going! You would break your neck."

I shook my head, and laughed bitterly.

"Have no fear of that, Madame," I said. "Those who least value their necks never happen to break them. See, I can spring out as we pass the next turning, and be out of sight in a moment."

"Indeed, I will not permit it. Oh, dear! we have already reached the Faubourg St. Germain. Stay--I have an idea I Do you know what o'clock it is?"

"I don't know how long I may have slept; but I think it must be quite three."

"***Bien***! The Countess de Blois has a ball to-night, and her visitors are sure not to disperse before four or five. My sister is there. I will send in to ask if she has yet gone home, and when the carriage stops you can slip out. Here is the Rue de Bac, and the door of her hotel is yet surrounded with equipages."

And with this, she let down a front window, desired the coachman to stop, leaned forward so as to hide me completely, and sent in her footman with the message. When the man had fairly entered the hall, she turned to me and said:--

"Now, Monsieur, fly! It is your only chance."

"I go, Madame; but before going, suffer me to assure you that I know neither your name, nor that of the person for whom you mistook me--that I have no idea of your place of residence--that I should not know you if I saw you again to-morrow--in short, that you are to me as entirely a stranger as if this adventure had never happened."

"Monsieur, I thank you for the assurance; but I see the servant returning. Pray, begone!"

I sprang out without another word, and, never once looking back, darted down a neighboring street and waited in the shadow of a doorway till I thought the carriage must be out of sight.

The night was now fine, the moon was up, and the sky was full of stars. But I heeded nothing, save my own perplexed and painful thoughts. Absorbed in these, I followed the course of the Rue du Bac till I came to the Pont National. There my steps were arrested by the sight of the eddying river, the long gleaming front of the Louvre, the quaint, glistening gables of the Tuilleries, the far-reaching trees of the Champs Elysees all silvered in the soft, uncertain moonlight. It was a most calm and beautiful picture; and I stood for a long time leaning against the parapet of the bridge, and looking dreamily at the scene before me. Then I heard the quarters chime from belfry to belfry all over the quiet city, and found that it was half-past three o'clock. Presently a patrol of ***gendarmes*** went by, and, finding that they paused and looked at me suspiciously, I turned away, and bent my steps homewards.

By the time I reached the Cite Bergere it was past four, and the early market-carts were already rumbling along the Rue du Faubourg Montmartre. Going up wearily to my apartments, I found a note waiting for me in Dalrymple's handwriting. It ran thus:--

"MY DEAR DAMON:--
"Do you know that it is nearly a month since I last saw you? Do you know that I have called twice at your lodgings without finding you at home? I hear of you as having been constantly seen, of late, in the society of a very pretty woman of our acquaintance; but I confess that I do not desire to see you go to the devil entirely without the friendly assistance of
"Yours faithfully,
"OSCAR DALRYMPLE."

I read the note twice. I could scarcely believe that I had so neglected my only friend. Had I been mad? Or a fool?--or both? Too anxious and unhappy to sleep, and too tired to sit up, I lit my lamp, threw myself upon the bed, and there lay repenting my wasted hours, my misplaced love and my egregious folly, till morning came with its sunshine and its traffic, and found me a "wiser," if not a "better man."

"Half-past seven!" exclaimed I to myself, as I jumped up and plunged my head into a basin of cold water. "Dr. Cheron shall see me before nine this morning. I'll call on Dalrymple at luncheon time; at three, I must get back for the afternoon lecture; and in the evening--in the evening, by Jove! Madame de Marignan must be content with her adorable Delaroche, for the deuce a bit of her humble servant will she ever see again!"

And away I went presently along the sunny streets, humming to myself those saucy and wholesome lines of good Sir Walter Raleigh's:--

"Shall I like a hermit dwell
On a rock, or in a cell,
Calling home the smallest part
That is missing of my heart,
To bestow it where I may

Meet a rival every day?
If she undervalues me,
What care I how fair she be?"

CHAPTER XVII.
THE WIDOW OF A MINISTER OF FINANCE.

You are just in time, Arbuthnot, to do me a service," said Dalrymple, looking up from his desk as I went in, and reaching out his hand to me over a barricade of books and papers.

"Then I am very glad I have come," I replied. "But what confusion is this? Are you going anywhere?"

"Yes--to perdition. There, kick that rubbish out of your way and sit down."

Never very orderly, Dalrymple's rooms were this time in as terrible a litter as can well be conceived. The table was piled high with bills, old letters, books, cigars, gloves, card-cases, and pamphlets. The carpet was strewn with portmanteaus, hat-cases, travelling-straps, old luggage labels, railway wrappers, and the like. The chairs and sofas were laden with wearing apparel. As for Dalrymple himself, he looked haggard and weary, as though the last four weeks had laid four years upon his shoulders.

"You look ill," I said clearing a corner of the sofa for my own accommodation; "or *ennuye*, which is much the same thing. What is the matter? And what can I do for you?"

"The matter is that I am going abroad," said he, with his chin resting moodily in his two palms and his elbows on the table.

"Going abroad! Where?"

"I don't know--

'Anywhere, anywhere, out of the world.'

It's of very little consequence whether I betake myself to the East or to the West; eat rice in the tropics, or drink train-oil at the Pole."

"But have you no settled projects?"

"None whatever."

"And don't care what becomes of you?"

"Not in the least."

"Then, in Heaven's name, what has happened?"

"The very thing that, three weeks ago, would have made me the happiest fellow in Christendom. What are you going to do to-morrow?"

"Nothing, beyond my ordinary routine of medical study."

"Humph! Could you get a whole holiday, for once?"

I remembered how many I had taken of late, and felt ashamed of the readiness with which I replied:--

"Oh yes! easily."

"Well, then, I want you to spend the day with me. It will be, perhaps, my last in Paris for many a month, or even many a year. I ... Pshaw! I may as well say it, and have done with it. I am going to be married."

"Married!" I exclaimed, in blank amazement; for it was the last thing I should have guessed.

Dalrymple tugged away at his moustache with both hands, as was his habit when perplexed or troubled, and nodded gloomily. "To whom?"

"To Madame de Courcelles."

"And are you not very happy?"

"Happy! I am the most miserable dog unhanged?"

I was more at fault now than ever.

"I ... judging from trifles which some would perhaps scarcely have observed," I said, hesitatingly, "I--I thought you were interested in Madame de Courcelles?"

"Interested!" cried he, pushing back his chair and springing to his feet, as if the word had stung him. "By heaven! I love that woman as I never loved in my life."

"Then why ..."

"I'll tell you why--or, at least, I will tell you as much as I may--as I can; for the affair is hers, and not mine. She has a cousin--curse him!--to whom she was betrothed from childhood. His estates adjoined hers; family interests were concerned in their union; and the parents on both sides arranged matters. When, however, Monsieur de Courcelles fell in love with her--a man much older than herself, but possessed of great wealth and immense political influence--her father did not hesitate to send the cousin to the deuce and marry his daughter to the Minister of Finance. The cousin, it seems, was then a wild young fellow; not particularly in love with her himself; and not at all inconsolable for her loss. When, however, Monsieur de Courcelles was good enough to die (which he had the bad taste to do very hastily, and without making, by any means, the splendid provision for his widow which he had promised), our friend, the cousin, comes forward again. By this time he is enough man of the world to appreciate the value of land--more especially as he has sold, mortgaged, played the mischief with nearly every acre of his own. He pleads the old engagement, and, as he is pleased to call it, the old love. Madame de Courcelles is a young widow, very solitary, with no one to love, no object to live for, and no experience of the world. Her pity is easily awaked; and the result is that she not only accepts the cousin, but lends him large sums of money; suffers the title-deeds of her estates to go into the hands of his lawyer; and is formally betrothed to him before the eyes of all Paris!"

"Who is this man? Where is he?" I asked, eagerly.

"He is an officer of Chasseurs, now serving with his regiment in Algiers--a daring, dashing, reckless fellow; heartless and dissipated enough; but a splendid soldier. However, having committed her property to his hands, and suffered her name to be associated publicly with his, Madame de Courcelles, during his absence in Algiers, has done me the honor to prefer me. I have the first real love of her life, and the short and long of it is, that we are to be privately married to-morrow."

"And why privately?"

"Ah, there's the pity of it! There's the disappointment and the bitterness!"

"Can't Madame de Courcelles write and tell this man that she loves somebody else better?"

"Confound it! no. The fellow has her too much in his power, and, if he chose to be dishonest, could half ruin her. At all events she is afraid of him; and I ... I am as helpless as a child in the matter. If I were a rich man, I would snap my fingers at him; but how can I, with a paltry eight hundred a year, provide for that woman? Pshaw! If I could but settle it with a pair of hair-triggers and twenty paces of turf, I'd leave little work for the lawyers!"

"Well, then, what is to be done?"

"Only this," replied he, striding impatiently to and fro, like a caged lion; "I must just bear with my helplessness, and leave the remedy to those who can oppose skill to skill, and lawyer to lawyer."

"At all events, you marry the lady."

"Ay--I marry the lady; but I start to-morrow night for Berlin, **en route** for anywhere that chance may lead me."

"Without her?"

"Without her. Do you suppose that I would stay in Paris--her husband--and live apart from her? Meet her, like an ordinary acquaintance? See others admiring her? Be content to lounge in and out of her *soirees*, or ride beside her carriage now and then, as you or fifty others might do? Perhaps, have even to endure the presence of De Caylus himself? *Merci*! Any number of miles, whether of land or sea, were better than a martyrdom like that!"

"De Caylus!" I repeated. "Where have I heard that name?"

"You may have heard of it in a hundred places," replied my friend. "As I said before, the man is a gallant soldier, and does gallant things. But to return to the present question--may I depend on you to-morrow? For we must have a witness, and our witness must be both discreet and silent."

"On my silence and discretion you may rely absolutely."

"And you can be here by nine?"

"By daybreak, if you please."

"I won't tax you to that extent. Nine will do quite well."

"Adieu, then, till nine."

"Adieu, and thank you."

With this I left him, somewhat relieved to find that I had escaped all cross-examination on the score of Madame Marignan.

"De Caylus!" I again repeated to myself, as I took my rapid way to the Hotel Dieu. "De Caylus! why, surely, it must have been that evening at Madame de Courcelles'...."

And then I recollected that De Caylus was the name of that officer who was said to have ridden by night, and single-handed, through the heart of the enemy's camp, somewhere in Algiers.

CHAPTER XVIII.
A MARRIAGE NOT "A LA MODE."

The marriage took place in a little out-of-the-way Protestant chapel beyond the barriers, at about a quarter before ten o'clock the next morning. Dalrymple and I were there first; and Madame de Courcelles, having, in order to avoid observation, come part of the distance in a cab and part on foot, arrived a few minutes later. She was very pale, and looked almost like a *religieuse*, with her black veil tied closely under her chin, and a dark violet dress, which might have passed for mourning. She gave her hand to Dalrymple without speaking; then knelt down at the communion-table, and so remained till we had all taken our places. As for Dalrymple, he had even less color than she, but held his head up haughtily, and betrayed no sign of the conflict within.

It was a melancholy little chapel, dusty and neglected, full of black and white funereal tablets, and damp as a vault. We shivered as we stood about the altar; the clergyman's teeth chattered as he began the marriage service; and the echoes of our responses reverberated forlornly up among the gothic rafters overhead. Even the sunbeams struggled sadly and palely down the upper windows, and the chill wind whistled in when the door was opened, bringing with it a moan of coming rain.

The ceremony over, the books signed in the vestry, and the clergyman, clerk, and pew-opener duly remunerated for their services, we prepared to be gone. For a couple of moments, Dalrymple and his bride stood apart in the shadow of the porch. I saw him take the hand on which he had just placed the ring, and look down upon it tenderly, wistfully--I saw him bend lower, and lower, whispering what no other ears might hear--saw their lips meet for one brief instant. Then the lady's veil was lowered; she turned hastily away; and Dalrymple was left standing in the doorway alone.

"By Heaven!" said he, grasping my hand as though he would crush it. "This is hard to bear."

I but returned the pressure of his hand; for I knew not with what words to comfort him. Thus we lingered for some minutes in silence, till the clergyman, having put off his surplice, passed us with a bow and went out; and the pew-opener, after pretending to polish the door-handle with her apron, and otherwise waiting about with an air of fidgety politeness, dropped a civil curtsey, and begged to remind us that the chapel must now be closed.

Dalrymple started and shook himself like a water-dog, as if he would so shake off "the slings and arrows of outrageous fortune."

"*Rex est qui metuit nihil*!" said he; "but I am a sovereign in bad circumstances, for all that. Heigho! Care will kill a cat. What shall we do with ourselves, old fellow, for the rest of the day?"

"I hardly know. Would you like to go into the country?"

"Nothing better. The air perhaps would exorcise some of these blue-devils."

"What say you to St. Germains? It looks as if it must rain before night; yet there is the forest and...."

"Excellent! We can do as we like, with nobody to stare at us; and I am in a horribly uncivilized frame of mind this morning."

With this, we turned once more toward Paris, and, jumping into the first cab that came by, were driven to the station. It happened that a train was then about to start; so we were off immediately.

There were no other passengers in the carriage, so Dalrymple infringed the company's mandate by lighting a cigar, and I, finding him disinclined for talk, did the same thing, and watched the passing country. Flat and uninteresting at first, it consisted of a mere sandy plain, treeless, hedgeless, and imperfectly cultivated with struggling strips of corn and vegetables. By and by came a line of stunted pollards, a hamlet, and a little dreary cemetery. Then the landscape improved. The straight line of the horizon broke into gentle undulations; the Seine, studded with islets, wound through the meadow-land at our feet; and a lofty viaduct carried us from height to height across the eddying river. Then we passed into the close green shade of a forest, which opened every here and there into long vistas, yielding glimpses of

"--verdurous glooms, and winding mossy ways."

Through this wood the line continued to run till we reached our destination. Here our first few steps brought us out upon the Place, directly facing the old red and black chateau of St. Germain-en-Laye. Leaving this and the little dull town behind us, we loitered for some time about the broad walks of the park, and then passed on into the forest. Although it was neither Sunday nor a fete-day, there were pleasure parties gipseying under trees--Parisian cockneys riding raw-boned steeds--pony-chaises full of laughing grisettes dashing up and down the broad roads that pierce the wood in various directions--old women selling cakes and lemonade--workmen gambling with half-pence on the smooth turf by the wayside--***bonnes***, comely and important, with their little charges playing round them, and their busy fingers plying the knitting-needles as they walked--young ladies sketching trees, and prudent governesses reading novels close by; in short, all the life and variety of a favorite suburban resort on an ordinarily fine day about the beginning of autumn.

Leaving the frequented routes to the right, we turned into one of the many hundred tracks that diverge in every direction from the beaten roads, and wandered deeper and deeper into the green shades and solitudes of the forest. Pausing, presently, to rest, Dalrymple threw himself at full length on the mossy ground, with his hands clasping the back of his head, and his hat over his eyes; whilst I found a luxurious arm-chair in the gnarled roots of a lichen-tufted elm. Thus we remained for a considerable time puffing away at our cigars in that sociable silence which may almost claim to be an unique privilege of masculine friendship. Women cannot sit together for long without talking; men can enjoy each other's companionship for hours with scarcely the interchange of an idea.

Meanwhile, I watched the squirrels up in the beech-trees and the dancing of the green leaves against the sky; and thought dreamily of home, of my father, of the far past, and the possible future. I asked myself how, when my term of study came to an end, I should ever again endure the old home-life at Saxonholme? How settle down for life as my father's partner, conforming myself to his prejudices, obeying all the demands of his imperious temper, and accepting for evermore the monotonous routine of a provincial practice! It was an intolerable prospect, but no less inevitable than intolerable. Pondering thus, I sighed heavily, and the sigh roused Dalrymple's attention.

"Why, Damon," said he, turning over on his elbow, and pushing up his hat to the level of his eyes, "what's the matter with you?"

"Oh, nothing--at least, nothing new."

"Well, new or old, what is it? A man must be either in debt, or in love, when he sighs in that way. You look as melancholy as Werter redivivus!"

"I--I ought not to be melancholy, I suppose; for I was thinking of home."

Dalrymple's face and voice softened immediately.

"Poor boy!" he said, throwing away the end of his cigar, "yours is not a bright home, I fear. You told me, I think, that you had lost your mother?"

"From infancy."

"And you have no sisters?"

"None. I am an only child."

"Your father, however, is living?"

"Yes, my father lives. He is a rough-tempered, eccentric man; misanthropic, but clever; kind enough, and generous enough, in his own strange way. Still--"

"Still what?"

--"I dread the life that lies before me! I dread the life without society, without ambition, without change--the dull house--the bounded sphere of action--the bondage.... But of what use is it to trouble you with these things?"

"This use, that it does you good to tell, and me to listen. Sympathy, like mercy, blesseth him that gives and him that takes; and if I cannot actually help you, I am, at all events, thankful to be taken out of myself. Go on--tell me more of your prospects. Have you no acquaintance at Saxonholme whose society will make the place pleasant to you? No boyish friends? No pretty cousins? No first-loves, from amongst whom to choose a wife in time to come?"

I shook my head sadly.

"Did I not tell you that my father was a misanthrope? He visits no one, unless professionally. We have no friends and no relations."

"Humph! that's awkward. However, it leaves you free to choose your own friends, when you go back. A medical man need never be without a visiting connection. His very profession puts a thousand opportunities in his way."

"That is true; but--"

"But what?"

"I am not fond of the profession. I have never liked it. I would give much to relinquish it altogether."

Dalrymple gave utterance to a prolonged and very dismal whistle.

"This," said he gravely, "is the most serious part of the business. To live in a dull place is bad enough--to live with dull people is bad enough; but to have one's thoughts perpetually occupied with an uncongenial subject, and one's energies devoted to an uncongenial pursuit, is just misery, and nothing short of it! In fact 'tis a moral injustice, and one that no man should be required to endure."

"Yet I must endure it."

"Why?"

"Because it is too late to do otherwise."

"It is never too late to repair an evil, or an error."

"Unless the repairing of it involved a worse evil, or a more fatal error! No--I must not dream now of turning aside from the path that has been chosen for me. Too much time and too much money have been given to the thing for that;--I must let it take its course. There's no help for it!"

"But, confound it, lad! you'd better follow the fife and drum, or go before the mast, than give up your life to a profession you hate!"

"Hate is a strong word," I replied. "I do not actually hate it--at all events I must try to make the best of it, if only for my father's sake. His heart is set on making a physician of me, and I dare not disappoint him."

Dalrymple looked at me fixedly, and then fell back into his old position.

"Heigho!" he said, pulling his hat once more over his eyes, "I was a disobedient son. My father intended me for the Church; I was expelled from College for fighting a duel before I was twenty, and then, sooner than go home disgraced, enlisted as a private soldier in a cavalry corps bound for foreign service. Luckily, they found me out before the ship sailed, and made the best of a bad bargain by purchasing me a cornetcy in a dragoon regiment. I would not advise you to be disobedient, Damon. My experience in that line has been bitter enough,"

"How so? You escaped a profession for which you were disinclined, and entered one for which you had every qualification."

"Ay; but think of the cursed *esclandre*--first the duel, then the expulsion, then my disappearance for two months ... My mother was in bad health at the time, too;

and I, her favorite son--I--in short, the anxiety was too much for her. She--she died before I had been six weeks in the regiment. There! we won't talk of it. It's the one subject that ..."

His voice faltered, and he broke off abruptly.

"I wish you were going with me to Berlin," said he, after a long silence which I had not attempted to interrupt.

"I wish with all my heart that I were!"

"And yet," he added, "I am glad on--on her account, that you remain in Paris. You will call upon her sometimes, Arbuthnot?"

"If Madame De Cour.... I mean, if Mrs. Dalrymple will permit me."

An involuntary smile flitted across his lips--the first I had seen there all the day.

"She will be glad--grateful. She knows that I value you, and she has proof that I trust you. You are the only possessor of our secret."

"It is as safe with me," I said, "as if I were dead, and in my grave."

"I know it, old fellow. Well--you will see her sometimes. You will write to me, and tell me how she is looking. If--if she were to fall ill, you would not conceal it from me? and in case of any emergency--any annoyance arising from De Caylus ..."

"Were she my own sister," I said, earnestly, "she would not find me readier to assist or defend her. Of this, Dalrymple, be assured."

"Thank you," he said, and stretched up his hand to me. "I do believe you are true--though there are few men, and still fewer women, of whom I should like to say as much. By the way, Arbuthnot, beware of that little flirt, Madame de Marignan. She has charming eyes, but no more heart than a vampire. Besides, an entanglement with a married woman!... *cela ne se peut pas, mon cher*. You are too young to venture on such dangerous ground, and too inexperienced."

I smiled--perhaps somewhat bitterly--for the wound was still fresh, and I could not help wincing when any hand came near it.

"You are right," I replied. "Madame de Marignan is a dangerous woman; but dangerous for me no longer. However, I have paid rather dearly for my safety."

And with this, I told him the whole story from beginning to end, confessing all my follies without reservation. Surprised, amused, sometimes unable to repress a smile, sometimes genuinely compassionate, he heard my narrative through, accompanying it from time to time with muttered comments and ejaculations, none of which were very flattering to Madame de Marignan. When I had done, he sprang to his feet, laid his hand heavily upon my shoulder, and said:--

"Damon, there are a great many disagreeable things in life which wise people say are good for us, and for which they tell us we ought to be grateful in proportion to our discomfort. For my own part, however, I am no optimist. I am not fond of mortifying the flesh, and the eloquence of Socrates would fail to persuade me that a carbuncle was a cheerful companion, or the gout an ailment to be ardently desired. Yet, for all this, I cannot say that I look upon your adventure in the light of a misfortune. You have lost time, spent money, and endured a considerable amount of aggravation; but you have, on the other hand, acquired ease of manner, facility of conversation, and just that necessary polish which fits a man for society. Come! you have received a valuable lesson both in morals and manners; so farewell to Madame de Marignan, and let us write *Pour acquit* against the score!"

Willing enough to accept this cheerful view, I flourished an imaginary autograph upon the air with the end of my cane, and laughingly dismissed the subject.

We then strolled back through the wood, treading the soft moss under our feet, startling the brown lizards from our path and the squirrels from the lower branches of the great trees, and, now and then, surprising a plump little green frog, which went skipping away into the long grass, like an animated emerald. Coming back to the gardens, we next lingered for some time upon the terrace, admiring the superb panorama of undulating woodland and cultivated champaign, which, seen through the golden haze of afternoon, stretched out in glory to the remotest horizon. To our right stood the prison-like chateau, flinging back the sunset from its innumerable casements, and seeming to drink in the warm glow at every pore of its old, red bricks. To our left, all lighted up against the sky, rose the lofty tree-tops of the forest which we had just quitted. Our shadows stretched behind us across the level terrace, like the shadows of giants. Involuntarily, we dropped our voices. It would have seemed almost like profanity to speak aloud while the first influence of that scene was upon us.

Going on presently towards the verge of the terrace, we came upon an artist who, with his camp-stool under his arm, and his portfolio at his feet, was, like ourselves, taking a last look at the sunset before going away. As we approached, he turned and recognised us. It was Herr Franz Mueller, the story-telling student of the *Chicards* club.

"Good-afternoon, gentlemen," said he, lifting his red cap, and letting it fall back again a little on one side. "We do not see many such sunsets in the course of the summer."

"Indeed, no," replied Dalrymple; "and ere long the autumn tints will be creeping over the landscape, and the whole scene will assume a different character. Have you been sketching in the forest?"

"No--I have been making a study of the chateau and terrace from this point, with the landscape beyond. It is for an historical subject which I have laid out for my winter's work."

And with this, he good-naturedly opened his folio and took out the sketch, which was a tolerably large one, and represented the scene under much the same conditions of light as we now saw it.

"I shall have a group of figures here," he said, pointing to a spot on the terrace, "and a more distant one there; with a sprinkling of dogs and, perhaps, a head or two at an open window of the chateau. I shall also add a flag flying on the turret, yonder."

"A scene, I suppose, from the life of Louis the Thirteenth," I suggested.

"No--I mean it for the exiled court of James the Second," replied he. "And I shall bring in the King, and Mary of Modena, and the Prince their son, who was afterwards the Pretender."

"It is a good subject," said Dalrymple. "You will of course find excellent portraits of all these people at Versailles; and a lively description of their court, mode of life, and so forth, if my memory serves me correctly, in the tales of Anthony, Count Hamilton. But with all this, I dare say, you are better acquainted than I."

"*Parbleu!* not I," said the student, shouldering his camp-stool as if it were a musket, and slinging his portfolio by a strap across his back; "therefore, I am all the more obliged to you for the information. My reading is neither very extensive nor very useful; and as for my library, I could pack it all into a hat-case any day, and find room for a few other trifles at the same time. Here is the author I chiefly study. He is my constant companion, and, like myself, looks somewhat the worse for wear."

Saying which, he produced from one of his pockets a little, greasy, dog-eared volume of Beranger, about the size of a small snuff-box, and began singing aloud, to a very cheerful air, a song of which a certain faithless Mademoiselle Lisette was the heroine, and of which the refrain was always:--

"Lisette! ma Lisette,
Tu m'as trompe toujours;
Je veux, Lisette,
Boire a nos amours."

To this accompaniment we walked back through the gardens to the railway station, where, being a quarter of an hour too soon, our companion amused himself by "chaffing," questioning, contradicting, and otherwise ingeniously tormenting the check-takers and porters of the establishment. One pompous official, in particular, became so helplessly indignant that he retired into a little office overlooking the platform, and was heard to swear fluently, all by himself, for several minutes. The time having expired and the doors being opened, we passed out with the rest of the home-going Parisians, and were about to take our places, when Mueller, climbing like a cat to the roof-seats on the top of the second-class carriages, beckoned us to follow.

"Who would be shut up with ten fat people and a baby, when fresh air can be breathed, and tobacco smoked, for precisely the same fare?" asked he. "You don't mean to say that you came down to St. Germains in one of the dens below?"

"Yes, we did," I replied; "but we had it to ourselves."

"So much the worse. Man is a gregarious animal, and woman also--which proves Zimmerman to have been neither, and accounts for the brotherhood of *Les Chicards*. Would you like to see how that old gentleman looks when he is angry?"

"Which? The one in the opposite corner?"

"The same."

"Well, that depends on circumstances. Why do you ask?"

"Because I'll engage to satisfy your curiosity in less than ten minutes."

"Oh, no, don't affront him," said I. "We shall only have a scene."

"I won't affront him. I promise not to utter a syllable, either offensive or defensive."

"Leave him alone, then, poor devil!"

"Nonsense! If he chooses to be annoyed, that's his business, and not mine. Now, you'll see."

And Mueller, alert for mischief, stared fixedly at the old gentleman in the opposite corner for some minutes--then sighed--roused himself as if from a profound reverie--seized his portfolio--took out a pencil and sketch-book--mended the pencil with an elaborate show of fastidiousness and deliberation--stared again--drew a deep breath--turned somewhat aside, as if anxious to conceal his object, and began sketching rapidly. Now and then he paused; stole a furtive glance over his shoulder; bit his lip; rubbed out; corrected; glanced again; and then went on rapidly as before.

In the meanwhile the old gentleman, who was somewhat red and irascible, began to get seriously uncomfortable. He frowned, fidgeted, coughed, buttoned and unbuttoned his coat, and jealously watched every proceeding of his tormentor. A general smile dawned upon the faces of the rest of the travellers. The priest over the way pinched his lips together, and looked down demurely. The two girls, next to the priest, tittered behind their handkerchiefs. The young man with the blue cravat sucked the top of his cane, and winked openly at his companions, both of whom were cracking nuts, and flinging the shells down the embankment. Presently Mueller threw his head back, held the drawing off, still studiously keeping the back of it towards the rest of the passengers; looked at it with half-closed eyes; stole another exceedingly cautious glance at his victim; and then, affecting for the first time to find himself observed, made a vast show of pretending to sketch the country through which we were passing.

The old gentleman could stand it no longer.

"Monsieur," said he, angrily. "Monsieur, I will thank you not to take my portrait. I object to it. Monsieur."

"Charming distance," said Mueller, addressing himself to me "Wants interest, however, in the foreground. That's a picturesque tree yonder, is it not?"

The old gentleman struck his umbrella sharply on the floor.

"It's of no use, Monsieur," he exclaimed, getting more red and excited. "You are taking my portrait, and I object to it. I know you are taking my portrait."

Mueller looked up dreamily.

"I beg your pardon, Monsieur," said he. "Did you speak?'

"Yes, Monsieur. I did speak. I repeat that you shall not take my portrait."

"Your portrait, Monsieur?"

"Yes, my portrait!"

"But, Monsieur," remonstrated the artist, with an air of mingled candor and surprise, "I never dreamed of taking your portrait!"

"*Sacre non*!" shouted the old gentleman, with another rap of the umbrella. "I saw you do it! Everybody saw you do It!"

"Nay, if Monsieur will but do me the honor to believe that I was simply sketching from nature, as the train...."

"An impudent subterfuge, sir!" interrupted the old gentleman. "An impudent subterfuge, and nothing less!"

Mueller drew himself up with immense dignity.

"Monsieur," he said, haughtily, "that is an expression which I must request you to retract. I have already assured you, on the word of a gentleman...."

"A gentleman, indeed! A pretty gentleman! He takes my portrait, and...."

"I have not taken your portrait, Monsieur."

"Good heavens!" cried the old gentleman, looking round, "was ever such assurance! Did not every one present see him in the act? I appeal to every one--to you, Monsieur--to you, Mesdames,--to you, reverend father,--did you not all see this person taking my portrait?"

"Nay, then, if it must come to this," said Mueller, "let the sketch be evidence, and let these ladies and gentlemen decide whether it is really the portrait of Monsieur--and if they think it like?"

Saying which, he held up the book, and displayed a head, sketched, it is true, with admirable spirit and cleverness, but--the head of an ass, with a thistle in its mouth!

A simultaneous explosion of mirth followed. Even the priest laughed till the tears ran down his cheeks, and Dalrymple, heavy-hearted as he was, could not help joining in the general shout. As for the old gentleman, the victim of this elaborate practical joke, he glared at us all round, swore that it was a premeditated insult from beginning to end, and, swelling with suppressed rage, flung himself back into his corner, and looked resolutely in the opposite direction.

By this time we were half-way to Paris, and the student, satisfied with his success, packed up his folio, brought out a great meerschaum with a snaky tube, and smoked like a factory-chimney.

When we alighted, it was nearly five o'clock.

"What shall we do next?" said Dalrymple, pulling drearily at his moustache. "I am so deuced dull to-day that I am ashamed to ask anybody to do me the charity to dine with me--especially a *bon garcon* like Herr Mueller."

"Don't be ashamed," said the student, laughingly, "I would dine with Pluto himself, if the dishes were good and my appetite as sharp as to-day."

"*Allons*, then! Where shall we go; to the *Trois Freres*, or the *Moulin Rouge*, or the *Maison Doree*?"

"The *Trois Freres*" said Mueller, with the air of one who deliberates on the fate of nations, "has the disadvantage of being situated in the Palais Royal, where the band still continues to play at half-past five every afternoon. Now, music should come on with the sweets and the champagne. It is not appropriate with soup or fish, and it distracts one's attention if injudiciously administered with the made dishes,"

"True. Then shall we try the *Moulin Rouge*?"

Mueller shook his head.

"At the *Moulin Rouge*" said he, gravely, "one can breakfast well; but their dinners are stereotyped. For the last ten years they have not added a new dish to their *carte*; and the discovery of a new dish, says Brillat Savarin, is of more importance to the human race than the discovery of a new planet. No--I should not vote for the *Moulin Rouge*."

"Well, then, Vefours, Very's, the Cafe Anglais?"

"Vefours is traditional; the Cafe Anglais is infested with English; and at Very's, which is otherwise a meritorious establishment, one's digestion is disturbed by the sight of omnivorous provincials, who drink champagne with the *roti*, and eat melon at dessert."

Dalrymple laughed outright.

"At this rate," said he, "we shall get no dinner at all! What is to become of us, if neither Very's, nor the *Trois Freres*, nor the *Moulin Rouge*, nor the *Maison Doree*...."

"*Halte-la!*" interrupted the student, theatrically; "for by my halidom, sirs, I said not a syllable in disparagement of the house yelept Doree! Is it not there that we eat of the crab of Bordeaux, succulent and roseate? Is it not there that we drink of Veuve Cliquot the costly, and of that Johannisberger, to which all other hocks are vinegar and water? Never let it be said that Franz Mueller, being of sound mind and body, did less than justice to the reputation of the *Maison Doree*."

"To the *Maison Doree*, then," said Dalrymple, "with what speed and appetite we may! By Jove! Herr Franz, you are a *connoisseur* in the matter of dining."

"A man who for twenty-nine days out of every thirty pays his sixty-five centimes for two dishes at a student's Restaurant in the Quartier Latin, knows better than most people where to go for a good dinner when he has the chance," said Mueller, philosophically. "The ragouts of the Temple--the *arlequins* of the *Cite*--the fried fish of the Odeon arcades--the unknown hashes of the *guingettes*, and the 'funeral baked meats' of the Palais Royal, are all familiar to my pocket and my palate. I do not scruple to confess that in cases of desperate emergency, I have even availed myself of the advantages of *Le hasard*."

"*Le hasard*." said I. "What is that?"

"*Le hasard de la fourchette*," replied the student, "is the resort of the vagabond, the *gamin*, and the *chiffonier*. It lies down by the river-side, near the Halles, and consists of nothing but a shed, a fire, and a caldron. In this caldron a seething sea of oleaginous liquid conceals an infinite variety of animal and vegetable substances. The arrangements of the establishment are beautifully simple. The votary pays his five centimes and is armed by the presiding genius of the place with a huge two-pronged iron fork. This fork he plunges in once;--he may get a calf's foot, or a potato, or a sheep's head, or a carrot, or a cabbage, or nothing, as fate and the fork direct. All men are gamblers in some way or another, and *Le hasard* is a game of gastronomic chance. But from the ridiculous to the sublime, it is but a step--and while talking of *Le hasard* behold, we have arrived at the *Maison Doree*."

CHAPTER XIX.
A DINNER AT THE MAISON DOREE AND
AN EVENING PARTY IN THE QUARTIER LATIN.

The most genial of companions was our new acquaintance, Franz Mueller, the art-student. Light-hearted, buoyant, unassuming, he gave his animal spirits full play, and was the life of our little dinner. He had more natural gayety than generally belongs to the German character, and his good-temper was inexhaustible. He enjoyed everything; he made the best of everything; he saw food for laughter in everything. He was always amused, and therefore was always amusing. Above all, there was a spontaneity in his mirth which acted upon others as a perpetual stimulant. He was in short, what the French call a ***bon garcon***, and the English a capital fellow; easy without assurance, comic without vulgarity, and, as Sydney Smith wittily hath it--"a great number of other things without a great number of other things."

Upon Dalrymple, who had been all day silent, abstracted, and unlike his usual self, this joyous influence acted like a tonic. As entertainer, he was bound to exert himself, and the exertion did him good. He threw off his melancholy; and with the help, possibly, of somewhat more than his usual quantity of wine, entered thoroughly into the passing joyousness of the hour. What a ***recherche***, luxurious extravagant little dinner it was, that evening at the Maison Doree! We had a charming little room overlooking the Boulevard, furnished with as much looking-glass, crimson-velvet, gilding, and arabesque painting as could be got together within the space of twelve-feet by eight. Our wine came to table in a silver cooler that Cellini might have wrought. Our meats were served upon porcelain that would have driven Palissy to despair. We had nothing that was in season, except game, and everything that was out; which, by-the-way, appears to be our modern criterion of excellence with respect to a dinner. Finally, we were waited upon by the most imposing of waiters--a waiter whose imperturbable gravity was not to be shaken by any amount of provocation, and whose neckcloth alone was sufficient to qualify him for the church.

How merry we were! How Mueller tormented that diplomatic waiter! What stories we told! what puns we made! What brilliant things we said, or fancied we said, over our Chambertin and Johannisberger! Mueller knew nothing of the substratum of sadness underlying all that jollity. He little thought how heavy Dalrymple's strong heart had been that morning. He had no idea that my friend and I were to part on the morrow, for months or years, as the case might be--he to carry his unrest hither and thither through distant lands; I to remain alone in a strange city, pursuing a distasteful study, and toiling onward to a future without fascination or hope. But, as the glass seals tell us, "such is life." We are all mysteries to one another. The pleasant fellow whom I invite to dinner because he amuses me, carries a scar on his soul which it would frighten me to see; and he in turn, when he praises my claret, little dreams of the carking care that poisons it upon my palate, and robs it of all its aroma. Perhaps the laughter-loving painter himself had his own little tragedy locked up in some secret corner of the heart that seemed to beat so lightly under that braided blouse of Palais Royal cut and Quartier Latin fashion! Who could tell? And of what use would it be, if it were told? Smiles carry one through the world more agreeably than tears, and if the skeleton is only kept decently out of sight in its own unsuspected closet, so much the better for you and me, and society at large.

Dinner over, and the serious waiter dismissed with the dessert and the empty bottles, we sat by the open window for a long time, sipping our coffee, smoking our cigars, and watching the busy life of the Boulevard below. There the shops were all alight and the passers-by more numerous than by day. Carriages were dashing along, full of opera-goers and ball-room beauties. On the pavement just under our window were seated the usual crowd of Boulevard idlers, sipping their *al fresco* absinthe, and *grog-au-vin.* In the very next room, divided from us by only a slender partition, was a noisy party of young men and girls. We could hear their bursts of merriment, the chinking of their glasses as they pledged one another, the popping of the champagne corks, and almost the very jests that passed from lip to lip. Presently a band came and played at the corner of an adjoining street. All was mirth, all was life, all was amusement and dissipation both in-doors and out-of-doors, in the "care-charming" city of Paris on that pleasant September night; and we, of course, were gay and noisy, like our neighbors. Dalrymple and Mueller could scarcely be called new acquaintances. They had met some few times at the **Chicards**, and also, some years before, in Rome. What stories they told of artists whom they had known! What fun they made of Academic dons and grave professors high in authority! What pictures they drew, of life in Rome--in Vienna--in Paris! Though we had no ladies of our party and were only three in number, I am not sure that the merry-makers in the next room laughed any louder or oftener than we!

At length the clock on the mantelpiece warned us that it was already half-past nine, and that we had been three hours at dinner. It was clearly time to vary the evening's amusement in some way or other, and the only question was what next to do? Should we go to a billiard-room? Or to the Salle Valentinois? Or to some of the cheap theatres on the Boulevard du Temple? Or to the Tableaux Vivants? Or the Cafe des Aveugles? Or take a drive round by the Champs Elysees in an open fly?

At length Mueller remembered that some fellow-students were giving a party that evening, and offered to introduce us.

"It is up five pairs of stairs, in the Quartier Latin," said he; "but thoroughly jolly--all students and grisettes. They'll be delighted to see us."

This admirable proposition was no sooner made than acted upon; so we started immediately, and Dalrymple, who seemed to be well acquainted with the usages of student-life, proposed that we should take with us a store of sweetmeats for the ladies.

"There subsists," observed he, "a mysterious elective affinity between the grisette and the chocolate bon-bon. He who can skilfully exhibit the latter, is almost certain to win the heart of the former. Where the chocolate fails, however, the **marron glace** is an infallible specific. I recommend that we lay in a liberal supply of both weapons."

"Carried by acclamation," said Mueller. "We can buy them on our way, in the Rue Vivienne. A capital shop; but one that I never patronize--they give no credit."

Chatting thus, and laughing, we made our way across the Boulevard and through a net-work of by-streets into the Rue Vivienne, where we laid siege to a

great bon-bon shop--a gigantic depot for dyspepsia at so much per kilogramme--
and there filled our pockets with sweets of every imaginable flavor and color. This
done, a cab conveyed us in something less than ten minutes across the Pont Neuf to
the Quartier Latin.

Mueller's friends were three in number, and all students--one of art, one of
law, and one of medicine. They lodged at the top of a dingy house near the Odeon,
and being very great friends and very near neighbors were giving this entertainment conjointly. Their names were Gustave, Jules, and Adrien. Adrien was the
artist, and lived in the garret, just over the heads of Gustave and Jules, which made
it very convenient for a party, and placed a *suite* of rooms at the disposal of their
visitors.

Long before we had achieved the five pairs of stairs, we heard the sound of
voices and the scraping of a violin, and on the fifth landing were received by a
pretty young lady in a coquettish little cap, whom Mueller familiarly addressed as
Annette, and who piloted us into a very small bed-room which was already full of
hats and coats, bonnets, shawls, and umbrellas. Having added our own paletots and
beavers to the general stock, and having each received a little bit of pasteboard in
exchange for the same, we were shown into the ball-room by Mademoiselle Annette, who appeared to fill the position of hostess, usher, and general superinten-
dent.

It was a good-sized room, somewhat low in the ceiling, and brilliantly lighted
with lots of tallow candles in bottles. The furniture had all been cleared out for the
dancers, except a row of benches round the walls, and a chest of draws in a recess
between the windows which served as a raised platform for the orchestra. The said
orchestra consisted of a violin and accordion, both played by amateurs, with an occasional *obligato* on the common comb. As for the guests, they were, as Mueller
had already told us, all students and grisettes--the former wearing every strange variety of beard and blouse; the latter in pretty light-colored muslins and bewitching
little caps, with the exception of two who wore flowers in their hair, and belonged
to the opera ballet. They were in the midst of a tremendous galop when we arrived;
so we stood at the door and looked on, and Dalrymple flirted with Mademoiselle
Annette. As soon as the galop was over, two of our hosts came forward to welcome
us.

"The Duke of Dalrymple and the Marquis of Arbuthnot--Messieurs Jules Char-pentier and Gustave Dubois," said Mueller, with the most ***degage*** air in the world.

Monsieur Jules, a tall young man with an enormous false nose of the regular carnival pattern, and Monsieur Gustave, who was short and stout, with a visible high-water mark round his throat and wrists, and curious leather mosaics in his boots, received us very cordially, and did not appear to be in the least surprised at the magnificence of the introduction. On the contrary, they shook hands with us; apologized for the absence of Adrien, who was preparing the supper upstairs; and offered to find us partners for the next valse. Dalrymple immediately proposed for the hand of Mademoiselle Annette. Mueller, declining adventitious aid, wandered among the ladies, making himself universally agreeable and trusting for a partner to his own unassisted efforts. For myself, I was indebted to Monsieur Gustave for an introduction to a very charming young lady whose name was Josephine, and with whom I fell over head and ears in love without a moment's warning.

She was somewhat under the middle height, slender, supple, rosy-lipped, and coquettish to distraction. Her pretty mouth dimpled round with smiles at every word it uttered. Her very eyes laughed. Her hair, which was more adorned than concealed by a tiny muslin cap that clung by some unseen agency to the back of her head, was of a soft, warm, wavy brown, with a woof of gold threading it here and there. Her voice was perhaps a little loud; her conversation rather childish; her ac-cent such as would scarcely have passed current in the Faubourg St. Germain--but what of that? One would be worse than foolish to expect style and cultivation in a grisette; and had I not had enough to disgust me with both in Madame de Mari-gnan? What more charming, after all, than youth, beauty, and lightheartedness? Were Noel and Chapsal of any importance to a mouth that could not speak without such a smile as Hebe might have envied?

I was, at all events, in no mood to take exception to these little defects. I am not sure that I did not even regard them in the light of additional attractions. That which in another I should have called ***bete***, I set down to the score of ***naivete*** in Mademoiselle Josephine. One is not diffident at twenty--by the way, I was now twenty-one--especially after dining at the Maison Doree.

Mademoiselle Josephine was frankness itself. Before I had enjoyed the pleasure of her acquaintance for ten minutes, she told me she was an artificial florist; that her *patronne* lived in the Rue Menilmontant; that she went to her work every morning at nine, and left it every evening at eight; that she lodged *sous les toits* at No. 70, Rue Aubry-le-Boucher; that her relations lived at Juvisy; and that she went to see them now and then on Sundays, when the weather and her funds permitted.

"Is the country pretty at Juvisy, Mademoiselle?" I asked, by way of keeping up the conversation.

"Oh, M'sieur, it is a real paradise. There are trees and fields, and there is the Seine close by, and a chateau, and a park, and a church on a hill, ... *ma foi!* there is nothing in Paris half so pretty; not even the Jardin des Plantes!"

"And have you been there lately?"

"Not for eight weeks, at the very least, M'sieur. But then it costs three francs and a half for the return ticket, and since I quarrelled with Emile...."

"Emile!" said I, quickly. "Who is he?"

"He is a picture-frame maker, M'sieur, and works for a great dealer in the Rue du Faubourg Montmartre. He was my sweetheart, and he took me out somewhere every Sunday, till we quarrelled."

"And what did you quarrel about, Mademoiselle?"

My pretty partner laughed and tossed her head.

"Eh, *mon Dieu*! he was jealous."

"Jealous of whom?"

"Of a gentleman--an artist--who wanted to paint me in one of his pictures. Emile did not like me to go to his *atelier* so often; and the gentleman gave me a shawl (such a pretty shawl!) and a canary in a lovely green and gold cage; and...."

"And Emile objected ?"

"Yes, M'sieur."

"How very unreasonable!"

"That's just what I said, M'sieur."

"And have you never seen him since!"

"Oh, yes--he keeps company now with my cousin Cecile, and she humors him in everything,"

"And the artist--what of him, Mademoiselle?"

"Oh, I sat to him every day, till his picture was finished. *Il etait bien gentil*. He took me to the theatre several times, and once to a fete at Versailles; but that was after Emile and I had broken it off."

"Did you find it tiresome, sitting as a model?"

"*Mais, comme ci, et comme ca*! It was a beautiful dress, and became me wonderfully. To be sure, it was rather cold!"

"May I ask what character you were supposed to represent, Mademoiselle?"

"He said it was Phryne. I have no idea who she was; but I think she must have found it very uncomfortable if she always wore sandals, and went without stockings."

I looked down at her little foot, and thought how pretty it must have looked in the Greek sandal. I pictured her to myself in the graceful Greek robe, with a chalice in her hand and her temples crowned with flowers. What a delicious Phryne! And what a happy fellow Praxiteles must have been!

"It was a privilege, Mademoiselle, to be allowed to see you in so charming a costume," I said, pressing her hand tenderly. "I envy that artist from the bottom of my heart."

Mademoiselle Josephine smiled, and returned the pressure.

"One might borrow it," said she, "for the Bal de l'Opera."

"Ah, Mademoiselle, if I dared only aspire to the honor of conducting you!"

"*Dame*! it is nearly four months to come!"

"True, but in the meantime, Mademoiselle----"

"In the meantime," said the fair Josephine, anticipating my hopes with all the unembarrassed straightforwardness imaginable, "I shall be delighted to improve M'sieur's acquaintance."

"Mademoiselle, you make me happy!"

"Besides, M'sieur is an Englishman, and I like the English so much!"

"I am delighted to hear it, Mademoiselle. I hope I shall never give you cause to alter your opinion."

"Last galop before supper!" shouted Monsieur Jules through, a brass speaking-trumpet, in order to make use of which he was obliged to hold up his nose with one hand. "Gentlemen, choose your partners. All couples to dance till they drop!"

There were a dozen up immediately, amongst whom Dalrymple and Mademoiselle Annette, and Mueller with one of the ballet ladies, were the first to start. As for Josephine, she proved to be a damsel of forty-galop power. She never wanted to rest, and she never cared to leave off. She did not even look warm when it was over. I wonder to this day how it was that I did not die on the spot.

When the galop was ended, we all went upstairs to Monsieur Adrien's garret, where Monsieur Adrien, who had red hair and wore glasses, received us in person, and made us welcome. Here we found the supper elegantly laid out on two doors which had been taken off their hinges for the purpose; but which, being supported from beneath on divers boxes and chairs of unequal heights, presented a painfully sloping surface, thereby causing the jellies to look like leaning towers of Pisa, and the spongecake (which was already professedly tipsy) to assume an air so unbecomingly convivial that it might almost have been called drunk.

Nobody thought of sitting down, and, if they did, there were no means of doing so; for Monsieur Adrien's garret was none of the largest, and, as in a small villa residence we sometimes see the whole house sacrificed to a winding staircase, so in this instance had the whole room been sacrificed to the splendor of the supper. For the inconvenience of standing, we were compensated, however, by the abundance and excellence of the fare. There were cold chickens, meat-pies, dishes of sliced ham, pyramids of little Bologna sausages, huge rolls of bread a yard in length, lobster salad, and cold punch in abundance.

The flirtations at supper were tremendous. In a bachelor establishment one cannot expect to find every convenience, and on this occasion the prevailing deficiencies were among the plates and glasses; so those who had been partners in the dance now became partners in other matters, eating off the same plate and drinking out of the same tumbler; but this only made it so much the merrier. By and by somebody volunteered a song, and somebody else made a speech, and then we went down again to the ball-room, and dancing recommenced.

The laughter now became louder, and the legs of the guests more vigorous than ever. The orchestra, too, received an addition to its strength in the person of a gentleman who, having drunk more cold punch than was quite consistent with the preservation of his equilibrium, was still sober enough to oblige us with a spirited accompaniment on the shovel and tongs, which, with the violin and accordion, and the comb *obligato* before mentioned, produced a startling effect, and reminded one of Turkish marches, Pantomime overtures, and the like barbaric music.

In the midst of the first polka, however, we were interrupted by a succession of furious double knocks on the floor beneath our feet. We stopped by involuntary consent--dancers, musicians, and all.

"It's our neighbor on the story below," said Monsieur Jules. "He objects to the dancing."

"Then we'll dance a little heavier, to teach him better taste," said a student, who had so little hair on his head and so much on his chin, that he looked as if his face had been turned upside down. "What is the name of the ridiculous monster?"

"Monsieur Bobinet."

"Ladies and gentlemen, let us dance for the edification of Monsieur Bobinet! Orchestra, strike up, in honor of Monsieur Bobinet! One, two, three, and away!"

Hereupon we uttered a general hurrah, and dashed off again, like a herd of young elephants. The knocking ceased, and we thought that Monsieur Bobinet had resigned himself to his fate, when, just as the polka ended and the dancers were promenading noisily round and round the room, the bombardment began afresh; and this time against the very door of the ball-room.

"*Par exemple*!" cries Monsieur Jules. "The enemy dares to attack us in our own lines!"

"Bolt the door, and let him knock till he's tired," suggested one.

"Open it suddenly, and deluge him with water!" cried another.

"Tar and feather him!" proposed a third.

In the meantime, Monsieur Bobinet, happily ignorant of these agreeable schemes for his reception, continued to thunder away upon the outer panels, accompanying the raps with occasional loud coughs, and hems, and stampings of the feet.

"Hush! do nothing violent," cried Mueller, scenting a practical joke. "Let us invite him in, and make fun of him. It will be ever so much more amusing!"

And with this he drove the rest somewhat back and threw open the door, upon the outer threshold of which, with a stick in one hand and a bedroom candle in the other, and a flowered dressing-gown tied round his ample waist by a cord and tassels, stood Monsieur Bobinet.

Mueller received him with a profound bow, and said:--

"Monsieur Bobinet, I believe?"

Monsieur Bobinet, who was very bald, very cross, and very stout, cast an irritable glance into the room, but, seeing so many people, drew back and said:--

"Yes, that is my name, Monsieur. I lodge on the fourth floor...."

"But pray walk in, Monsieur Bobinet," said Mueller, opening the door still wider and bowing still more profoundly.

"Monsieur," returned the fourth-floor lodger, "I--I only come to complain...."

"Whatever the occasion of this honor, Monsieur," pursued the student, with increasing politeness, "we cannot suffer you to remain on the landing. Pray do us the favor to walk in."

"Oh, walk in--pray walk in, Monsieur Bobinet," echoed Jules, Gustave, and Adrien, all together.

The fourth-floor lodger hesitated; took a step forward; thought, perhaps, that, since we were all so polite, he would do his best to conciliate us; and, glancing down nervously at his dressing-gown and slippers, said:--

"Really, gentlemen, I should have much pleasure, but I am not prepared...."

"Don't mention it, Monsieur Bobinet," said Mueller. "We are delighted to receive you. Allow me to disembarrass you of your candle."

"And permit me," said Jules, "to relieve you of your stick."

"Pray, Monsieur Bobinet, do you never dance the polka?" asked Gustave.

"Bring Monsieur Bobinet a glass of cold punch," said Adrien.

"And a plate of lobster salad," added the bearded student.

Monsieur Bobinet, finding the door already closed behind him, looked round nervously; but encountering only polite and smiling faces, endeavored to seem at his ease, and to put a good face upon the matter.

"Indeed, gentlemen, I must beg you to excuse me," said he. "I never drink at night, and I never eat suppers. I only came to request...."

"Nay, Monsieur Bobinet, we cannot suffer you to leave us without taking a glass of cold punch," pursued Mueller.

"Upon my word," began the lodger, "I dare not...."

"A glass of white wine, then?"

"Or a cup of coffee?"

"Or some home-made lemonade?"

Monsieur Bobinet cast a look of helpless longing towards the door.

"If you really insist, gentlemen," said he, "I will take a cup of coffee; but indeed...."

"A cup of coffee for Monsieur Bobinet!" shouted Mueller.

"A large cup of coffee for Monsieur Bobinet!" repeated Jules.

"A strong cup of coffee for Monsieur Bobinet!" cried Gustave, following up the lead of the other two.

The fourth-floor lodger frowned and colored up, beginning to be suspicious of mischief. Seeing this, Mueller hastened to apologize.

"You must pardon us, Monsieur Bobinet," he said with the most winning amiability, "if we are all in unusually high spirits to-night. You are not aware, perhaps, that our friend Monsieur Jules Charpentier was married this morning, and that we are here in celebration of that happy event. Allow me to introduce you to the bride."

And turning to one of the ballet ladies, he led her forward with exceeding gravity, and presented her to Monsieur Bobinet as Madame Charpentier.

The fourth-floor lodger bowed, and went through the usual congratulations. In the meantime, some of the others had prepared a mock sofa by means of two chairs set somewhat wide apart, with a shawl thrown over the whole to conceal the space between. Upon one of these chairs sat a certain young lady named Louise, and upon the other Mam'selle Josephine. As soon as it was ready, Muller, who had been only waiting for it, affected to observe for the first time that Monsieur Bobinet was still standing.

"***Mon Dieu***!" he exclaimed, "has no one offered our visitor a chair? Monsieur Bobinet, I beg a thousand pardons. Pray do us the favor to be seated. Your coffee will be here immediately, and these ladies on the sofa will be delighted to make room for you."

"Oh yes, pray be seated, Monsieur Bobinet," cried the two girls. "We shall be charmed to make room for Monsieur Bobinet!"

More than ever confused and uncomfortable, poor Monsieur Bobinet bowed; sat down upon the treacherous space between the two chairs; went through immediately; and presented the soles of his slippers to the company in the least picturesque manner imaginable. This involuntary performance was greeted with a shout of wild delight.

"Bravo, Monsieur Bobinet!"

"***Vive*** Monsieur Bobinet!"

"Three cheers for Monsieur Bobinet!"

Scarlet with rage, the fourth-floor lodger sprang to his feet and made a rush to the door; but he was hemmed in immediately. In vain he stormed; in vain he swore. We joined hands; we called for music; we danced round him; we sang; and at last, having fairly bumped and thumped and hustled him till we were tired, pushed him out on the landing, and left him to his fate.

After this interlude, the mirth grew fast and furious. ***Valse*** succeeded ***valse***, and galop followed galop, till the orchestra declared they could play no longer, and the gentleman with the shovel and tongs collapsed in a corner of the room and went to sleep with his head in the coal-scuttle. Then the ballet-ladies were prevailed upon to favor us with a ***pas de deux***; after which Mueller sang a comic song with a chorus, in which everybody joined; and then the orchestra was bribed with hot brandy-and-water, and dancing commenced again. By this time the visitors began to drop away in twos and threes, and even the fair Josephine, to whom I had never ceased paying the most devoted attention, declared she could not stir another step. As for Dalrymple, he had disappeared during supper, without a word of leave-taking to any one.

Matters being at this pass, I looked at my watch, and found that it was already half-past six o'clock; so, having bade good-night, or rather good-morning, to Messieurs Jules, Gustave, and Adrien, and having, with great difficulty, discovered my own coat and hat among the miscellaneous collection in the adjoining bed-room, I prepared to escort Mademoiselle Josephine to her home.

"Going already?" said Mueller, encountering us on the landing, with a roll in one hand and a Bologna sausage in the other.

"Already! Why, my dear fellow, it is nearly seven o'clock!"

"***Qu'importe***? Come up to the supper-room and have some breakfast!"

"Not for the world!"

"Well, ***chacun a son gout***. I am as hungry as a hunter."

"Can I not take you any part of your way?"

"No, thank you. I am a Quartier Latinist, ***pur sang***, and lodge only a street or two off. Stay, here is my address. Come and see me--you can't think how glad I shall be!"

"Indeed, I will come---and here is my card in exchange. Good-night, Herr Mueller."

"Good-night, Marquis of Arbuthnot. Mademoiselle Josephine, *au plaisir*."

So we shook hands and parted, and I saw my innamorata home to her residence at No. 70, Rue Aubry le Boucher, which opened upon the Marche des Innocents. She fell asleep upon my shoulder in the cab, and was only just sufficiently awake when I left her, to accept all the *marrons glaces* that yet remained in the pockets of my paletot, and to remind me that I had promised to take her out next Sunday for a drive in the country, and a dinner at the Moulin Rouge.

The fountain in the middle of the Marche was now sparkling in the sunshine like a shower of diamonds, and the business of the market was already at its height. The shops in the neighboring streets were opening fast. The "iron tongue" of St. Eustache was calling the devout to early prayer. Fagged as I was, I felt that a walk through the fresh air would do me good; so I dismissed the cab, and reached my lodgings just as the sleepy *concierge* had turned out to sweep the hall, and open the establishment for the day. When I came down again two hours later, after a nap and a bath, I found a *commissionnaire* waiting for me.

"*Tiens*!" said Madame Bouisse (Madame Bouisse was the wife of the *concierge*). "*V'la*! here is M'sieur Arbuthnot."

The man touched his cap, and handed me a letter.

"I was told to deliver it into no hands but those of M'sieur himself," said he.

The address was in Dalrymple's writing. I tore the envelope open. It contained only a card, on the back of which, scrawled hastily in pencil, were the following words:

"To have said good-bye would have made our parting none the lighter. By the time you decipher this hieroglyphic I shall be some miles on my way: Address Hotel de Russie, Berlin. Adieu, Damon; God bless you. O.D."

"How long is it since this letter was given to you?" said I, without taking my eyes from the card.

The *commissionnaire* made no reply. I repeated the question, looked up impatiently, and found that the man was already gone.

CHAPTER XX.
THE CHATEAU DE SAINTE AULAIRE.

"Mark yon old mansion frowning through the trees,
Whose hollow turret wooes the whistling breeze."

My acquaintance with Mademoiselle Josephine progressed rapidly; although, to confess the truth, I soon found myself much less deeply in love than I had at first supposed. For this disenchantment, fate and myself were alone to blame. It was not her fault if I had invested her with a thousand imaginary perfections; nor mine if the spell was broken as soon as I discovered my mistake.

Too impatient to wait till Sunday, I made my way on Saturday afternoon to Rue Aubry-le-Boucher. I persuaded myself that I was bound to call on her, in order to conclude our arrangements for the following day. At all events, I argued, she might forget the engagement, or believe that I had forgotten it. So I went, taking with me a magnificent bouquet, and an embroidered satin bag full of *marrons glaces*.

My divinity lived, as she had told me, *sous les toits*--and *sous les toits*, up seven flights of very steep and dirty stairs, I found her. It was a large attic with a sloping roof, overlooking a bristling expanse of chimney-pots, and commanding the twin towers of Notre Dame. There were some colored prints of battles and ship-wrecks wafered to the walls; a couple of flower-pots in the narrow space between the window-ledge and the coping outside; a dingy canary in a wire cage; a rival mechanical cuckoo in a Dutch clock in the corner; a little bed with striped hangings; a rush-bottomed *prie-dieu* chair in front of a plain black crucifix, over which drooped a faded branch of consecrated palm; and some few articles of household furniture of the humblest description. In all this there was nothing vulgar. Under other circumstances I might, perhaps, have even elicited somewhat of grace and poetry from these simple materials. But conceive what it was to see them through an atmosphere of warm white steam that left an objectionable clamminess on the backs of the chairs and caused even the door-handle to burst into a tepid perspiration. Conceive what it was to behold my adored one standing in the middle of the room, up to her elbows in soap-suds, washing out the very dress in which she was to appear on the morrow.... Good taste defend us! Could anything be more cruelly calculated to disturb the tender tenor of a lover's dreams? Fancy what Leander would have felt, if, after swimming across the Hellespont, he had surprised Hero at the washing-tub! Imagine Romeo's feelings, if he had scaled the orchard-walls only to find Juliet helping to hang out the family linen!

The worst of it was that my lovely Josephine was not in the least embarrassed. She evidently regarded the washing-tub as a desirable piece of furniture, and was not even conscious that the act of "soaping in," was an unromantic occupation!

Such was the severity of this first blow that I pleaded an engagement, presented my offerings (how dreadfully inappropriate they seemed!), and hurried away to a lecture on *materia medica* at the *Ecole Pratique*; that being a good, congenial, dismal entertainment for the evening!

Sunday came with the sunrise, and at midday, true as the clock of St. Eustache, I knocked once more at the door of the *mansarde* where my Josephine dwelt. This time, my visit being anticipated, I found her dressed to receive me. She looked more fresh and charming than ever; and the lilac muslin which I had seen in the washing-tub some eighteen or twenty hours before, became her to perfection. So did her pretty green shawl, pinned closely at the throat and worn as only a French-woman would have known how to wear it. So did the white camellia and the moss-rose buds which she had taken out of my bouquet, and fastened at her waist.

What I was not prepared for, however, was her cap. I had forgotten that your Parisian grisette[1] would no more dream of wearing a bonnet than of crowning her head with feathers and adorning her countenance with war-paint. It had totally escaped me that I, a bashful Englishman of twenty-one, nervously sensitive to ridicule and gifted by nature with but little of the spirit of social defiance, must in broad

---

1   The grisette of twenty years ago, *bien entendu*. I am writing, be it remembered, of "The days of my youth."

daylight make my appearance in the streets of Paris, accompanied by a bonnetless grisette! What should I do, if I met Dr. Cheron? or Madame de Courcelles? or, worse than all, Madame de Marignan? My obvious resource was to take her in whatever direction we should be least likely to meet any of my acquaintances. Where, oh fate! might that obscurity be found which had suddenly become the dearest object of my desires?

"*Eh bien*, Monsieur Basil," said Josephine, when my first compliments had been paid. "I am quite ready. Where are we going?"

"We shall dine, *mon cher ange*," said I, absently, "at--let me see--at...."

"At the Moulin Rouge," interrupted she. "But that is six hours to come. In the meantime--"

"In the meantime? Ay, in the meantime...what a delightful day for the time of year!"

"Shall it be Versailles?" suggested Josephine.

"Heaven forbid!"

Josephine opened her large eyes.

"*Mon Dieu!*" said she. "What is there so very dreadful in Versailles?"

I made no reply. I was passing all the suburbs in review before my mind's eye,-- Bellevue, Enghien, Fontenay-aux-Roses, St. Germains, Sceaux; even Fontainebleau and Compiegne.

The grisette pouted, and glanced at the clock.

"If Monsieur is as slow to start as he is to answer," said she, "we shall not get beyond the barriers to-day."

At this moment, I remembered to have heard of Montlhery as a place where there was a forest and a feudal ruin; also, which was more to the purpose, as lying at least six-and-twenty miles south of Paris.

"My dear Mademoiselle Josephine," I said, "forgive me. I have planned an excursion which I am sure will please you infinitely better than a mere common-place trip to Versailles. Versailles, on Sunday, is vulgar. You have heard, of course, of Montlhery--one of the most interesting places near Paris."

"I have read a romance called *The Tower of Montlhery*" said Josephine.

"And that tower--that historical and interesting tower--is still standing! How delightful to wander among the ruins--to recall the stirring events which caused it to be besieged in the reign of--of either Louis the Eleventh, or Louis the Fourteenth; I don't remember which, and it doesn't signify--to explore the picturesque village, and ramble through the adjoining woods of St. Genevieve--to visit..."

"I wonder if we shall find any donkeys to ride," interrupted Josephine, upon whom my eloquence was taking the desired effect.

"Donkeys!" I exclaimed, drawing, I am ashamed to say, upon my imagination. "Of course--hundreds of them!"

"*Ah, ca*! Then the sooner we go the better. Stay, I must just lock my door, and leave word with my neighbor on the next floor that I am gone out for the day,"

So she locked the door and left the message, and we started. I was fortunate enough to find a close cab at the corner of the *marche*--she would have preferred an open one, but I overruled that objection on the score of time--and before very long we were seated in the cushioned fauteuils of a first-class compartment on the Orleans Railway, and speeding away towards Montlhery.

It was with no trifling sense of relief that I found the place really picturesque, when we arrived. We had, it is true, to put up with a comfortless drive of three or four miles in a primitive, jolting, yellow omnibus, which crawled at stated hours of the day between the town and the station; but that was a minor evil, and we made the best of it. First of all, we strolled through the village--the clean, white, sunny village, where the people were sitting outside their doors playing at dominoes, and the cocks and hens were walking about like privileged inhabitants of the market-place. Then we had luncheon at the *auberge* of the "Lion d'Or." Then we looked in at the little church (still smelling of incense from the last service) with its curious old altar-piece and monumental brasses. Then we peeped through the iron gate of the melancholy *cimetiere*, which was full of black crosses and wreaths of *immortelles*. Last of all, we went to see the ruin, which stood on the summit of a steep and solitary rock in the midst of a vast level plain. It proved to be a round keep of gigantic strength and height, approached by two courtyards and surrounded by the weed-grown and fragmentary traces of an extensive stronghold, nothing of which now remained save a few broken walls, three or four embrasured loopholes, an ancient well of incalculable depth, and the rusted teeth of a formidable portcullis. Here we paused awhile to rest and admire the view; while Josephine, pleased as a child on a holiday, flung pebbles into the well, ate sugar-plums, and amused herself with my pocket-telescope.

"*Regardez*!" she cried, "there is the dome of the Pantheon. I am sure it is the Pantheon--and to the right, far away, I see a town!--little white houses, and a steeple. And there goes a steamer on the river--and there is the railway and the railway station, and the long road by which we came in the omnibus. Oh, how nice it is, Monsieur Basil, to look through a telescope!"

"Do me the favor, *ma belle*, to accept it--for my sake," said I, thankful to find her so easily entertained. I was lying in a shady angle of old wall, puffing away at a cigar, with my hat over my eyes, and the soles of my boots levelled at the view. It is difficult to smoke and make love at the same time; and I preferred the tobacco.

Josephine was enchanted, and thanked me in a thousand pretty, foolish phrases. She declared she saw ever so much farther and clearer with the glass, now that it was her own. She looked at me through it, and insisted that I should look at her. She picked out all sorts of marvellous objects, at all sorts of incredible distances. In short, she prattled and chattered till I forgot all about the washing-tub, and again began to think her quite charming. Presently we heard wandering sounds of music among the trees at the foot of the hill--sounds as of a violin and bagpipes; now coming with the wind from the west, now dying away to the north, now bursting out afresh more merrily than ever, and leading off towards the village.

"*Tiens*! that must be a wedding!" said Josephine, drumming with her little feet against the side of the old well on which she was sitting.

"A wedding! what connection subsists, pray, between the bonds of matrimony, and a tune on the bagpipes?"

"I don't know what you mean by bagpipes--I only know that when people get married in the country, they go about with the musicians playing before them. What you hear yonder is a violin and a *cornemuse*."

"A *cornemuse!*" I repeated. "What's that?"

"Oh, country music. A thing you blow into with your mouth, and play upon with your fingers, and squeeze under your arm--like this."

"Then it's the same thing, *ma chere*," said I. "A bagpipes and a *cornemuse*--a *cornemuse* and bagpipes. Both of them national, popular, and frightful."

"I'm so fond of music," said Josephine.

Not wishing to object to her tastes, and believing that this observation related to the music then audible, I made no reply.

"And I have never been to an opera," added she.

I was still silent, though from another motive.

"You will take me one night to the Italiens, or the Opera Comique, will you not, Monsieur Basil?" pursued she, determined not to lose her opportunity.

I had now no resource but to promise; which I did, very reluctantly.

"You would enjoy the Opera Comique far more than the Italiens," said I, remembering that Madame de Marignan had a box at the Italiens, and rapidly weighing the chances for and against the possibility of recognition. "At the first they sing in French--at the last, in Italian,"

"Ah, bah! I should prefer the French," replied she, falling at once into the snare. "When shall it be--this week?"

"Ye--es; one evening this week."

"What evening?"

"Well, let me see--we had better wait, and consult the advertisements."

"*Dame*! never mind the advertisements. Let it be Tuesday."

"Why Tuesday?"

"Because it is soon; and because I can get away early on Tuesdays if I ask leave."

I had, plainly, no chance of escape.

"You would not prefer to see the great military piece at the Porte St. Martin?" I suggested. "There are three hundred real soldiers in it, and they fire real cannon."

"Not I! I have been to the Porte St. Martin, over and over again. Emile knew one of the scene-painter's assistants, and used to get tickets two or three times a month."

"Then it shall be the Opera Comique," said I, with a sigh.

"And on Tuesday evening next."

"On Tuesday evening next."

At this moment the piping and fiddling broke out afresh, and Josephine, who had scarcely taken the little telescope from her eye all the time, exclaimed that she saw the wedding party going through the market-place of the town.

"There they are--the musicians first; the bride and bridegroom next; and eight friends, all two and two! There will be a dance, depend on it! Let us go down to the town, and hear all about it! Perhaps they might invite us to join them--who knows?"

"But you would not dance before dinner?"

"*Eh, mon Dieu*! I would dance before breakfast, if I had the chance. Come along. If we do not make haste, we may miss them."

I rose, feeling, and I daresay, looking, like a martyr; and we went down again into the town.

There we inquired of the first person who seemed likely to know--he was a dapper hairdresser, standing at his shop-door with his hands in his apron pockets and a comb behind his ear--and were told that the wedding-party had just passed through the village, on their way to the Chateau of Saint Aulaire.

"The Chateau of St. Aulaire!" said Josephine. "What are they going to do there? What is there to see?"

"It is an ancient mansion, Mademoiselle, much visited by strangers," replied the hairdresser with exceeding politeness. "Worthy of Mademoiselle's distinguished attention--and Monsieur's. Contains old furniture, old paintings, old china--stands in an extensive park--one of the lions of this neighborhood, Mademoiselle--also Monsieur."

"To whom does it belong?" I asked, somewhat interested in this account.

"That, Monsieur, is a question difficult to answer," replied the fluent hairdresser, running his fingers through his locks and dispersing a gentle odor of rose-oil. "It was formerly the property of the ancient family of Saint Aulaire. The last Marquis de Saint Aulaire, with his wife and family, were guillotined in 1793. Some say that the young heir was saved; and an individual asserting himself to be that heir did actually put forward a claim to the estate, some twenty, or five-and-twenty years ago, but lost his cause for want of sufficient proof. In the meantime, it had passed into the hands of a wealthy republican family, descended, it is said, from General Dumouriez. This family held it till within the last four years, when two or three fresh claimants came forward; so that it is now the object of a lawsuit which may last till every brick of it falls to ruin, and every tree about it withers away. At present, a man and his wife have charge of the place, and visitors are permitted to see it any day between twelve and four."

"I should like to see the old place," said I.

"And I should like to see how the bride is dressed," said Josephine, "and if the bridegroom is handsome."

"Well, let us go--not forgetting to thank Monsieur *le Perruquier* for his polite information."

Monsieur *le Perruquier* fell into what dancing-masters call the first position, and bowed elaborately.

"Most welcome, Mademoiselle--and Monsieur," said he. "Straight up the road--past the orchard about a quarter of a mile--old iron gates--can't miss it. Good-afternoon, Mademoiselle--also Monsieur."

Following his directions, we came presently to the gates, which were rusty and broken-hinged, with traces of old gilding still showing faintly here and there upon their battered scrolls and bosses. One of them was standing open, and had evidently been standing so for years; while the other had as evidently been long closed, so that the deep grass had grown rankly all about it, and the very bolt was crusted over with a yellow lichen. Between the two, an ordinary wooden hurdle had been put up, and this hurdle was opened for us by a little blue-bloused urchin in a pair of huge *sabots*, who, thinking we belonged to the bridal party, pointed up the dusky avenue, and said, with a grin:--

"*Tout droit, M'sieur--ils sont passes par la!*"

Par la, "under the shade of melancholy boughs," we went accordingly. Far away on either side stretched dim vistas of neglected park-land, deep with coarse grass and weeds and, where the trees stood thickest, all choked with a brambly undergrowth. After about a quarter of a mile of this dreary avenue, we came to a broad area of several acres laid out in the Italian style with fountains and terraces, at the upper end of which stood the house--a feudal, *moyen-age* French chateau, with irregular wings, steep slated roofings, innumerable windows, and fantastic steeple-topped turrets sheeted with lead and capped with grotesque gilded weathercocks. The principal front had been repaired in the style of the Renaissance and decorated with little foliated entablatures above the doors and windows; whilst a double flight of steps leading up to a grand entrance on the level of the first story, like the famous double staircase of Fontainebleau, had been patched on in the very centre, to the manifest disfigurement of the building. Most of the windows were shuttered up, and as we drew nearer, the general evidences of desolation became more apparent. The steps of the terraces were covered with patches of brown and golden moss. The stone urns were some of them fallen in the deep grass, and some broken. There were gaps in the rich balustrade here and there; and the two great fountains on either side of the lower terrace had long since ceased to fling up their feathery columns towards the sun. In the middle of one a broken Pan, noseless and armless, turned up a stony face of mute appeal, as if imploring us to free him from the parasitic jungle of aquatic plants which flourished rankly round him in the basin. In the other, a stalwart river-god with his finger on his lip, seemed listening for the music of those waters which now scarcely stirred amid the tangled weeds that clustered at his feet.

Passing all these, passing also the flower-beds choked with brambles and long waving grasses, and the once quaintly-clipped myrtle and box-trees, all flinging out fantastic arms of later growth, we came to the upper terrace, which was paved in curious patterns of stars and arabesques, with stones alternately round and flat. Here a good-humored, cleanly peasant woman came clattering out in her *sabots* from a side-door, key in hand, preceded us up the double flight of steps, unlocked the great door, and admitted us.

The interior, like the front, had been modernized about a hundred and fifty years before, and resembled a little formal Versailles or miniature Fontainebleau. Dismantled halls paved with white marble; panelled ante-chambers an inch deep in dust; dismal *salons* adorned with Renaissance arabesques and huge looking-glasses, cracked and mildewed, and mended with pasted seams of blue paper; boudoirs with faded Watteau panellings; corridors with painted ceilings where mythological divinities, marvellously foreshortened on a sky-blue ground, were seen surrounded by rose-colored Cupids and garlanded with ribbons and flowers; innumerable bedrooms, some containing grim catafalques of beds with gilded cornices and funereal plumes, some empty, some full of stored-up furniture fast going to decay--all these in endless number we traversed, conducted by the good-tempered *concierge*, whose heavy *sabots* awakened ghostly echoes from floor to floor.

At length, through an ante-chamber lined with a double file of grim old family portraits--some so blackened with age and dust as to be totally indistinguishable, and others bulging hideously out of their frames--we came to the library, a really noble room, lofty, panelled with walnut wood, floored with polished oak, and looking over a wide expanse of level country. Long ranges of empty book-shelves fenced in with broken wire-work ran round the walls. The painted ceiling represented, as usual, the heavens and some pagan divinities. A dumb old time-piece, originally constructed to tell the months, the days of the year, and the hours, stood on a massive corner bracket near the door. Long antique mirrors in heavy black frames reached from floor to ceiling between each of the windows; and in the centre of the room, piled all together and festooned with a thick drapery of cobwebs, stood a dozen or so of old carved chairs, screens, and foot-stools, rich with velvet, brocade, and gilded leather, but now looking as if a touch would crumble them to dust. Over the great carved fireplace, however, hung a painting upon which my attention became riveted as soon as I entered the room--a painting yellow with age; covered with those minute cracks which are like wrinkles on the face of antique art, coated with dust, and yet so singularly attractive that, having once noticed it, I looked at nothing else.

It was the half-length portrait of a young lady in the costume of the reign of Louis XVI. One hand rested on a stone urn; the other was raised to her bosom, holding a thin blue scarf that seemed to flutter in the wind. Her dress was of white satin, cut low and square, with a stomacher of lace and pearls. She also wore pearls in her hair, on her white arms, and on her whiter neck. Thus much for the mere adjuncts; as for the face--ah, how can I ever describe that pale, perfect, tender face, with its waving brown hair and soft brown eyes, and that steadfast perpetual smile that seemed to light the eyes from within, and to dwell in the corners of the lips without parting or moving them? It was like a face seen in a dream, or the imperfect image which seems to come between us and the page when we read of Imogen asleep.

"Who was this lady?" I asked, eagerly.

The *concierge* nodded and rubbed her hands.

"Aha! M'sieur," said she, "'tis the best painting in the chateau, as folks tell me. M'sieur is a connoisseur."

"But do you know whose portrait it is?"

"To be sure I do, M'sieur. It's the portrait of the last Marquise--the one who was guillotined, poor soul, with her husband, in--let me see--in 1793!"

"What an exquisite creature! Look, Josephine, did you ever see anything so beautiful?"

"Beautiful!" repeated the grisette, with a sidelong glance at one of the mirrors.

"Beautiful, with such a coiffure and such a bodice! *Ciel!* how tastes differ!"

"But her face, Josephine!"

"What of her face? I'm sure it's plain enough."

"Plain! Good heavens! what..."

But it was not worth while to argue upon it. I pulled out one of the old chairs, and so climbed near enough to dust the surface of the painting with my handkerchief.

"I wish I could buy it!" I exclaimed.

Josephine burst into a loud laugh.

"*Grand Dieu!*" said she, half pettishly, "if you are so much in love with it as all that, I dare say it would not be difficult!"

The *concierge* shook her head.

"Everything on this estate is locked up," said she. "Nothing can be sold, nothing given away, nothing even repaired, till the *proces* is ended."

I sighed, and came down reluctantly from my perch. Josephine was visibly impatient. She had seen the wedding-party going down one of the walks at the back of the house; and the *concierge* was waiting to let us out. I drew her aside, and slipped a liberal gratuity into her hand.

"If I were to come down here some day with a friend of mine who is a painter," I whispered, "would you have any objection, Madame, to allow him to make a little sketch of that portrait?"

The *concierge* looked into her palm, and seeing the value of the coin, smiled, hesitated, put her finger to her lip, and said:--

"*Ma foi*, M'sieur, I believe I have no business to allow it; but--to oblige a gentleman like you--if there was nobody about--"

I nodded. We understood each other sufficiently, and no more was needed.

Once out of the house, Medemoiselle Josephine pouted, and took upon herself to be sulky--a disposition which was by no means lessened when, after traversing the park in various directions in search of the bridal company, we found that they had gone out long ago by a gate at the other side of the estate, and were by this time piping, most probably, in the adjoining parish.

It was now five o'clock; so we hastened back through the village, cast a last glance at the grim old tower on its steep solitude, consigned ourselves to the yellow omnibus, and in due time were once more flying along the iron road towards Paris. The rapid motion, the dignity of occupying a first-class seat, and, above all, the prospects of an excellent dinner, soon brought my fair companion round again, and by the time we reached the Moulin Rouge, she was all vivacity and good temper. The less I say about that dinner the better. I am humiliated when I recall all that I suffered, and all that she did. I blush even now when I remember how she blew upon her soup, put her knife in her mouth, and picked her teeth with her shawl-pin. What possessed her that she would persist in calling the waiter "Monsieur?" And why, in Heaven's name, need she have clapped her hands when I ordered the champagne? To say that I had no appetite--that I wished myself at the antipodes--that I longed to sink into my boots, to smother the waiter, or to do anything equally desperate and unreasonable, is to express but a tithe of the anguish I endured. I bore it, however, in silence, little dreaming what a much heavier trial was yet in store for me.

CHAPTER XXI.
I FALL A SACRIFICE TO MRS. GRUNDY.

A word with you, if you please, Basil Arbuthnot," said Dr. Cheron, "when you have finished copying those prescriptions."

Dr. Cheron was standing with his feet firmly planted in the tiger-skin rug and his back to the fireplace. I was busy writing at the study table, and glancing anxiously from time to time at the skeleton clock upon the chimney-piece; for it was getting on fast towards five, and at half-past six I was to take Josephine to the Opera Comique. As perverse fortune would have it, the Doctor had this afternoon given me more desk-work than usual, and I began to doubt whether I should be able to dine, dress, and reach the theatre in time if he detained me much longer.

"But you need be in no haste," he added, looking at his watch. "That is to say, upon my account."

I bowed nervously--I was always nervous in his presence--and tried to write faster than ever; but, feeling his cold blue eye upon me, made a blot, smeared it with my sleeve, left one word out, wrote another twice over, and was continually tripped up by my pen, which sputtered hideously and covered the page with florid passages in little round spots, which only needed tails to become crotchets and quavers. At length, just as the clock struck the hour, I finished my task and laid aside my pen.

Dr. Cheron coughed preparatorily.

"It is some time," said he, "since you have given me any news of your father. Do you often hear from him?"

"Not very often, sir," I replied. "About once in every three weeks. He dislikes letter-writing."

Dr. Cheron took a packet of papers from his breast-pocket, and ruffling them over, said, somewhat indifferently:--

"Very true--very true. His notes are brief and few; but always to the purpose. I heard from him this morning."

"Indeed, sir?"

"Yes--here is his letter. It encloses a remittance of seventy-five pounds; fifty of which are for you. The remaining twenty-five being reserved for the defrayal of your expenses at the Ecole de Medecine and the Ecole Pratique."

I was delighted.

"Both are made payable through my banker," continued Dr. Cheron, "and I am to take charge of your share till you require it; which cannot be just yet, as I understand from this letter that your father supplied you with the sum of one hundred and five pounds on leaving England."

My delight went down to zero.

"Does my father say that I am not to have it now, sir?" I asked, hesitatingly.

"He says, as I have already told you, that it is to be yours when you require it."

"And if I require it very shortly, sir--in fact, if I require it now?"

"You ought not to require it now," replied the Doctor, with a cold, scrutinizing stare. "You ought not to have spent one hundred and five pounds in five months."

I looked down in silence. I had more than spent it long since; and I had to thank Madame de Marignan for the facility with which it had flown. It was not to be denied that my course of lessons in practical politeness had been somewhat expensive.

"How have you spent it?" asked Dr. Cheron, never removing his eyes from my face.

I might have answered, in bouquets, opera stalls, and riding horses; in dress coats, tight boots, and white kid gloves; in new books, new music, bon-bons, cabs, perfumery, and the like inexcusable follies. But I held my tongue instead, and said nothing.

Dr. Cheron looked again at his watch.

"Have you kept any entries of your expenses since you came to Paris?" said he.

"Not with--with any regularity, sir," I replied.

He took out his pencil-case and pocket-book.

"Let us try, then," said he, "to make an average calculation of what they might be in five months."

I began to feel very uncomfortable.

"I believe your father paid your travelling expenses?"

I bowed affirmatively.

"Leaving you the clear sum of one hundred and five pounds." I bowed again.

"Allowing, then, for your rent--which is, I believe, twenty francs per week," said he, entering the figures as he went on, "there will be four hundred francs spent in five months. For your living, say thirty francs per week, which makes six hundred. For your clothing, seventy-five per month, which makes three hundred and seventy-five, and ought to be quite enough for a young man of moderate tastes. For your washing and firewood, perhaps forty per month, which makes two hundred-- and for your incidental expenses, say fifteen per week, which makes three hundred. We thus arrive at a total of one thousand eight hundred and seventy-five francs, which, reduced to English money at the average standard of twenty-five francs to the sovereign, represents the exact sum of seventy-five pounds. Do I make myself understood?"

I bowed for the third time.

"Of the original one hundred and five pounds, we now have thirty not accounted for. May I ask how much of that surplus you have left?"

"About--not more than--than a hundred and twenty francs," I replied, stripping the feathers off all the pens in succession, without knowing it.

"Have you any debts?"

"A--a few."

"Tailors' bills?"

"Yes, sir."

"What others?"

"A--a couple of months' rent, I believe, sir."

"Is that all?"

"N--not quite."

Dr. Cheron frowned, and looked again at his watch.

"Be good enough, Mr. Arbuthnot," he said, "to spare me this amount of useless interrogation by at once stating the nature and amount of the rest."

"I--I cannot positively state the amount, sir," I said, absurdly trying to get the paper-weight into my waistcoat pocket, and then putting it down in great confusion. "I--I have an account at Monceau's in the Rue Duphot, and..."

"I beg your pardon," interrupted Dr. Cheron: "but who is Monceau?"

"Monceau's--Monceau's livery-stables, sir."

Dr. Cheron slightly raised his eye-brows, and entered the name.

"And at Lavoisier's, on the Boulevard Poissonniere--"

"What is sold, pray, at Lavoisier's?"

"Gloves, perfumes, hosiery, ready-made linen..."

"Enough--you can proceed."

"I have also a bill at--at Barbet's, in the Passage de l'Opera."

"And Barbet is--?"

"A--a florist!" I replied, very reluctantly.

"Humph!--a florist!" observed Dr. Cheron, again transfixing me with the cold, blue eye. "To what amount do you suppose you are indebted to Monsieur Barbet?"

I looked down, and became utterly unintelligible.

"Fifty francs?"

"I--I fear, more than--than--"

"A hundred? A hundred and fifty? Two hundred?"

"About two hundred, I suppose, sir," I said desperately.

"Two hundred francs--that is to say, eight pounds English--to your florist! Really, Mr. Arbuthnot, you must be singularly fond of flowers!"

I looked down in silence.

"Have you a conservatory attached to your rooms?"

The skeleton clock struck the half hour.

"Excuse me, sir," I said, driven now to the last extremity, "but--but I have an engagement which--in short, I will, if you please, make out a list of--of these items, ascertaining the correct amount of each; and when once paid, I will endeavor--I mean, it is my earnest desire, to--to limit my expenditure strictly to--in short, to study economy for the future. If, in the meantime, you will have the goodness to excuse me...."

"One word, young man. Will the fifty pounds cover your debts?"

"Quite, sir, I am confident."

"And leave you something in hand for your current expenses?"

"Indeed, I fear very little."

"In that case what will you do?"

This was a terrible question, and one for which I could find no answer.

"Write to your father for another remittance--eh?"

"I--upon my word, I dare not, sir," I faltered.

"Then you would go in debt again?"

"I really fear--even with the strictest economy--I--"

"Be so obliging as to let me have your seat," said Dr. Cheron, thrusting the obnoxious note-book into his pocket and taking my place at the desk, from which he brought out a couple of cards, and a printed paper.

"This ticket," said he, "admits the holder to the anatomical course for the term now beginning, and this to the lectures at the Ecole Pratique. Both are in my gift. The first is worth two hundred francs, and the second two hundred and fifty. I ought, perhaps, in strict justice, to bestow them upon some needy and deserving individual: however, to save you from debt, or a very unpleasant alternative, I will fill them in with your name, and, when you bring me all your bills receipted, I will transfer to your account the four hundred and fifty francs which I must, otherwise, have paid for your courses out of the remittance forwarded by your father for that purpose. Understand, however, that I must first have the receipts, and that I expect you, on the word of a gentleman, to commit no more follies, and to contract no more debts."

"Oh, sir!" I exclaimed, "how can I ever--"

"No thanks, I beg," interposed Dr. Cheron. "Prove your gratitude by your conduct; do not trouble yourself to talk about it."

"Indeed, sir, you may depend--"

"And no promises either, if you please. I attach no kind of value to them. Stay--here is my check for the fifty pounds forwarded by your father. With that sum extricate yourself from debt. You know the rest."

Hereupon Dr. Cheron replaced the cards and the printed form, double-locked his desk, and, with a slight gesture of the hand, frigidly dismissed me.

I left the house quite chopfallen. I was relieved, it is true, from the incubus of debt; but then how small a figure I had cut in the eyes of Dr. Cheron! Besides, I was small for the second time--reproved for the second time--lectured, helped, put down, and poohpoohed, for the second time! Could I have peeped at myself just then through the wrong end of a telescope, I vow I could not have looked smaller in my own eyes.

I had no time to dine; so I despatched a cup of coffee and a roll on my way home, and went hungry to the theatre.

Josephine was got up with immense splendor for this occasion; greatly to her own satisfaction and my disappointment. Having hired a small private box in the least conspicuous part of the theatre, I had committed the cowardly mistake of endeavoring to transform my grisette into a woman of fashion. I had bought her a pink and white opera cloak, a pretty little fan, a pair of white kid gloves, and a bouquet. With these she wore a decent white muslin dress furnished out of the limited resources of her own wardrobe, and a wreath of pink roses, the work of her own clever fingers. Thus equipped, she was far less pretty than in her coquettish little every-day cap, and looked, I regret to say, more like an *ouvriere* than ever. Aggravating above all else, however, was her own undisguised delight in her appearance.

"Are my flowers all right? Is my dress tumbled? Is the hood of my cloak in the middle of my back?" were the questions she addressed to me every moment. In the ante-room she took advantage of each mirror we passed. In the lobby I caught her trying to look at her own back. When we reached our box she pulled her chair to the very centre of it, and sat there as if she expected to be admired by the whole audience.

"My dear Josephine," I remonstrated, "sit back here, facing the stage. You will see much better--besides, it is your proper seat, being the only lady in the box."

"Ah, *mon Dieu!* then I cannot see the house--and how pretty it is! Ever so much prettier than the Gaiete, or the Porte St. Martin!"

"You can see the house by peeping behind the curtain."

"As if I were ashamed to be seen! *Par exemple*!"

"Nay, as you please. I only advise you according to custom and fashion."

Josephine pouted, and unwillingly conceded a couple of inches.

"I wish I had brought the little telescope you gave me last Sunday," said she, presently. "There is a gentleman with one down there in the stalls."

"A telescope at the opera--the gods forbid! Here, however, is my opera-glass, if you like to use it."

Josephine turned it over curiously, and peeped first through one tube and then through the other.

"Which ought I to look through?" asked she.

"Both, of course."

"Both! How can I?"

"Why thus--as you look through a pair of spectacles."

"*Ciel!* I can't manage that! I can never look through anything without covering up one eye with my hand."

"Then I think you had better be contented with your own charming eyes, *ma belle*" said I, nervously. "How do you like your bouquet?"

Josephine sniffed at it as if she were taking snuff, and pronounced it perfect. Just then the opera began. I withdrew into the shade, and Josephine was silenced for a while in admiration of the scenery and the dresses. By and by, she began to yawn.

"Ah, *mon Dieu!*" said she, "when will they have done singing? I have not heard a word all this time."

"But everything is sung, *ma chere*, in an opera."

"What do you mean? Is there no play?"

"This is the play; only instead of speaking their words, they sing them."

Josephine shrugged her shoulders.

"Ah, bah!" said she. "How stupid! I had rather have seen the *Closerie des Genets* at the Graiete, if that is to be the case the whole evening. Oh, dear! there is such a pretty lady come into the opposite box, in such a beautiful blue *glace*, trimmed with black velvet and lace!"

"Hush! you must not talk while they are singing!"

"*Tiens!* it is no pleasure to come out and be dumb. But do just see the lady in the opposite box! She looks exactly as if she had walked out of a fashion-book."

"My dear child, I don't care one pin to look at her," said I, preferring to keep as much out of sight as possible. "To admire your pretty face is enough for me."

Josephine squeezed my hand affectionately.

"That is just as Emile used to talk to me," said she.

I felt by no means flattered.

"*Regardez done!*" said she, pulling me by the sleeve, just as I was standing up, a little behind her chair, looking at the stage. "That lady in the blue *glace* never takes her eyes from our box! She points us out to the gentleman who is with her-- do look!"

I turned my glass in the direction to which she pointed, and recognised Madame de Marignan!

I turned hot and cold, red and white, all in one moment, and shrank back like a snail that has been touched, or a sea-anemone at the first dig of the naturalist.

"Does she know you?" asked Josephine.

"I--I--probably--that is to say--I have met her in society."

"And who is the gentleman?"

That was just what I was wondering. It was not Delaroche. It was no one whom I had ever seen before. It was a short, fat, pale man, with a bald head, and a ribbon in his button-hole.

"Is he her husband?" pursued Josephine.

The suggestion flashed upon me like a revelation. Had I not heard that M. de Marignan was coming home from Algiers? Of course it was he. No doubt of it. A little vulgar, fat, bald man.... Pshaw, just the sort of a husband that she deserved!

"How she looks at me!" said Josephine.

I felt myself blush, so to speak, from head to foot.

"Good Heavens! my dear girl," I exclaimed, "take your elbows off the front of the box!"

Josephine complied, with a pettish little grimace.

"And, for mercy's sake, don't hold your head as if you feared it would tumble off!"

"It is the flowers," said she. "They tickle the back of my neck, whenever I move my head. I am much more comfortable in my cap."

"Never mind. Make the best of it, and listen to this song."

It was the great tenor ballad of the evening. The house was profoundly silent; the first wandering chords of a harp were heard behind the scenes; and Duprez began. In the very midst of one of his finest and tenderest *sostenuto* passages, Josephine sneezed--and such a sneeze! you might have heard it out in the lobbies. An audible titter ran round the house. I saw Madame de Marignan cover her face with her handkerchief, and yield to an irrepressible fit of laughter. As for the tenor, he cast a withering glance up at the box, and made a marked pause before resuming his song. Merciful powers! what crime had I committed that I should be visited with such a punishment as this?

"Wretched girl!" I exclaimed, savagely, "what have you done?"

"Done, ***mon ami!***" said Josephine, innocently. "Why, I fear I have taken cold."

I groaned aloud.

"Taken cold!" I muttered to myself. "Would to Heaven you had taken prussic acid!"

"*Qu'est ce que c'est?*" asked she.

But it was not worth while to reply. I gave myself up to my fate. I determined to remonstrate no more. I flung myself on a seat at the back of the box, and made up my mind to bear all that might yet be in store for me. When she openly ate a stick of ***sucre d'orge*** after this, I said nothing. When she applauded with both hands, I endured in silence. At length the performance came to a close and the curtain fell. Madame de Marignan had left before the last act, so I ran no danger of encountering her on the way out; but I was profoundly miserable, nevertheless. As for Josephine, she, poor child, had not enjoyed her evening at all, and was naturally out of temper. We quarrelled tremendously in the cab, and parted without having made it up. It was all my own fault. How could I be such a fool as to suppose that, with a few shreds and patches of finery, I could make a fine lady of a grisette?

CHAPTER XXII.
HIGH ART IN THE QUARTIER LATIN.

B ut, my dear fellow, what else could you have expected? You took Mam'selle Josephine to the **Opera Comique. *Eh bien!*** you might as well have taken an oyster up Mount Vesuvius. Our fair friend was out of her element. ***Voila tout***."

"Confound her and her element!" I exclaimed with a groan. "What the deuce *is* her element--the Quartier Latin?"

"The Quartier Latin is to some extent her habitat--but then Mam'selle Josephine belongs to a genus of which you, **cher** Monsieur Arbuthnot, are deplorably ignorant--the genus grisette. The grisette from a certain point of view is the ***chef-d'oeuvre*** of Parisian industry; the bouquet of Parisian civilization. She is indigenous to the ***mansarde*** and the ***pave***--bears no transplantation--flourishes in ***the premiere balconie***, the suburban ***guingette***, and the Salle Valentinois; but degenerates at a higher elevation. To improve her is to spoil her. In her white cap and muslin gown, the Parisian grisette is simply delicious. In a smart bonnet, a Cashmere and a brougham, she is simply detestable. Fine clothes vulgarize her. Fine surroundings demoralize her. Lodged on the sixth story, rich in the possession of a cuckoo-clock, a canary, half a dozen pots of mignonette, and some bits of cheap furniture in imitation mahogany, she has every virtue and every fault that is charming in woman--childlike gaiety; coquetry; thoughtless generosity; the readiest laugh, the readiest tear, and the warmest heart in the world. Transplant her to the Chaussee d'Antin, instil the taste for diamonds, truffles, and Veuve Clicquot, and you poison her whole nature. She becomes false, cruel, greedy, prodigal of your money, parsimonious of her own--a vampire--a ghoul--the hideous thing we call in polite parlance a *Fille de Marbre.*"

Thus, with much gravity and emphasis, spoke Herr Franz Mueller, lying on his back upon a very rickety sofa, and smoking like a steam-engine. A cup of half-cold coffee, and a bottle of rum three parts emptied stood beside him on the floor. These were the remains of his breakfast; for it was yet early in the morning of the day following my great misadventure at the Opera Comique, and I had sought him out at his lodgings in the Rue Clovis at an hour when the Quartier Latin was for the most part in bed.

"Josephine, at all events, is not of the stuff that *Filles de Marbre* are made of," I said, smiling.

"Perhaps not--*mais, que voulez-vous?* We are what we are. A grisette makes a bad fine lady. A fine lady would make a still worse grisette. The Archbishopric of Paris is a most repectable and desirable preferment; but your humble servant, for instance, would hardly suit the place,"

"And the moral of this learned and perspicuous discourse?"

"*Tiens*! the moral, is--keep our fair friend in her place. Remember that a dinner at thirty sous in the Palais Royal, or a fete with fireworks at Mabille, will give her ten times more pleasure than the daintiest repast you could order at the Maison Doree, or the choicest night of the season at either opera house. And how should it be otherwise? One must understand a thing to be able to enjoy it; and I'll be sworn Mam'selle Josephine was infinitely more bored last night than yourself."

Our conversation, or rather his monologue, was here interrupted by the ringing of the outer bell.

The artist sat up, took his pipe from his lips, and looked considerably disturbed.

"*Mille tonnerres*!" said he in a low tone. "Who can it be?... so early in the day ... not yet ten o'clock ... it is very mysterious."

"It is only mysterious," said I, "as long as you don't open the door. Shall I answer the bell?"

"No--yes--wait a moment ... suppose it is that demon, my landlord, or that archfiend, my tailor--then you must say ... holy St. Nicholas! you must say I am in bed with small-pox, or that I've broken out suddenly into homicidal delirium, and you're my keeper."

"Unfortunately I should not know either of your princes of darkness at first sight."

"True--and it might be Dupont, who owes me thirty francs, and swore by the bones of his aunt (an excellent person, who keeps an estaminet in the Place St. Sulpice) that he would pay me this week. ***Diable***! there goes the bell again."

"It would perhaps be safest," I suggested, "to let M. or N. ring on till he is tired of the exercise."

"But conceive the horrid possibility of letting thirty francs ring themselves out of patience! No, ***mon ami***--I will dare the worst that may happen. Wait here for me--I will answer the door myself,"

Now it should be explained that Mueller's apartments consisted of three rooms. First, a small outer chamber which he dignified with the title of Salle d'Attente, but which, as it was mainly furnished with old boots, umbrellas and walking-sticks, and contained, by way of accommodation for visitors only a three-legged stool and a door-mat, would have been more fitly designated as the hall. Between this Salle d'Attente and the den in which he slept, ate, smoked, and received his friends, lay the studio--once a stately salon, now a wilderness of litter and dilapidation. On one side you beheld three windows closely boarded up, with strips of newspaper pasted over the cracks to exclude every gleam of day. Overhead yawned a huge, dusty skylight, to make way for which a fine old painted ceiling had been ruthlessly knocked away. On the walls were pinned and pasted all sorts of rough sketches and studies in color and crayon. In one corner lolled a despondent-looking lay-figure in a moth-eaten Spanish cloak; in another lay a heap of plaster-casts, gigantic hands and feet, broken-nosed masks of the Apollo, the Laocoon, the Hercules Farnese, and other foreigners of distinction. Upon the chimney-piece were displayed a pair of foils, a lute, a skull, an antique German drinking-mug, and several very modern empty bottles. In the middle of the room stood two large easels, a divan, a round table, and three or four chairs; while the floor was thickly strewn with empty color-tubes, bits of painting-rag, corks, cigar-ends, and all kinds of miscellaneous litter.

All these things I had observed as I passed in; for this, be it remembered, was my first visit to Mueller in his own territory.

I heard him go through the studio and close the door behind him, and then I heard him open the door upon the public staircase. Presently he came back, shutting the door behind him as before.

"My dear fellow," he exclaimed, breathlessly, "you have brought luck with you! What do you think? A sitter--positively, a sitter! Wants to be sketched in at once-- *Vive la France*!"

"Man or woman? Young or old? Plain or pretty?"

"Elderly half-length, feminine gender--Madame Tapotte. They are both there, Monsieur and Madame Excellent couple--redolent of the country--husband bucolic, adipose, auriferous--wife arrayed in all her glory, like the Queen of Sheba. I left them in the Salle d'Attente--told them I had a sitter--time immensely occupied-- half-lengths furiously in demand ... *Will* you oblige me by performing the part for a few minutes, just to carry out the idea?"

"What part?"

"The part of sitter."

"Oh, with pleasure," I replied, laughing. "Do with me what you please,"

"You don't mind? Come! you are the best fellow in the world. Now, if you'll sit in that arm-chair facing the light--head a little thrown back, arms folded, chin up ... Capital! You don't know what an effect this will have upon the provincial mind!"

"But you're not going to let them in! You have no portrait of me to be at work upon!"

"My dear fellow, I've dozens of half-finished studies, any one of which will answer the purpose. *Voila*! here is the very thing."

And snatching up a canvas that had been standing till now with its face to the wall, he flourished it triumphantly before my eyes, and placed it on the easel.

"Heavens and earth!" I exclaimed, "that's a copy of the Titian in the Louvre-- the 'Young Man with the Glove!'"

"What of that? Our Tapottes will never find out the difference. By the way, I told them you were a great English Milord, so please keep up the character."

"I will try to do credit to the peerage."

"And if you would not mind throwing in a word of English every now and then ... a little Goddam, for instance.. . Eh?"

I laughed and shook my head.

"I will pose for you as Milord with all the pleasure in life," I said; "only I cannot undertake to pose for the traditional Milord of the Bouffes Parisiens! However, I will speak some English, and, if you like, I'll know no French."

"No, no--*diable*! you must know a little, or I can't exchange a word with you. But very little--the less the better. And now I'll let them in."

They came; Madame first--tall, buxom, large-featured, fresh-colored, radiant in flowers, lace, and Palais Royal jewelry; then Monsieur--short, fat, bald, rosy and smiling, with a huge frill to his shirt-front and a nankeen waistcoat.

Mueller introduced them with much ceremony and many apologies.

"Permit me, milord," he said, "to present Monsieur and Madame Tapotte-- Monsieur and Madame Tapotte; Milord Smithfield."

I rose and bowed with the gravity becoming my rank.

"I have explained to milord," continued Mueller, addressing himself partly to the new-comers, partly to me, and chiefly to the study on the easel, "that having no second room in which to invite Monsieur and Madame to repose themselves, I am compelled to ask them into the studio--where, however, his lordship is so very kind as to say that they are welcome." (Hereupon Madame Tapotte curtsied again, and Monsieur ducked his bald head, and I returned their salutations with the same dignity as before.) "If Monsieur and Madame will be pleased to take seats, however, his lordship's sitting will be ended in about ten minutes. *Mille pardons*, the face, milord, a little more to the right. Thank you--thank you very much. And if you will do me the favor to look at me ... for the expression of the eye--just so--thank you! A most important point, milord, is the expression of the eye. When I say the expression, I mean the fire, the sparkle, the liquidity ... *enfin* the expression!"

Here he affected to put in some touches with immense delicacy--then retreated a couple of yards, the better to contemplate his work--pursed up his mouth--ran his fingers through his hair--shaded his eyes with his hand--went back and put in another touch--again retreated--again put in a touch; and so on some three or four times successively.

Meanwhile Monsieur and Madame Tapotte were fidgeting upon their chairs in respectful silence. Every now and then they exchanged glances of wonder and admiration. They were evidently dying to compare my august features with my portrait, but dared not take the liberty of rising. At length the lady's curiosity could hold out no longer.

"*Ah, mon Dieu!*" she said; "but it must be very fatiguing to sit so long in the same position. And to paint.... *Oiel!* what practice! what perseverance! what patience! *Avec permission*, M'sieur..."

And with this she sidled up to Mueller's elbow, leaving Monsieur Tapotte thunderstruck at her audacity.

Then for a moment she stood silent; but during that moment the eager, apologetic smile vanished suddenly out of her face, and was succeeded by an expression of blank disappointment.

"*Tiens*!" she said bluntly. "I don't see one bit of likeness."

I turned hot from head to foot, but Mueller's serene effrontery was equal to the occasion.

"I dare say not, Madame," he replied, coolly. "I dare say not. This portrait is not intended to be like."

Madame Tapotte's eyes and mouth opened simultaneously.

"*Comment*!" she exclaimed.

"I should be extremely sorry," continued Mueller, loftily, "and his lordship would be extremely sorry, if there were too much resemblance."

"But a--a likeness--it seems to me, should at all events be--like," stammered Madame Tapotte, utterly bewildered.

"And if M'sieur is to paint my wife," added Monsieur Tapotte, who had by this time joined the group at the easel, "I--I...*Dame*! it must be a good deal more like than this."

Mueller drew himself up with an air of great dignity.

"Sir," he said, "if Madame does me the honor to sit to me for her portrait--for her *own* portrait, observe--I flatter myself the resemblance will be overwhelming. But you must permit me to inform you that Milord Smithfield is not sitting for his own portrait."

The Tapottes looked at each other in a state bordering on stupefaction.

"His lordship," continued Mueller, "is sitting for the portrait of one of his illustrious ancestors--a nobleman of the period of Queen Elizabeth."

Tapotte *mari* scratched his head, and smiled feebly.

"*Parbleu*!" said he, "*mais c'est bien drole, ca*!"

The artist shrugged his shoulders.

"It so happens," said he, "that his lordship's gallery at Smithfield Castle has unhappily been more than half destroyed by fire. Two centuries of family portraits reduced to ashes! Terrible misfortune! Only one way of repairing the loss--that is of partially repairing it. I do my best. I read the family records--I study the history of the period--his lordship sits to me daily--I endeavor to give a certain amount of family likeness; sometimes more, you observe, sometimes less ... enormous responsibility, Monsieur Tapotte!"

"Oh, enormous!"

"The taste for family portraits," continued Mueller, still touching up the Titian, "is a very natural one--and is on the increase. Many gentlemen of--of somewhat recent wealth, come to me for their ancestors."

"No!"

"*Foi d'honneur*. Few persons, however, are as conscientious as his lordship in the matter of family resemblance. They mostly buy up their forefathers ready-made--adopt them, christen them, and ask no questions."

Monsieur and Madame Tapotte exchanged glances.

"*Tiens, mon ami*, why should we not have an ancestor or two, as well as other folks," suggested the lady, in a very audible whisper.

Monsieur shook his head, and muttered something about the expense.

"There is no harm, at all events," urged madame, "in asking the price."

"My charge for gallery portraits, madame, varies from sixty to a hundred francs," said Mueller.

"Heavens! how dear! Why, my own portrait is to be only fifty."

"Sixty, Madame, if we put in the hands and the jewelry," said Mueller, blandly.

"*Eh bien*!--sixty. But for these other things.... bah! *ils sont fierement chers*."

"*Pardon*, madame! The elegancies and superfluities of life are, by a just rule of political economy, expensive. It is right that they should be so; as it is right that the necessaries of life should be within the reach of the poorest. Bread, for instance, is strictly necessary, and should be cheap. A great-grandfather, on the contrary, is an elegant superfluity, and may be put up at a high figure."

"There is some truth in that," murmured Monsieur Tapotte.

"Besides, in the present instance, one also pays for antiquity."

"*C'est juste--C'est juste*."

"At the same time," continued Mueller, "if Monsieur Tapotte were to honor me with a commission for, say, half a dozen family portraits, I would endeavor to put them in at forty francs apiece--including, at that very low price, a Revolutionary Deputy, a beauty of the Louis Quinze period, and a Marshal of France."

"*Tiens*! that's a fair offer enough," said madame. "What say you, *mon ami*?"

But Monsieur Tapotte, being a cautious man, would say nothing hastily. He coughed, looked doubtful, declined to commit himself to an opinion, and presently drew off into a corner for the purpose of holding a whispered consultation with his wife.

Meanwhile Mueller laid aside his brushes and palette, informed me with a profound bow that my lordship had honored him by sitting as long as was strictly necessary, and requested my opinion upon the progress of the work.

I praised it rapturously. You would have thought, to hear me, that for drawing, breadth, finish, color, composition, chiaroscuro, and every other merit that a painting could possess, this particular *chef-d'oeuvre* excelled all the masterpieces of Europe.

Mueller bowed, and bowed, and bowed, like a Chinaman at a visit of ceremony; He was more than proud; he was overwhelmed, *accable*, et caetera, et caetera.

The Tapottes left off whispering, and listened breathlessly.

"He is evidently a great painter, *not' jeune homme*!" said Madame in one of her large whispers.

To which Monsieur replied as audibly:--"*Ca se voit, ma femme--sacre nom d'une pipe*!"

"Milford will do me the favor to sit again on Friday?" said Mueller, as I took up my hat and gloves.

I replied with infinite condescension that I would endeavor to do so. I then made the stiffest of stiff bows to the excellent Tapottes, and, ushered to the door by Mueller, took my departure majestically in the character of Lord Smithfield.

CHAPTER XXIII.
THE QUARTIER LATIN.

The dear old Quartier Latin of my time--the Quartier Latin of Balzac, of Beranger, of Henry Murger---the Quartier Latin where Franz Mueller had his studio; where Messieurs Gustave; Jules, and Adrien gave their unparalleled *soirees dansantes*; where I first met my ex-flame Josephine--exists no longer. It has been improved off the face of the earth, and with it such a gay bizarre, improvident world of youth and folly as shall never again be met together on the banks of the Seine.

Ah me! how well I remember that dingy, delightful Arcadia--the Rue de la Vieille Boucherie, narrow, noisy, crowded, with projecting upper stories and Gothic pent-house roofs--the Rue de la Parcheminerie, unchanged since the Middle Ages--the Rue St. Jacques, steep, interminable, dilapidated; with its dingy cabarets, its brasseries, its cheap restaurants, its grimy shop windows filled with colored prints, with cooked meats, with tobacco, old books, and old clothes; its ancient colleges and hospitals, time-worn and weather-beaten, frowning down upon the busy thoroughfare and breaking the squalid line of shops; its grim old hotels swarming with lodgers, floor above floor, from the cobblers in the cellars to the grisettes in the attics! Then again, the gloomy old Place St. Michel, its abundant fountain ever flowing, ever surrounded by water-carts and water-carriers, by women with pails, and bare-footed street urchins, and thirsty drovers drinking out of iron cups chained to the wall. And then, too, the Rue de la Harpe....

I close my eyes, and the strange, precipitous, picturesque, decrepit old street, with its busy, surging crowd, its street-cries, its street-music, and its indescribable union of gloom and gayety, rises from its ashes. Here, grand old dilapidated mansions with shattered stone-carvings, delicate wrought-iron balconies all rust-eaten and broken, and windows in which every other pane is cracked or patched, alternate with more modern but still more ruinous houses, some leaning this way, some that, some with bulging upper stories, some with doorways sunk below the level of the pavement. Yonder, gloomy and grim, stands the College of Saint Louis. Dark alleys open off here and there from the main thoroughfare, and narrow side streets, steep as flights of steps. Low sheds and open stalls cling, limpet-like, to every available nook and corner. An endless procession of trucks, wagons, water-carts, and fiacres rumbles perpetually by. Here people live at their windows and in the doorways-- the women talking from balcony to balcony, the men smoking, reading, playing at dominoes. Here too are more cafes and cabarets, open-air stalls for the sale of fried fish, and cheap restaurants for workmen and students, where, for a sum equivalent to sevenpence half-penny English, the Quartier Latin regales itself upon meats and drinks of dark and enigmatical origin. Close at hand is the Place and College of the Sorbonne--silent in the midst of noisy life, solitary in the heart of the most crowded quarter of Paris. A sombre mediaeval gloom pervades that ancient quadrangle; scant tufts of sickly grass grow here and there in the interstices of the pavement; the dust of centuries crust those long rows of windows never opened. A little further on is the Rue des Gres, narrow, crowded, picturesque, one uninterrupted perspective of bookstalls and bookshops from end to end. Here the bookseller occasionally pursues a two-fold calling, and retails not only literature but a cellar of *petit vin bleu*; and here, overnight, the thirsty student exchanges for a bottle of Macon the "Code Ci-vile" that he must perforce buy back again at second-hand in the morning.

A little farther on, and we come to the College Saint Louis, once the old Col-lege Narbonne; and yet a few yards more, and we are at the doors of the Theatre du Pantheon, once upon a time the Church of St. Benoit, where the stage occupies the site of the altar, and an orchestra stall in what was once the nave, may be had for seventy-five centimes. Here, too, might be seen the shop of the immortal Lesage, renowned throughout the Quartier for the manufacture of a certain kind of tran-scendental ham-patty, peculiarly beloved by student and grisette; and here, cluster-ing within a stone's throw of each other, were to be found those famous restaurants, Pompon, Viot, Flicoteaux, and the "Boeuf Enrage," where, on gala days, many an Alphonse and Fifine, many a Theophile and Cerisette, were wont to hold high feast and festival--terms sevenpence half-penny each, bread at discretion, water gratis, wine and toothpicks extra.

But it was in the side streets, courts, and *impasses* that branched off to the left and right of the main arteries, that one came upon the very heart of the old Pays Latin; for the Rue St. Jacques, the Rue de la Harpe, the Rue des Gres, narrow, steep, dilapidated though they might be, were in truth the leading thoroughfares--the Boulevards, so to speak--of the Student Quartier. In most of the side alleys, however, some of which dated back as far, and farther, than the fifteenth century, there was no footway for passengers, and barely space for one wheeled vehicle at a time. A filthy gutter invariably flowed down the middle of the street. The pavement, as it peeped out here and there through a *moraine* of superimposed mud and offal, was seen to consist of small oblong stones, like petrified kidney potatoes. The houses, some leaning this way, some that, with projecting upper stories and over-hanging gable-roofs, nodded together overhead, leaving but a narrow strip of sky down which the sunlight strove in vain to struggle. Long poles upon which were suspended old clothes hung out to air, and ragged linen to dry, stood out like tattered banners from the attic windows. Here, too, every ground-floor was a shop, open, unglazed, cavernous, where the dealer lay *perdu* in the gloom of midday, like a spider in the midst of his web, surrounded by piles of old bottles, old iron, old clothes, old furniture, or whatever else his stock in trade might consist of.

Of such streets--less like streets, indeed, than narrow, overhanging gorges and ravines of damp and mouldering stone--of such streets, I say, intricate, winding, ill-lighted, unventilated, pervaded by an atmosphere compounded of the fumes of fried fish, tobacco, old leather, mildew and dirt, there were hundreds in the Quartier Latin of my time:--streets to the last degree unattractive as places of human habitation, but rich, nevertheless, in historic associations, in picturesque detail, and in archaeological interest. Such a street, for instance, was the Rue du Fouarre (scarcely a feature of which has been modernized to this day), where Dante, when a student of theology in Paris, attended the lectures of one Sigebert, a learned monk of Gemblours, who discoursed to his scholars in the open air, they sitting round him the while upon fresh straw strewn upon the pavement. Such a street was the Rue des Cordiers, close adjoining the Rue des Gres, where Rousseau lived and wrote; and the Rue du Dragon, where might then be seen the house of Bernard Palissy; and the Rue des Macons, where Racine lived; and the Rue des Marais, where Adrienne

Lecouvreur--poor, beautiful, generous, ill-fated Adrienne Lecouvreur!--died. Here, too, in a blind alley opening off the Rue St. Jacques, yet stands part of that Carmelite Convent in which, for thirty years, Madame de la Valliere expiated the solitary frailty of her life. And so at every turn! Not a gloomy by-street, not a dilapidated fountain, not a grim old college facade but had its history, or its legend. Here the voice of Abelard thundered new truths, and Rabelais jested, and Petrarch discoursed with the doctors. Here, in the Rue de l'Ancienne Comedie, walked the shades of Racine, of Moliere, of Corneille, of Voltaire. Dear, venerable, immortal old Quartier Latin! Thy streets were narrow, but they were the arteries through which, century after century, circulated all the wisdom and poetry, all the art, and science, and learning of France! Their gloom, their squalor, their very dirt was sacred. Could I have had my will, not a stone of the old place should have been touched, not a pavement widened, not a landmark effaced.

Then beside, yet not apart from, all that was mediaeval and historic in the Pays Latin, ran the gay, effervescent, laughing current of the life of the *jeunessed' aujour d'hui.* Here beat the very heart of that rare, that immortal, that unparalleled *vie de Boheme*, the vagabond poetry of which possesses such an inexhaustible charm for even the soberest imagination. What brick and mortar idylls, what romances *au cinquieme*, what joyous epithalamiums, what gay improvident *menages*, what kisses, what laughter, what tears, what lightly-spoken and lightly-broken vows those old walls could have told of!

Here, apparelled in all sorts of unimaginable tailoring, in jaunty colored cap or flapped sombrero, his pipe dangling from his button-hole, his hair and beard displaying every eccentricity under heaven, the Paris student, the *Pays Latiniste pur sang*, lived and had his being. Poring over the bookstalls in the Place du Pantheon or the Rue des Gres--hurrying along towards this or that college with a huge volume under each arm, about nine o'clock in the morning--haunting the cafes at midday and the restaurants at six--swinging his legs out of upper windows and smoking in his shirt-sleeves in the summer evenings--crowding the pit of the Odeon and every part of the Theatre du Pantheon--playing wind instruments at dead of night to the torment of his neighbors, or, in vocal mood, traversing the Quartier with a society of musical friends about the small hours of the morning--getting into scuffles with the gendarmes--flirting, dancing, playing billiards and the deuce; falling in love and in debt; dividing his time between Aristotle and Mademoiselle Mimi Pinson ... here, and here only, in all his phases, at every hour of the day and night, he swarmed, ubiquitous.

And here, too (a necessary sequence), flourished the fair and frail grisette. Her race, alas! is now all but extinct--the race of Fretillon, of Francine, of Lisette, Musette, Rosette, and all the rest of that too fascinating terminology--the race immortalized again and again by Beranger, Gavarni, Balzac, De Musset; sketched by a hundred pencils and described by a hundred pens; celebrated in all manner of metres and set to all manner of melodies; now caricatured and now canonized; now painted wholly *en noir* and now all *couleur de rose*; yet, however often described, however skilfully analyzed, remaining for ever indescribable, and for ever defying analysis!

"De tous les produits Parisiens," says Monsieur Jules Janin (himself the quintessence of everything most Parisian), "le produit le plus Parisien, sans contredit, c'est la grisette." True; but our epigrammatist should have gone a step farther. He should have added that the grisette *pur sang* is to be found nowhere except in Paris; and (still a step farther) nowhere in Paris save between the Pont Neuf and the Barriere d'Enfer. There she reigns; there (ah! let me use the delicious present tense--let me believe that I still live in Arcadia!)--there she lights up the old streets with her smile; makes the old walls ring with her laughter; flits over the crossings like a fairy; wears the most coquettish of little caps and the daintiest of little shoes; rises to her work with the dawn; keeps a pet canary; trains a nasturtium round her window; loves as heartily as she laughs, and almost as readily; owes not a sou, saves not a centime; sews on Adolphe's buttons, like a good neighbor; is never so happy as when Adolphe in return takes her to Tivoli or the Jardin Turc; adores *galette, sucre d'orge*, and Frederick Lemaitre; and looks upon a masked ball and a debardeur dress as the summit of human felicity.

Vive la grisette! Shall I not follow many an illustrious example and sing my modest paean in her praise? Frown not, august Britannia! Look not so severely askance upon my poor little heroine of the Quartier Latin! Thinkest thou because thou art so eminently virtuous that she who has many a serviceable virtue of her own, shall be debarred from her share in this world's cakes and ale?

Vive la grisette! Let us think and speak no evil of her. "Elle ne tient au vice que par un rayon, et s'en eloigne par les mille autres points de la circonference sociale." The world sees only her follies, and sees them at first sight; her good qualities lie hidden in the shade. Is she not busy as a bee, joyous as a lark, helpful, pitiful, unselfish, industrious, contented? How often has she not slipped her last coin into the alms-box at the hospital gate, and gone supperless to bed? How often sat up all night, after a long day's toil in a crowded work-room, to nurse Victorine in the fever? How often pawned her Sunday gown and shawl, to redeem that coat without which Adolphe cannot appear before the examiners to-morrow morning? Granted, if you will, that she has an insatiable appetite for sweets, cigarettes, and theatrical admissions--shall she not be welcome to her tastes? And is it her fault if her capacity in the way of miscellaneous refreshments partakes of the nature of the miraculous--somewhat to the inconvenience of Adolphe, who has overspent his allowance? Supposing even that she may now and then indulge (among friends) in a very modified can-can at the Chaumiere--what does that prove, except that her heels are as light as her heart, and that her early education has been somewhat neglected?

But I am writing of a world that has vanished as completely as the lost Pleiad. The Quartier Latin of my time is no more. The Chaumiere is no more. The grisette is fast dying out. Of the Rue de la Harpe not a recognisable feature is left. The old Place St. Michel, the fountain, the Theatre du Pantheon, are gone as if they had never been. Whole streets, I might say whole parishes, have been swept away--whole chapters of mediaeval history erased for ever.

Well, I love to close my eyes from time to time, and evoke the dear old haunts from their ruins; to descend once more the perilous steeps of the Rue St. Jacques, and to thread the labyrinthine by-streets that surround the Ecole de Medecine. I see them all so plainly! I look in at the familiar print-shops--I meet many a long-forgotten face--I hear many a long-forgotten voice--I am twenty years of age and a student again!

Ah me! what a pleasant time, and what a land of enchantment! Dingy, dilapidated, decrepit as it was, that graceless old Quartier Latin, believe me, was paved with roses and lighted with laughing gas.

CHAPTER XXIV.
THE FETE AT COURBEVOIE.

"*Halte la*! I thought I should catch you about this time! They've been giving you unconscionable good measure to-day, though, haven't they? I thought Bollinet's lecture was always over by three; and here I've been moralizing on the flight of Time for more than twenty minutes."

So saying, Mueller, having stopped me as I was coming down the steps of the Hotel Dieu, linked his arm in mine, drew me into a shady angle under the lee of Notre Dame, and, without leaving me time to reply, went on pouring out his light, eager chatter as readily as a mountain-spring bubbles out its waters.

"I thought you'd like to know about the Tapottes, you see--and I was dying to tell you. I went to your rooms last night between eight and nine, and you were out; so I thought the only sure way was to come here--I know you never miss Bollinet's Lectures. Well, as I was saying, the Tapottes.... Oh, *mon cher*! I am your debtor for life in that matter of Milord Smithfield. It has been the making of me. What do you think? Tapotte is not only going to sit for a companion half-length to Madame's portrait, but he has given me a commission for half-a-dozen ancestors. Fancy-- half-a-dozen illustrious dead-and-done Tapottes! What a scope for the imagination! What a bewildering vista of *billets de banque*! I feel--ah, *mon ami*! I feel that the wildest visions of my youth are about to be realized, and that I shall see my tailor's bill receipted before I die!"

"I'm delighted," said I, "that Tapotte has turned up a trump card."

"A trump card? Say a California--a Pactolus--a Golden Calf. Nay, hath not Tapotte two golden calves? Is he not of the precious metal all compact? Stands he not, in the amiable ripeness of his years, a living representative of the Golden Age? *'O bella eta dell' oro*!'"

And to my horror, he then and there executed a frantic **pas seul**.

"Gracious powers!" I exclaimed. "Are you mad?"

"Yes--raving mad. Have you any objection?"

"But, my dear fellow--in the face of day--in the streets of Paris! We shall get taken up by the police!"

"Then suppose we get out of the streets of Paris? I'm tired enough, Heaven knows, of cultivating the arid soil of the Pave. See, it's a glorious afternoon. Let's go somewhere."

"With all my heart. Where?"

"*Ah, mon Dieu! ca m'est egal*. Enghien--Vincennes--St. Cloud--Versailles ... anywhere you like. Most probably there's a fete going on somewhere, if we only knew where,"

"Can't we find out?"

"Oh, yes--we can drop into a Cafe and look at the **Petites Affiches**; only that entails an absinthe; or we can go into the nearest Omnibus Bureau and see the notices on the walls, which will be cheaper."

So we threaded our way along the narrow thoroughfares of the Ile de la Cite, and came presently to an Omnibus Bureau on the Quai de l'Horloge, overlooking the Pont Neuf and the river. Here the first thing we saw was a flaming placard setting forth the pleasures and attractions of the great annual fete at Courbevoie; a village on the banks of the Seine, a mile or two beyond Neuilly.

"*Voila, notre affaire*!" said Mueller, gaily. "We can't do better than steer straight for Courbevoie."

Saying which, he hailed a passing fiacre and bade the coachman drive to the Embarcadere of the Rive Droite.

"We shall amuse ourselves famously at Courbevoie," he said, as we rattled over the stones. "We'll dine at the Toison d'Or--an excellent little restaurant overlooking the river; and if you're fond of angling, we can hire a punt and catch our own fish for dinner. Then there will be plenty of fiddling and dancing at the guingettes and gardens in the evening. By the way, though, I've no money! That is to say, none worth speaking of--**voila!**... one franc, one piece of fifty centimes, another of twenty centimes, and some sous. I hope your pockets are better lined than mine."

"Not much, I fear," I replied, pulling out my porte-monnaie, and emptying the contents into my hand. They amounted to nine francs and seventy-five centimes.

"*Parbleu*! we've just eleven francs and a half between us," said Mueller. "A modest sum-total; but we must make it as elastic as we can. Let me see, there'll be a franc for the fiacre, four francs for our return tickets, four for our dinner, and two and a half to spend as we like in the fair. Well, we can't commit any great extravagance with that amount of floating capital."

"Better turn back and go to my rooms for some more money?" I exclaimed. "I've two Napoleons in my desk."

"No, no--we should miss the three-fifty train, and not get another till between five and six."

"But we shall have no fun if we have no money!"

"I dissent entirely from that proposition, Monsieur Englishman. I have always had plenty of fun, and I have been short of cash since the hour of my birth. Come, it shall be my proud task to-day to prove to you the pleasures of impecuniosity!"

So with our eleven francs and a half we went on to the station, and took our places for Courbevoie.

We travelled, of course, by third class in the open wagons; and it so happened that in our compartment we had the company of three pretty little chattering grisettes, a fat countrywoman with a basket, and a quiet-looking elderly female with her niece. These last wore bonnets, and some kind of slight mourning. They belonged evidently to the small bourgeoise class, and sat very quietly in the corner of the carriage, speaking to no one. The three grisettes, however, kept up an incessant fire of small talk and squabble.

"I was on this very line last Sunday," said one. "I went with Julie to Asnieres, and we were so gay! I wonder if it will be very gay at Courbevoie."

"*Je m'en doute*," replied another, whom they called Lolotte. "I came to one of the Courbevoie fetes last spring, and it was not gay at all. But then, to be sure, I was with Edouard, and he is as dull as the first day in Lent. Where were you last Sunday, Adele?"

"I did not go beyond the barriers. I went to the Cirque with my cousin, and we dined in the Palais Royal. We enjoyed ourselves so much! You know my cousin?"

"Ah! yes--the little fellow with the curly hair and the whiskers, who waits for you at the corner when we leave the workshop."

"The same--Achille."

"Your Achille is nice-looking," said Mademoiselle Lolotte, with a somewhat critical air. "It is a pity he squints."

"He does not squint, mam'selle."

"Oh, ***ma chere***! I appeal to Caroline."

"I am not sure that he actually squints," said Mam'selle Caroline, speaking for the first time; "but he certainly has one eye larger than the other, and of quite a different color."

"***Tiens***, Caroline--it seems to me that you look very closely into the eyes of young men," exclaims Adele, turning sharply upon this new assailant.

"At all events you admit that Caroline is right," cries Lolotte, triumphantly.

"I admit nothing of the kind. I say that you are both very ill-natured, and that you say what is not true. As for you, Lolotte, I don't believe you ever had the chance of seeing a young man's eyes turned upon you, or you would not be so pleased with the attentions of an old one."

"An ***old*** one!" shrieked Mam'selle Lolotte. "Ah, ***mon Dieu***! Is a man old at forty-seven? Monsieur Durand is in the prime of life, and there isn't a girl in the Quartier who would not be proud of his attentions!"

"He's sixty, if an hour," said the injured Adele. "And as for you, Caroline, who have never had a beau in your life...."

"***Ciel***! what a calumny!--I--never had a ... Holy Saint Genevieve! why, it was only last Thursday week...."

Here the train stopped at the Asnieres station, and two privates of the Garde Imperiale got into the carriage. The horizon cleared as if by magic. The grisettes suddenly forgot their differences, and began to chat quite amicably. The soldiers twirled their mustachios, listened, smiled, and essayed to join in the conversation. In a few minutes all was mirth and flirtation.

Meanwhile Mueller was casting admiring glances on the young girl in the corner, whilst the fat countrywoman, pursing up her mouth, and watching the grisettes and soldiers, looked the image of offended virtue.

"Dame! Madame," she said, addressing herself to the old lady in the bonnet, "girls usen't to be so forward in the days when you and I were young!"

To which the old lady in the bonnet, blandly smiling, replied:--

"Beautiful, for the time of year."

"Eh? For the time of year? Dame! I don't see that the time of year has anything to do with it," exclaimed the fat countrywoman.

Here the young girl in the corner, blushing and smiling very sweetly, interposed with--"Pardon, Madame--my aunt is somewhat deaf. Pray, excuse her."

Whereupon the old lady, watching the motion of her niece's lips, added--

"Ah, yes--yes! I am a poor, deaf old woman--I don't understand what you say. Talk to my little Marie, here--she can answer you."

"I, for one, desire nothing better than permission to talk to Mademoiselle," said Mueller, gallantly.

"Mais, Monsieur..."

"Mademoiselle, with Madame her aunt, are going to the fete at Courbevoie?"

"Yes, Monsieur."

"The river is very pretty thereabouts, and the walks through the meadows are delightful."

"Indeed, Monsieur!"

"Mademoiselle does not know the place?"

"No, Monsieur."

"Ah, if I might only be permitted to act as guide! I know every foot of the ground about Courbevoie."

Mademoiselle Marie blushed again, looked down, and made no reply.

"I am a painter," continued Mueller; "and I have sketched all the windings of the Seine from Neuilly to St. Germains. My friend here is English--he is a student of medicine, and speaks excellent French."

"What is the gentleman saying, *mon enfant*?" asked the old lady, somewhat anxiously.

"Monsieur says that the river is very pretty about Courbevoie, *ma tante*," replied Mademoiselle Marie, raising her voice.

"Ah! ah! and what else?"

"Monsieur is a painter."

"A painter? Ah, dear me! it's an unhealthy occupation. My poor brother Pierre might have been alive to this day if he had taken to any other line of business! You must take great care of your lungs, young man. You look delicate."

Mueller laughed, shook his head, and declared at the top of his voice that he had never had a day's illness in his life.

Here the pretty niece again interposed.

"Ah, Monsieur," she said, "my aunt does not understand....My--my uncle Pierre was a house-painter."

"A very respectable occupation, Mademoiselle," replied Mueller, politely. "For my own part, I would sooner paint the insides of some houses than the outsides of some people."

At this moment the train began to slacken pace, and the steam was let off with a demoniac shriek.

"*Tiens, mon enfant*," said the old lady, turning towards her niece with affectionate anxiety. "I hope you have not taken cold."

The excellent soul believed that it was Mademoiselle Marie who sneezed.

And now the train had stopped--the porters were running along the platform, shouting "Courbevoie! Courbevoie!"--the passengers were scrambling out *en masse*--and beyond the barrier one saw a confused crowd of *charrette* and omnibus-drivers, touters, fruit-sellers, and idlers of every description. Mueller handed out the old lady and the niece; the fat countrywoman scrambled up into a kind of tumbril driven by a boy in *sabots*; the grisettes and soldiers walked off together; and the tide of holiday-makers, some on foot, some in hired vehicles, set towards the village. In the meanwhile, what with the crowd on the platform and the crowd outside the barrier, and what with the hustling and pushing at the point where the tickets were taken, we lost sight of the old lady and her niece.

"What the deuce has become of *ma tante*?" exclaimed Mueller, looking round.

But neither *ma tante* nor Mademoiselle Marie were anywhere to be seen. I suggested that they must have gone on in the omnibus or taken a *charrette*, and so have passed us unperceived.

"And, after all," I added, "we didn't want to enter upon an indissoluble union with them for the rest of the day. *Ma tante's* deafness is not entertaining, and *la petite* Marie has nothing to say."

"*La petite* Marie is uncommonly pretty, though," said Mueller. "I mean to dance a quadrille with her by-and-by, I promise you."

"*A la bonne heure*! We shall be sure to chance upon them again before long."

We had come by this time to a group of pretty villa-residences with high garden walls and little shady side-lanes leading down to the river. Then came a church and more houses; then an open Place; and suddenly we found ourselves in the midst of the fair.

It was just like any other of the hundred and one fetes that take place every summer in the environs of Paris. There was a merry-go-round and a greasy pole; there was a juggler who swallowed knives and ribbons; there were fortune-tellers without number; there were dining-booths, and drinking-booths, and dancing-booths; there were acrobats, organ-boys with monkeys, and Savoyards with white mice; there were stalls for the sale of cakes, fruit, sweetmeats, toys, combs, cheap jewelry, glass, crockery, boots and shoes, holy-water vessels, rosaries, medals, and little colored prints of saints and martyrs; there were brass bands, and string bands, and ballad-singers everywhere; and there was an atmosphere compounded of dust, tobacco-smoke, onions, musk, and every objectionable perfume under heaven.

"Dine at the Restaurant de l'Empire, Messieurs," shouted a shabby touter in a blouse, thrusting a greasy card into our faces. "Three dishes, a dessert, a half-bottle, and a band of music, for one franc-fifty. The cheapest dinner in the fair!"

"The cheapest dinner in the fair is at the Belle Gabrielle!" cried another. "We'll give you for the same money soup, fish, two dishes, a dessert, a half-bottle, and take your photograph into the bargain!"

"Bravo! *mon vieux*--you first poison them with your dinner, and then provide photographs for the widows and children," retorts touter number one. "That's justice, anyhow."

Whereupon touter number two shrieks out a torrent of abuse, and we push on, leaving them to settle their differences after their own fashion.

At the next booth we are accosted by a burly fellow daubed to the eyes with red and blue paint, and dressed as an Indian chief.

"*Entrez, entrez, Messieurs et Mesdames*" he cries, flourishing a war-spear some nine feet in length. "Come and see the wonderful Peruvian maiden of Tanjore, with webbed fingers and toes, her mouth in the back of her head, and her eyes in the soles of her feet! Only four sous each, and an opportunity that will never occur again!"

"Only fifty centimes!" shouts another public orator; "the most ingenious little machine ever invented! Goes into the waistcoat pocket--is wound up every twenty-four hours--tells the day of the month, the day of the year, the age of the moon, the state of the Bourse, the bank rate of discount, the quarter from which the wind is blowing, the price of new-laid eggs in Paris and the provinces, the rate of mortality in the Fee-jee islands, and the state of your sweetheart's affections!"

A little further on, by dint of much elbowing, we made our way into a crowded booth where, for the modest consideration of two sous per head, might be seen a Boneless Youth and an Ashantee King. The performances were half over when we went in. The Boneless Youth had gone through his feats of agility, and was lying on a mat in a corner of the stage, the picture of limp incapability. The Ashantee monarch was just about to make his appearance. Meanwhile, a little man in fleshings and a cocked hat addressed the audience.

"Messieurs and Mesdames--I have the honor to announce that Caraba Rado-kala, King of Ashantee, will next appear before you. This terrific native sovereign was taken captive by that famous Dutch navigator, the Mynheer Van Dunk, in his last voyage round the globe. Van Dunk, having brought his prisoner to Europe in an iron cage, sold him to the English government in 1840; who sold him again to Milord Barnum, the great American philanthropist, in 1842; who sold him again to Franconi of the Cirque Olympique; who finally sold him to me. At the time of his capture, Caraba Radokala was the most treacherous, barbarous, and sanguinary monster upon record. He had three hundred and sixty-five wives--a wife, you observe, for every day in the year. He lived exclusively upon human flesh, and consumed, when in good health, one baby per diem. His palace in Ashantee was built entirely of the skulls and leg-bones of his victims. He is now, however, much less ferocious; and, though he feeds on live pigeons, rabbits, dogs, mice, and the like, he has not tasted human flesh since his captivity. He is also heavily ironed. The distinguished company need therefore entertain no apprehensions. Pierre--draw the bolt, and let his majesty loose!"

A savage roar was now heard, followed by a rattling of chains. Then the curtains were suddenly drawn back, and the Ashantee king--crowned with a feather head-dress, loaded with red and blue war-paint, and chained from ankle to ankle--

bounded on the stage.

Seeing the audience before him, he uttered a terrific howl. The front rows were visibly agitated. Several young women faintly screamed.

The little man in the cocked hat rushed to the front, protesting that the ladies had no reason to be alarmed. Caraba Radokala, if not wantonly provoked, was now quite harmless--a little irritable, perhaps, from being waked too suddenly--would be as gentle as a lamb, if given something to eat:--"Pierre, quiet his majesty with a pigeon!"

Pierre, a lank lad in motley, hereupon appeared with a live pigeon, which immediately escaped from his hands and perched on the top of the proscenium. Caraba Radokala yelled; the little man in the cocked hat raved; and Pierre, in default of more pigeons, contritely reappeared with a lump of raw beef, into which his majesty ravenously dug his royal teeth. The pigeon, meanwhile, dressed its feathers and looked complacently down, as if used to the incident.

"Having fed, Caraba Radokala will now be quite gentle and good-humored," said the showman. "If any lady desires to shake hands with him, she may do so with perfect safety. Will any lady embrace the opportunity?"

A faint sound of tittering was heard in various parts of the booth; but no one came forward.

"Will *no* lady be persuaded? Well, then, is there any gentleman present who speaks Ashantee?"

Mueller gave me a dig with his elbow, and started to his feet.

"Yes," he replied, loudly. "I do."

Every head was instantly turned in our direction.

The showman collapsed with astonishment. Even the captive, despite his ignorance of the French tongue, looked considerably startled.

"*Comment*!" stammered the cocked hat. "Monsieur speaks Ashantee?"

"Fluently."

"Is it permitted to inquire how and when monsieur acquired this very unusual accomplishment?"

"I have spoken Ashantee from my infancy," replied Mueller, with admirable aplomb. "I was born at sea, brought up in an undiscovered island, twice kidnapped by hostile tribes before attaining the age of ten years, and have lived among savage nations all my life."

A murmur of admiration ran through the audience, and Mueller became, for the time, an object of livelier interest than Caraba Radokala himself. Seeing this, the indignant monarch executed a warlike *pas*, and rattled his chains fiercely.

"In that case, monsieur, you had better come upon the stage, and speak to his majesty," said the showman reluctantly.

"With all the pleasure in life."

"But I warn you that his temper is uncertain."

"Bah!" said Mueller, working his way round through the crowd, "I'm not afraid of his temper."

"As monsieur pleases--but, if monsieur offends him, *I* will not be answerable for the consequences."

"All right--give us a hand up, *mon vieux*!" And Muller, having clambered upon the stage, made a bow to the audience and a salaam to his majesty.

"Chickahominy chowdar bang," said he, by way of opening the conversation.

The ex-king of Ashantee scowled, folded his arms, and maintained a haughty silence.

"Hic hac horum, high cockalorum," continued Mueller, with exceeding suavity.

The captive monarch stamped impatiently, ground his teeth, but still made no reply.

"Monsieur had better not aggravate him," said the showman. "On the contrary--I am overwhelming him with civilities Now observe--I condole with him upon his melancholy position. I inquire after his wives and children; and I remark how uncommonly well he is looking."

And with this, he made another salaam, smiled persuasively, and said--

"Alpha, beta, gamma, delta--chin-chin--Potz tausend!--Erin-go-bragh!"

"Borriobooloobah!" shrieked his majesty, apparently stung to desperation.

"Rocofoco!" retorted Mueller promptly.

But as if this last was more than any Ashantee temper could bear, Caraba Rodokala clenched both his fists, set his teeth hard, and charged down upon Mueller like a wild elephant. Being met, however, by a well-planted blow between the eyes, he went down like a ninepin--picked himself up,--rushed in again, and, being forcibly seized and held back by the cocked hat, Pierre of the pigeons, and a third man who came tumbling up precipitately from somewhere behind the stage, vented his fury, in a torrent of very highly civilized French oaths.

"Eh, *sacredieu*!" he cried, shaking his fist in Mueller's face, "I've not done with you yet, *diable de galerien*!"

Whereupon there burst forth a general roar--a roar like the "inextinguishable laughter" of Olympus.

"*Tiens*!" said Mueller, "his majesty speaks French almost as well as I speak Ashantee!"

"*Bourreau! Brigand! Assassin*!" shrieked his Ferocity, as his friends hustled him off the stage.

The curtains then fell together again; and the audience, still laughing vociferously, dispersed with cries of "Vive Caraba Rodokala!" "Kind remembrances to the Queens of Ashantee!" "What's the latest news from home?" "Borriobooloo-bah--ah--ah!"

Elbowing our way out with the crowd, we now plunged once more into the press of the fair. Here our old friends the dancing dogs of the Champs Elysees, and the familiar charlatan of the Place du Chatelet with his chariot and barrel-organ, transported us from Ashantee to Paris. Next we came to a temporary shooting-gallery, adorned over the entrance with a spirited cartoon of a Tyrolean sharpshooter; and then to an exhibition of cosmoramas; and presently to a weighing machine, in which a great, rosy-cheeked, laughing Normandy peasant girl, with her high cap, blue skirt, massive gold cross and heavy ear-rings, was in the act of being weighed.

"*Tiens! Mam'selle est joliment solide*!" remarks a saucy bystander, as the owner of the machine piles on weight after weight.

"Perhaps if I had no more brains than m'sieur, I should weigh as light!" retorts the damsel, with a toss of her high cap.

"*Pardon*! it is not a question of brains--it is a question of hearts," interposes an elderly exquisite in a white hat. "Mam'selle has captured so many that she is completely over weighted."

"Twelve stone six ounces," pronounces the owner of the machine, adjusting the last weight.

Whereupon there is a burst of ironical applause, and the big *paysanne*, half laughing, half angry, walks off, exclaiming, "***Eh bien! tant mieux***! I've no mind to be a scarecrow--***moi***!"

By this time we have both had enough of the fair, and are glad to make our way out of the crowd and down to the riverside. Here we find lovers strolling in pairs along the towing-path; family groups pic-nicking in the shade; boats and punts for hire, and a swimming-match just coming off, of which all that is visible are two black heads bobbing up and down along the middle of the stream.

"And now, ***mon ami***, what do you vote for?" asks Mueller. "Boating or fishing? or both? or neither?"

"Both, if you like--but I never caught anything in my life,"

"The pleasure of fishing, I take it," says Mueller, "is not in the fish you catch, but in the fish you miss. The fish you catch is a poor little wretch, worth neither the trouble of landing, cooking, nor eating; but the fish you miss is always the finest fellow you ever saw in your life!"

"***Allons donc***! I know, then, which of us two will have most of the pleasure to-day," I reply, laughing. "But how about the expense?"

To which Mueller, with a noble recklessness, answers:--

"Oh, hang the expense! Here, boatman! a boat ***a quatre rames***, and some fish-ing-tackle--by the hour."

Now it was undoubtedly a fine sentiment this of Mueller's, and had we but fetched my two Napoleons before starting, I should have applauded it to the echo; but when I considered that something very nearly approaching to a franc had already filtered out of our pockets in passing through the fair, and that the hour of dinner was looming somewhat indefinitely in the distance, I confess that my soul became disquieted within me.

"Don't forget, for heaven's sake," I said, "that we must keep something for din-ner!"

"My dear fellow," he replied, "I have already a tremendous appetite for dinner--that *is* something."

After this, I resigned myself to whatever might happen.

We then rowed up the river for about a mile beyond Courbevoie. moored our boat to a friendly willow, put our fishing-tackle together, and composed ourselves for the gentle excitement that waits upon the gudgeon and the minnow.

"I haven't yet had a single nibble," said Mueller, when we had been sitting to our work for something less than ten minutes.

"Hush!" I said. "You mustn't speak, you know."

"True--I had forgotten. I'll sing instead. Fishes, I have been told, are fond of music.

'Fanfan, je vous aimerais bien;
Contre vous je n'ai nul caprice;
Vous etes gentil, j'en convien....'"

"Come, now!" I exclaimed pettishly, "this is really too bad. I had a bite--a most decided bite--and if you had only kept quiet"....

"Nonsense, my dear fellow! I tell you again--and I have it on the best authority--fishes like music. Did you never hear of Arion! Have you forgotten about the Syrens? Believe me, your gudgeon nibbled because I sang him to the surface--just as the snakes come out for the song of the snake-charmer. I'll try again!"

And with this he began:--

"Jeannette est une brune
Qui demeure a Pantin,
Ou toute sa fortune
Est un petit jardin!"

"Well, if you go on like that, all I have to say is, that not a fish will come within half a mile of our bait," said I, with tranquil despair.

"Alas! **mon cher**, I am grieved to observe in your otherwise estimable character, a melancholy want of faith," replied Mueller "Without faith, what is friendship? What is angling? What is matrimony? Now, I tell you that with regard to the finny tribe, the more I charm them, the more enthusiastically they will flock to be caught. We shall have a miraculous draught in a few minutes, if you are but patient."

And then he began again:--

"Mimi Pinson est une blonde,

Une blonde que l'on connait.
Elle n'a qu'une robe au monde,
Landerirette!
Et qu'un bonnet."

I laid aside my rod, folded my arms, and when he had done, applauded ironically.

"Very good," I said. "I understand the situation. We are here, at some--indeed, I may say, considering the state of our exchequer, at a considerable mutual expense; not to catch fish, but to afford Herr Mueller an opportunity of exercising his extensive memory, and his limited baritone voice. The entertainment is not without its **agrements**, but I find it dear at the price."

"*Tiens*, Arbuthnot! let us fish seriously. I promise not to open my lips again till you have caught something."

"Then, seriously, I believe you would have to be silent the whole night, and all I should catch would be the rheumatism. I am the worst angler in the world, and the most unlucky."

"Really and truly?"

"Really and truly. And you?"

"As bad as yourself. If a tolerably large and energetic fish did me the honor to swallow my bait, the probability is that he would catch me. I certainly shouldn't know what to do with him."

"Then the present question is--what shall we do with ourselves?"

"I vote that we row up as far as yonder bend in the river, just to see what lies beyond; and then back to Courbevoie."

"Heaven only grant that by that time we shall have enough money left for dinner!" I murmured with a sigh.

We rowed up the river as far as the first bend, a distance of about half a mile; and then we rowed on as far as the next bend. Then we turned, and, resting on our oars, drifted slowly back with the current. The evening was indescribably brilliant and serene. The sky was cloudless, of a greenish blue, and full of light. The river was clear as glass. We could see the flaccid water-weeds swaying languidly with the current far below, and now and then a shoal of tiny fish shooting along half-way between the weeds and the surface. A rich fringe of purple iris, spear-leaved sagit-tarius, and tufted meadow-sweet (each blossom a bouquet on a slender thyrsus) bordered the towing-path and filled the air with perfume. Here the meadows lay open to the water's edge; a little farther on, they were shut off by a close rampart of poplars and willows whose leaves, already yellowed by autumn, were now fiery in the sunset. Joyous bands of gnats, like wild little intoxicated maenads, circled and hummed about our heads as we drifted slowly on; while, far away and mellowed by distance, we heard the brazen music of the fair.

We were both silent. Mueller pulled out a small sketch-book and made a rapid study of the scene--the reach in the river; the wooded banks; the green flats tra-versed by long lines of stunted pollards; the church-tops and roofs of Courbevoie beyond.

Presently a soft voice, singing, broke upon the silence. Mueller stopped invol-untarily, pencil in hand. I held my breath, and listened. The tune was flowing and sweet; and as our boat drifted on, the words of the singer became audible.

"O miroir ondoyant!
Je reve en te voyant
Harmonie et lumiere,
O ma riviere,
O ma belle riviere!

"On voit se reflechir
Dans ses eaux les nuages;
Elle semble dormir
Entre les paturages

Ou paissent les grands boeufs
Et les grasses genisses.
Au patres amoureux
Que ses bords sont propices!"

"A woman's voice," said Mueller. "Dupont's words and music. She must be young and pretty ... where has she hidden herself?"

The unseen singer, meanwhile, went on with another verse.

"Pres des iris du bord,
Sous une berge haute,
La carpe aux reflets d'or
Ou le barbeau ressaute,
Les goujons font le guet,
L'Ablette qui scintille
Fuit le dent du brochet;
Au fond rampe l'anguille!

"O miroir ondoyant!
Je reve en te voyant
Harmonic et lumiere,
O ma riviere,
O ma belle riviere!"

"Look!" said Mueller. "Do you not see them yonder--two women under the trees? By Jupiter! it's *ma tante* and *la petite* Marie!"

Saying which, he flung himself upon his oars and began pulling vigorously towards the shore.

CHAPTER XXV.
THAT TERRIBLE MUeLLER.

La petite Marie broke off at the sound of our oars, and blushed a becoming rose-color.

"Will these ladies do us the honor of letting us row them back to Courbevoie?" said Mueller, running our boat close in against the sedges, and pulling off his hat as respectfully as if they were duchesses.

Mademoiselle Marie repeated the invitation to her aunt, who accepted it at once.

"*Tres volontiers, tres volontiers, messieurs*" she said, smiling and nodding. "We have rambled out so far--so far! And I am not as young as I was forty years ago. *Ah, mon Dieu*! how my old bones ache! Give me thy hand, Marie, and thank the gentlemen for their politeness."

So Mam'selle Marie helped her aunt to rise, and we steadied the boat close under the bank, at a point where the interlacing roots of a couple of sallows made a kind of natural step by means of which they could easily get down.

"Oh, dear! dear! it will not turn over, will it, my dear young man? *Ciel*! I am slipping ... Ah, *Dieu, merci*!--Marie, *mon cher enfant*, pray be careful not to jump in, or you will upset us all!"

And *ma tante*, somewhat tremulous from the ordeal of embarking, settled down in her place, while Mueller lifted Mam'selle Marie into the boat, as if she had been a child. I then took the oars, leaving him to steer; and so we pursued our way towards Courbevoie.

"Mam'selle has of course seen the fair?" said Mueller, from behind the old lady's back.

"No, monsieur,"

"No! Is it possible?"

"There was so much crowd, monsieur, and such a noise ... we were quite too much afraid to venture in."

"Would you be afraid, mam'selle, to venture with me?"

"I--I do not know, monsieur."

"Ah, mam'selle, you might be very sure that I would take good care of you!"

"*Mais ... monsieur*"...

"These gentlemen, I see, have been angling," said the old lady, addressing me very graciously. "Have you caught many fish?"

"None at all, madame!" I replied, loudly.

"*Tiens*! so many as that?"

"*Pardon*, madame," I shouted at the top of my voice. "We have caught noth-ing--nothing at all."

Ma tante smiled blandly.

"Ah, yes," she said; "and you will have them cooked presently for dinner, *n'est-ce pas*? There is no fish so fresh, and so well-flavored, as the fish of our own catch-ing."

"Will madame and mam'selle do us the honor to taste our fish and share our modest dinner?" said Mueller, leaning forward in his seat in the stern, and deliver-ing his invitation close into the old lady's ear.

To which *ma tante*, with a readiness of hearing for which no one would have given her credit, replied:--

"But--but monsieur is very polite--if we should not be inconveniencing these gentlemen"....

"We shall be charmed, madame--we shall be honored!"

"*Eh bien!* with pleasure, then--Marie, my child, thank the gentlemen for their amiable invitation."

I was thunderstruck. I looked at Mueller to see if he had suddenly gone out of his senses. Mam'selle Marie, however, was infinitely amused.

"*Fi donc!* monsieur," she said. "You have no fish. I heard the other gentleman say so."

"The other gentleman, mam'selle," replied Mueller, "is an Englishman, and troubled with the spleen. You must not mind anything he says."

Troubled with the spleen! I believe myself to be as even-tempered and as ready to fall in with a joke as most men; but I should have liked at that moment to punch Franz Mueller's head. Gracious heavens! into what a position he had now brought us! What was to be done? How were we to get out of it? It was now just seven; and we had already been upon the water for more than an hour. What should we have to pay for the boat? And when we had paid for the boat, how much money should we have left to pay for the dinner? Not for our own dinners--ah, no! For *ma tante's* dinner (and *ma tante* had a hungry eye) and for *la petite* Marie's dinner; and *la petite* Marie, plump, rosy, and well-liking, looked as if she might have a capital appetite upon occasion! Should we have as much as two and a half francs? I doubted it. And then, in the absence of a miracle, what could we do with two and a half francs, if we had them? A miserable sum!--convertible, perhaps, into as much bouilli, bread and cheese, and thin country wine as might have satisfied our own hunger in a prosaic and commonplace way; but for four persons, two of them women!...

And this was not the worst of it. I thought I knew Mueller well enough by this time to feel that he would entirely dismiss this minor consideration of ways and means; that he would order the dinner as recklessly as if we had twenty francs apiece in our pockets; and that he would not only order it, but eat it and preside at it with all the gayety and audacity in life.

Then would come the horrible retribution of the bill!

I felt myself turn red and hot at the mere thought of it.

Then a dastardly idea insinuated itself into my mind. I had my return-ticket in my waistcoat-pocket:--what if I slipped away presently to the station and went back to Paris by the next train, leaving my clever friend to improvise his way out of his own scrape as best he could?

In the meanwhile, as I was rowing with the stream, we soon got back to Courbevoie.

"*Are* you mad?" I said, as, having landed the ladies, Mueller and I delivered up the boat to its owner.

"Didn't I admit it, two or three hours ago?" he replied. "I wonder you don't get tired, *mon cher*, of asking the same question so often."

"Four francs, fifty centimes, Messieurs," said the boatman, having made fast his boat to the landing-place.

"Four francs, fifty centimes!" I echoed, in dismay.

Even Mueller looked aghast.

"My good fellow," he said, "do you take us for coiners?"

"Hire of boat, two francs the hour. These gentlemen have been out nearly one hour and a half--three francs. Hire of bait and fishing-tackle, one franc fifty. Total, four francs and a half," replied the boatman, putting out a great brown palm.

Mueller, who was acting as cashier and paymaster, pulled out his purse, deposited one solitary half-franc in the middle of that brown palm, and suggested that the boatman and he should toss up for the remaining four francs--or race for them--or play for them--or fight for them. The boatman, however, indignantly rejected each successive proposal, and, being paid at last, retired with a ***decrescendo*** of oaths.

"***Tiens!***" said Mueller, reflectively. "We have but one franc left. One franc, two sous, and a centime. ***Vive la France!***"

"And you have actually asked that wretched old woman and her niece to dinner!"

"And I have actually solicited that excellent and admirable woman, Madame Marotte, relict of the late lamented Jacques Marotte, umbrella maker, of number one hundred and two, Rue du Faubourg St. Denis, and her beautiful and accomplished niece, Mademoiselle Marie Charpentier, to honor us with their company this evening. ***Dis-donc,*** what shall we give them for dinner?"

"Precisely what you invited them to, I should guess--the fish we caught this afternoon."

"Agreed. And what else?"

"Say--a dish of invisible greens, and a phoenix ***a la Marengo***."

"You are funny, ***mon cher***."

"Then, for fear I should become too funny--good afternoon."

"What do you mean?"

"I mean that I have no mind to dine first, and be kicked out of doors afterwards. It is one of those aids to digestion that I can willingly dispense with."

"But if I guarantee that the dinner shall be paid for--money down!"

"Tra la la!"

"You don't believe me? Well, come and see."

With this, he went up to Madame Marotte, who, with her niece, had sat down on a bench under a walnut-tree close by, waiting our pleasure.

"Would not these ladies prefer to rest here, while we seek for a suitable restaurant and order the dinner?" said Mueller insinuatingly.

The old lady looked somewhat blank. She was not too tired to go on--thought it a pity to bring us all the way back again--would do, however, as "*ces messieurs*" pleased; and so was left sitting under the walnut-tree, reluctant and disconsolate.

"*Tiens! mon enfant*" I heard her say as we turned away, "suppose they don't come back again!"

We had promised to be gone not longer, than twenty minutes, or at most half an hour. Mueller led the way straight to the *Toison d' Or*.

I took him by the arm as we neared the gate.

"Steady, steady, *mon gaillard*" I said. "We don't order our dinner, you know, till we've found the money to pay for it."

"True--but suppose I go in here to look for it?"

"Into the restaurant garden?"

"Precisely."

CHAPTER XXVI.
THE PETIT COURIER ILLUSTRE.

THE *Toison d' Or* was but a modest little establishment as regarded the house, but it was surrounded on three sides by a good-sized garden overlooking the river. Here, in the trellised arbors which lined the lawn on either side, those customers who preferred the open air could take their dinners, coffees, and absinthes *al fresco*.

The scene when we arrived was at its gayest. There were dinners going on in every arbor; waiters running distractedly to and fro with trays and bottles; two women, one with a guitar, the other with a tamborine, singing under a tree in the middle of the garden; while in the air there reigned an exhilarating confusion of sounds and smells impossible to describe.

We went in. Mueller paused, looked round, captured a passing waiter, and asked for Monsieur le proprietaire. The waiter pointed over his shoulder towards the house, and breathlessly rushed on his way.

Mueller at once led the way into a salon on the ground-floor looking over the garden.

Here we found ourselves in a large low room containing some thirty or forty tables, and fitted up after the universal restaurant pattern, with cheap-looking glasses, rows of hooks, and spittoons in due number. The air was heavy with the combined smells of many dinners, and noisy with the clatter of many tongues. Behind the fruits, cigars, and liqueur bottles that decorated the *comptoir* sat a plump, black-eyed little woman in a gorgeous cap and a red silk dress. This lady welcomed us with a bewitching smile and a gracious inclination of the head.

"*Ces messieurs*," she said, "will find a vacant table yonder, by the window."

Mueller bowed majestically.

"Madame," he said, "I wish to see Monsieur le proprietaire."

The dame de comptoir looked very uneasy.

"If Monsieur has any complaint to make," she said, "he can make it to me."

"Madame, I have none."

"Or if it has reference to the ordering of a dinner...."

Mueller smiled loftily.

"Dinner, Madame," he said, with a disdainful gesture, "is but one of the accidents common to humanity. A trifle! A trifle always humiliating--sometimes inconvenient--occasionally impossible. No, Madame, mine is a serious mission; a mission of the highest importance, both socially and commercially. May I beg that you will have the goodness to place my card in the hands of Monsieur le proprietaire, and say that I request the honor of five minutes' interview."

The little woman's eyes had all this time been getting rounder and blacker. She was evidently confounded by my friend's grandiloquence.

"*Ah! mon Dieu! M'sieur*," she said, nervously, "my husband is in the kitchen. It is a busy day with us, you understand--but I will send for him."

And she forthwith despatched a waiter for "Monsieur Choucru."

Mueller seized me by the arm.

"Heavens!" he exclaimed, in a very audible aside, "did you hear? She is his wife! She is Madame Choucru?"

"Well, and what of that?"

"What of that, indeed? *Mais, mon ami*, how can you ask the question? Have you no eyes? Look at her! Such a remarkably handsome woman--such a *tournure*--such eyes--such a figure for an illustration! Only conceive the effect of Madame Choucru--in medallion!"

"Oh, magnificent!" I replied. "Magnificent--in medallion."

But I could not, for the life of me, imagine what he was driving at.

"And it would make the fortune of the *Toison d'Or*" he added, solemnly.

To which I replied that it would undoubtedly do so.

Monsieur Choucru now came upon the scene; a short, rosy, round-faced little man in a white flat cap and bibbed apron--like an elderly cherub that had taken to cookery. He hung back upon the threshold, wiping his forehead, and evidently unwilling to show himself in his shirt-sleeves.

"Here, **mon bon**," cried Madame, who was by this time crimson with gratified vanity, and in a fever of curiosity; "this way--the gentleman is waiting to speak to you!"

Monsieur, the cook and proprietor, shuffled his feet to and fro in the doorway, but came no nearer.

"*Parbleu*!" he said, "if M'sieur's business is not urgent."

"It is extremely urgent, Monsieur Choucru," replied Mueller; "and, moreover, it is not so much my business as it is yours,"

"Ah bah! if it is my business, then, it may stand over till to-morrow," replied the little man, impatiently. "To-day I have eighty dinners on hand, and with M'sieur's permission"....

But Mueller strode to the door and caught him by the shoulder.

"No, Monsieur Choucru," he said sternly, "I will not let you ruin yourself by putting off till to-morrow what can only be done to-day. I have come here, Monsieur Choucru, to offer you fame. Fame and fortune, Monsieur Choucru!--and I will not suffer you, for the sake of a few miserable dinners, to turn your back upon the most brilliant moment of your life!"

"*Mais, M'sieur*--explain yourself" ... stammered the proprietaire.

"You know who I am, Monsieur Choucru?"

"No, M'sieur--not in the least."

"I am Mueller--Franz Mueller--landscape painter, portrait painter, historical painter, caricaturist, artist **en chef** to the **Petit Courier Illustre**"

"*Hein! M'sieur est peintre*!"

"Yes, Monsieur Choucru--and I offer you my protection."

Monsieur Choucru scratched his ear, and smiled doubtfully.

"Now listen, Monsieur Choucru--I am here to-day in the interests of the **Petit Courier Illustre**. I take the Courbevoie fete for my subject. I sketch the river, the village, the principal features of the-scene; and on Saturday my designs are in the hands of all Paris. Do you understand me?"

"I understand that M'sieur is all this time talking to me of his own business, while mine, **la bas**, is standing still!" exclaimed the proprietaire, in an agony of impatience. "I have the honor to wish M'sieur good-day."

But Mueller seized him again, and would not let him escape.

"Not so fast, Monsieur Choucru," he said; "not so fast! Will you answer me one question before you go?"

"*Eh, mon Dieu*! Monsieur."

"Will you tell me, Monsieur Choucru, what is to prevent me from giving a view of the best restaurant in Courbevoie?"

Madame Choucru, from behind the *comptoir*, uttered a little scream.

"A design in the *Petit Courier Illustre*, I need scarcely tell you," pursued Mueller, with indescribable pomposity, "is in itself sufficient to make the fortune not only of an establishment, but of a neighborhood. I am about to make Courbevoie the fashion. The sun of Asnieres, of Montmorency, of Enghien has set--the sun of Courbevoie is about to rise. My sketches will produce an unheard-of effect. All Paris will throng to your fetes next Sunday and Monday--all Paris, with its inexhaustible appetite for *bifteck aux pommes frites*--all Paris with its unquenchable thirst for absinthe and Bavarian beer! Now, Monsieur Choucru, do you begin to understand me?"

"*Mais*, Monsieur, I--I think...."

"You think you do, Monsieur Choucru? Very good. Then will you please to answer me one more question. What is to prevent me from conferring fame, fortune, and other benefits too numerous to mention on your excellent neighbor at the corner of the Place--Monsieur Coquille of the Restaurant *Croix de Malte*?"

Monsieur Choucru scratched his ear again, stared helplessly at his wife, and said nothing. Madame looked grave.

"Are we to treat this matter on the footing of a business transaction, Monsieur!" she asked, somewhat sharply. "Because, if so, let Monsieur at once name his price for me...."

"'PRICE,' Madame!" interrupted Mueller, with a start of horror. "Gracious powers! this to me--to Franz Mueller of the *Petit Courier Illustre*! 'No, Madame--you mistake me--you wound me--you touch the honor of the Fine Arts! Madame, I am incapable of selling my patronage."

Madame clasped her hands; raised her voice; rolled her black eyes; did everything but burst into tears. She was shocked to have offended Monsieur! She was profoundly desolated! She implored a thousand pardons! And then, like a true French-woman of business, she brought back the conversation to the one important point:--since money was not in question, upon what consideration would Monsieur accord his preference to the ***Toison d' Or*** instead of to the ***Croix de Malte***?

Mueller bowed, laid his hand upon his heart, and said:--

"I will do it, ***pour les beaux yeux de Madame***."

And then, in graceful recognition of the little man's rights as owner of the eyes in question, he bowed to Monsieur Choucru.

Madame was inexpressibly charmed. Monsieur smiled, fidgeted, and cast longing glances towards the door.

"I have eighty dinners on hand," he began again, "and if M'sieur will excuse me...."

"One moment more, my dear Monsieur Choucru," said Mueller, slipping his hand affectionately through the little man's arm. "For myself, as I have already told you, I can accept nothing--but I am bound in honor not to neglect the interests of the journal I represent. You will of course wish to express your sense of the compliment paid to your house by adding your name to the subscription list of the ***Petit Courier Illustre***?"

"Oh, by--by all means--with pleasure," faltered the proprietaire.

"For how many copies, Monsieur Choucru? Shall we say--six?"

Monsieur looked at Madame. Madame nodded. Mueller took out his pocket-book, and waited, pencil in hand.

"Eh--***parbleu***!--let it be for six, then," said Monsieur Choucru, somewhat reluctantly.

Mueller made the entry, shut up the pocket-book, and shook hands boisterously with his victim.

"My dear Monsieur Choucru," he said, "I cannot tell you how gratifying this is to my feelings, or with what disinterested satisfaction I shall make your establishment known to the Parisian public. You shall be immortalized, my dear fellow--positively immortalized!"

"***Bien oblige, M'sieur--bien oblige***. Will you not let my wife offer you a glass of liqueure?"

"Liqueure, ***mon cher***!" exclaimed Mueller, with an outburst of frank cordiality--"hang liqueure!--WE'LL DINE WITH YOU!"

"Monsieur shall be heartily welcome to the best dinner the ***Toison d'Or*** can send up; and his friend also," said Madame, with her sweetest smile.

"Ah, Madame!"

"And M'sieur Choucru shall make you one of his famous cheese souffles. ***Tiens, mon bon***, go down and prepare a cheese souffle for two."

Mueller smote his forehead distractedly.

"For two!" he cried. "Heavens! I had forgotten my aunt and my cousin!"

Madame looked up inquiringly.

"Monsieur has forgotten something?"

"Two somethings, Madame--two somebodies! My aunt--my excellent and admirable maternal aunt,--and my cousin. We left them sitting under a tree by the river-side, more than half an hour ago. But the fault, Madame, is yours."

"How, Monsieur?"

"Yes; for in your charming society I forget the ties of family and the laws of politeness. But I hasten to fetch my forgotten relatives. With what pleasure they will share your amiable hospitality! ***Au revoir***, Madame. In ten minutes we shall be with you again!"

Madame Choucru looked grave. She had not bargained to entertain a party of four; yet she dared not disoblige the ***Petit Courier Illustre***. She had no time, however, to demur to the arrangement; for Mueller, ingeniously taking her acquiescence for granted, darted out of the room without waiting for an answer.

"Miserable man!" I exclaimed, as soon as we were outside the doors, "what will you do now?"

"Do! Why, fetch my admirable maternal aunt and my interesting cousin, to be sure."

"But you have raised a dinner under false pretences!"

"I, ***mon cher***? Not a bit of it."

"Have you, then, really anything to do with the ***Petit Courier Illustre***?"

"The Editor of the ***Petit Courier Illustre*** is one of the best fellows in the world, and occasionally (when my pockets represent that vacuum which Nature very properly abhors) he advances me a couple of Napoleons. I wipe out the score from time to time by furnishing a design for the paper. Now to-day, you see, I'm in luck. I shall pay off two obligations at once--to say nothing of Monsieur Choucru's six-fold subscription to the P.C., on which the publishers will allow me a douceur of thirty francs. Now, confess that I'm a man of genius!"

In less than a quarter of an hour we were all four established round one of Madame Choucru's comfortable little dining-tables, in a snug recess at the farthest end of the salon. Here, being well out of reach of our hostess's black eyes, Mueller assumed all the airs of a liberal entertainer. He hung up *ma cousine's* bonnet; fetched a footstool for *ma tante*; criticised the sauces; presided over the wine; cut jokes with the waiter; and pretended to have ordered every dish beforehand. The stewed kidneys with mushrooms were provided especially for Madame Marotte; the fricandeau was selected in honor of Mam'selle Marie (had he not an innate presentiment that she loved fricandeau?); and as for the soles *au gratin*, he swore, in defiance of probability and all the laws of nature, that they were the very fish we had just caught in the Seine. By-and-by came Monsieur Choucru's famous cheese *souffle*; and then, with a dish of fruit, four cups of coffee, and four glasses of liqueure, the banquet came to an end.

As we sat at desert, Mueller pulled out his book and pencilled a rapid but flattering sketch of the dining-room interior, developing a perspective as long as the Rue de Rivoli, and a *mobilier* at least equal in splendor to that of the *Trois Freres*.

At sight of this *chef d'oeuvre*, Madame Choucru was moved almost to tears. Ah, Heaven! if Monsieur could only figure to himself her admiration for his *beau talent*! But alas! that was impossible--as impossible as that Monsieur Choucru should ever repay this unheard-of obligation!

Mueller laid his hand upon his heart, and bowed profoundly.

"Ah! Madame," he said, "it is not to Monsieur Choucru that I look for repayment--it is to you."

"To me, Monsieur? *Dieu merci! Monsieur se moque de moi*!"

And the Dame de Comptoir, intrenched behind her fruits and liqueure bottles, shot a Parthian glance from under her black eye-lashes, and made believe to blush.

"Yes, Madame, to you. I only ask permission to come again very soon, for the purpose of executing a little portrait of Madame--a little portrait which, alas! *must* fail to render adequate justice to such a multitude of charms."

And with this choice compliment, Mueller bowed again, took his leave, bestowed a whole franc upon the astonished waiter, and departed from the *Toison d'Or* in an atmosphere of glory.

The fair, or rather that part of the fair where the dancers and diners most did congregate, was all ablaze with lights, and noisy with brass bands as we came out. *Ma tante*, who was somewhat tired, and had been dozing for the last half hour over her coffee and liqueure, was impatient to get back to Paris. The fair Marie, who was not tired at all, confessed that she should enjoy a waltz above everything. While Mueller, who professed to be an animated time-table, swore that we were just too late for the ten minutes past ten train, and that there would be no other before eleven forty-five. So Madame Marotte was carried off, *bon gre, mal gre*, to a dancing-booth, where gentlemen were admitted on payment of forty centimes per head, and ladies went in free.

Here, despite the noise, the dust, the braying of an abominable band, the overwhelming smell of lamp-oil, and the clatter, not only of heavy walking-boots, but even of several pairs of sabots upon an uneven floor of loosely-joined planks--*ma tante*, being disposed of in a safe corner, went soundly to sleep.

It was a large booth, somewhat over-full; and the company consisted mainly of Parisian blue blouses, little foot-soldiers, grisettes (for there were grisettes in those days, and plenty of them), with a sprinkling of farm-boys and dairy-maids from the villages round about. We found this select society caracoling round the booth in a thundering galop, on first going in. After the galop, the conductor announced a *valse a deux temps*. The band struck up--one--two--three. Away went some thirty couples--away went Mueller and the fair Marie--and away went the chronicler of this modest biography with a pretty little girl in green boots who waltzed remarkably well, and who deserted him in the middle of the dance for a hideous little French soldier about four feet and a half high.

After this rebuff (having learned, notwithstanding my friend's representations to the contrary, that a train ran from Courbevoie to Paris every half-hour up till midnight) I slipped away, leaving Mueller and *ma cousine* in the midst of a furious flirtation, and Madame Marotte fast asleep in her corner.

The clocks were just striking twelve as I passed under the archway leading to the Cite Bergere.

"*Tiens*!" said the fat concierge, as she gave me my key and my candle. "Monsieur has perhaps been to the theatre this evening? No!--to the country--to the fete at Courbevoie! Ah, then, I'll be sworn that M'sieur has had plenty of fun!"

But had I had plenty of fun? That was the question. That Mueller had had plenty of flirting and plenty of fun was a fact beyond the reach of doubt. But a flirtation, after all, unless in a one-act comedy, is not entertaining to the mere looker-on; and oh! must not those bridesmaids who sometimes accompany a happy couple in their wedding-tour, have a dreary time of it?

CHAPTER XXVII.
THE ECOLE DE NATATION.

It seemed to me that I had but just closed my eyes, when I was waked by a hand upon my shoulder, and a voice calling me by my name. I started up to find the early sunshine pouring in at the window, and Franz Mueller standing by my bedside.

"*Tiens*!" said he. "How lovely are the slumbers of innocence! I was hesitating, *mon cher*, whether to wake or sketch you."

I muttered something between a growl and a yawn, to the effect that I should have been better satisfied if he had left me alone.

"You prefer everything that is basely self-indulgent, young man," replied Mueller, making a divan of my bed, and coolly lighting his pipe under my very nose. "Contrary to all the laws of *bon-camaraderie*, you stole away last night, leaving your unprotected friend in the hands of the enemy. And for what?--for the sake of a few hours' ignominious oblivion! Look at me--I have not been to bed all night, and I am as lively as a lobster in a lobster-pot."

"How did you get home?" I asked, rubbing my eyes; "and when?"

"I have not got home at all yet," replied my visitor. "I have come to breakfast with you first."

Just at this moment, the *pendule* in the adjoining room struck six.

"To breakfast!" I repeated. "At this hour?--you who never breakfast before midday!"

"True, *mon cher*; but then you see there are reasons. In the first place, we danced a little too long, and missed the last train, so I was obliged to bring the dear creatures back to Paris in a fiacre. In the second place, the driver was drunk, and the horse was groggy, and the fiacre was in the last stage of dilapidation. The powers below only know how many hours we were on the road; for we all fell asleep, driver included, and never woke till we found ourselves at the Barriere de l'Etoile at the dawn of day."

"Then what have you done with Madame Marotte and Mademoiselle Marie?"

"Deposited them at their own door in the Rue du Faubourg St. Denis, as was the bounden duty of a ***preux chevalier***. But then, ***mon cher***, I had no money; and having no money, I couldn't pay for the fiacre; so I drove on here--and here I am--and number One Thousand and Eleven is now at the door, waiting to be paid."

"The deuce he is!"

"So you see, sad as it was to disturb the slumbers of innocence, I couldn't possibly let you go on sleeping at the rate of two francs an hour."

"And what is the rate at which you have waked me?"

"Sixteen francs the fare, and something for the driver--say twenty in all."

"Then, my dear fellow, just open my desk and take one of the two Napoleons you will see lying inside, and dismiss number One Thousand and Eleven without loss of time; and then...."

"A thousand thanks! And then what?"

"Will you accept a word of sound advice?"

"Depends on whether it's pleasant to follow, ***caro mio***"

"Go home; get three or four hours' rest; and meet me in the Palais Royal about twelve for breakfast."

"In order that you may turn round and go to sleep again in comfort? No, young man, I will do nothing of the kind. You shall get up, instead, and we'll go down to Molino's."

"To Molino's?"

"Yes--don't you know Molino's--the large swimming-school by the Pont Neuf. It's a glorious morning for a plunge in the Seine."

A plunge in the Seine! Now, given a warm bed, a chilly autumn morning, and a decided inclination to quote the words of the sluggard, and "slumber again," could any proposition be more inopportune, savage, and alarming? I shuddered; I protested; I resisted; but in vain.

"I shall be up again in less time than it will take you to tell your beads, ***mon*** *gaillard*' said Mueller the ferocious, as, having captured my Napoleon, he prepared to go down and liquidate with number One Thousand and Eleven. "And it's of no use to bolt me out, because I shall hammer away till you let me in, and that will wake your fellow-lodgers. So let me find you up, and ready for the fray."

And then, execrating Mueller, and Molino, and Molino's bath, and Molino's customers, and all Molino's ancestors from the period of the deluge downwards, I reluctantly complied.

The air was brisk, the sky cloudless, the sun coldly bright; and the city wore that strange, breathless, magical look so peculiar to Paris at early morning. The shops were closed; the pavements deserted; the busy thoroughfares silent as the avenues of Pere la Chaise. Yet how different from the early stillness of London! London, before the world is up and stirring, looks dead, and sullen, and melancholy; but Paris lies all beautiful, and bright, and mysterious, with a look as of dawning smiles upon her face; and we know that she will wake presently, like the Sleeping Beauty, to sudden joyousness and activity.

Our road lay for a little way along the Boulevards, then down the Rue Vivienne, and through the Palais Royal to the quays; but long ere we came within sight of the river this magical calm had begun to break up. The shop-boys in the Palais Royal were already taking down the shutters--the great book-stall at the end of the Galerie Vitree showed signs of wakefulness; and in the Place du Louvre there was already a detachment of brisk little foot-soldiers at drill. By the time we had reached the open line of the quays, the first omnibuses were on the road; the water-carriers were driving their carts and blowing their shrill little bugles; the washer-women, hard at work in their gay, oriental-looking floating kiosques, were hammering away, mallet in hand, and chattering like millions of magpies; and the early matin-bell was ringing to prayers as we passed the doors of St. Germain L'Auxerrois.

And now we were skirting the Quai de l'Ecole, looking down upon the bath known in those days as Molino's--a hugh, floating quadrangular structure, surrounded by trellised arcades and rows of dressing-rooms, with a divan, a cafe restaurant, and a permanent corps of cooks and hair-dressers on the establishment. For your true Parisian has ever been wedded to his Seine, as the Venetian to his Adriatic; and the Ecole de Natation was then, as now, a lounge, a reading-room, an adjunct of the clubs, and one of the great institutions of the capital.

Some bathers, earlier than ourselves, were already sauntering about the galleries in every variety of undress, from the simple *calecon* to the gaudiest version of Turkish robe and Algerian *kepi*. Some were smoking; some reading the morning papers; some chatting in little knots; but as yet, with the exception of two or three school-boys (called, in the *argot* of the bath, *moutards*), there were no swimmers in the water.

With some of these loungers Mueller exchanged a nod or a few words as we passed along the platform; but shook hands cordially with a bronzed, stalwart man, dressed like a Venetian gondolier in the frontispiece to a popular ballad, with white trousers, blue jacket, anchor buttons, red sash, gold ear-rings, and great silver buckles in his shoes. Mueller introduced this romantic-looking person to me as "Monsieur Barbet."

"My friend, Monsieur Barbet," said he, "is the prince of swimming-masters. He is more at home in the water than on land, and knows more about swimming than a fish. He will calculate you the specific gravity of the heaviest German metaphysician at a glance, and is capable of floating even the works of Monsieur Thiers, if put to the test."

"Monsieur can swim?" said the master, addressing me, with a nautical scrape.

"I think so," I replied.

"Many gentlemen think so," said Monsieur Barbet, "till they find themselves in the water."

"And many who wish to be thought accomplished swimmers never venture into it on that account," added Mueller. "You would scarcely suppose," he continued, turning to me, "that there are men here--regular *habitues* of the bath--who never go into the water, and yet give themselves all the airs of practised bathers. That tall man, for instance, with the black beard and striped *peignoir*, yonder--there's a fellow who comes once or twice a week all through the season, goes through the ceremony of undressing, smokes, gossips, criticises, is looked up to as an authority, and has never yet been seen off the platform. Then there's that bald man in the white robe--his name's Giroflet--a retired stockbroker. Well, that fellow robes himself like an ancient Roman, puts himself in classical attitudes, affects taciturnity, models himself upon Brutus, and all that sort of thing; but is as careful not to get his feet wet as a cat. Others, again, come simply to feed. The restaurant is one of the choicest in Paris, with this advantage over Vefour or the Trois Freres, that it is the only place where you may eat and drink of the best in hot weather, with nothing on but the briefest of ***calecons***"

Thus chattering, Mueller took me the tour of the bath, which now began to fill rapidly. We then took possession of two little dressing-rooms no bigger than sentry-boxes, and were presently in the water.

The scene now became very animated. Hundreds of eccentric figures crowded the galleries--some absurdly fat, some ludicrously thin; some old, some young; some bow-legged, some knock-kneed; some short, some tall; some brown, some yellow; some got up for effect in gorgeous wrappers; and all more or less hideous.

"An amusing sight, isn't it?" said Mueller, as, having swum several times round the bath, we sat down for a few moments on one of the flights of steps leading down to the water.

"It is a sight to disgust one for ever with human-kind," I replied.

"And to fill one with the profoundest respect for one's tailor. After all, it's broad-cloth makes the man."

"But these are not men--they are caricatures."

"Every man is a caricature of himself when you strip him," said Mueller, epi-grammatically. "Look at that scarecrow just opposite. He passes for an Adonis, ***de par le monde***."

I looked and recognised the Count de Rivarol, a tall young man, an ***elegant*** of the first water, a curled darling of society, a professed lady-killer, whom I had met many a time in attendance on Madame de Marignan. He now looked like a monkey:--

.... "long, and lank and brown,
As in the ribb'd sea sand!"

"Gracious heavens!" I exclaimed, "what would become of the world, if clothes went out of fashion?"

"Humph!--one half of us, my dear fellow, would commit suicide."

At the upper end of the bath was a semicircular platform somewhat loftier than the rest, called the Amphitheatre. This, I learned, was the place of honor.

Here clustered the *elite* of the swimmers; here they discussed the great principles of their art, and passed judgment on the performances of those less skilful than themselves. To the right of the Amphitheatre rose a slender spiral staircase, like an openwork pillar of iron, with a tiny circular platform on the top, half surrounded by a light iron rail. This conspicuous perch, like the pillar of St. Simeon Stylites, was every now and then surmounted by the gaunt figure of some ambitious plunger who, after attitudinizing awhile in the pose of Napoleon on the column Vendome, would join his hands above his head and take a tremendous "header" into the gulf below. When this feat was successfully performed, the *elite* in the Amphitheatre applauded graciously.

And now, what with swimming, and lounging, and looking on, some two hours had slipped by, and we were both hungry and tired, Mueller proposed that we should breakfast at the Cafe Procope.

"But why not here?" I asked, as a delicious breeze from the buffet came wafting by "like a steam of rich distilled perfumes."

"Because a breakfast *chez* Molino costs at least twenty-five francs per head-- BECAUSE I have credit at Procope--BECAUSE I have not a *sou* in my pocket--and BECAUSE, milord Smithfield, I aspire to the honor of entertaining your lordship on the present occasion!" replied Mueller, punctuating each clause of his sentence with a bow.

If Mueller had not a *sou*, I, at all events, had now only one Napoleon; so the Cafe Procope carried the day.

CHAPTER XXVIII.
THE RUE DE L'ANCIENNE COMEDIE AND THE CAFE PROCOPE.

The Rue des Fosses-Saint-Germain-des-Pres and the Rue de l'Ancienne Comedie are one and the same. As the Rue des Fosses-Saint-Germain-des-Pres, it dates back to somewhere about the reign of Philippe Auguste; and as the Rue de l'Ancienne Comedie it takes its name and fame from the year 1689, when the old Theatre Francais was opened on the 18th of April by the company known as Moliere's troupe--Moliere being then dead, and Lully having succeeded him at the Theatre du Palais Royal.

In the same year, 1689, one Francois Procope, a Sicilian, conceived the happy idea of hiring a house just opposite the new theatre, and there opening a public refreshment-room, which at once became famous, not only for the excellence of its coffee (then newly introduced into France), but also for being the favorite resort of all the wits, dramatists, and beaux of that brilliant time. Here the latest epigrams were circulated, the newest scandals discussed, the bitterest literary cabals set on foot. Here Jean Jacques brooded over his chocolate; and Voltaire drank his mixed with coffee; and Dorat wrote his love-letters to Mademoiselle Saunier; and Marmontel wrote praises of Mademoiselle Clairon; and the Marquis de Bievre made puns innumerable; and Duclos and Mercier wrote satires, now almost forgotten; and Piron recited those verses which are at once his shame and his fame; and the Chevalier de St. Georges gave fencing lessons to his literary friends; and Lamothe, Freron, D'Alembert, Diderot, Helvetius, and all that wonderful company of wits, philosophers, encyclopaedists, and poets, that lit up as with a dying glory the last decades of the old *regime*, met daily, nightly, to write, to recite, to squabble, to lampoon, and some times to fight.

The year 1770 beheld, in the closing of the Theatre Francais, the extinction of a great power in the Rue des Fosses-Saint-Germain-des-Pres--for it was not, in fact, till the theatre was no more a theatre that the street changed its name, and became the Rue de L'Ancienne Comedie. A new house (to be on first opening invested with the time-honored title of Theatre Francais, but afterwards to be known as the Odeon) was now in progress of erection in the close neighborhood of the Luxembourg. The actors, meanwhile, repaired to the little theatre of the Tuilleries. At length, in 1782,[2] the Rue de L'Ancienne Comedie was one evening awakened from its two years' lethargy by the echo of many footfalls, the glare of many flambeaux, and the rattle of many wheels; for all Paris, all the wits and critics of the Cafe Procope, all the fair shepherdesses and all the beaux seigneurs of the court of Marie Antoinette and Louis XVI., were hastening on foot, in chairs, and in chariots, to the opening of the new house and the performance of a new play! And what a play! Surely, not to consider it too curiously, a play which struck, however sportively, the key-note of the coming Revolution;--a play which, for the first time, displayed society literally in a state of ***bouleversement***;--a play in which the greed of the courtier, the venality of the judge, the empty glitter of the crown, were openly held up to scorn;--a play in which all the wit, audacity, and success are on the side of the ***canaille***;--a play in which a lady's-maid is the heroine, and a valet canes his master, and a great nobleman is tricked, outwitted, and covered with ridicule!

This play, produced for the first time under the title of ***La Folle Journee***, was written by one Caron de Beaumarchais--a man of wit, a man of letters, a man of the people, a man of nothing--and was destined to achieve immortality under its later title of ***Le Mariage de Figaro***.

A few years later, and the Rue de l'Ancienne Comedie echoed daily and nightly to the dull rumble of Revolutionary tumbrils, and the heavy tramp of Revolutionary mobs. Danton and Camille Desmoulins must have passed through it habitually on their way to the Revolutionary Tribunal. Charlotte Corday (and this is a matter of history) did pass through it that bright July evening, 1793, on her way to a certain gloomy house still to be seen in the adjoining Rue de l'Ecole de Medecine, where she stabbed Marat in his bath.

---

2   1782 is the date given by M. Hippolyte Lucas. Sainte-Beuve places it two years later.

But throughout every vicissitude of time and politics, though fashion deserted the Rue de l'Ancienne Comedie, and actors migrated, and fresh generations of wits and philosophers succeeded each other, the Cafe Procope still held its ground and maintained its ancient reputation. The theatre (closed in less than a century) became the studio first of Gros and then of Gerard, and was finally occupied by a succession of restaurateurs but the Cafe Procope remained the Cafe Procope, and is the Cafe Procope to this day.

The old street and all belonging to it--especially and peculiarly the Cafe Procope---was of the choicest Quartier Latin flavor in the time of which I write; in the pleasant, careless, impecunious days of my youth. A cheap and highly popular restaurateur named Pinson rented the old theatre. A ***costumier*** hung out wigs, and masks, and debardeur garments next door to the restaurateur. Where the fatal tumbril used to labor past, the frequent omnibus now rattled gayly by; and the pavements trodden of old by Voltaire, and Beaumarchais, and Charlotte Corday, were thronged by a merry tide of students and grisettes. Meanwhile the Cafe Procope, though no longer the resort of great wits and famous philosophers, received within its hospitable doors, and nourished with its indifferent refreshments, many a now celebrated author, painter, barrister, and statesman. It was the general rendezvous for students of all kinds--poets of the Ecole de Droit, philosophers of the Ecole de Medecine, critics of the Ecole des Beaux Arts. It must however be admitted that the poetry and criticism of these future great men was somewhat too liberally perfumed with tobacco, and that into their systems of philosophy there entered a considerable element of grisette.

Such, at the time of my first introduction to it, was the famous Cafe Procope.

CHAPTER XXIX.
THE PHILOSOPHY OF BREAKFAST.

Now this, *mon cher*," said Mueller, taking off his hat with a flourish to the young lady at the *comptoir*, "is the immortal Cafe Procope."

I looked round, and found myself in a dingy, ordinary sort of Cafe, in no wise differing from any other dingy, ordinary sort of Cafe in that part of Paris. The decorations were ugly enough to be modern. The ceiling was as black with gas-fumes and tobacco smoke as any other ceiling in any other estaminet in the Quartier Latin. The waiters looked as waiters always look before midday-- sleepy, discontented, and unwashed. A few young men of the regular student type were scattered about here and there at various tables, reading, smoking, chatting, breakfasting, and reading the morning papers. In an alcove at the upper end of the second room (for there were two, one opening from the other) stood a blackened, broken-nosed, plaster bust of Voltaire, upon the summit of whose august wig some irreverent customer had perched a particularly rakish-looking hat. Just in front of this alcove and below the bust stood a marble-topped table, at one end of which two young men were playing dominoes to the accompaniment of the matutinal absinthe.

"And this," said Mueller, with another flourish, "is the still more immortal table of the still more supremely immortal Voltaire. Here he was wont to rest his sublime elbows and sip his *demi-tasse*. Here, upon this very table, he wrote that famous letter to Marie Antoinette that Freron stole, and in revenge for which he wrote the comedy called *l'Ecossaise*; but of this admirable satire you English, who only know Voltaire in his Henriade and his history of Charles the Twelfth, have probably never heard till this moment! *Eh bien*! I'm not much wiser than you--so never mind. I'll be hanged if I've ever read a line of it. Anyhow, here is the table, and at this other end of it we'll have our breakfast."

It was a large, old-fashioned, Louis Quatorze piece of furniture, the top of which, formed from a single slab of some kind of gray and yellow marble, was stained all over with the coffee, wine, and ink-splashes of many generations of customers. It looked as old--nay, older--than the house itself.

The young men who were playing at dominoes looked up and nodded, as three or four others had done in the outer room when we passed through.

"*Bonjour, l'ami*," said the one who seemed to be winning. "Hast thou chanced to see anything of Martial, coming along!"

"I observed a nose defiling round the corner of the Rue de Bussy," replied Mueller, "and it looked as if Martial might be somewhere in the far distance, but I didn't wait to see. Are you expecting him?"

"Confound him--yes! We've been waiting more than half an hour."

"If you have invited him to breakfast," said Mueller, "he is sure to come."

"On the contrary, he has invited us to breakfast."

"Ah, that alters the case," said Mueller, philosophically. "Then he is sure *not* to come." "Garcon!"

A bullet-headed, short-jacketed, long-aproned waiter, who looked as if he had not been to bed since his early youth, answered the summons,

"M'sieur!"

"What have you that you can especially recommend this morning?"

The waiter, with that nasal volubility peculiar to his race, rapidly ran over the whole vegetable and animal creation.

Mueller listened with polite incredulity.

"Nothing else?" said he, when the other stopped, apparently from want of breath.

"*Mais oui, M'sieur*!" and, thus stimulated, the waiter, having "exhausted worlds and then imagined new," launched forth into a second and still more impossible catalogue.

Mueller turned to me.

"The resources of this establishment, you observe," he said, very gravely, "are inexhaustible. One might have a Roc's egg a la Sindbad for the asking."

The waiter looked puzzled, shuffled his slippered feet, and murmured something about "*oeufs sur le plat*."

"Unfortunately, however," continued Mueller, "we are but men--not fortresses provisioning for a siege. Antoine, *mon enfant*, we know thee to be a fellow of incontestible veracity, and thy list is magnificent; but we will be content with a *vol-au-vent* of fish, a *bifteck aux pommes frites*, an *omelette sucree*, and a bottle of thy 1840 Bordeaux with the yellow seal. Now vanish!"

The waiter, wearing an expression of intense relief, vanished accordingly.

Meanwhile more students had come in, and more kept coming. Hats and caps cropped up rapidly wherever there were pegs to hang them on, and the talking became fast and furious.

I soon found that everybody knew everybody at the Cafe Procope, and that the specialty of the establishment was dominoes--just as the specialty of the Cafe de la Regence is chess. There were games going on before long at almost every table, and groups of lookers-on gathered about those who enjoyed the reputation of being skilful players.

Gradually breakfast after breakfast emerged from some mysterious nether world known only to the waiters, and the war of dominoes languished.

"These are all students, of course," I said presently, "and yet, though I meet a couple of hundred fellows at our hospital lectures, I don't see a face I know."

"You would find some by this time, I dare say, in the other room," replied Mueller. "I brought you in here that you might sit at Voltaire's table, and eat your steak under the shadow of Voltaire's bust; but this salon is chiefly frequented by law-students--the other by medical and art students. Your place, *mon cher*, as well as mine, is in the outer sanctuary."

"That infernal Martial!" groaned one of the domino-players at the other end of the table. "So ends the seventh game, and here we are still. *Parbleu!* Horace, hasn't that absinthe given you an inconvenient amount of appetite?"

"Alas! my friend--don't mention it. And when the absinthe is paid for, I haven't a sou."

"My own case precisely. What's to be done?"

"Done!" echoed Horace, pathetically. "Shade of Apicius! inspire me...but, no--he's not listening."

"Hold! I have it. We'll make our wills in one another's favor, and die."

"I should prefer to die when the wind is due East, and the moon at the full," said Horace, contemplatively.

"True--besides, there is still *la mere* Gaudissart. Her cutlets are tough, but her heart is tender. She would not surely refuse to add one more breakfast to the score!"

Horace shook his head with an air of great despondency.

"There was but one Job," said he, "and he has been dead some time. The patience of *la mere* Gaudissart has long since been entirely exhausted."

"I am not so sure of that. One might appeal to her feelings, you know--have a presentiment of early death--wipe away a tear... Bah! it is worth the effort, anyhow."

"It is a forlorn hope, my dear fellow, but, as you say, it is worth the effort. *Allons donc!* to the storming of *la mere* Gaudissart!"

And with this they pushed aside the dominoes, took down their hats, nodded to Mueller, and went out.

"There go two of the brightest fellows and most improvident scamps in the whole Quartier," said my companion. "They are both studying for the bar; both under age; both younger sons of good families; and both destined, if I am not much mistaken, to rise to eminence by-and-by. Horace writes for *Figaro* and the *Petit Journal pour Rire*--Theophile does *feuilleton* work--romances, chit-chat, and political squibs--rubbish, of course; but clever rubbish, and wonderful when one considers what boys they both are, and what dissipated lives they lead. The amount of impecuniosity those fellows get through in the course of a term is something inconceivable. They have often only one decent suit between them--and sometimes not that. To-day, you see, they are at their wits' end for a breakfast. They have run their credit dry at Procope and everywhere else, and are gone now to a miserable little den in the Rue du Paon, kept by a fat good-natured old soul called *la mere* Gaudissart. She will perhaps take compassion on their youth and inexperience, and let them have six sous worth of horsebeef soup, stale bread, and the day before yesterday's vegetables. Nay, don't look so pitiful! We poor devils of the Student Quartier hug our Bohemian life, and exalt it above every other. When we have money, we cannot find windows enough out of which to fling it--when we have none, we start upon *la chasse au diner*, and enjoy the pleasures of the chase. We revel in the extremes of fasting and feasting, and scarcely know which we prefer."

"I think your friends Horace and Theophile are tolerably clear as to which **they** prefer," I remarked, with a smile.

"Bah! they would die of **ennui** if they had always enough to eat! Think how it sharpens a man's wits if--given the time, the place, and the appetite--he has every day to find the credit for his dinners! Show me a mathematical problem to compare with it as a popular educator of youth!"

"But for young men of genius, like Horace and Theophile..."

"Make yourself quite easy, **mon cher**. A little privation will do them no kind of harm. They belong to that class of whom it has been said that 'they would borrow money from Harpagon, and find truffles on the raft of the Medusa.' But hold! we are at the end of our breakfast. What say you? Shall we take our **demi-tasse** in the next room, among our fellow-students of physic and the fine arts?"

CHAPTER XXX.
A MAN WITH A HISTORY.

The society of the outer salon differed essentially from the society of the inner salon at the Cafe Procope. It was noisier--it was shabbier--it was smokier. The conversation in the inner salon was of a general character on the whole, and, as one caught sentences of it here and there, seemed for the most part to relate to the literature and news of the day--to the last important paper in the Revue des Deux Mondes, to the new drama at the Odeon, or to the article on foreign politics in the *Journal des Debats*. But in the outer salon the talk was to the last degree shoppy, and overflowed with the argot of the studios. Some few medical students were clustered, it is true, in a corner near the door; but they were so outnumbered by the artists at the upper end of the room, that these latter seemed to hold complete possession, and behaved more like the members of a recognised club than the casual customers of a cafe. They talked from table to table. They called the waiters by their Christian names. They swaggered up and down the middle of the room with their hats on their heads, their hands in their pockets, and their pipes in their mouths, as coolly as if it were the broad walk of the Luxembourg gardens.

And the appearance of these gentlemen was not less remarkable than their deportment. Their hair, their beards, their clothes, were of the wildest devising. They seemed one and all to have started from a central idea, that central idea being to look as unlike their fellow-men as possible; and thence to have diverged into a variety that was nothing short of infinite. Each man had evidently modelled himself upon his own ideal, and no two ideals were alike. Some were picturesque, some were grotesque; and some, it must be admitted, were rather dirty ideals, into the realization of which no such paltry considerations as those of soap, water, or brushes were permitted to enter.

Here, for instance, were Roundhead crops and flowing locks of Cavalier re-dundancy--steeple-crowned hats, and Roman cloaks draped bandit-fashion--moustachios frizzed and brushed up the wrong way in the style of Louis XIV.--pointed beards and slouched hats, after the manner of Vandyke---patriarchal beards *a la Barbarossa*--open collars, smooth chins, and long undulating locks of the Raffaelle type--coats, blouses, paletots of inconceivable cut, and all kinds of unusual colors--in a word, every eccentricity of clothing, short of fancy costume, in which it was practicable for men of the nineteenth century to walk abroad and meet the light of day.

We had no sooner entered this salon, taken possession of a vacant table, and called for coffee, than my companion was beset by a storm of greetings.

"Hola! Mueller, where hast thou been hiding these last few centuries, *mon gaillard?*"

"*Tiens!* Mueller risen from the dead!"

"What news from *la bas,* old fellow?"

To all which ingenious pleasantries my companion replied in kind--introducing me at the same time to two or three of the nearest speakers. One of these, a dark young man got up in the style of a Byzantine Christ, with straight hair parted down the middle, a bifurcated beard, and a bare throat, was called Eugene Droz. Another--big, burly, warm-complexioned, with bright open blue eyes, curling reddish beard and moustache, slouched hat, black velvet blouse, immaculate linen, and an abundance of rings, chains, and ornaments--was made up in excellent imitation of the well-known portrait of Rubens. This gentleman's name, as I presently learned, was Caesar de Lepany.

When we came in, these two young men, Droz and De Lepany, were discussing, in enthusiastic but somewhat unintelligible language, the merits of a certain Monsieur Lemonnier, of whom, although till that moment ignorant of his name and fame, I at once perceived that he must be some celebrated *chef de cuisine*.

"He will never surpass that last thing of his," said the Byzantine youth. "Heavens! How smooth it is! How buttery! How pulpy!"

"Ay--and yet with all that lusciousness of quality, he never wants piquancy," added De Lepany.

"I think his greens are apt to be a little raw," interposed Mueller, taking part in the conversation.

"Raw!" echoed the first speaker, indignantly. "*Eh, mon Dieu!* What can you be thinking of! They are almost too hot!"

"But they were not so always, Eugene," said he of the Rubens make-up, with an air of reluctant candor. "It must be admitted that Lemonnier's greens used formerly to be a trifle--just a trifle--raw. Evidently Monsieur Mueller does not know how much he has taken to warming them up of late. Even now, perhaps, his olives are a little cold."

"But then, how juicy his oranges are!" exclaimed young Byzantine.

"True--and when you remember that he never washes--!"

"Ah, *sacredie!* yes--there is the marvel!"

And Monsieur Eugene Droz held up his hands and eyes with all the reverent admiration of a true believer for a particularly dirty dervish.

"Who, in Heaven's name, is this unclean individual who used to like his vegetables underdone, and never washes?" whispered I in Mueller's ear.

"What--Lemonnier! You don't mean to say you never heard of Lemonnier?"

"Never, till now. Is he a cook?"

Mueller gave me a dig in the ribs that took my breath away.

"*Goguenard!*" said he. "Lemonnier's an artist--the foremost man of the water-color school. But I wouldn't be too funny if I were you. Suppose you were to burst your jocular vein--there'd be a catastrophe!"

Meanwhile the conversation of Messieurs Droz and Lepany had taken a fresh turn, and attracted a little circle of listeners, among whom I observed an eccentric-looking young man with a club-foot, an enormously long neck, and a head of short, stiff, dusty hair, like the bristles of a blacking-brush.

"Queroulet!" said Lepany, with a contemptuous flourish of his pipe. "Who spoke of Queroulet? Bah!--a miserable plodder, destitute of ideality--a fellow who paints only what he sees, and sees only what is commonplace--a dull, narrow-souled, un-imaginative handicraftsman, to whom a tree is just a tree; and a man, a man; and a straw, a straw, and nothing more!"

"That's a very low-souled view to take of art, no doubt," croaked in a grating treble voice the youth with the club-foot; "but if trees and men and straws are not exactly trees and men and straws, and are not to be represented as trees and men and straws, may I inquire what else they are, and how they are to be pictorially treated?"

"They must be ideally treated, Monsieur Valentin," replied Lepany, majestically.

"No doubt; but what will they be like when they are ideally treated? Will they still, to the vulgar eye, be recognisable for trees and men and straws?"

"I should scarcely have supposed that Monsieur Valentin would jest upon such a subject as a canon of the art he professes," said Lepany, becoming more and more dignified.

"I am not jesting," croaked Monsieur Valentin; "but when I hear men of your school talk so much about the Ideal, I (as a realist) always want to know what they themselves understand by the phrase."

"Are you asking me for my definition of the Ideal, Monsieur Valentin?"

"Well, if it's not giving you too much trouble--yes."

Lepany, who evidently relished every chance of showing off, fell into a picturesque attitude and prepared to hold forth. Valentin winked at one or two of his own clique, and lit a cigar.

"You ask me," began Lepany, "to define the Ideal--in other words, to define the indefinite, which alas! whether from a metaphysical, a philosophical, or an aesthetic point of view, is a task transcending immeasurably my circumscribed powers of expression."

"Gracious heavens!" whispered Mueller in my ear. "He must have been reared from infancy on words of five syllables!"

"What shall I say?" pursued Lepany. "Shall I say that the Ideal is, as it were, the Real distilled and sublimated in the alembic of the imagination? Shall I say that the Ideal is an image projected by the soul of genius upon the background of the universe? That it is that dazzling, that unimaginable, that incommunicable goal towards which the suns in their orbits, the stars in their courses, the spheres with all their harmonies, have been chaotically tending since time began! Ideal, say you? Call it ideal, soul, mind, matter, art, eternity,... what are they all but words? What are words but the weak strivings of the fettered soul that fain would soar to those empyrean heights where Truth, and Art, and Beauty are one and indivisible? Shall

I say all this..."

"My dear fellow, you have said it already--you needn't say it again," inter-rupted Valentin.

"Ay; but having said it--having expressed myself, perchance with some obscu-rity...."

"With the obscurity of Erebus!" said, very deliberately, a fat student in a blouse.

"Monsieur!" exclaimed De Lepany, measuring the length and breadth of the fat student with a glance of withering scorn.

The Byzantine was no less indignant.

"Don't heed them, **mon ami**!" he cried, enthusiastically. "Thy definition is sublime-eloquent!"

"Nay," said Valentin, "we concede that Monsieur de Lepany is sublime; we recognise with admiration that he is eloquent; but we submit that he is wholly un-intelligible."

And having delivered this parting shot, the club-footed realist slipped his arm through the arm of the fat student, and went off to a distant table and a game at dominoes.

Then followed an outburst of offended idealism. His own clique crowded round Lepany as the champion of their school. They shook hands with him. They embraced him. They fooled him to the top of his bent. Presently, being not only as good-natured as he was conceited, but (rare phenomenon in the Quartier Latin!) a rich fellow into the bargain, De Lepany called for champagne and treated his admir-ers all around.

In the midst of the chatter and bustle which this incident occasioned, a pale, earnest-looking man of about five-and-thirty, coming past our table on his way out of the Cafe, touched Mueller on the arm, bent down, and said quietly:--

"Mueller, will you do me a favor!"

"A hundred, Monsieur," replied my companion; half rising, and with an air of unusual respect and alacrity.

"Thanks, one will be enough. Do you see that man yonder, sitting alone in the corner, with his back to the light?"

"I do."

"Good--don't look at him again, for fear of attracting his attention. I have been trying for the last half hour to get a sketch of his head, but I think he suspected me. Anyhow he moved so often, and so hid his face with his hands and the newspaper, that I was completely baffled. Now it is a remarkable head--just the head I have been wanting for my Marshal Romero--and if, with your rapid pencil and your skill in seizing expression, you could manage this for me...."

"I will do my best," said Mueller.

"A thousand thanks. I will go now; for when I am gone he will be off his guard. You will find me in the den up to three o'clock. Adieu."

Saying which, the stranger passed on, and went out.

"That's Flandrin!" said Mueller.

"Really?" I said. "Flandrin! And you know him?"

But in truth I only answered thus to cover my own ignorance; for I knew little at that time of modern French art, and I had never even heard the name of Flandrin before.

"Know him!" echoed Mueller. "I should think so. Why, I worked in his studio for nearly two years."

And then he explained to me that this great painter (great even then, though as yet appreciated only in certain choice Parisian circles, and not known out of France) was at work upon a grand historical subject connected with the Spanish persecutions in the Netherlands--the execution of Egmont and Horn, in short, in the great square before the Hotel de Ville in Brussels.

"But the main point now," said Mueller, "is to get the sketch--and how? Confound the fellow! while he keeps his back to the light and his head down like that, the thing is impossible. Anyhow I can't do it without an accomplice. You must help me."

"I! What can I do?"

"Go and sit near him--speak to him--make him look up--keep him, if possible, for a few minutes in conversation--nothing easier."

"Nothing easier, perhaps, if I were you; but, being only myself, few things more difficult!"

"Nevertheless, my dear boy, you must try, and at once. Hey --presto!--away!"

Placed where we were, the stranger was not likely to have observed us; for we had come into the room from behind the corner in which he was sitting, and had taken our places at a table which he could not have seen without shifting his own position. So, thus peremptorily commanded, I rose; slipped quietly back into the inner salon, made a pretext of looking at the clock over the door; and came out again, as if alone and looking for a vacant seat.

The table at which he had placed himself was very small--only just big enough to stand in a corner and hold a plate and a coffee-cup; but it was supposed to be large enough for two, and there were evidently two chairs belonging to it. On one of these, being alone, the stranger had placed his overcoat and a small black bag. I at once saw and seized my opportunity.

"Pardon, Monsieur," I said, very civilly, "will you permit me to hang these things up?"

He looked up, frowned, and said abruptly:--

"Why, Monsieur?"

"That I may occupy this chair."

He glanced round; saw that there was really no other vacant; swept off the bag and coat with his own hands; hung them on a peg overhead; dropped back into his former attitude, and went on reading.

"I regret to have given you the trouble, Monsieur," I said, hoping to pave the way to a conversation.

But a little quick, impatient movement of the hand was his only reply. He did not even raise his head. He did not even lift his eyes from the paper.

I called for a demi-tasse and a cigar; then took out a note-book and pencil, assumed an air of profound abstraction, and affected to become absorbed in calculations.

In the meanwhile, I could not resist furtively observing the appearance of this man whom a great artist had selected as his model for one of the darkest characters of mediaeval history.

He was rather below than above the middle height; spare and sinewy; square in the shoulders and deep in the chest; with close-clipped hair and beard; grizzled moustache; high cheek-bones; stern impassive features, sharply cut; and deep-set restless eyes, quick and glancing as the eyes of a monkey. His face, throat, and hands were sunburnt to a deep copper-color, as if cast in bronze. His age might have been from forty-five to fifty. He wore a thread-bare frock-coat buttoned to the chin; a stiff black stock revealing no glimpse of shirt-collar; a well-worn hat pulled low over his eyes; and trousers of dark blue cloth, worn very white and shiny at the knees, and strapped tightly down over a pair of much-mended boots.

The more I looked at him, the less I was surprised that Flandrin should have been struck by his appearance. There was an air of stern poverty and iron resolution about the man that arrested one's attention at first sight. The words "*ancien militaire*" were written in every furrow of his face; in every seam and on every button of his shabby clothing. That he had seen service, missed promotion, suffered unmerited neglect (or, it might be, merited disgrace), seemed also not unlikely.

Watching him as he sat, half turned away, half hidden by the newspaper he was reading, one elbow resting on the table, one brown, sinewy hand supporting his chin and partly concealing his mouth, I told myself that here, at all events, was a man with a history--perhaps with a very dark history. What were the secrets of his past? What had he done? What had he endured? I would give much to know.

My coffee and cigar being brought, I asked for the *Figaro*, and holding the paper somewhat between the stranger and myself, watched him with increasing interest.

I now began to suspect that he was less interested in his own newspaper than he appeared to be, and that his profound abstraction, like my own, was assumed. An indefinable something in the turn of his head seemed to tell me that his attention was divided between whatever might be going forward in the room and what he was reading. I cannot describe what that something was; but it gave me the impression that he was always listening. When the outer door opened or shut, he stirred uneasily, and once or twice looked sharply round to see what new-comer entered the cafe. Was he anxiously expecting some one who did not come? Or was he dreading the appearance of some one whom he wished to avoid? Might he not be a political refugee? Might he not be a spy?

"There is nothing of interest in the papers to-day, Monsieur," said, making another effort to force him into conversation.

He affected not to hear me.

I drew my chair a little nearer, and repeated the observation.

He frowned impatiently, and without looking up, replied:--

"*Eh, mon Dieu*, Monsieur!--when there is a dearth of news!"

"There need not, even so, be a dearth of wit. *Figaro* is as heavy to-day as a government leader in the *Moniteur*."

He shrugged his shoulders and moved slightly round, apparently to get a better light upon what he was reading, but in reality to turn still more away from me. The gesture of avoidance was so marked, that with the best will in the world, it would have been impossible for me to address him again. I therefore relapsed into silence.

Presently I saw a sudden change flash over him.

Now, in turning away from myself, he had faced round towards a narrow looking-glass panel which reflected part of the opposite side of the room; and chancing, I suppose, to lift his eyes from the paper, he had seen something that arrested his attention. His head was still bent; but I could see that his eyes were riveted upon the mirror. There was alertness in the tightening of his hand before his mouth--in the suspension of his breathing.

Then he rose abruptly, brushed past me as if I were not there, and crossed to where Mueller, sketch-book in hand, was in the very act of taking his portrait.

I jumped up, almost involuntarily, and followed him. Mueller, with an unsuccessful effort to conceal his confusion, thrust the book into his pocket.

"Monsieur," said the stranger, in a low, resolute voice, "I protest against what you have been doing. You have no right to take my likeness without my permission."

"Pardon, Monsieur, I--I beg to assure you--" stammered Mueller.

"That you intended no offence? I am willing to suppose so. Give me up the sketch, and I am content."

"Give up the sketch!" echoed Mueller.

"Precisely, Monsieur."

"Nay--but if, as an artist, I have observed that which leads me to desire a--a memorandum--let us say of the pose and contour of a certain head," replied Mueller, recovering his self-possession, "it is not likely that I shall be disposed to part from my memorandum."

"How, Monsieur! you refuse?"

"I am infinitely sorry, but--"

"But you refuse?"

"I certainly cannot comply with Monsieur's request."

The stranger, for all his bronzing, grew pale with rage.

"Do not compel me, Monsieur, to say what I must think of your conduct, if you persist in this determination," he said fiercely.

Mueller smiled, but made no reply.

"You absolutely refuse to yield up the sketch?"

"Absolutely."

"Then, Monsieur, *c'est une infamie--et vous etes un lache*!"

But the last word had scarcely hissed past his lips before Mueller dashed his coffee dregs full in the stranger's face.

In one second, the table was upset--blows were exchanged--Mueller, pinned against the wall with his adversary's hands upon his throat, was striking out with the desperation of a man whose strength is overmatched--and the whole room was in a tumult.

In vain I attempted to fling myself between them. In vain the waiters rushed to and fro, imploring "ces Messieurs" to interpose. In vain a stout man pushed his way through the bystanders, exclaiming angrily:--

"Desist, Messieurs! Desist, in the name of the law! I am the proprietor of this establishment--I forbid this brawling--I will have you both arrested! Messieurs, do you hear?"

Suddenly the flush of rage faded out of Mueller's face. He gasped--became livid. Lepany, Droz, myself, and one or two others, flew at the stranger and dragged him forcibly back.

"Assassin!" I cried, "would you murder him?"

He flung us off, as a baited bull flings off a pack of curs. For myself, though I received only a backhanded blow on the chest, I staggered as if I had been struck with a sledgehammer.

Mueller, half-fainting, dropped into a chair.

There was a tramp and clatter at the door--a swaying and parting of the crowd.

"Here are the sergents de ville!" cried a trembling waiter.

"He attacked me first," gasped Mueller. "He has half strangled me."

"*Qu'est ce que ca me fait*!" shouted the enraged proprietor. "You are a couple of *canaille*! You have made a scandal in my Cafe. Sergents, arrest both these gentlemen!"

The police--there were two of them, with their big cocked hats on their heads and their long sabres by their sides--pushed through the circle of spectators. The first laid his hand on Mueller's shoulder; the second was about to lay his hand on mine, but I drew back.

"Which is the other?" said he, looking round.

"*Sacredie*!" stammered the proprietor, "he was here--there--not a moment ago!"

"*Diable*!" said the sergent de ville, stroking his moustache, and staring fiercely about him. "Did no one see him go?"

There was a chorus of exclamations--a rush to the inner salon--to the door--to the street. But the stranger was nowhere in sight; and, which was still more incomprehensible, no one had seen him go!

"*Mais, mon Dieu*!" exclaimed the proprietor, mopping his head and face violently with his pocket-handkerchief, "was the man a ghost, that he should vanish into the air?"

"*Parbleu*! a ghost with muscles of iron," said Mueller. "Talk of the strength of a madman--he has the strength of a whole lunatic asylum!"

"He gave me a most confounded blow in the ribs, anyhow!" said Lepany.

"And nearly broke my arm," added Eugene Droz.

"And has given me a pain in my chest for a week," said I, in chorus.

"If he wasn't a ghost," observed the fat student sententiously, "he must certainly be the devil."

The sergents de ville grinned.

"Do we, then, arrest this gentleman?" asked the taller and bigger of the two, his hand still upon my friend's shoulder.

But Mueller laughed and shook his head.

"What!" said he, "arrest a man for resisting the devil? Nonsense, *mes amis*, you ought to canonize me. What says Monsieur le proprietaire?"

Monsieur the proprietor smiled.

"I am willing to let the matter drop," he replied, "on the understanding that Monsieur Mueller was not really the first offender."

"*Foi d'honneur*! He insulted me--I threw some coffee in his face--he flung himself upon me like a tiger, and almost choked me, as all here witnessed. And for what? Because I did him the honor to make a rough pencilling of his ugly face ... ***Mille tonnerres***!--the fellow has stolen my sketch-book!"

CHAPTER XXXI.
FANCIES ABOUT FACES.

The sketch-book was undoubtedly gone, and the stranger had undoubtedly taken it. How he took it, and how he vanished, remained a mystery. The aspect of affairs, meanwhile, was materially changed. Mueller no longer stood in the position of a leniently-treated offender. He had become accuser, and plaintiff. A grave breach of the law had been committed, and he was the victim of a bold and skilful *tour de main*.

The police shook their heads, twirled their moustaches, and looked wise.

It was a case of premeditated assault--in short, of robbery with violence. It must be inquired into--reported, of course, at head-quarters, without loss of time. Would Monsieur be pleased to describe the stolen sketch-book? An oblong, green volume, secured by an elastic band; contains sketches in pencil and water-colors; value uncertain--Good. And the accused ... would Monsieur also be pleased to describe the person of the accused? His probable age, for instance; his height; the color of his hair, eyes, and beard? Good again. Lastly, Monsieur's own name and address, exactly and in full. *Tres-bon.* It might, perhaps, be necessary for Monsieur to enter a formal deposition to-morrow morning at the Prefecture of Police, in which case due notice would be given.

Whereupon he who seemed to be chief of the twain, having entered Mueller's replies in a greasy pocket-book of stupendous dimensions, which he seemed to wear like a cuirass under the breast of his uniform, proceeded to interrogate the proprietor and waiters.

Was the accused an habitual frequenter of the cafe?--No. Did they remember ever to have seen him there before?--No. Should they recognise him if they saw him again? To this question the answers were doubtful. One waiter thought he should recognise the man; another was not sure; and Monsieur the proprietor admitted that he had himself been too angry to observe anything or anybody very minutely.

Finally, having made themselves of as much importance and asked as many questions as possible, the sergents de ville condescended to accept a couple of petits verres a-piece, and then, with much lifting of cocked hats and clattering of sabres, departed.

Most of the students had ere this dropped off by twos and threes, and were gone to their day's work, or pleasure--to return again in equal force about five in the afternoon. Of those that remained, some five or six came up when the police were gone, and began chatting about the robbery. When they learned that Flandrin had desired to have a sketch of the man's head; when Mueller described his features, and I his obstinate reserve and semi-military air, their excitement knew no bounds. Each had immediately his own conjecture to offer. He was a political spy, and therefore fearful lest his portrait should be recognised. He was a conspirator of the Fieschi school. He was Mazzini in person.

In the midst of the discussion, a sudden recollection flashed upon me.

"A clue! a clue!" I shouted triumphantly. "He left his coat and black bag hanging up in the corner!"

Followed by the others, I ran to the spot where I had been sitting before the affray began. But my exultation was shortlived. Coat and bag, like their owner, had disappeared.

Mueller thrust his hands into his pockets, shook his head, and whistled dismally.

"I shall never see my sketch-book again, **parbleu!**" said he. "The man who could not only take it out of my breast-pocket, but also in the very teeth of the police, secure his property and escape unseen, is a master of his profession. Our friends in the cocked hats have no chance against him."

"And Flandrin, who is expecting the sketch," said I; "what of him?"

Mueller shrugged his shoulders.

"Next to being beaten," growled he, "there's nothing I hate like confessing it. However, it has to be done--so the sooner the better. Would you like to come with me? You'll see his studio."

I was only too glad to accompany him; for to me, as to most of us, there was ever a nameless charm in the picturesque litter of an artist's studio. Mueller's own studio, however, was as yet the only one I had seen. He laughed when I said this.

"If your only notion of a studio is derived from that specimen," said he, "you will be agreeably surprised by the contrast. He calls his place a 'den,' but that's a metaphor. Mine is a howling wilderness."

Arriving presently at a large house at the bottom of a courtyard in the Rue Vaugirard, he knocked at a small side-door bearing a tiny brass plate not much larger than a visiting-card, on which was engraved--"Monsieur Flandrin."

The door opened by some invisible means from within, and we entered a passage dimly lighted by a painted glass door at the farther end. My companion led the way down this passage, through the door, and into a small garden containing some three or four old trees, a rustic seat, a sun-dial on an antique-looking fragment of a broken column, and a little weed-grown pond about the size of an ordinary drawing-room table, surrounded by artificial rock-work.

At the farther extremity of this garden, filling the whole space from wall to wall, and occupying as much ground as must have been equal to half the original enclosure, stood a large, new, windowless building, in shape exactly like a barn, lighted from a huge skylight in the roof, and entered by a small door in one corner. I did not need to be told that this was the studio.

But if the outside was like a barn, the inside was like a beautiful mediaeval interior by Cattermole--an interior abounding in rich and costly detail; in heavy crimson draperies, precious old Italian cabinets, damascened armor, carved chairs with upright backs and twisted legs, old paintings in massive Florentine frames, and strange quaint pieces of Elizabethan furniture, like buffets, with open shelves full of rare and artistic things--bronzes, ivory carvings, unwieldy Majolica jars, and lovely goblets of antique Venetian glass laced with spiral ornaments of blue and crimson and that dark emerald green of which the secret is now lost for ever.

Then, besides all these things, there were great folios leaning piled against the walls, one over the other; and Persian rugs of many colors lying here and there about the floor; and down in one corner I observed a heap of little models, useful, no doubt, as accessories in pictures--gondolas, frigates, foreign-looking carts, a tiny sedan chair, and the like.

But the main interest of the scene concentrated itself in the unfinished picture, the hired model (a brawny fellow in a close-fitting suit of black, leaning on a huge two-handed sword), and the artist in his holland blouse, with the palette and brushes in his hand.

It was a very large picture, and stood on a monster easel, somewhat towards the end of the studio. The light from above poured full upon the canvas, while beyond lay a background of shadow. Much of the subject was as yet only indicated, but enough was already there to tell the tragic story and display the power of the painter. There, high above the heads of the mounted guards and the assembled spectators, rose the scaffold, hung with black. Egmont, wearing a crimson tabard, a short black cloak embroidered with gold, and a hat ornamented with black and white plumes, stood in a haughty attitude, as if facing the square and the people. Two other figures, apparently of an ecclesiastic and a Spanish general, partly in outline, partly laid in with flat color, were placed to the right of the principal character. The headsman stood behind, leaning upon his sword. The slender spire of the Hotel de Ville, surmounted by its gilded archangel glittering in the morning sun, rose high against a sky of cloudless blue; while all around was seen the well-known square with its sculptured gables and decorated facades--every roof, window, and balcony crowded with spectators.

Unfinished though it was, I saw at once that I was brought face to face with what would some day be a famous work of art. The figures were grandly grouped; the heads were noble; the sky was full of air; the action of the whole scene informed with life and motion.

I stood admiring and silent, while Mueller told his tale, and Flandrin paused in his work to listen.

"It is horribly unlucky," said he. "I had not been able to find a portrait of Romero and, *faute de mieux*, have been trying for days past to invent the right sort of head for him--of course, without success. You never saw such a heap of failures! But as for that man at the cafe, if Providence had especially created him for my purpose, he could not have answered it better."

"I believe I am as sorry as you can possibly be," said Mueller.

"Then you are very sorry indeed," replied the painter; and he looked even more disappointment than he expressed.

"I'm afraid I can't do it," said Mueller, after a moment's silence; "but if you'll give me a pencil and a piece of paper, and credit me with the will in default of the deed, I will try to sketch the head from memory."

"Ah? if you can only do that! Here is a drawing block--choose what pencils you prefer--or here are crayons, if you like them better."

Mueller took the pencils and block, perched himself on the corner of a table, and began. Flandrin, breathless with expectation, looked over his shoulder. Even the model (in the grim character of Egmont's executioner) laid aside his two-handed sword, and came round for a peep.

"Bravo! that's just his nose and brow," said Flandrin, as Mueller's rapid hand flew over the paper. "Yes--the likeness comes with every touch ... and the eyes, so keen and furtive. ... Nay, that eyelid should be a little more depressed at the corner.... Yes, yes--just so. Admirable! There!--don't attempt to work it up. The least thing might mar the likeness. My dear fellow, what a service you have rendered me!"

"*Quatre-vingt mille diables*!" ejaculated the model, his eyes riveted upon the sketch.

Mueller laughed and looked.

"*Tiens*! Guichet," said he, "is that meant for a compliment?"

"Where did you see him?" asked the model, pointing down at the sketch.

"Why? Do you know him?"

"Where did you see him, I say?" repeated Guichet, impatiently.

He was a rough fellow, and garnished every other sentence with an oath; but he did not mean to be uncivil.

"At the Cafe Procope."

"When?"

"About an hour ago. But again, I repeat--do you know him?"

"Do I know him? *Tonnerre de Dieu*!"

"Then who and what is he?"

The model stroked his beard; shook his head; declined to answer.

"Bah!" said he, gloomily, "I may have seen him, or I may be mistaken. 'Tis not my affair."

"I suspect Guichet knows something against this interesting stranger," laughed Flandrin. "Come, Guichet, out with it! We are among friends."

But Guichet again looked at the drawing, and again shook his head.

"I'm no judge of pictures, messieurs," said he. "I'm only a poor devil of a model. How can I pretend to know a man from such a ***griffonage*** as that?"

And, taking up his big sword again, he retreated to his former post over against the picture. We all saw that he was resolved to say no more.

Flandrin, delighted with Mueller's sketch, put it, with many thanks and praises, carefully away in one of the great folios against the wall.

"You have no idea, ***mon cher*** Mueller," he said, "of what value it is to me. I was in despair about the thing till I saw that fellow this morning in the Cafe; and he looked as if he had stepped out of the Middle Ages on purpose for me. It is quite a mediaeval face--if you know what I mean by a mediaeval face."

"I think I do," said Mueller. "You mean that there was a moyen-age type, as there was a classical type, and as there is a modern type."

"Just so; and therein lies the main difficulty that we historical painters have to encounter. When we cannot find portraits of our characters, we are driven to invent faces for them--and who can invent what he never sees? Invention must be based on some kind of experience; and to study old portraits is not enough for our purpose, except we frankly make use of them as portraits. We cannot generalize upon them, so as to resuscitate a vanished type."

"But then has it really vanished?" said Mueller. "And how can we know for certain that the mediaeval type did actually differ from the type we see before us every day?"

"By simple and direct proof--by studying the epochs of portrait painting. Take Holbein's heads, for instance. Were not the people of his time grimmer, harder-visaged, altogether more unbeautiful than the people of ours? Take Petitot's and Sir Peter Lely's. Can you doubt that the characteristics of their period were entirely different? Do you suppose that either race would look as we look, if resuscitated and clothed in the fashion of to-day?"

"I am not at all sure that we should observe any difference," said Mueller, doubtfully.

"And I feel sure we should observe the greatest," replied Flandrin, striding up and down the studio, and speaking with great animation. "I believe, as regards the men and women of Holbein's time, that their faces were more lined than ours; their eyes, as a rule, smaller--their mouths wider--their eyebrows more scanty--their ears larger--their figures more ungainly. And in like manner, I believe the men and women of the seventeenth century to have been more fleshy than either Holbein's people or ourselves; to have had rounder cheeks, eyes more prominent and heavy-lidded, shorter noses, more prominent chins, and lips of a fuller and more voluptuous mould."

"Still we can't be certain how much of all this may be owing to the mere mannerisms of successive schools of art," urged Mueller, sticking manfully to his own opinion. "Where will you find a more decided mannerist than Holbein? And because he was the first portrait-painter of his day, was he not reproduced with all his faults of literalness and dryness by a legion of imitators? So with Sir Peter Lely, with Petitot, with Vandyck, with every great artist who painted kings and queens and court beauties. Then, again, a certain style of beauty becomes the rage, and-a skilful painter flatters each fair sitter in turn by bringing up her features, or her expression, or the color of her hair, as near as possible to the fashionable standard. And further, there is the dress of a period to be taken into account. Think of the family likeness that pervades the flowing wigs of the courts of Louis Quatorze and Charles the Second--see what powder did a hundred years ago to equalize mankind."

Flandrin shook his head.

"Ingenious, ***mon garcon***" said he; "ingenious, but unsound The cut of a fair lady's bodice never yet altered the shape of her nose; neither was it the fashion of their furred surtouts that made Erasmus and Sir Thomas More as like as twins. What you call the 'mannerism' of Holbein is only his way of looking at his fellow-creatures. He and Sir Antonio More were the most faithful of portrait-painters. They didn't know how to flatter. They painted exactly what they saw--no more, and no less; so that every head they have left us is a chapter in the history of the Middle Ages. The race--depend on't--the race was unbeautiful; and not even the picturesque dress of the period (which, according to your theory, should have helped to make the wearers of it more attractive) could soften one jot of their plainness."

"I can't bring myself to believe that we were all so ugly--French, English, and Germans alike--only a couple of centuries ago," said Mueller.

"That is to say, you prefer to believe that Holbein, and Lucas Cranach, and Sir Antonio More, and all their school, were mannerists. Nonsense, my dear fellow--

nonsense! *It is Nature who is the mannerist*. She loves to turn out a certain generation after a particular pattern; and when she is tired of that pattern, she invents another. Her fancies last, on the average about, a hundred years. Sometimes she changes the type quite abruptly; sometimes modifies it by gentle, yet always perceptible, degrees. And who shall say what her secret processes are? Education, travel, intermarriage with foreigners, the introduction of new kinds of food) the adoption of new habits, may each and all have something to do with these successive changes; but of one point at least we may be certain--and that is, that we painters are not responsible for her caprices. Our mission is to interpret Dame Nature more or less faithfully, according to our powers; but beyond interpretation we cannot go. And now (for you know I am as full of speculations as an experimental philosopher) I will tell you another conclusion I have come to with regard to this subject; and that is that national types were less distinctive in mediaeval times than in ours. The French, English, Flemish, and Dutch of the Middle Ages, as we see them in their portraits, are curiously alike in all outward characteristics. The courtiers of Francis the First and their (James, and the lords and ladies of the court of Henry the Eighth, resemble each other as people of one nation. Their features are, as it were, cast in one mould. So also with the courts of Louis Quatorze and Charles the Second. As for the regular French face of to-day, with its broad cheek-bones and high temples running far up into the hair on either side, that type does not make its appearance till close upon the advent of the Reign of Terror. But enough! I shall weary you with theories, and wear out the patience of our friend Guichet, who is sufficiently tired already with waiting for a head that never comes to be cut off as it ought. Adieu--adieu. Come soon again, and see how I get on with Marshal Romero."

Thus dismissed, we took our leave and left the painter to his work.

"An extraordinary man!" said Mueller, as we passed out again through the neglected garden and paused for a moment to look at some half-dozen fat gold and silver fish that were swimming lazily about the little pond. "A man made up of contradictions--abounding in energy, yet at the same time the dreamiest of speculators. An original thinker, too; but wanting that basis which alone makes original thinking of any permanent value."

"But," said I, "he is evidently an educated man."

"Yes--educated as most artists are educated; but Flandrin has as strong a bent for science as for art, and deserved something better. Five years at a German university would have made of him one of the most remarkable men of his time. What did you think of his theory of faces?"

"I know nothing of the subject, and cannot form a judgment; but it sounded as if it might be true."

"Yes--just that. It may be true, and it may not. If true, then for my own part I should like to pursue his theory a step further, and trace the operation of these secret processes by means of which I am, happily, such a much better-looking fellow than my great-great-great-great-grandfather of two hundred years ago. What, for instance, has the introduction of the potato done for the noses of mankind?"

Chatting thus, we walked back as far as the corner of the Rue Racine, where we parted; I to attend a lecture at the Ecole de Medecine, and Mueller to go home to his studio in the Rue Clovis.

CHAPTER XXXII.
RETURNED WITH THANKS.

A week or two had thus gone by since the dreadful evening at the Opera Comique, and all this time I had neither seen nor heard more of the fair Josephine. My acquaintance with Franz Mueller and the life of the Quartier Latin had, on the contrary, progressed rapidly. Just as the affair of the Opera had dealt a final blow to my romance *a la grisette* on the one hand, so had the excursion to Courbevoie, the visit to the Ecole de Natation, and the adventure of the Cafe Procope, fostered my intimacy with the artist on the other. We were both young, somewhat short of money, and brimful of fun. Each, too, had a certain substratum of earnestness underlying the mere surface-gayety of his character. Mueller was enthusiastic for art; I for poetry; and both for liberty. I fear, when I look back upon them, that we talked a deal of nonsense about Brutus, and the Rights of Man, and the noble savage, and all that sort of thing, in those hot-headed days of our youth. It was a form of political measles that the young men of that time were quite as liable to as the young men of our own; and, living as we then were in the heart of the most revolutionary city in Europe, I do not well see how we could have escaped the infection. Mueller (who took it worse than I did, and was very rabid indeed when I first knew him) belonged just then not only to the honorable brotherhood of Les Chicards, but also to a small debating club that met twice a week in a private room at the back of an obscure Estaminet in the Rue de la Harpe. The members of this club were mostly art-students, and some, like himself, Chicards--generous, turbulent, high-spirited boys, with more enthusiasm than brains, and a flow of words wholly out of proportion to the bulk of their ideas. As I came to know him more intimately, I used sometimes to go there with Mueller, after our cheap dinner in the Quartier and our evening stroll along the Boulevards or the

Champs Elysees; and I am bound to admit that I never, before or since, heard quite so much nonsense of the declamatory sort as on those memorable occasions. I did not think it nonsense then, however. I admired it with all my heart; applauded the nursery eloquence of these sucking Mirabeaus and Camille Desmoulins as frantically as their own vanity could desire; and was even secretly chagrined that my own French was not yet fluent enough to enable me to take part in their discussions.

In the meanwhile, my debts were paid; and, having dropped out of society when I fell out of love with Madame de Marignan, I no longer overspent my allowance. I bought no more bouquets, paid for no more opera-stalls, and hired no more prancing steeds at seven francs the hour. I bade adieu to picture-galleries, flower-shows, morning concerts, dress boots, white kid gloves, elaborate shirt-fronts, and all the vanities of the fashionable world. In a word, I renounced the Faubourg St. Germain for the Quartier Latin, and applied myself to such work and such pleasures as pertained to the locality. If, after a long day at Dr. Cheron's, or the Hotel Dieu, or the Ecole de Medecine, I did waste a few hours now and then, I, at least, wasted them cheaply. Cheaply, but oh, so pleasantly! Ah me! those nights at the debating club, those evenings at the Chicards, those student's balls at the Chaumiere, those third-class trips to Versailles and Fontainebleau, those one-franc pit seats at the Gaiete and the Palais Royal, those little suppers at Pompon's and Flicoteau's--how delightful they were! How joyous! How free from care! And even when we made up a party and treated the ladies (for to treat the ladies is *de rigueur* in the code of Quartier Latin etiquette), how little it still cost, and what a world of merriment we had for the money!

It was well for me, too, and a source of much inward satisfaction, that my love-affair with Mademoiselle Josephine had faded and died a natural death. We never made up that quarrel of the Opera Comique, and I had not desired that we should make it up. On the contrary, I was exceedingly glad of the opportunity of withdrawing my attentions; so I wrote her a polite little note, in which I expressed my regret that our tastes were so dissimilar and our paths in life so far apart; wished her every happiness; assured her that I should ever remember her with friendly regard; and signed my name with a tremendous flourish at the bottom of the second page. With the note, however, I sent her a raised pie and a red and green shawl, of which I begged her acceptance in token of amity; and as neither of those gifts was returned, I concluded that she ate the one and wore the other, and that there was peace between us.

But the scales of fortune as they go up for one, go down for another. This man's luck is balanced by that man's ruin--Orestes falls sick, and Pylades returns from Kissingen cured of his lumbago--old Croesus dies, and little Miss Kilmansegg comes into the world with a golden spoon in her mouth, So it fell out with Franz Mueller and myself. As I happily steered clear of Charybdis, he drifted into Scylla--in other words, just as I recovered from my second attack of the tender passion, he caught the epidemic and fancied himself in love with the fair Marie.

I say "fancied," because his way of falling in love was so unlike my way, that I could scarcely believe it to be the same complaint. It affected neither his appetite, nor his spirits, nor his wardrobe. He made as many puns and smoked as many pipes as usual. He did not even buy a new hat. If, in fact, he had not told me himself, I should never have guessed that anything whatever was the matter with him.

It came out one day when he was pressing me to go with him to a certain tea-party at Madame Marotte's, in the Rue St. Denis.

"You see," said he, "it is *la petite* Marie's fete; and the party's in her honor; and they'd be so proud if we both went to it; and--and, upon my soul, I'm awfully fond of that little girl"....

"Of Marie Marotte?"

He nodded.

"You are not serious," I said.

"I am as serious," he replied, "as a dancing dervish."

And then, for I suppose I looked incredulous, he went on to justify himself.

"She's very good," he said, "and very pretty. Quite a Madonna face, to my thinking."

"You may see a dozen such Madonna faces among the nurses in the Luxembourg Gardens, every afternoon of your life," said I.

"Oh, if you come to that, every woman is like every other woman, up to a certain point."

"*Les femmes se suivent et se ressemblent toujours*," said I, parodying a well-known apothegm.

"Precisely, but then they wear their rue, or cause you to wear yours, 'with a difference.' This girl, however, escapes the monotony of her sex by one or two peculiarities:--she has not a bit of art about her, nor a shred of coquetry. She is as simple and as straightforward as an Arcadian. She doesn't even know when she is being made love to, or understand what you mean, when you pay her a compliment."

"Then she's a phenomenon--and what man in his senses would fall in love with a phenomenon?"

"Every man, ***mon cher enfant***, who falls in love at all! The woman we worship is always a phenomenon, whether of beauty, or grace, or virtue--till we find her out; and then, probably, she becomes a phenomenon of deceit, or slovenliness, or bad temper! And now, to return to the point we started from--will you go with me to Madame Marotte's tea-party to-morrow evening at eight? Don't say 'No,' there's a good fellow."

"I'll certainly not say No, if you particularly want me to say Yes," I replied, "but--"

"Prythee, no buts! Let it be Yes, and the thing is settled. So--here we are. Won't you come in and smoke a pipe with me? I've a bottle of capital Rhenish in the cupboard."

We had met near the Odeon, and, as our roads lay in the same direction, had gone on walking and talking till we came to Mueller's own door in the Rue Clovis. I accepted the invitation, and followed him in. The ***portiere***, a sour-looking, bent old woman with a very dirty duster tied about her head, hobbled out from her little dark den at the foot of the stairs, and handed him the key of his apartment.

"***Tiens***!" said she, "wait a moment--there's a parcel for you, M'sieur Mueller."

And so, hobbling back again, she brought out a small flat brown paper-packet sealed at both ends.

"Ah, I see--from the Emperor!" said Mueller. "Did he bring it himself, Madame Duphot, or did he send it by the Archbishop of Paris?"

A faint grin flitted over the little old woman's withered face.

"Get along with you, M'sieur Mueller," she said. "You're always playing the ***farceur***! The parcel was brought by a man who looked like a stonemason."

"And nobody has called?"

"Nobody, except M'sieur Richard."

"Monsieur Richard's visits are always gratifying and delightful--may the *diable* fly away with him!" said Mueller. "What did dear Monsieur Richard want to-day, Madame Duphot?"

"He wanted to see you, and the third-floor gentleman also--about the rent."

"Dear Richard! What an admirable memory he has for dates! Did he leave any message, Madame Duphot?"

The old woman looked at me, and hesitated.

"He says, M'sieur Mueller--he says ..."

"Nay, this gentleman is a friend--you may speak out. What does our beloved and respected *proprietaire* say, Madame Duphot?"

"He says, if you don't both of you pay up the arrears by midday on Sunday next, he'll seize your goods, and turn you into the street."

"Ah, I always said he was the nicest man I knew!" observed Mueller, gravely. "Anything else, Madame Duphot?"

"Only this, Monsieur Mueller--that if you didn't go quietly, he'd take your windows out of the frames and your doors off the hinges."

"*Comment*! He bade you give me that message, the miserable old son of a spider! *Quatre-vingt mille plats de diables aux truffes*! Take my windows out of the frames, indeed! Let him try, Madame Duphot--that's all--let him try!"

And with this, Mueller, in a towering rage, led the way upstairs, muttering volleys of the most extraordinary and eccentric oaths of his own invention, and leaving the little old *portiere* grinning maliciously in the hall.

"But can't you pay him?" said I.

"Whether I can, or can't, it seems I must," he replied, kicking open the door of his studio as viciously as if it were the corporeal frame of Monsieur Richard. "The only question is--how? At the present moment, I haven't five francs in the till."

"Nor have I more than twenty. How much is it?"

"A hundred and sixty--worse luck!"

"Haven't the Tapottes paid for any of their ancestors yet?"

"Confound it!--yes; they've paid for a Marshal of France and a Farmer General, which are all I've yet finished and sent home. But there was the washerwoman, and the *traiteur*, and the artist's colorman, and, *enfin*, the devil to pay--and the money's gone, somehow!"

"I've only just cleared myself from a lot of debts," I said, ruefully, "and I daren't ask either my father or Dr. Cheron for an advance just at present. What is to be done?"

"Oh, I don't know. I must raise the money somehow. I must sell something--there's my copy of Titian's 'Pietro Aretino.' It's worth eighty francs, if only for a sign. And there's a Madonna and Child after Andrea del Sarto, worth a fortune to any enterprising sage-femme with artistic proclivities. I'll try what Nebuchadnezzar will do for me."

"And who, in the name of all that's Israelitish, is Nebuchadnezzar?"

"Nebuchadnezzar, my dear Arbuthnot, is a worthy Shylock of my acquaintance--a gentleman well known to Bohemia--one who buys and sells whatever is purchasable and saleable on the face of the globe, from a ship of war to a comic paragraph in the *Charivari*. He deals in bric-a-brac, sermons, government sinecures, pugs, false hair, light literature, patent medicines, and the fine arts. He lives in the Place des Victoires. Would you like to be introduced to him?"

"Immensely."

"Well, then, be here by eight to-morrow morning, and I'll take you with me. After nine he goes out, or is only visible to buyers. Here's my bottle of Rhenish--genuine Assmanshauser. Are you hungry?"

I admitted that I was not unconscious of a sensation akin to appetite.

He gazed steadfastly into the cupboard, and shook his head.

"A box of sardines," he said, gloomily, "nearly empty. Half a loaf, evidently disinterred from Pompeii. An inch of Lyons sausage, saved from the ark; the remains of a bottle of fish sauce, and a pot of currant jelly. What will you have?"

I decided for the relics of Pompeii and the deluge, and we sat down to discuss those curious delicacies. Having no corkscrew, we knocked off the neck of the bottle, and being short of glasses, drank our wine out of teacups.

"But you have never opened your parcel all this time," I said presently. "It may be full of *billets de banque*--who can tell?"

"That's true," said Mueller; and broke the seals.

"By all the Gods of Olympus!" he shouted, holding up a small oblong volume bound in dark green cloth. "My sketch-book!"

He opened it, and a slip of paper fell out. On this slip of paper were written, in a very neat, small hand, the words, "***Returned with thanks***;" but the page that contained the sketch made in the Cafe Procope was missing.

CHAPTER XXXIII.
AN EVENING PARTY AMONG
THE PETIT-BOURGEOISIE.

Madame Marotte, as I have already mentioned more than once, lived in the Rue du Faubourg St. Denis; which, as all the world knows, is a prolongation of the Rue St. Denis--just as the Rue St. Denis was, in my time, a transpontine continuation of the old Rue de la Harpe. Beginning at the Place du Chatelet as the Rue St. Denis, opening at its farther end on the Boulevart St. Denis and passing under the triumphal arch of Louis le Grand (called the Porte St. Denis), it there becomes first the Rue du Faubourg St. Denis, and then the interminable Grande Route du St. Denis which drags its slow length along all the way to the famous Abbey outside Paris.

The Rue du Faubourg St. Denis is a changed street now, and widens out, prim, white, and glittering, towards the new barrier and the new Rond Point. But in the dear old days of which I tell, it was the sloppiest, worst-paved, worst-lighted, noisiest, narrowest, and most crowded of all the great Paris thoroughfares north of the Seine. All the country traffic from Chantilly and Compiegne came lumbering this way into the city; diligences, omnibuses, wagons, fiacres, water-carts, and all kinds of vehicles thronged and blocked the street perpetually; and the sound of wheels ceased neither by night nor by day. The foot-pavements of the Rue du Faubourg St. Denis, too, were always muddy, be the weather what it might; and the gutters were always full of stagnant pools. An ever-changing, never-failing stream of rustics from the country, workpeople from the factories of the *banlieu*, grisettes, commercial travellers, porters, commissionaires, and *gamins* of all ages here flowed to and fro. Itinerant venders of cakes, lemonade, cocoa, chickweed, *allumettes*, pin-cushions, six-bladed penknives, and never-pointed pencils filled the air with their cries, and made both day and night hideous. You could not walk a dozen yards at any time without falling down a yawning cellar-trap, or being run over by a porter with a huge load upon his head, or getting splashed from head to foot by the sudden pulling-up of some cart in the gutter beside you.

It was among the peculiarities of the Rue du Faubourg St. Denis that everybody was always in a hurry, and that nobody was ever seen to look in at the shop-windows. The shops, indeed, might as well have had no windows, since there were no loungers to profit by them. Every house, nevertheless, was a shop, and every shop had its window. These windows, however, were for the most part of that kind before which the passer-by rarely cares to linger; for the commerce of the Rue du Faubourg St. Denis was of that steady, unpretending, money-making sort that despises mere shop-front attractions. Grocers, stationers, corn-chandlers, printers, cutlers, leather-sellers, and such other inelegant trades, here most did congregate; and to the wearied wayfarer toiling along the dead level of this dreary pave, it was quite a relief to come upon even an artistically-arranged *Magasin de Charcuterie*, with its rows of glazed tongues, mighty Lyons sausages, yellow *terrines* of Strasbourg pies, fantastically shaped pickle-jars, and pyramids of silvery sardine boxes.

It was at number One Hundred and Two in this agreeable thoroughfare that my friend's innamorata resided with her maternal aunt, the worthy relict of Monsieur Jacques Marotte, umbrella-maker, deceased. Thither, accordingly, we wended our miry way, Mueller and I, after dining together at one of our accustomed haunts on the evening following the events related in my last chapter. The day had been dull and drizzly, and the evening had turned out duller and more drizzly still. We had not had rain for some time, and the weather had been (as it often is in Paris in October) oppressively hot; and now that the rain had come, it did not seem to cool the air at all, but rather to load it with vapors, and make the heat less endurable than before.

Having toiled all the way up from the Rue de la Harpe on the farther bank of the Seine, and having forded the passage of the Arch of Louis le Grand, we were very wet and muddy indeed, very much out of breath, and very melancholy objects to behold.

"It's dreadful to think of going into any house in this condition, Mueller," said

I, glancing down ruefully at the state of my boots, and having just received a copious spattering of mud all down the left side of my person. "What is to be done?"

"We've only to go to a boot-cleaning and brushing-up shop," replied Mueller. "There's sure to be one close by somewhere."

"A boot-cleaning and brushing-up shop!" I echoed.

"What--didn't you know there were lots of them, all over Paris? Have you never noticed places that look like shops, with ground glass windows instead of shop-fronts, on which are painted up the words, '*cirage des bottes?*'"

"Never, that I can remember."

"Then be grateful to me for a piece of very useful information! Suppose we turn down this by-street--it's mostly to the seclusion of by-streets and passages that our bashful sex retires to renovate its boots and its broadcloth."

I followed him, and in the course of a few minutes we found the sort of place of which we were in search. It consisted of one large, long room, like a shop without goods, counters, or shelves. A single narrow bench ran all round the walls, raised on a sort of wooden platform about three feet in width and three feet from the ground. Seated upon this bench, somewhat uncomfortably, as it seemed, with their backs against the wall, sat some ten or a dozen men and boys, each with an attendant shoeblack kneeling before him, brushing away vigorously. Two or three other customers, standing up in the middle of the shop, like horses in the hands of the groom, were having their coats brushed instead of their boots. Of those present, some looked like young shopmen, some were of the *ouvrier* class, and one or two looked like respectable small tradesmen and fathers of families. The younger men were evidently smartening up for an hour or two at some cheap ball or Cafe-Concert, now that the warehouse was closed, and the day's work was over.

Our boots being presently brought up to the highest degree of polish, and our garments cleansed of every disfiguring speck, we paid a few sous apiece and turned out again into the streets. Happily, we had not far to go. A short cut brought us into the midst of the Rue de Faubourg St. Denis, and within a few yards of a gloomy-looking little shop with the words "*Veuve Marotte*" painted up over the window, and a huge red and white umbrella dangling over the door. A small boy in a shiny black apron was at that moment putting up the shutters; the windows of the front room over the shop were brightly lit from within; and a little old gentleman in goloshes and a large blue cloak with a curly collar, was just going in at the private door. We meekly followed him, and hung up our hats and overcoats, as he did, in the passage.

"After you, Messieurs," said the little old gentleman, skipping politely back, and flourishing his hand in the direction of the stairs. "After you!"

We protested vehemently against this arrangement, and fought quite a skirmish of civilities at the foot of the stairs.

"I am at home here, Messieurs," said the little old gentleman, who, now that he was divested of hat, cloak, and goloshes, appeared in a flaxen *toupet*, an antiquated blue coat with brass buttons, a profusely frilled shirt, and low-cut shoes with silver buckles. "I am an old friend of the family--a friend of fifty years. I hold myself privileged to do the honors, Messieurs;--a friend of fifty years may claim to have his privileges."

With this he smirked, bowed, and backed against the wall, so that we were obliged to precede him. When we reached the landing, however, he (being evidently an old gentleman of uncommon politeness and agility) sprang forward, held open the door for us, and insisted on ushering us in.

It was a narrow, long-shaped room, the size of the shop, with two windows looking upon the street; a tiny square of carpet in the middle of the floor; boards highly waxed and polished; a tea-table squeezed up in one corner; a somewhat ancient-looking, spindle-legged cottage piano behind the door; a mirror and an ornamental clock over the mantelpiece; and a few French lithographs, colored in imitation of crayon drawings, hanging against the walls.

Madame Marotte, very deaf and fussy, in a cap with white ribbons, came forward to receive us. Mademoiselle Marie, sitting between two other young women of her own age, hung her head, and took no notice of our arrival.

The rest of the party consisted of a gentleman and two old ladies. The gentleman (a plump, black-whiskered elderly Cupid, with a vast expanse of shirt-front like an immense white ace of hearts, and a rose in his button-hole) was standing on the hearth-rug in a graceful attitude, with one hand resting on his hip, and the other under his coat-tails. Of the two old ladies, who seemed as if expressly created by nature to serve as foils to one another, one was very fat and rosy, in a red silk gown and a kind of black velvet hat trimmed with white marabout feathers and

Roman pearls; while the other was tall, gaunt, and pale, with a long nose, a long upper lip, and supernaturally long yellow teeth. She wore a black gown, black cotton gloves, and a black velvet band across her forehead, fastened in the centre with a black and gold clasp containing a ghastly representation of a human eye, apparently purblind--which gave this lady the air of a serious Cyclops.

Madame Marotte was profuse of thanks, welcomes, apologies, and curtseys. It was so good of these gentlemen to come so far--and in such unpleasant weather, too! But would not these Messieurs give themselves the trouble to be seated? And would they prefer tea or coffee--for both were on the table? And where was Marie? Marie, whose *fete*-day it was, and who should have come forward to welcome these gentlemen, and thank them for the honor of their company!

Thus summoned, Mademoiselle Marie emerged from between the two young women, and curtsied demurely.

In the meanwhile, the little old gentleman who had ushered as in was bustling about the room, shaking hands with every one, and complimenting the ladies.

"Ah, Madame Desjardins," he said, addressing the stout lady in the hat, "enchanted to see you back from the sea-side!--you and your charming daughter. I do not know which looks the more young and blooming."

Then, turning to the grim lady in black:--

"And I am charmed to pay my homage to Madame de Montparnasse. I had the pleasure of being present at the brilliant *debut* of Madame's gifted daughter the other evening at the private performance of the pupils of the Conservatoire. Mademoiselle Honoria inherits the *grand air*, Madame, from yourself."

Then, to the plump gentleman with the shirt-front:--

"And Monsieur Philomene!--this is indeed a privilege and a pleasure. Bad weather, Monsieur Philomene, for the voice!"

Then, to the two girls:--

"Mesdemoiselles--Achille Dorinet prostrates himself at the feet of youth, beauty, and talent! Mademoiselle Honoria, I salute in you the future Empress of the tragic stage. Mademoiselle Rosalie, modesty forbids me to extol the acquired graces of even my most promising pupil; but I may be permitted to adore in you the graces of nature."

While I was listening to these scraps of salutation, Mueller was murmuring tender nothings in the ear of the fair Marie, and Madame Marotte was pouring out the coffee.

Monsieur Achille Dorinet, having gone the round of the company, next addressed himself to me.

"Permit me, Monsieur," he said, bringing his heels together and punctuating his sentences with little bows, "permit me, in the absence of a master of the ceremonies, to introduce myself--Achille Dorinet, Achille Dorinet, whose name may not, perhaps, be wholly unknown to you in connection with the past glories of the classical ballet. Achille Dorinet, formerly *premier sujet* of the Opera Francais-- now principal choreographic professor at the Conservatoire Imperiale de Musique. I have had the honor, Monsieur, of dancing at Erfurth before their Imperial Majesties the Emperors Napoleon and Alexander, and a host of minor sovereigns. Those, Monsieur, were the high and palmy days of the art. We performed a ballet descriptive of the siege of Troy, and I undertook the part of a river god--the god Scamander, *en effet*. The great ladies of the court, Monsieur, were graciously pleased to admire my proportions as the god Scamander. I wore a girdle of sedges, a wreath of water-lilies, and a scarf of blue and silver. I have reason to believe that the costume became me."

"Sir," I replied gravely, "I do not doubt it."

"It is a noble art, Monsieur, *l'art de la dame*" said the former *premier sujet*, with a sigh; "but it is on the decline. Of the grand style of fifty years ago, only myself and tradition remain."

"Monsieur was, doubtless, a contemporary of Vestris, the famous dancer," I said.

"The illustrious Vestris, Monsieur," said the little old gentleman, "was, next to Louis the Fourteenth, the greatest of Frenchmen. I am proud to own myself his disciple, as well as his contemporary."

"Why next to Louis the Fourteenth, Monsieur Dorinet?" I asked, keeping my countenance with difficulty. "Why not next to Napoleon the First, who was a still greater conqueror?"

"But no dancer, Monsieur!" replied the ex-god Scamander, with a kind of half pirouette; "whereas the Grand Monarque was the finest dancer of his epoch."

Madame Marotte had by this time supplied all her guests with tea and coffee, while Monsieur Philomene went round with the cakes and bread and butter. Madame Desjardins spread her pocket-handkerchief on her lap--a pocket-handker-chief the size of a small table-cloth. Madame de Montparnasse, more mindful of her gentility, removed to a corner of the tea-table, and ate her bread and butter in her black cotton gloves.

"We hope we have another bachelor by-and-by," said Madame Marotte, ad-dressing herself to the young ladies, who looked down and giggled. "A charming man, mesdemoiselles, and quite the gentleman--our *locataire*, M'sieur Lenoir. You know him, M'sieur Dorinet--pray tell these demoiselles what a charming man M'sieur Lenoir is!"

The little dancing-master bowed, coughed, smiled, and looked somewhat em-barrassed.

"Monsieur Lenoir is no doubt a man of much information," he said, hesitat-ingly; "a traveller--a reader--a gentleman--oh! yes, certainly a gentleman. But to say that he is a--a charming man ... well, perhaps the ladies are the best judges of such nice questions. What says Mam'selle Marie?"

Thus applied to, the fair Marie became suddenly crimson, and had not a word to reply with. Monsieur Dorinet stared. The young ladies tittered. Madame Ma-rotte, deaf as a post and serenely unconscious, smiled, nodded, and said "Ah, yes, yes--didn't I tell you so?"

"Monsieur Dorinet has, I fear, asked an indiscreet question," said Mueller, boil-ing over with jealousy.

"I--I have not observed Monsieur Lenoir sufficiently to--to form an opinion," faltered Marie, ready to cry with vexation.

Mueller glared at her reproachfully, turned on his heel, and came over to where I was standing.

"You saw how she blushed?" he said in a fierce whisper. "*Sacredie*! I'll bet my head she's an arrant flirt. Who, in the name of all the fiends, is this lodger she's been carrying on with? A lodger, too--oh! the artful puss!"

At this awkward moment, Monsieur Dorinet, with considerable tact, asked Monsieur Philomene for a song; and Monsieur Philomene (who as I afterwards learned was a favorite tenor at fifth-rate concerts) was graciously pleased to comply.

Not, however, without a little preliminary coquetry, after the manner of ten-ors. First he feared he was hoarse; then struck a note or two on the piano, and tried his falsetto; then asked for a glass of water; and finally begged that one of the young ladies would be so amiable as to accompany him.

Mademoiselle Honoria, inheriting rigidity from the maternal Cyclops, drew herself up and declined stiffly; but the other, whom the dancing-master had called Rosalie, got up directly and said she would do her best.

"Only," she added, blushing, "I play so badly!"

Monsieur Philomene was provided with two copies of his song--one for the accompanyist and one for himself; then, standing well away from the piano with his face to the audience, he balanced his music in his hand, made his little professional bow, coughed, ran his fingers through his hair, and assumed an expression of tender melancholy.

"One--two--three," began Mdlle. Rosalie, her little fat fingers staggering helplessly among the first cadenzas of the symphony. "One--two--three. One" ...

Monsieur Philomene interrupted with a wave of the hand, as if conducting an orchestra.

"Pardon, Mademoiselle," he said, "not quite so fast, if you please! Andantino--andantino--one--two--three ... Just so! A thousand thanks!"

Again Mdlle. Rosalie attacked the symphony. Again Monsieur Philomene cleared his voice, and suffered a pensive languor to cloud his manly brow.

"*Revenez, revenez, beaux jours de mon enfance,*"
he began, in a small, tremulous, fluty voice.

"They'll have a long road to travel back, *parbleu*!" muttered Mueller.

"*De votre aspect riant charmer ma souvenance!*"

Here Mdlle. Rosalie struck a wrong chord, became involved in hopeless difficulties, and gasped audibly.

Monsieur Philomene darted a withering glance at her, and went on:--

"*Mon coeur; mon pauvre coeur*" ...

More wrong chords, and a smothered "*mille pardons*!" from Mdlle. Rosalie.

"Mon coeur, mon pauvre coeur a la tristesse en proie,
En fouillant le passe"....

A dead stop on the part of Mdlle. Rosalie.

"*En fouillant le passe*"....

repeated the tenor, with the utmost severity of emphasis.

"*Mais, mon Dieu*, Rosalie! what are you doing?" cried Madame Desjardins, angrily. "Why don't you go on?"

Mdlle. Rosalie burst into a flood of tears.

"I--I can't!" she sobbed. "It's so--so very difficult--and"...

Madame Desjardins flung up her hands in despair.

"*Ciel*!" she cried, "and I have been paying three francs a lesson for you, Mademoiselle, twice a week for the last six years!"

"*Mais, maman*"....

"*Fi done*, Mademoiselle! I am ashamed of you. Make a curtsey to Monsieur Philomene this moment, and beg his pardon; for you have spoiled his beautiful song!"

But Monsieur Philomene would hear of no such expiation. His soul, to use his own eloquent language, recoiled from it with horror! The accompaniment, *a vrai dire*, was not easy, and *la bien aimable* Mam'selle Rosalie had most kindly done her best with it. *Allons donc!*--on condition that no more should be said on the subject, Monsieur Philomene would volunteer to sing a little unaccompanied romance of his own composition--a mere *bagatelle*; but a tribute to "*les beaux yeux de ces cheres dames*!"

So Mam'selle Rosalie wiped away her tears, and Madame Desjardins smoothed her ruffled feathers, and Monsieur Philomene warbled a plaintive little ditty in which "*coeur*" rhymed to "*peur*" and "*amours*" to "*toujours*" and "*le sort*" to "*la mort*" in quite the usual way; so giving great satisfaction to all present, but most, perhaps, to himself.

And now, hospitably anxious that each of her guests should have a chance of achieving distinction, Madame Marotte invited Mdlle. Honoria to favor the company with a dramatic recitation.

Mdlle. Honoria hesitated; exchanged glances with the Cyclops; and, in order to enhance the value of her performance, began raising all kinds of difficulties. There was no stage, for instance; and there were no footlights; but M. Dorinet met these objections by proposing to range all the seats at one end of the room, and to divide the stage off by a row of lighted candles.

"But it is so difficult to render a dramatic scene without an interlocutor!" said the young lady.

"What is it you require, ***ma chere demoiselle?***" asked Madame Marotte.

"I have no interlocutor," said Mdlle. Honoria.

"No what, my love?"

"No interlocutor," repeated Mdlle. Honoria, at the top of her voice.

"Dear! dear! what a pity! Can't we send the boy for it? Marie, my child, bid Jacques run to Madame de Montparnasse's ***appartement*** in the Rue" ...

But Madame Marotte's voice was lost in the confusion; for Monsieur Dorinet was already deep in the arrangement of the room, and we were all helping to move the furniture. As for Mademoiselle's last difficulty, the little dancing-master met that by offering to read whatever was necessary to carry on the scene.

And now, the stage being cleared, the audience placed, and Monsieur Dorinet provided with a volume of Corneille, Mademoiselle Honoria proceeded to drape herself in an old red shawl belonging to Madame Marotte.

The scene selected is the fifth of the fourth act of Horace, where Camille, meeting her only surviving brother, upbraids him with the death of Curiace.

Mam'selle Honoria, as Camille, with clasped hands and tragic expression, stalks in a slow and stately manner towards the footlights.

(Breathless suspense of the audience.)

M. Dorinet, who should begin by vaunting his victory over the Curiatii, stops to put on his glasses, finds it difficult to read with all the candles on the ground, and mutters something about the smallness of the type.

Mdlle. Honoria, not to keep the audience waiting, surveys the ex-god Seamander with a countenance expressive of horror; starts; and takes a turn across the stage.

"*Ma soeur,*" begins M. Dorinet, holding the book very much on one side, so as to catch the light upon the page, "*ma soeur, voici le bras*"....

"Ah, Heaven! my dear Mademoiselle, take care of the candles!" cries Madame Marotte in a shrill whisper.

... "le bras qui venge nos deux freres,
Le bras qui rompt le cours de nos destins contraires,
Qui nous rend"...

Here he lost his place; stammered; and recovered it with difficulty.

"Qui nous rend maitres d'Albe"....

Madame Marotte groans aloud in an agony of apprehension

"*Ah, mon Dieu!*" she exclaims, gaspingly, "if they didn't flare so, it wouldn't be half so dangerous!"

Here M. Dorinet dropped his book, and stooping to pick up the book, dropped his spectacles.

"I think," said Mdlle. Honoria, indignantly, "we had better begin again. Monsieur Dorinet, pray read with the help of a candle *this* time!"

And, with an angry toss of her head, Mdlle. Honoria went up the stage, put on her tragedy face again, and prepared once more to stalk down to the footlights.

Monsieur Dorinet, in the meanwhile, had snatched up a candle, readjusted his spectacles, and found his place.

"*Ma soeur*" he began again, holding the book close to his eyes and the candle just under his nose, and nodding vehemently with every emphasis:--

"Ma soeur, voici le bras qui venge nos deux freres,
Le bras qui rompt le cours de nos destins contraires,
Qui nous rend maitres d'Albe" ...

A piercing scream from Madame Marotte, a general cry on the part of the audience, and a strong smell of burning, brought the dancing-master to a sudden stop. He looked round, bewildered.

"Your wig! Your wig's on fire!" cried every one at once.

Monsieur Dorinet clapped his hand to his head, which was now adorned with a rapidly-spreading glory; burned his fingers; and cut a frantic caper.

"Save him! save him!" yelled Madame Marotte.

But almost before the words were out of her mouth, Mueller, clearing the candles at a bound, had rushed to the rescue, scalped Monsieur Dorinet by a ***tour de main***, cast the blazing wig upon the floor, and trampled out the fire.

Then followed a roar of "inextinguishable laughter," in which, however, neither the tragic Camille nor the luckless Horace joined.

"Heavens and earth!" murmured the little dancing-master, ruefully surveying the ruins of his blonde peruke. And then he put his hand to his head, which was as bald as an egg.

In the meanwhile Mdlle. Honoria, who had not yet succeeded in uttering a syllable of her part, took no pains to dissemble her annoyance; and was only pacified at last by a happy proposal on the part of Monsieur Philomene, who suggested that "this gifted demoiselle" should be entreated to favor the society with a soliloquy.

Thus invited, she draped herself again, stalked down to the footlights for the third time, and in a high, shrill voice, with every variety of artificial emphasis and studied gesture, recited Voltaire's famous "Death of Coligny," from the ***Henriade***.

In the midst of this performance, just at that point when the assassins are described as falling upon their knees before their victim, the door of the room was softly opened, and another guest slipped in unseen behind us. Slipped in, indeed, so quietly that (the backs of the audience being turned that way) no one seemed to hear, and no one looked round but myself.

Brief as was that glance, and all in the shade as he stood, I recognised him instantly.

It was the mysterious stranger of the Cafe Procope.

CHAPTER XXXIV.
MY AUNT'S FLOWER GARDEN.

Having despatched the venerable Coligny much to her own satisfaction and apparently to the satisfaction of her hearers, Mdlle. Honoria returned to private life; Messieurs Philomene and Dorinet removed the footlights; the audience once more dispersed itself about the room; and Madame Marotte welcomed the new-comer as Monsieur Lenoir.

"*Monsieur est bien aimable*," she said, nodding and smiling, and, with tremulous hands, smoothing down the front of her black silk gown. "I had told these young ladies that we hoped for the honor of Monsieur's society. Will Monsieur permit me to introduce him?"

"With pleasure, Madame Marotte."

And M. Lenoir--white cravatted, white kid-gloved, hat in hand, perfectly well-dressed in full evening black, and wearing a small orange-colored rosette at his button-hole--bowed, glanced round the room, and, though his eyes undoubtedly took in both Mueller and myself, looked as if he had never seen either of us in his life.

I< saw Mueller start, and the color fly into his face.

"By Heaven!" he exclaimed, "it is--it must be ... look at him, Arbuthnot! If that isn't the man who stole my sketch-book, I'll eat my head!"

"It *is* the man," I replied. "I recognised him ten minutes ago, when he first came in."

"You are certain?"

"Quite certain."

"And yet--there is something different!"

There *was* something different; but, at the same time, much that was identical. There was the same strange, inscrutable look, the same bronzed complexion, the same military bearing. M. Lenoir, it was true, was well, and even elegantly dressed; whereas, the stranger of the Cafe Procope bore all the outward stigmata of penury; but that was not all. There was yet "something different." The one looked like a man who had done, or suffered, a wrong in his time; who had an old quarrel with the world; and who only sought to hide himself, his poverty, and his bitter pride from the observation of his fellow men. The other stood before us dignified, *decore*, self-possessed, a man not only of the world, but apparently no stranger to that small section of it called "the great world." In a word, the man of the Cafe, sunken, sullen, threadbare as he was, would have been almost less out of his proper place in Madame Marotte's society of small trades-people and minor professionals, than was M. Lenoir with his *grand air* and his orange-colored ribbon.

"It's the same man," said Mueller; "the same, beyond a doubt. The more I look at him, the more confident I am."

"And the more I look at him," said I, "the more doubtful I get."

Madame Marotte, meanwhile, had introduced M. Lenoir to the two Conservatoire pupils and their mammas; Monsieur Dorinet had proposed some "*petits jeux*;" and Monsieur Philomene was helping him to re-arrange the chairs--this time in a circle.

"Take your places, Messieurs et Mesdames--take your places!" cried Monsieur Dorinet, who had by this time resumed his wig, singed as it was, and shorn of its fair proportions. "What game shall we play at?"

"*Pied de Boeuf*" "*Colin Maillard*" and other games were successively proposed and rejected.

"We have a game in Alsace called 'My Aunt's Flower Garden'" said Mueller. "Does any one know it?"

"'My Aunt's Flower Garden?'" repeated Monsieur Dorinet. "I never heard of it."

"It sounds pretty," said Mdlle. Rosalie.

"Will M'sieur teach it to us, if it is not very difficult?" suggested Mdlle. Rosalie's mamma.

"With pleasure, Madame. It is not a bad game--and it is extremely easy. We will sit in a circle, if you please--the chairs as they are placed will do quite well."

We were just about to take our places when Madame Marotte seized the opportunity to introduce Mueller and myself to M. Lenoir.

"We have met before, Monsieur," said Mueller, pointedly.

"I am ashamed to confess, Monsieur, that I do not remember to have had that pleasure," replied M. Lenoir, somewhat stiffly.

"And yet, Monsieur, it was but the other day," persisted Mueller.

"Monsieur, I can but reiterate my regret."

"At the Cafe Procope."

M. Lenoir stared coldly, slightly shrugged his shoulders, and said, with the air of one who repudiates a discreditable charge:--

"Monsieur, I do not frequent the Cafe Procope."

"If Monsieur Mueller is to teach us the game, Monsieur Mueller must begin it!" said Monsieur Dorinet.

"At once," replied Mueller, taking his place in the circle.

As ill-luck would have it (the rest of us being already seated), there were but two chairs left; so that M. Lenoir and Mueller had to sit side by side.

"I begin with my left-hand neighbor," said Mueller, addressing himself with a bow to Mdlle. Rosalie; "and the circle will please to repeat after me:--'I have the four corners of my Aunt's Flower Garden for sale--

thee, and lov'd thee, and ne'er can forget.'"

MDLLE. ROSALIE *to* M. PHILOMENE.--I have the four corners of my Aunt's Flower Garden for sale--

thee, and lov'd thee, and ne'er can forget.'

M. PHILOMENE *to* MADAME DE MONTPARNASSE.--I have the four corners of my Aunt's Flower Garden, etc., etc.

MADAME DE MONTPARNASSE *to* M. DORINET.--I have the four corners of my Aunt's Flower Garden, etc., etc.

Monsieur Dorinet repeats the formula to Madame Desjardins; Madame Desjardins passes it on to me; I proclaim it at the top of my voice to Madame Marotte; Madame Marotte transfers it to Mdlle. Honoria; Mdlle. Honoria delivers it to the fair Marie; the fair Marie tells it to M. Lenoir, and the first round is completed.

Mueller resumes the lead :--

"In the second grow heartsease and wild eglantine;
Fair exchange is no theft--for my heart, give me thine."

MDLLE. ROSALIE *to* M. PHILOMENE:--

"In the second grow heartsease and wild eglantine;
Fair exchange is no theft--for my heart, give me thine."

M. PHILOMENE *to* MDLLE. DE MONTPARNASSE:--

"*In the second grow heartsease*," &c., &c.
And so on again, till the second round is done. Then Mueller began again:--

"In the third of these corners pale primroses grow;
Now tell me thy secret, and whisper it low."

Mdlle. Rosalie was about to repeat these lines as before; but he stopped her.
"No, Mademoiselle, not till you have told me the secret."
"The secret, M'sieur? What secret?"
"Nay, Mademoiselle, how can I tell that till you have told me? You must whisper something to me--something very secret, which you would not wish any one else to hear--before you repeat the lines. And when you repeat them, Monsieur Philomene must whisper his secret to you--and so on through the circle."
Mdlle. Rosalie hesitated, smiled, whispered something in Mueller's ear, and went on with:--

"In the third of these corners pale primroses grow;
Now tell me thy secret, and whisper it low."

Monsieur Philomene then whispered his secret to Mdlle. Rosalie, and so on again till it ended with M. Lenoir and Mueller.
"I don't think it is a very amusing game," said Madame Marotte; who, being

deaf, had been left out of the last round, and found it dull.

"It will be more entertaining presently, Madame," shouted Mueller, with a malicious twinkle about his eyes. "Pray observe the next lines, Messieurs et Mesdames, and follow my lead as before:--

'Roses bloom in the fourth; and your secret, my dear,
Which you whisper'd so softly just now in my ear,
I repeat word for word, for the others to hear!'

Mademoiselle Rosalie (whose pardon I implore!) whispered to me that Monsieur Philomene dyed his moustache and whiskers."

There was a general murmur of alarm tempered with tittering. Mademoiselle Rosalie was dumb with confusion. Monsieur Philomene's face became the color of a full-blown peony. Madame de Montparnasse and Mdlle. Honoria turned absolutely green.

"*Comment!*" exclaimed one or two voices. "Is everything to be repeated?"

"Everything, Messieurs et Mesdames," replied Mueller--"everything--without reservation. I call upon Mdlle. Rosalie to reveal the secret of Monsieur Philomene."

MDLLE. ROSALIE (*with great promptitude*):--Monsieur Philomene whispered to me that Honoria was the most disagreeable girl in Paris, Marie the dullest, and myself the prettiest.

M. PHILOMENE (*in an agony of confusion*):--I beseech you, Mam'selle Honoria ... I entreat you, Mam'selle Marie, not for an instant to suppose....

MDLLE. HONORIA (*drawing herself up and smiling acidly*):--Oh, pray do not give yourself the trouble to apologize, Monsieur Philomene. Your opinion, I assure you, is not of the least moment to either of us. Is it, Marie?

But the fair Marie only smiled good-naturedly, and said:--

"I know I am not clever. Monsieur Philomene is quite right; and I am not at all angry with him."

"But--but, indeed, Mesdemoiselles, I--I--am incapable...." stammered the luckless tenor, wiping the perspiration from his brow. "I am incapable...."

"Silence in the circle!" cried Mueller, authoritatively. "Private civilities are forbidden by the rules of the game. I call Monsieur Philomene to order, and I demand from him the secret of Madame de Montparnasse."

M. Philomene looked even more miserable than before.

"I--I ... but it is an odious position! To betray the confidence of a lady ... Heavens! I cannot."

"The secret!--the secret!" shouted the others, impatiently.

Madame de Montparnasse pursed up her parchment lips, glared upon us defiantly, and said:--

"Pray don't hesitate about repeating my words, M'sieur Philomene. I am not ashamed of them."

M. PHILOMENE (*reluctantly*):--Madame de Montparnasse observed to me that what she particularly disliked was a mixed society like--like the present; and that she hoped our friend Madame Marotte would in future be less indiscriminate in the choice of her acquaintances.

MULLER (*with elaborate courtesy*):--We are all infinitely obliged to Madame de Montparnasse for her opinion of us--(I speak for the society, as leader of the circle)--and beg to assure her that we entirely coincide in her views. It rests with Madame to carry on the game, and to betray the confidence of Monsieur Dorinet.

MADAME DE MONTPARNASSE (*with obvious satisfaction*):--Monsieur Dorinet told me that Rosalie Desjardin's legs were ill-made, and that she would never make a dancer, though she practised from now till doomsday.

M. DORINET (*springing to his feet as if he had been shot*):--Heavens and earth! Madame de Montparnasse, what have I done that you should so pervert my words? Mam'selle Rosalie--*ma chere eleve*, believe me, I never....

"Silence in the circle!" shouted Mueller again.

M. DORINET:--But, M'sieur, in simple self-defence....

MULLER:--Self-defence, Monsieur Dorinet, is contrary to the rules of the game. Revenge only is permitted. Revenge yourself on Madame Desjardins, whose secret it is your turn to tell.

M. DORINET:--Madame Desjardins drew my attention to the toilette of Madame de Montparnasse. She said: "*Mon Dieu!* Monsieur Dorinet, are you not tired of seeing La Montparnasse in that everlasting old black gown? My Rosalie says she is in mourning for her ugliness."

MADAME DESJARDINS (*laughing heartily*):--*Eh bien--oui!* I don't deny it;

and Rosalie's *mot* was not bad. And now, M'sieur the Englishman (*turning to me*), it is your turn to be betrayed. Monsieur, whose name I cannot pronounce, said to me:--"Madame, the French, *selon moi*, are the best dressed and most *spirituel* people of Europe. Their very silence is witty; and if mankind were, by universal consent, to go without clothes to-morrow, they would wear the primitive costume of Adam and Eve more elegantly than the rest of the world, and still lead the fashion,"

(*A murmur of approval on the part of the company, who take the compliment entirely aux serieux*.)

MYSELF (*agreeably conscious of having achieved popularity*):--Our hostess's deafness having unfortunately excluded her from this part of the game, I was honored with the confidence of Mdlle. Honoria, who informed me that she is to make her *debut* before long at the Theatre Francais, and hoped that I would take tickets for the occasion.

MDLLE. ROSALIE (*satirically*):--*Brava*, Honoria! What a woman of business you are!

MDLLE. HONORIA (*affecting not to hear this observation*)--

"Roses bloom in the fourth, and your secret, my dear,
Which you whispered so softly just now in my ear,
I repeat word for word for the others to hear."

Marie said to me.... *Tiens*! Marie, don't pull my dress in that way. You shouldn't have said it, you know, if it won't bear repeating! Marie said to me that she could have either Monsieur Mueller or Monsieur Lenoir, by only holding up her finger-- but she couldn't make up her mind which she liked best.

MDLLE. MARIE (*half crying*):--Nay, Honoria--how can you be so--so unkind ... so spiteful? I--I did not say I could have either M'sieur Mueller or... or...

M. LENOIR (*with great spirit and good breeding*):--Whether Mademoiselle used those words or not is of very little importance. The fact remains the same; and is as old as the world. Beauty has but to will and to conquer.

MULLER:--Order in the circle! The game waits for Mademoiselle Marie.

MARIE (*hesitatingly*):--

"*Roses bloom in the fourth, and your secret*"

M'sieur Lenoir said that--that he admired the color of my dress, and that blue became me more than lilac.

MULLER: (*coldly*)--*Pardon*, Mademoiselle, but I happened to overhear what Monsieur Lenoir whispered just now, and those were not his words. Monsieur Lenoir said, "Look in"... but perhaps Mademoiselle would prefer me not to repeat more?

MARIE--(*in great confusion*):--As--as you please, M'sieur.

MULLER:--Then, Mademoiselle, I will be discreet, and I will not even impose a forfeit upon you, as I might do, by the laws of the game. It is for Monsieur Lenoir to continue.

M. LENOIR:--I do not remember what Monsieur Mueller whispered to me at the close of the last round.

MULLER (*pointedly*):--*Pardon,* Monsieur, I should have thought that scarcely possible.

M. LENOIR:--It was perfectly unintelligible, and therefore left no impression on my memory.

MULLER:--Permit me, then, to have the honor of assisting your memory. I said to you--"Monsieur, if I believed that any modest young woman of my acquaintance was in danger of being courted by a man of doubtful character, do you know what I would do? I would hunt that man down with as little remorse as a ferret hunts down a rat in a drain."

M. LENOIR:--The sentiment does you honor, Monsieur; but I do not see the application,

MULLER:--Vous ne le trouvez pas, Monsieur?

M. LENOIR--(*with a cold stare, and a scarcely perceptible shrug of the shoulders*):--Non, Monsieur.

Here Mdlle. Rosalie broke in with:--"What are we to do next, M'sieur Mueller? Are we to begin another round, or shall we start a fresh game?"

To which Mueller replied that it must be "*selon le plaisir de ces dames*;" and put the question to the vote.

But too many plain, unvarnished truths had cropped up in the course of the last round of my Aunt's Flower Garden; and the ladies were out of humor. Madame de Montparnasse, frigid, Cyclopian, black as Erebus, found that it was time to go home; and took her leave, bristling with gentility. The tragic Honoria stalked majestically after her. Madame Desjardins, mortally offended with M. Dorinet on the score of Rosalie's legs, also prepared to be gone; while M. Philomene, convicted of hair-dye and *brouille* for ever with "the most disagreeable girl in Paris," hastened to make his adieux as brief as possible.

"A word in your ear, mon cher Dorinet," whispered he, catching the little dancing-master by the button-hole. "Isn't it the most unpleasant party you were ever at in your life?"

The ex-god Scamander held up his hands and eyes.

"*Eh, mon Dieu!*" he replied. "What an evening of disasters! I have lost my best pupil and my second-best wig!"

In the meanwhile, we went up like the others, and said good-night to our hostess.

She, good soul! in her deafness, knew nothing about the horrors of the evening, and was profuse of her civilities. "So amiable of these gentlemen to honor her little soiree--so kind of M'sieur Mueller to have exerted himself to make things go off pleasantly--so sorry we would not stay half an hour longer," &c., &c.

To all of which Mueller (with a sly grimace expressive of contrition) replied only by a profound salutation and a rapid retreat. Passing M. Lenoir without so much as a glance, he paused a moment before Mdlle. Marie who was standing near the door, and said in a tone audible only to her and myself:--

"I congratulate you, Mademoiselle, on your admirable talent for intrigue. I trust, when you look in the usual place and find the promised letter, it will prove agreeable reading. J'ai l'honneur, Mademoiselle, de vous saluer."

I saw the girl flush crimson, then turn deadly white, and draw back as if his hand had struck her a sudden blow. The next moment we were half-way down the stairs.

"What, in Heaven's name, does all this mean?" I said, when we were once more in the street.

"It means," replied Mueller fiercely, "that the man's a scoundrel, and the woman, like all other women, is false."

"Then the whisper you overheard" ...

"Was only this:--'***Look in the usual place, and you will find a letter***.' Not many words, ***mon cher***, but confoundedly comprehensive! And I who believed that girl to be an angel of candor! I who was within an ace of falling seriously in love with her! ***Sacredie***! what an idiot I have been!"

"Forget her, my dear fellow," said I. "Wipe her out of your memory (which I think will not be difficult), and leave her to her fate."

He shook his head.

"No," he said, gloomily, "I won't do that. I'll get to the bottom of that man's mystery; and if, as I suspect, there's that about his past life which won't bear the light of day--I'll save her, if I can."

CHAPTER XXXV.
WEARY AND FAR DISTANT.

Twice already, in accordance with my promise to Dalrymple, I had called upon Madame de Courcelles, and finding her out each time, had left my card, and gone away disappointed. From Dalrymple himself, although I had written to him several times, I heard seldom, and always briefly. His first notes were dated from Berlin, and those succeeding them from Vienna. He seemed restless, bitter, dissatisfied with himself, and with the world. Naturally unfit for a lounging, idle life, his active nature, now that it had to bear up against the irritation of hope deferred, chafed and fretted for work.

"My sword-arm," he wrote in one of his letters, "is weary of its holiday. There are times when I long for the smell of gunpowder, and the thunder of battle. I am sick to death of churches and picture-galleries, operas, dilettantism, white-kid-glovism, and all the hollow shows and seemings of society. Sometimes I regret having left the army--at others I rejoice; for, after all, in these piping times of peace, to be a soldier is to be a mere painted puppet--a thing of pipe-clay and gold bullion--an expensive scarecrow--an elegant Guy Fawkes--a sign, not of what is, but of what has been, and yet may be again. For my part, I care not to take the livery without the service. Pshaw! will things never mend! Are the good old times, and the good old international hatreds, gone by for ever? Shall we never again have a thorough, seasonable, wholesome, continental war? This place (Vienna) would be worth fighting for, if one had the chance. I sometimes amuse myself by planning a siege, when I ride round the fortifications, as is my custom of an afternoon."

In another, after telling me that he had been reading some books of travel in Egypt and Central America, he said:--

"Next to a military life I think that of a traveller--a genuine traveller, who turns his back upon railroads and guides--must be the most exciting and the most enviable under heaven. Since reading these books, I dream of the jungle and the desert, and fancy that a buffalo-hunt must be almost as fine sport as a charge of cavalry. Oh, what a weary exile this is! I feel as if the very air were stagnant around me, and I, like the accursed vessel that carried the ancient mariner,--

> As idle as a painted ship,
> Upon a painted ocean.'"

Sometimes, though rarely, he mentioned Madame de Courcelles, and then very guardedly: always as "Madame de Courcelles," and never as his wife.

"That morning," he wrote, "comes back to me with all the vagueness of a dream--you will know what morning I mean, and why it fills so shadowy a page in the book of my memory. And it might as well have been a dream, for aught of present peace or future hope that it has brought me. I often think that I was selfish when I exacted that pledge from her. I do not see of what good it can be to either her or me, or in what sense I can be said to have gained even the power to protect and serve her. Would that I were rich; or that she and I were poor together, and dwelling far away in some American wild, under the shade of primeval trees, the world forgetting; by the world forgot! I should enjoy the life of a Canadian settler--so free, so rational, so manly. How happy we might be--she with her children, her garden, her books; I with my dogs, my gun, my lands! What a curse it is, this spider's web of civilization, that hems and cramps us in on every side, and from which not all the armor of common-sense is sufficient to preserve us!"

Sometimes he broke into a strain of forced gayety, more sad, to my thinking, than the bitterest lamentations could have been.

"I wish to Heaven," he said, in one of his later letters--"I wish to Heaven I had no heart, and no brain! I wish I was, like some worthy people I know, a mere human zoophyte, consisting of nothing but a mouth and a stomach. Only conceive how it must simplify life when once one has succeeded in making a clean sweep of all those finer emotions which harass more complicated organisms! Enviable zoophytes, that live only to digest!--who would not be of the brotherhood?"

In another he wrote:--

"I seem to have lived years in the last five or six weeks, and to have grown suddenly old and cynical. Some French writer (I think it is Alphonse Karr) says, 'Nothing in life is really great and good, except what is not true. Man's greatest treasures are his illusions.' Alas! my illusions have been dropping from me in showers of late, like withered leaves in Autumn. The tree will be bare as a gallows ere long, if these rough winds keep on blowing. If only things would amuse me as of old! If there was still excitement in play, and forgetfulness in wine, and novelty in travel! But there is none--and all things alike are 'flat, stale, and unprofitable,' The truth is, Damon, I want but one thing--and wanting that, lack all."

Here is one more extract, and it shall be the last:--

"You ask me how I pass my days--in truth, wearily enough. I rise with the dawn, but that is not very early in September; and I ride for a couple of hours before breakfast. After breakfast I play billiards in some public room, consume endless pipes, read the papers, and so on. Later in the day I scowl through a picture-gallery, or a string of studios; or take a pull up the river; or start off upon a long, solitary objectless walk through miles and miles of forest. Then comes dinner--the inevitable, insufferable, interminable German table-d'hote dinner--and then there is the evening to be got through somehow! Now and then I drop in at a theatre, but generally take refuge in some plebeian Lust Garten or Beer Hall, where amid clouds of tobacco-smoke, one may listen to the best part-singing and zitter-playing in Europe. And so my days drag by--who but myself knows how slowly? Truly, Damon, there comes to every one of us, sooner or later, a time when we say of life as Christopher Sly said of the comedy--''Tis an excellent piece of work. Would 'twere done!'"

CHAPTER XXXVI.
THE VICOMTE DE CAYLUS.

It was after receiving the last of these letters that I hazarded a third visit to Madame de Courcelles. This time, I ventured to present myself at her door about midday, and was at once ushered upstairs into a drawing-room looking out on the Rue Castellane.

Seeing her open work-table, with the empty chair and footstool beside it, I thought at the first glance that I was alone in the room, when a muttered "Sacr-r-r-re! Down, Bijou!" made me aware of a gentleman extended at full length upon a sofa near the fireplace, and of a vicious-looking Spitz crouched beneath it.

The gentleman lifted his head from the sofa-cusion; stared at me; bowed carelessly; got upon his feet; and seizing the poker, lunged savagely at the fire, as if he had a spite against it, and would have put it out, if he could. This done, he yawned aloud, flung himself into the nearest easy-chair, and rang the bell.

"More coals, Henri," he said, imperiously; "and--stop! a bottle of Seltzer-water."

The servant hesitated.

"I don't think, Monsieur le Vicomte," he said, "that Madame has any Seltzer-water in the house; but ..."

"Confound you!--you never have anything in the house at the moment one wants it," interrupted the gentleman, irritably.

"I can send for some, if Monsieur le Vicomte desires it."

"Send for it, then; and remember, when I next ask for it, let there be some at hand."

"Yes, Monsieur le Vicomte."

"And--Henri!"

"Yes, Monsieur le Vicomte."

"Bid them be quick. I hate to be kept waiting!"

The servant murmured his usual "Yes, Monsieur le Vicomte," and disappeared; but with a look of such subdued dislike and impatience in his face, as would scarcely have flattered Monsieur le Vicomte had he chanced to surprise it.

In the meantime the dog had never ceased growling; whilst I, in default of something better to do, turned over the leaves of an album, and took advantage of a neighboring mirror to scrutinize the outward appearance of this authoritative occupant of Madame de Courcelles' drawing-room.

He was a small, pallid, slender man of about thirty-five or seven years of age, with delicate, effeminate features, and hair thickly sprinkled with gray. His fingers, white and taper as a woman's, were covered with rings. His dress was careless, but that of a gentleman. Glancing at him even thus furtively, I could not help observing the worn lines about his temples, the mingled languor and irritability of his every gesture; the restless suspicion of his eye; the hard curves about his handsome mouth.

"*Mille tonnerres*!" said he, between his teeth "come out, Bijou--come out, I say!"

The dog came out unwillingly, and changed the growl to a little whine of apprehension. His master immediately dealt him a smart kick that sent him crouching to the farther corner of the room, where he hid himself under a chair.

"I'll teach you to make that noise," muttered he, as he drew his chair closer to the fire, and bent over it, shiveringly. "A yelping brute, that would be all the better for hanging."

Having sat thus for a few moments, he seemed to grow restless again, and, pushing back his chair, rose, looked out of the window, took a turn or two across the room, and paused at length to take a book from one of the side-tables. As he did this, our eyes met in the looking-glass; whereupon he turned hastily back to the window, and stood there whistling till it occurred to him to ring the bell again.

"Monsieur rang?" said the footman, once more making his appearance at the door.

"*Mort de ma vie*! yes. The Seltzer-water."

"I have sent for it, Monsieur le Vicomte."

"And it is not yet come?"

"Not yet, Monsieur le Vicomte."

He muttered something to himself, and dropped back into the chair before the fire.

"Does Madame de Courcelles know that I am here?" he asked, as the servant, after lingering a moment, was about to leave the room.

"I delivered Monsieur le Vicomte's message, and brought back Madame's reply," said the man, "half an hour ago."

"True--I had forgotten it. You may go."

The footman closed the door noiselessly, and had no sooner done so than he was recalled by another impatient peal.

"Here, Henri--have you told Madame de Courcelles that this gentleman is also waiting to see her?"

"Yes, Monsieur le Vicomte."

"*Eh bien*?"

"And Madame said she should be down in a few moments."

"*Sacredie*! go back, then, and inquire if...."

"Madame is here."

As the footman moved back respectfully, Madame de Courcelles came into the room. She was looking perhaps somewhat paler, but, to my thinking, more charming than ever. Her dark hair was gathered closely round her head in massive braids, displaying to their utmost advantage all the delicate curves of her throat and chin; while her rich morning dress, made of some dark material, and fastened at the throat by a round brooch of dead gold, fell in loose and ample folds, like the drapery of a Roman matron. Coming at once to meet me, she extended a cordial hand, and said:--

"I had begun to despair of ever seeing you again. Why have you always come when I was out?"

"Madame," I said, bending low over the slender fingers, that seemed to linger kindly in my own, "I have been undeservedly unfortunate."

"Remember for the future," she said, "that I am always at home till midday, and after five."

Then, turning to her other visitor, she said:--

"*Mon cousin*, allow me to present my friend. Monsieur Arbuthnot--Monsieur le Vicomte Adrien de Caylus."

I had suspected as much already. Who but he would have dared to assume these airs of insolence? Who but her suitor and my friend's rival? I had disliked him at first sight, and now I detested him. Whether it was that my aversion showed itself in my face, or that Madame de Courcelles's cordial welcome of myself annoyed him, I know not; but his bow was even cooler than my own.

"I have been waiting to see you, Helene," said he, looking at his watch, "for nearly three-quarters of an hour."

"I sent you word, *mon cousin*, that I was finishing a letter for the foreign post," said Madame de Courcelles, coldly, "and that I could not come sooner."

Monsieur de Caylus bit his lip and cast an impatient glance in my direction.

"Can you spare me a few moments alone, Helene?" he said.

"Alone, *mon cousin*?"

"Yes, upon a matter of business."

Madame de Courcelles sighed.

"If Monsieur Arbuthnot will be so indulgent as to excuse me for five minutes," she replied. "This way, *mon cousin*."

So saying, she lifted a dark green curtain, beneath which they passed to a farther room out of sight and hearing.

They remained a long time away. So long, that I grew weary of waiting, and, having turned over all the illustrated books upon the table, and examined every painting on the walls, turned to the window, as the idler's last resource, and watched the passers-by.

What endless entertainment in the life-tide of a Paris street, even though but a branch from one of the greater arteries! What color--what character--what animation--what variety! Every third or fourth man is a blue-bloused artisan; every tenth, a soldier in a showy uniform. Then comes the grisette in her white cap; and the lemonade-vender with his fantastic pagoda, slung like a peep-show across his shoulders; and the peasant woman from Normandy, with her high-crowned head-dress; and the abbe, all in black, with his shovel-hat pulled low over his eyes; and the mountebank selling pencils and lucifer-matches to the music of a hurdy-gurdy; and the gendarme, who is the terror of street urchins; and the gamin, who is the torment of the gendarme; and the water-carrier, with his cart and his cracked bugle; and the elegant ladies and gentlemen, who look in at shop windows and hire seats at two sous each in the Champs Elysees; and, of course, the English tourist reading "Galignani's Guide" as he goes along. Then, perhaps, a regiment marches past with colors flying and trumpets braying; or a fantastic-looking funeral goes by, with a hearse like a four-post bed hung with black velvet and silver; or the peripatetic showman with his company of white rats establishes himself on the pavement opposite, till admonished to move on by the sergent de ville. What an ever-shifting panorama! What a kaleidoscope of color and character! What a study for the humorist, the painter, the poet!

Thinking thus, and watching the overflowing current as it hurried on below, I became aware of a smart cab drawn by a showy chestnut, which dashed round the corner of the street and came down the Rue Castellane at a pace that caused every head to turn as it went by. Almost before I had time to do more than observe that it was driven by a moustachioed and lavender-kidded gentleman, it drew up before the house, and a trim tiger jumped down, and thundered at the door. At that moment, the gentleman, taking advantage of the pause to light a cigar, looked up, and I recognised the black moustache and sinister countenance of Monsieur de Simoncourt.

"A gentleman for Monsieur le Vicomte," said the servant, drawing back the green curtain and opening a vista into the room beyond.

"Ask him to come upstairs," said the voice of De Caylus from within.

"I have done so, Monsieur; but he prefers to wait in the cabriolet."

"Pshaw!--confound it!--say that I'm coming."

The servant withdrew.

I then heard the words "perfectly safe investment--present convenience--unexpected demand," rapidly uttered by Monsieur de Caylus; and then they both came back; he looked flushed and angry--she calm as ever.

"Then I shall call on you again to-morrow, Helene," said he, plucking nervously at his glove. "You will have had time to reflect. You will see matters differently."

Madame Courcelles shook her head.

"Reflection will not change my opinion," she said gently.

"Well, shall I send Lejeune to you? He acts as solicitor to the company, and ..."

"***Mon cousin***" interposed the lady, "I have already given you my decision--

why pursue the question further? I do not wish to see Monsieur Lejeune, and I have no speculative tastes whatever."

Monsieur de Caylus, with a suppressed exclamation that sounded like a curse, rent his glove right in two, and then, as if annoyed at the self-betrayal, crushed up the fragments in his hand, and laughed uneasily.

"All women are alike," he said, with an impatient shrug. "They know nothing of the world, and place no faith in those who are competent to advise them. I had given you credit, my charming cousin, for broader views."

Madame de Courcelles smiled without replying, and caressed the little dog, which had come out from under the sofa to fondle round her.

"Poor Bijou!" said she. "Pretty Bijou! Do you take good care of him, ***mon cousin***?"

"Upon my soul, not I," returned De Caylus, carelessly. "Lecroix feeds him, I believe, and superintends his general education."

"Who is Lecroix?"

"My valet, courier, body-guard, letter-carrier, and general ***factotum***. A useful vagabond, without whom I should scarcely know my right hand from my left!"

"Poor Bijou! I fear, then, your chance of being remembered is small indeed!" said Madame de Courcelles, compassionately.

But Monsieur le Vicomte only whistled to the dog; bowed haughtily to me; kissed, with an air of easy familiarity, before which she evidently recoiled, first the hand and then the cheek of his beautiful cousin, and so left the room. The next moment I saw him spring into the cabriolet, take his place beside Monsieur de Simoncourt, and drive away, with Bijou following at a pace that might almost have tried a greyhound.

"My cousin, De Caylus, has lately returned from Algiers on leave of absence," said Madame de Courcelles, after a few moments of awkward silence, during which I had not known what to say. "You have heard of him, perhaps?"

"Yes, Madame, I have heard of Monsieur de Caylus."

"From Captain Dalrymple?

"From Captain Dalrymple, Madame; and in society."

"He is a brave officer," she said, hesitatingly, "and has greatly distinguished himself in this last campaign."

"So I have heard, Madame."

She looked at me, as if she would fain read how much or how little Dalrymple had told me.

"You are Captain Dalrymple's friend, Mr. Arbuthnot," she said, presently, "and I know you have his confidence. You are probably aware that my present position with regard to Monsieur de Caylus is not only very painful, but also very difficult."

"Madame, I know it."

"But it is a position of which I have the command, and which no one understands so well as myself. To attempt to help me, would be to add to my embarrassments. For this reason it is well that Captain Dalrymple is not here. His presence just now in Paris could do no good--on the contrary, would be certain to do harm. Do you follow my meaning, Monsieur Arbuthnot?"

"I understand what you say, Madame; but...."

"But you do not quite understand why I say it? *Eh bien*, Monsieur, when you write to Captain Dalrymple.... for you write sometimes, do you not?"

"Often, Madame."

"Then, when you write, say nothing that may add to his anxieties. If you have reason at any time to suppose that I am importuned to do this or that; that I am annoyed; that I have my own battle to fight--still, for his sake as well as for mine, be silent. It *is* my own battle, and I know how to fight it."

"Alas! Madame...."

She smiled sadly.

"Nay," she said, "I have more courage than you would suppose; more courage and more will. I am fully capable of bearing my own burdens; and Captain Dalrymple has already enough of his own. Now tell me something of yourself. You are here, I think, to study medicine. Are you greatly devoted to your work? Have you many friends?"

"I study, Madame--not always very regularly; and I have one friend."

"An Englishman?"

"No, Madame--a German."

"A fellow-student, I presume."

"No, Madame--an artist."

"And you are very happy here?"

"I have occupations and amusements; therefore, if to be neither idle nor dull is to be happy. I suppose I am happy."

"Nay," she said quickly, "be sure of it. Do not doubt it. Who asks more from Fate courts his own destruction."

"But it would be difficult, Madame, to go through life without desiring something better, something higher--without ambition, for instance--without love."

"Ambition and love!" she repeated, smiling sadly. "There speaks the man. Ambition first--the aim and end of life; love next--the pleasant adjunct to success! Ah, beware of both."

"But without either, life would be a desert."

"Life *is* a desert," she replied, bitterly. "Ambition is its mirage, ever beckoning, ever receding--love its Dead Sea fruit, fair without and dust within. You look surprised. You did not expect such gloomy theories from me--yet I am no cynic. I have lived; I have suffered; I am a woman--*voila tout*. When you are a few years older, and have trodden some of the flinty ways of life, you will see the world as I see it."

"It may be so, Madame; but if life is indeed a desert, it is, at all events, some satisfaction to know that the dwellers in tents become enamored of their lot, and, content with what the desert has to give, desire no other. It is only the neophyte who rides after the mirage and thirsts for the Dead Sea apple."

She smiled again.

"Ah!" she said, "the gifts of the desert are two-fold, and what one gets depends on what one seeks. For some the wilderness has gifts of resignation, meditation, peace; for others it has the horse, the tent, the pipe, the gun, the chase of the panther and antelope. But to go back to yourself. Life, you say, would be barren without ambition and love. What is your ambition?"

"Nay, Madame, that is more than I can tell you--more than I know myself."

"Your profession...."

"If ever I dream dreams, Madame," I interrupted quickly, "my profession has no share in them. It is a profession I do not love, and which I hope some day to abandon."

"Your dreams, then?"

I shook my head.

"Vague--unsubstantial--illusory--forgotten as soon as dreamt! How can I analyze them? How can I describe them? In childhood one says--'I should like to be a soldier, and conquer the world;' or 'I should like to be a sailor, and discover new Continents;' or 'I should like to be a poet, and wear a laurel wreath, like Petrarch and Dante;' but as one gets older and wiser (conscious, perhaps, of certain latent energies, and weary of certain present difficulties and restraints), one can only wait, as best one may, and watch for the rising of that tide whose flood leads on to fortune."

With this I rose to take my leave. Madame de Courcelles smiled and put out her hand.

"Come often," she said; "and come at the hours when I am at home. I shall always be glad to see you. Above all, remember my caution--not a word to Captain Dalrymple, either now or at any other time."

"Madame, you may rely upon me. One thing I ask, however, as the reward of my discretion."

"And that one thing?"

"Permission, Madame, to serve you in any capacity, however humble--in any strait where a brother might interfere, or a faithful retainer lay down his life in your service."

With a sweet earnestness that made my heart beat and my cheeks glow, she thanked and promised me.

"I shall look upon you henceforth," she said, "as my knight *sans peur et sans reproche*."

Heaven knows that not all the lessons of all the moralists that ever wrote or preached since the world began, could just then have done me half such good service as did those simple words. They came at the moment when I most needed them--when I had almost lost my taste for society, and was sliding day by day into habits of more confirmed idleness and Bohemianism. They roused me. They made a man of me. They recalled me to higher aims, "purer manners, nobler laws." They clothed me, so to speak, in the *toga virilis* of a generous devotion. They made me long to prove myself "*sans peur*," to merit the "*sans reproche.*" They marked an era in my life never to be forgotten or effaced.

Let it not be thought for one moment that I loved her--or fancied I loved her. No, not so far as one heart-beat would carry me; but I was proud to possess her confidence and her friendship. Was she not Dalrymple's wife, and had not he asked me to watch over and protect her? Nay, had she not called me her knight and accepted my fealty?

Nothing perhaps, is so invaluable to a young man on entering life as the friendship of a pure-minded and highly-cultivated woman who, removed too far above him to be regarded with passion, is yet beautiful enough to engage his admiration; whose good opinion becomes the measure of his own self-respect; and whose confidence is a sacred trust only to be parted from with loss of life or honor.

Such an influence upon myself at this time was the friendship of Madame de Courcelles. I went out from her presence that morning morally stronger than before, and at each repetition of my visit I found her influence strengthen and increase. Sometimes I met Monsieur de Caylus, on which occasions my stay was ever of the briefest; but I most frequently found her alone, and then our talk was of books, of art, of culture, of all those high and stirring things that alike move the sympathies of the educated woman and rouse the enthusiasm of the young man. She became interested in me; at first for Dalrymple's sake, and by-and-by, however little I deserved it, for my own--and she showed that interest in many ways inexpressibly valuable to me then and thenceforth. She took pains to educate my taste; opened to me hitherto unknown avenues of study; led me to explore "fresh fields and pastures new," to which, but for her help, I might not have found my way for many a year to come. My reading, till now, had been almost wholly English or classical; she sent me to the old French literature--to the ***Chansons de Geste***; to the metrical romances of the Trouveres; to the Chronicles of Froissart, Monstrelet, and Philip de Comines, and to the poets and dramatists that immediately succeeded them.

These books opened a new world to me; and, having daily access to two fine public libraries, I plunged at once into a course of new and delightful reading, ranging over all that fertile tract of song and history that begins far away in the morning land of mediaeval romance, and leads on, century after century, to the new era that began with the Revolution.

With what avidity I devoured those picturesque old chronicles--those autobiographies--those poems, and satires, and plays that I now read for the first time! What evenings I spent with St. Simon, and De Thou, and Charlotte de Baviere! How I relished Voltaire! How I laughed over Moliere! How I revelled in Montaigne! Most of all, however, I loved the quaint lore of the earlier literature:--

"Old legends of the monkish page,
Traditions of the saint and sage,
Tales that have the rime of age,
And Chronicles of Eld."

Nor was this all. I had hitherto loved art as a child or a savage might love it, ignorantly, half-blindly, without any knowledge of its principles, its purposes, or its history. But Madame de Courcelles put into my hands certain books that opened my eyes to a thousand wonders unseen before. The works of Vasari, Nibby, Winkelman and Lessing, the aesthetic writings of Goethe and the Schlegels, awakened in me, one after the other, fresher and deeper revelations of beauty.

I wandered through the galleries of the Louvre like one newly gifted with sight. I haunted the Venus of Milo and the Diane Chasseresse like another Pygmalion. The more I admired, the more I found to admire. The more I comprehended, the more I found there remained for me to comprehend. I recognised in art the Sphinx whose enigma is never solved. I learned, for the first time, that poetry may be committed to imperishable marble, and steeped in unfading colors. By degrees, as I followed in the footsteps of great thinkers, my insight became keener and my perceptions more refined. The symbolism of art evolved itself, as it were, from below the surface; and instead of beholding in paintings and statues mere studies of outward beauty, I came to know them as exponents of thought--as efforts after ideal truth--as aspirations which, because of their divineness, can never be wholly expressed; but whose suggestiveness is more eloquent than all the eloquence of words.

Thus a great change came upon my life--imperceptibly at first, and by gradual degrees; but deeply and surely. To apply myself to the study of medicine became daily more difficult and more distasteful to me. The boisterous pleasures of the Quartier Latin lost their charm for me. Day by day I gave myself up more and more passionately to the cultivation of my taste for poetry and art. I filled my little sitting-room with casts after the antique. I bought some good engravings for my walls, and hung up a copy of the Madonna di San Sisto above the table at which I wrote and read. All day long, wherever I might be--at the hospital, in the lecture-room, in the laboratory--I kept looking longingly forward to the quiet evening by-and-by when, with shaded lamp and curtained window, I should again take up the studies of the night before.

Thus new aims opened out before me, and my thoughts flowed into channels ever wider and deeper. Already the first effervescence of youth seemed to have died off the surface of my life, as the "beaded bubbles" die off the surface of champagne. I had tried society, and wearied of it. I had tried Bohemia, and found it almost as empty as the Chaussee d'Autin. And now that life which from boyhood I had ever looked upon as the happiest on earth, the life of the student, was mine. Could I have devoted it wholly and undividedly to those pursuits which were fast becoming to me as the life of my life, I would not have exchanged my lot for all the wealth of the Rothschilds. Somewhat indolent, perhaps, by nature, indifferent to achieve, ambitious only to acquire, I asked nothing better than a life given up to the worship of all that is beautiful in art, to the acquisition of knowledge, and to the development of taste. Would the time ever come when I might realize my dream? Ah! who could tell? In the meanwhile ... well, in the meanwhile, here was Paris--here were books, museums, galleries, schools, golden opportunities which, once past, might never come again. So I reasoned; so time went on; so I lived, plodding on by day in the Ecole de Medecine, but, when evening came, resuming my studies at the leaf turned down the night before, and, like the visionary in "The Pilgrims of the Rhine," taking up my dream-life at the point where I had been last awakened.

CHAPTER XXXVII.
GUICHET THE MODEL.

To the man who lives alone and walks about with his eyes open, the mere bricks and mortar of a great city are instinct with character. Buildings become to him like living creatures. The streets tell him tales. For him, the house-fronts are written over with hieroglyphics which, to the passing crowd, are either unseen or without meaning. Fallen grandeur, pretentious gentility, decent poverty, the infamy that wears a brazen front, and the crime that burrows in darkness--he knows them all at a glance. The patched window, the dingy blind, the shattered doorstep, the pot of mignonette on the garret ledge, are to him as significant as the lines and wrinkles on a human face. He grows to like some houses and to dislike others, almost without knowing why--just as one grows to like or dislike certain faces in the parks and clubs. I remember now, as well as if it were yesterday, how, during the first weeks of my life in Paris, I fell in love at first sight with a wee *maisonnette* at the corner of a certain street overlooking the Luxembourg gardens--a tiny little house, with soft-looking blue silk window-curtains, and cream-colored jalousies, and boxes of red and white geraniums at all the windows. I never knew who lived in that sunny little nest; I never saw a face at any of those windows; yet I used to go out of my way in the summer evenings to look at it, as one might go to look at a beautiful woman behind a stall in the market-place, or at a Madonna in a shop-window.

At the time about which I write, there was probably no city in Europe of which the street-scenery was so interesting as that of Paris. I have already described the Quartier Latin, joyous, fantastic, out-at-elbows; a world in itself and by itself; unlike anything else in Paris or elsewhere. But there were other districts in the great city--now swept away and forgotten--as characteristic in their way as the Quartier

Latin. There was the Ile de Saint Louis, for instance--a **Campo Santo** of decayed nobility--lonely, silent, fallen upon evil days, and haunted here and there by ghosts of departed Marquises and Abbes of the *vieille ecole*. There was the debateable land to the rear of the Invalides and the Champ de Mars. There was the Faubourg St. Germain, fast falling into the sere and yellow leaf, and going the way of the Ile de Saint Louis. There was the neighborhood of the Boulevart d'Aulnay, and the Rue de la Roquette, ghastly with the trades of death; a whole Quartier of monumental sculptors, makers of iron crosses, weavers of funereal chaplets, and wholesale coffin-factors. And beside and apart from all this, there were (as in all great cities) districts of evil report and obscure topography--lost islets of crime, round which flowed and circled the daily tide of Paris life; flowed and circled, yet never penetrated. A dark arch here and there--the mouth of a foul alley--a riverside vista of gloom and squalor, marked the entrance to these Alsatias. Such an Alsatia was the Rue Pierre Lescot, the Rue Sans Nom, and many more than I can now remember--streets into which no sane man would venture after nightfall without the escort of the police.

Into the border land of such a neighborhood--a certain congeries of obscure and labyrinthine streets to the rear of the old Halles--I accompanied Franz Mueller one wintry afternoon, about an hour before sunset, and perhaps some ten days after our evening in the Rue du Faubourg St. Denis. We were bound on an expedition of discovery, and the object of our journey was to find the habitat of Guichet the model.

"I am determined to get to the bottom of this Lenoir business," said Mueller, doggedly; "and if the police won't help me, I must help myself."

"You have no case for the police," I replied.

"So says the **chef de bureau**; but I am of the opposite opinion. However, I shall make my case out clearly enough before long. This Guichet can help me, if he will. He knows Lenoir, and he knows something against him; that is clear. You saw how cautious he was the other day. The difficulty will be to make him speak."

"I doubt if you will succeed."

"I don't, **mon cher**. But we shall see. Then, again, I have another line of evidence open to me. You remember that orange-colored rosette in the fellow's button-hole?"

"Certainly I do."

"Well, now, I happen, by the merest chance, to know what that rosette means. It is the ribbon of the third order of the Golden Palm of Mozambique--a Portuguese decoration. They give it to diplomatic officials, eminent civilians, distinguished for-eigners, and the like. I know a fellow who has it, and who belongs to the Portuguese Legation here. *Eh bien!* I went to him the other day, and asked him about our said friend--how he came by it, who he is, where he comes from, and so forth. My Portuguese repeats the name--elevates his eyebrows--in short, has never heard of such a person. Then he pulls down a big book from a shelf in the secretary's room--turns to a page headed 'Golden Palm of Mozambique'--runs his finger along the list of names--shakes his head, and informs me that no Lenoir is, or ever has been, received into the order. What do you say to that, now?"

"It is just what I should have expected; but still it is not a ease for the police. It concerns the Portuguese minister; and the Portuguese minister is by no means likely to take any trouble about the matter. But why waste all this time and care? If I were you, I would let the thing drop. It is not worth the cost."

Mueller looked grave.

"I would drop it this moment," he said, "if--if it were not for the girl."

"Who is still less worth the cost,"

"I know it," he replied, impatiently. "She has a pretty, sentimental Madonna face; a sweet voice; a gentle manner--*et voila tout*. I'm not the least bit in love with her now. I might have been. I might have committed some great folly for her sake; but that danger is past, *Dieu merci!* I couldn't love a girl I couldn't trust, and that girl is a flirt. A flirt of the worst sort, too--demure, serious, conventional. No, no; my fancy for the fair Marie has evaporated; but, for all that, I don't relish the thought of what her fate might be if linked for life to an unscrupulous scoundrel like Lenoir. I must do what I can, my dear fellow--I must do what I can."

We had by this time rounded the Halles, and were threading our way through one gloomy by-street after another. The air was chill, the sky low and rainy; and already the yellow glow of an oil-lamp might be seen gleaming through the inner darkness of some of the smaller shops. Meanwhile, the dusk seemed to gather at our heels, and to thicken at every step.

"You are sure you know your way?" I asked presently, seeing Mueller look up at the name at the corner of the street.

"Why, yes; I think I do," he answered, doubtfully.

"Why not inquire of that man just ahead?" I suggested.

He was a square-built, burly, shabby-looking fellow, and was striding along so fast that we had to quicken our pace in order to come up with him. All at once Mueller fell back, laid his hand on my arm, and said:--

"Stop! It is Guichet himself. Let him go on, and we'll follow."

So we dropped into the rear and followed him. He turned presently to the right, and preceded us down a long and horribly ill-favored street, full of mean cabarets and lodging-houses of the poorest class, where, painted in red letters on broken lamps above the doors, or printed on cards wafered against the window-panes, one saw at almost every other house, the words, "*Ici on loge la nuit.*" At the end of this thoroughfare our unconscious guide plunged into a still darker and fouler *impasse*, hung across from side to side with rows of dingy linen, and ornamented in the centre with a mound of decaying cabbage-leaves, potato-parings, oyster-shells, and the like. Here he made for a large tumble-down house that closed the alley at the farther end, and, still followed by ourselves, went in at an open doorway, and up a public staircase dimly lighted by a flickering oil-lamp at every landing. At his own door he paused, and just as he had turned the key, Mueller accosted him.

"Is that you, Guichet?" he said. "Why, you are the very man I want! If I had come ten minutes sooner, I should have missed you."

"Is it M'sieur Mueller?" said Guichet, bending his heavy brows and staring at us in the gloom of the landing.

"Ay, and with me the friend you saw the other day. So, this is your den? May we come in?"

He had been standing till now with his hand on the key and the closed door at his back, evidently not intending to admit us; but thus asked, he pushed the door open, and said, somewhat ungraciously:--

"It is just that, M'sieur Mueller--a den; not fit for gentlemen like you. But you can go in, if you please."

We did not wait for a second invitation, but went in immediately. It was a long, low, dark room, with a pale gleam of fading daylight struggling in through a tiny window at the farther end. We could see nothing at first but this gleam; and it was not till Guichet had raked out the wood ashes on the hearth, and blown them into a red glow with his breath, that we could distinguish the form or position of anything in the room. Then, by the flicker of the fire, we saw a low truckle-bed close under the window; a kind of bruised and battered seaman's chest in the middle of the room; a heap of firewood in one corner; a pile of old packing-cases; old sail-cloth, old iron, and all kinds of rubbish in another; a few pots and pans over the fire-place; and a dilapidated stool or two standing about the room. Avoiding these latter, we set ourselves down upon the edge of the chest; while Guichet, having by this time lit a piece of candle-end in a tin sconce against the wall, stood before us with folded arms, and stared at us in silence.

"I want to know, Guichet, if you can give me some sittings," said Mueller, by way of opening the conversation.

"Depends on when, M'sieur Mueller," growled the model.

"Well--next week, for the whole week."

Guichet shook his head. He was engaged to Monsieur Flandrin *la bas*, for the next month, from twelve to three daily, and had only his mornings and evenings to dispose of; in proof of which he pulled out a greasy note-book and showed where the agreement was formally entered. Mueller made a grimace of disappointment.

"That man's head takes a deal of cutting off, **mon ami**," he said. "Aren't you tired of playing executioner so long?"

"Not I, M'sieur! It's all the same to me--executioner or victim, saint or devil."

Mueller, laughing, offered him a cigar.

"You've posed for some queer characters in your time, Guichet," said he.

"Parbleu, M'sieur!"

"But you've not been a model all your life?"

"Perhaps not, M'sieur."

"You've been a sailor once upon a time, haven't you?"

The model looked up quickly.

"How did you know that?" he said, frowning.

"By a number of little things--by this, for instance," replied Mueller, kicking his heels against the sea-chest; "by certain words you make use of now and then; by the way you walk; by the way you tie your cravat. **Que diable**! you look at me as if you took me for a sorcerer!"

The model shook his head.

"I don't understand it," he said, slowly.

"Nay, I could tell you more than that if I liked," said Mueller, with an air of mystery.

"About myself?"

"Ay, about yourself, and others."

Guichet, having just lighted his cigar, forgot to put it to his lips.

"What others?" he asked, with a look half of dull bewilderment and half of apprehension.

Mueller shrugged his shoulders.

"Pshaw!" said he; "I know more than you think I know, Guichet. There's our friend, you know--he of whom I made the head t'other day ... you remember?"

The model, still looking at him, made no answer.

"Why didn't you say at once where you had met him, and all the rest of it, **mon vieux**? You might have been sure I should find out for myself, sooner or later."

The model turned abruptly towards the fire-place, and, leaning his head against the mantel-shelf, stood with his back towards us, looking down into the fire.

"You ask me why I did not tell you at once?" he said, very slowly.

"Ay--why not?"

"Why not? Because--because when a man has begun to lead an honest life, and has gone on leading an honest life, as I have, for years, he is glad to put the past behind him--to forget it, and all belonging to it. How was I to guess you knew anything about--about that place *la bas*?"

"And why should I not know about it?" replied Mueller, flashing a rapid glance at me.

Guichet was silent.

"What if I tell you that I am particularly interested in--that place *la bas*?"

"Well, that may be. People used to come sometimes, I remember--artists and writers, and so on."

"Naturally."

"But I don't remember to have ever seen you, M'sieur Mueller."

"You did not observe me, **mon cher**--or it may have been before, or after your time."

"Yes, that's true," replied Guichet, ponderingly. "How long ago was it, M'sieur

Mueller?"

Mueller glanced at me again. His game, hitherto so easy, was beginning to grow difficult.

"Eh, *mon Dieu!*" he said, indifferently, "how can I tell? I have knocked about too much, now here, now there, in the course of my life, to remember in what particular year this or that event may have happened. I am not good at dates, and never was."

"But you remember seeing me there?"

"Have I not said so?"

Guichet took a couple of turns about the room. He looked flushed and embarrassed.

"There is one thing I should like to know," he said, abruptly. "Where was I? What was I doing when you saw me?"

Mueller was at fault now, for the first time.

"Where were you?" he repeated. "Why, there--where we said just now. *La bas*."

"No, no--that's not what I mean. Was I .... was I in the uniform of the Garde Chiourme?"

The color rushed into Mueller's face as, flashing a glance of exultation at me, he replied:--

"Assuredly, *mon ami*. In that, and no other."

The model drew a deep breath.

"And Bras de Fer?" he said. "Was he working in the quarries ?"

"Bras de Fer! Was that the name he went by in those days?"

"Ay--Bras de Fer--*alias* Coupe-gorge--*alias* Triphot--*alias* Lenoir--*alias* a hundred other names. Bras de Fer was the one he went by at Toulon--and a real devil he was in the Bagnes! He escaped three times, and was twice caught and brought back again. The third time he killed one sentry, injured another for life, and got clear off. That was five years ago, and I left soon after. I suppose, if you saw him in Paris the other day, he has kept clear of Toulon ever since."

"But was he in for life?" said Mueller, eagerly.

"*Travaux forces a perpetuite*," replied Guichet, touching his own shoulder significantly with the thumb of his right hand.

Mueller sprang to his feet.

"Enough," he said. "That is all I wanted to know. Guichet, ***mon cher***, I am your debtor for life. We will talk about the sittings when you have more time to dispose of. Adieu."

"But, M'sieur Mueller, you won't get me into trouble!" exclaimed the model, eagerly. "You won't make any use of my words?"

"Why, supposing I went direct to the Prefecture, what trouble could I possibly get you into, ***mon ami?***" replied Mueller.

The model looked down in silence.

"You are a brave man. You do not fear the vengeance of Bras de Fer, or his friends?"

"No, M'sieur---it's not that."

"What is it, then?"

"M'sieur...."

"Pshaw, man! Speak up."

"It is not that you would get me personally into trouble, M'sieur Mueller," said Guichet, slowly. "I am no coward, I hope--a coward would make a bad Garde Chiourme at Toulon, I fancy. And I'm not an escaped *forçat*. But--but, you see, I've worked my way into a connection here in Paris, and I've made myself a good name among the artists, and ... and I hold to that good name above everything in the world."

"Naturally--rightly. But what has that to do with Lenoir?"

"Ah, M'sieur Mueller, if you knew more about me, you would not need telling how much it has to do with him! I was not always a Garde Chiourme at Toulon. I was promoted to it after a time, for good conduct, you know, and that sort of thing. But--but I began differently--I began by wearing the prison dress, and working in the quarries."

"My good fellow," said Mueller, gently, "I half suspected this--I am not sur-prised; and I respect you for having redeemed that past in the way you have re-deemed it."

"Thank you, M'sieur Mueller; but you see, redeemed or unredeemed, I'd rather be lying at the bottom of the Seine than have it rise up against me now,"

"We are men of honor," said Mueller, "and your secret is safe with us."

"Not if you go to the Prefecture and inform against Bras de Fer on my words," exclaimed the model, eagerly. "How can I appear against him--Guichet the model--Guichet the Garde Chiourme--Guichet the *forcat?* M'sieur Mueller, I could never hold my head up again. It would be the ruin of me."

"You shall not appear against him, and it shall not be the ruin of you. Guichet," said Mueller. "That I promise you. Only assure me that what you have said is strictly correct--that Bras de Fer and Lenoir are one and the same person--an escaped *forcat*, condemned for life to the galleys."

"That's as true, M'sieur Mueller, as that God is in heaven," said the model, emphatically.

"Then I can prove it without your testimony--I can prove it by simply summoning any of the Toulon authorities to identify him."

"Or by stripping his shirt off his back, and showing the brand on his left shoulder," said Guichet. "There you'll find it, T.F. as large as life--and if it don't show at first, just you hit him a sharp blow with the flat of your hand, M'sieur Mueller, and it will start out as red and fresh as if it had been done only six months ago. *Parbleu!* I remember the day he came in, and the look in his face when the hot iron hissed into his flesh! They roar like bulls, for the most part; but he never flinched or spoke. He just turned a shade paler under the tan, and that was all."

"Do you remember what his crime was?" asked Mueller

Guichet shook his head.

"Not distinctly," he said. "I only know that he was in for a good deal, and had a lot of things proved against him on his trial. But you can find all that out for yourself, easily enough. He was tried in Paris, about fourteen years ago, and it's all in print, if you only know where to look for it."

"Then I'll find it, if I have to wade through half the Bibliotheque Nationale!" said Mueller. "Adieu, Guichet--you have done me a great service, and you may be sure I will do nothing to betray you. Let us shake hands upon it."

The color rushed into the model's swarthy cheeks.

"*Comment*, M'sieur Mueller!" he said, hesitatingly. "You offer to shake hands with me--after what I have told you?"

"Ten times more willing than before, *mon ami*," said Mueller. "Did I not tell you just now that I respected you for having redeemed that past, and shall I not give my hand where I give my respect?"

The model grasped his outstretched hand with a vehemence that made Mueller wince again.

"Thank you," he said, in a low, deep voice. "Thank you. Death of my life! M'sieur Mueller, I'd go to the galleys again for you, after this--if you asked me."

"Agreed. Only when I do ask you, it shall be to pay a visit of ceremony to Monsieur Bras de Fer, when he is safely lodged again at Toulon with a chain round his leg, and a cannon-ball at the end of it."

And with this Mueller turned away laughingly, and I followed him down the dimly-lighted stairs.

"By Jove!" he said, "what a grip the fellow gave me! I'd as soon shake hands with the Commendatore in Don Giovanni."

CHAPTER XXXVIII.
NUMBER TWO HUNDRED AND SEVEN.

Mueller, when he so confidently proposed to visit Bras de Fer in his future retirement at Toulon, believed that he had only to lodge his information with the proper authorities, and see the whole affair settled out of hand. He had not taken the bureaucratic system into consideration; and he had forgotten how little positive evidence he had to offer. It was no easier then than now to inspire the official mind with either insight or decision; and the police of Paris, inasmuch as they in no wise differed from the police of to-day, yesterday, or to-morrow, were slow to understand, slow to believe, and slower still to act.

An escaped convict? Monsieur le Chef du Bureau, upon whom we took the liberty of waiting the next morning, could scarcely take in the bare possibility of such a fact. An escaped convict? Bah! no convict could possibly escape under the present admirable system. ***Comment***! He effected his escape some years ago? How many years ago? In what yard, in what ward, under what number was he entered in the official books? For what offence was he convicted? Had Monsieur seen him at Toulon?--and was Monsieur prepared to swear that Lenoir and Bras de Fer were one and the same person? How! Monsieur proposed to identify a certain individual, and yet was incapable of replying to these questions! Would Monsieur be pleased to state upon what grounds he undertook to denounce the said individual, and what proof he was prepared to produce in confirmation of the same?

To all which official catechizing, Mueller, who (wanting Guichet's testimony) had nothing but his intense personal conviction to put forward, could only reply that he was ready to pledge himself to the accuracy of his information; and that if Monsieur the Chef du Bureau would be at the pains to call in any Toulon official of a few years' standing, he would undoubtedly find that the person now described as calling himself Lenoir, and the person commonly known in the Bagnes as Bras de Fer, were indeed "one and the same."

Whereupon Monsieur le Chef--a pompous personage, with a bald head and a white moustache--shrugged his shoulders, smiled incredulously, had the honor to point out to Monsieur that the Government could by no means be at the expense of conveying an inspector from Toulon to Paris on so shadowy and unsupported a statement, and politely bowed us out.

Thus rebuffed, Mueller began to despair of present success; whilst I, in default of any brighter idea, proposed that he should take legal advice on the subject. So we went to a certain avocat, in a little street adjoining the Ecole de Droit, and there purchased as much wisdom as might be bought for the sum of five francs sterling.

The avocat, happily, was fertile in suggestions. This, he said, was not a case for a witness. Here was no question of appearing before a court. With the foregone offences of either Lenoir or Bras de Fer, we had nothing to do; and to convict them of such offences formed no part of our plan. We only sought to show that Lenoir and Bras de Fer were in truth "one and the same person," and we could only do so upon the authority of some third party who had seen both. Now Monsieur Mueller had seen Lenoir, but not Bras de Fer; and Guichet had seen Bras de Fer, but not Lenoir. Here, then, was the real difficulty; and here, he hoped, its obvious solution. Let Guichet be taken to some place where, being himself unseen, he may obtain a glimpse of Lenoir. This done, he can, in a private interview of two minutes, state his conviction to Monsieur the Chef de Bureau--*voila tout*! If, however, the said Guichet can be persuaded by no considerations either of interest or justice, then another very simple course remains open. Every newly-arrived convict in every penal establishment throughout France is photographed on his entrance into the Bagne, and these photographs are duly preserved for purposes of identification like the present. Supposing therefore Bras de Fer had not escaped from Toulon before the introduction of this system, his portrait would exist in the official books to this day, and might doubtless be obtained, if proper application were made through an official channel.

Armed with this information, and knowing that any attempt to induce Guichet to move further in the matter would be useless, we then went back to the Bureau, and with much difficulty succeeded in persuading M. le Chef to send to Toulon for the photograph. This done, we could only wait and be patient.

Briefly, then, we did wait and were patient--though the last condition was not easy; for even I, who was by no means disposed to sympathize with Mueller in his solicitude for the fair Marie, could not but feel a strange contagion of excitement in this ***chasse au forcat***. And so a week or ten days went by, till one memorable afternoon, when Mueller came rushing round to my rooms in hot haste, about an hour before the time when we usually met to go to dinner, and greeted me with--

"Good news, ***mon vieux***! good news! The photograph has come--and I have been to the Bureau to see it--and I have identified my man--and he will be arrested to-night, as surely as that he carries T.F. on his shoulder!"

"You are certain he is the same?" I said.

"As certain as I am of my own face when I see it in the looking-glass."

And then he went on to say that a party of soldiers were to be in readiness a couple of hours hence, in a shop commanding Madame Marot's door; that he, Mueller, was to be there to watch with them till Lenoir either came out from or went into the house; and that as soon as he pointed him out to the sergeant in command, he was to be arrested, put into a cab waiting for the purpose, and conveyed to La Roquette.

Behold us, then, at the time prescribed, lounging in the doorway of a small shop adjoining the private entrance to Madame Marot's house; our hands in our pockets; our cigars in our mouths; our whole attitude expressive of idleness and unconcern. The wintry evening has closed in rapidly. The street is bright with lamps, and busy with passers-by. The shop behind us is quite dark--so dark that not the keenest observer passing by could detect the dusky group of soldiers sitting on the counter within, or the gleaming of the musket-barrels which rest between their knees. The sergeant in command, a restless, black-eyed, intelligent little Gascon, about five feet four in height, with a revolver stuck in his belt, paces impatiently to and fro, and whistles softly between his teeth. The men, four in number, whisper together from time to time, or swing their feet in silence.

Thus the minutes go by heavily; for it is weary work waiting in this way, uncertain how long the watch may last, and not daring to relax the vigilance of eye and ear for a single moment. It may be for an hour, or for many hours, or it may be for only a few minutes-who can tell? Of Lenoir's daily haunts and habits we know nothing. All we do know is that he is wont to be out all day, sometimes returning only to dress and go out again; sometimes not coming home till very late at night; sometimes absenting himself for a day and a night, or two days and two nights together. With this uncertain prospect before us, therefore, we wait and watch, and watch and wait, counting the hours as they strike, and scanning every face that gleams past in the lamplight.

So the first hour goes by, and the second. Ten o'clock strikes. The traffic in the street begins perceptibly to diminish. Shops close here and there (Madame Marot's shutters have been put up by the boy in the oilskin apron more than an hour ago), and the *chiffonnier*, sure herald of the quieter hours of the night, flits by with rake and lanthorn, observant of the gutters.

The soldiers on' the counter yawn audibly from time to time; and the sergeant, who is naturally of an impatient disposition, exclaims, for the twentieth time, with an inexhaustible variety, however, in the choice of expletives:--

"*Mais; nom de deux cent mille petards*! will this man of ours never come?"

To which inquiry, though not directly addressed to myself, I reply, as I have already replied once or twice before, that he may come immediately, or that he may not come for hours; and that all we can do is to wait and be patient. In the midst of which explanation, Mueller suddenly lays his hand on my arm, makes a sign to the sergeant, and peers eagerly down the street.

There is a man coming up quickly on the opposite side of the way. For myself, I could recognise no one at such a distance, especially by night; but Mueller's keener eye, made keener still by jealousy, identifies him at a glance.

It is Lenoir.

He wears a frock coat closely buttoned, and comes on with a light, rapid step, suspecting nothing. The sergeant gives the word--the soldiers spring to their feet--I draw back into the gloom of the shop-and only Mueller remains, smoking his cigarette and lounging against the door-post.

Then Lenoir crosses over, and Mueller, affecting to observe him for the first time, looks up, and without lifting his hat, says loudly:--

"*Comment*! have I the honor of saluting Monsieur Lenoir?"

Whereupon Lenoir, thrown off his guard by the suddenness of the address, hesitates--seems about to reply--checks himself--quickens his pace, and passes without a word.

The next instant he is surrounded. The butt ends of four muskets rattle on the pavement--the sergeant's hand is on his shoulder--the sergeant's voice rings in his ear.

"Number two hundred and seven, you are my prisoner!"

CHAPTER XXXIX.
THE END OF BRAS BE FER.

LENOIR's first impulse was to struggle in silence; then, finding escape hopeless, he folded his arms and submitted.

"So, it is Monsieur Mueller who has done me this service," he said coldly; but with a flash in his eye like the sudden glint in the eye of a cobra di capello. "I will take care not to be unmindful of the obligation."

Then, turning impatiently upon the sergeant:--

"Have you no carriage at hand?" he said, sharply; "or do you want to collect a crowd in the street?"

The cab, however, which had been waiting a few doors lower down, drove up while he was speaking. The sergeant hurried him in; the half-dozen loiterers who had already gathered about us pressed eagerly forward; two of the soldiers and the sergeant got inside; Mueller and I scrambled up beside the driver; word was given "to the Prefecture of Police;" and we drove rapidly away down the Rue du Faubourg St. Denis, through the arch of Louis Quatorze, out upon the bright noisy Boulevard, and on through thoroughfares as brilliant and crowded as at midday, towards the quays and the river.

Arrived at the Quai des Ortevres, we alighted at the Prefecture, and were conducted through a series of ante-rooms and corridors into the presence of the same bald-headed Chef de Bureau whom we had seen on each previous occasion. He looked up as we came in, pressed the spring of a small bell that stood upon his desk, and growled something in the ear of a clerk who answered the summons.

"Sergeant," he said, pompously, "bring the prisoner under the gas-burner."

Lenoir, without waiting to be brought, took a couple of steps forward, and placed himself in the light.

Monsieur le Chef then took out his double eye-glass, and proceeded to compare Lenoir's face, feature by feature, with a photograph which he took out of his pocket-book for the purpose.

"Are you prepared, Monsieur," he said, addressing Mueller for the first time--"are you, I say, prepared to identify the prisoner upon oath?"

"Within certain limitations--yes," replied Mueller.

"Certain limitations!" exclaimed the Chef, testily. "What do you mean by 'certain limitations?' Here is the man whom you accuse, and here is the photograph. Are you, I repeat, prepared to make your deposition before Monsieur le Prefet that they are one and the same person?"

"I am neither more nor less prepared, Monsieur," said Mueller, "than you are; or than Monsieur le Prefet, when he has the opportunity of judging. As I have already had the honor of informing you, I saw the prisoner for the first time about two months since. Having reason to believe that he was living in Paris under an assumed name, and wearing a decoration to which he had no right, I prosecuted certain inquiries about him. The result of those inquiries led me to conclude that he was an escaped convict from the Bagnes of Toulon. Never having seen him at Toulon, I was unable to prove this fact without assistance. You, Monsieur, have furnished that assistance, and the proof is now in your hand. It only remains for Monsieur le Prefet and yourself to decide upon its value."

"Give me the photograph, Monsieur Marmot," said a pale little man in blue spectacles, who had come in unobserved from a door behind us, while Mueller was speaking.

The bald-headed Chef jumped up with great alacrity, bowed like a second Sir Pertinax, and handed over the photograph.

"The peculiar difficulty of this case, Monsieur le Prefet" ... he began.

The Prefet waved his hand.

"Thanks, Monsieur Marmot," he said, "I know all the particulars of this case. You need not trouble to explain them. So this is the photograph forwarded from Toulon. Well--well! Sergeant, strip the prisoner's shoulders."

A sudden quiver shot over Lenoir's face at this order, and his cheek blenched under the tan; but he neither spoke nor resisted. The next moment his coat and waistcoat were lying on the ground; his shirt, torn in the rough handling, was hanging round his loins, and he stood before us naked to the waist, lean, brown, muscular--a torso of an athlete done in bronze.

We pressed round eagerly. Monsieur le Chef put up his double eye-glass; Monsier le Prefet took off his blue spectacles.

"So--so," he said, pointing with the end of his glasses towards a whitish, indefinite kind of scar on Lenoir's left shoulder, "here is a mark like a burn. Is this the brand?"

The sergeant nodded.

"V'la, M'sieur le Prefet!" he said, and struck the spot smartly with his open palm. Instantly the smitten place turned livid, while from the midst of it, like the handwriting on the wall, the fatal letters T. F. sprang out in characters of fire.

Lenoir flashed a savage glance upon us, and checked the imprecation that rose to his lips. Monsieur le Prefet, with a little nod of satisfaction, put on his glasses again, went over to the table, took out a printed form from a certain drawer, dipped a pen in the ink, and said:--

"Sergeant, you will take this order, and convey Number Two Hundred and Seven to the Bicetre, there to remain till Thursday next, when he will be drafted back to Toulon by the convict train, which leaves two hours after midnight. Monsieur Mueller, the Government is indebted to you for the assistance you have rendered the executive in this matter. You are probably aware that the prisoner is a notorious criminal, guilty of one proved murder, and several cases of forgery, card-sharping, and the like. The Government is also indebted to Monsieur Marmot" (here he inclined his head to the bald-headed Chef), "who has acted with his usual zeal and intelligence."

Monsieur Marmot, murmuring profuse thanks, bowed and bowed again, and followed Monsieur le Prefet obsequiously to the door. On the threshold, the great little man paused, turned, and said very quietly: "You understand, sergeant, this prisoner does *not* escape again;" and so vanished; leaving Monsieur Marmot still bowing in the doorway.

Then the sergeant hurried on Lenoir's coat and waistcoat, clapped a pair of handcuffs on his wrists, thrust his hat on his head, and prepared to be gone; Monsieur, the bald-headed, looking on, meanwhile, with the utmost complacency, as if taking to himself all the merit of discovery and capture.

"Pardon, Messieurs," said the serjeant, when all was ready. "Pardon--but here is a fellow for whom I am responsible now, and who must be strictly looked after. I shall have to put a gendarme on the box from here to the Bicetre, instead of you two gentlemen."

"All right, **mon ami**" said Mueller. "I suppose we should not have been admitted if we had gone with you?"

"Nay, I could pass you in, Messieurs, if you cared to see the affair to the end, and followed in another **fiacre**."

So we said we would see it to the end, and following the prisoner and his guard through all the rooms and corridors by which we had come, picked up a second cab on the Quai des Orfevres, just outside the Prefecture of Police.

It was now close upon midnight. The sky was flecked with driving clouds. The moon had just risen above the towers of Notre Dame. The quays were silent and deserted. The river hurried along, swirling and turbulent. The sergeant's cab led the way, and the driver, instead of turning back towards the Pont Neuf, followed the line of the quays along the southern bank of the Ile de la Cite; passing the Morgue--a mass of sinister shadow; passing the Hotel Dieu; traversing the Parvis Notre Dame; and making for the long bridge, then called the Pont Louis Philippe, which connects the two river islands with the northern half of Paris.

"It is a wild-looking night," said Mueller, as we drove under the mountainous shadow of Notre Dame and came out again in sight of the river.

"And it is a wild business to be out upon," I added. "I wonder if this is the end of it?"

The words were scarcely past my lips when the door of the cab ahead flew suddenly open, and a swift something, more like a shadow than a man, darted across the moonlight, sprang upon the parapet of the bridge, and disappeared!

In an instant we were all out--all rushing to and fro--all shouting--all wild with surprise and confusion.

"One man to the Pont d'Arcole!" thundered the sergeant, running along the perapet, revolver in hand. "One to the Quai Bourbon--one to the Pont de la Cite! Watch up stream and down! The moment he shows his head above water, fire!"

"But, in Heaven's name, how did he escape?" exclaimed Mueller.

"**Grand Dieu**! who can tell--unless he is the very devil?" cried the sergeant, distractedly. "The handcuffs were on the floor, the door was open, and he was gone in a breath! Hold! What's that?"

The soldier on the Pont de la Cite gave a shout and fired. There was a splash--a plunge--a rush to the opposite parapet.

"There he goes!"

"Where?"

"He has dived again!"

"Look--look yonder--between the floating bath and the bank!"

The sergeant stood motionless, his revolver ready cocked--the water swirled and eddied, eddied and parted--a dark dot rose for a second to the surface!

Three shots fired at the same moment (one by the sergeant, two by the soldiers) rang sharply through the air, and were echoed with startling suddenness again and again from the buttressed walls of Notre Dame. Ere the last echo had died away, or the last faint smoke-wreath had faded, two boats were pulling to the spot, and all the quays were alive with a fast-gathering crowd. The sergeant beckoned to the gendarme who had come upon the box.

"Bid the boatmen drag the river just here between the two bridges," he said, "and bring the body up to the Prefecture." Then, turning to Mueller and myself, "I am sorry to trouble you again, Messieurs," he said, "but I must ask you to come back once more to the Quai des Orfevres, to depose to the facts which have just happened."

"But is the man shot, or has he escaped?" asked a breathless bystander.

"Both," said the sergeant, with a grim smile, replacing his revolver in his belt. "He has escaped Toulon; but he has gone to the bottom of the Seine with something like six ounces of lead in his skull."

CHAPTER XL
THE ENIGMA OF THE THIRD STORY.

Who ever loved, that loved not at first sight?--MARLOWE.

In Paris, a lodging-house (or, as they prefer to style it, a ***hotel meuble***) is a little town in itself; a beehive swarming from basement to attic; a miniature model of the great world beyond, with all its loves and hatreds, jealousies, aspirations, and struggles. Like that world, it contains several grades of society, but with this difference, that those who therein occupy the loftiest position are held in the lowest estimation. Thus, the fifth-floor lodgers turn up their noses at the inhabitants of the attics; while the fifth-floor is in its turn scorned by the fourth, and the fourth is despised by the third, and the third by the second, down to the magnificent dwellers on ***the premier etage***, who live in majestic disdain of everybody above or beneath them, from the grisettes in the garret, to the ***concierge*** who has care of the cellars.

The house in which I lived in the Cite Bergere was, in fact, a double house, and contained no fewer than thirty tenants, some of whom had wives, children, and servants. It consisted of six floors, and each floor contained from eight to ten rooms. These were let in single chambers, or in suites, as the case might be; and on the outer doors opening round the landings were painted the names, or affixed the visiting-cards, of the dwellers within. My own third-floor neighbors were four in number. To my left lived a certain Monsieur and Madame Lemercier, a retired couple from Alsace. Opposite their door, on the other side of the well staircase, dwelt one Monsieur Cliquot, an elderly ***employe*** in some public office; next to him, Signor Milanesi, an Italian refugee who played in the orchestra at the ***Varietes*** every night, was given to practising the violoncello by day, and wore as much hair about his face as a Skye-terrier. Lastly, in the apartment to my right, resided a lady, upon whose door was nailed a small visiting-card engraved with these words:--

MLLE. HORTENSE DUFRESNOY.

Teacher of Languages.

I had resided in the house for months before I ever beheld this Mademoiselle Hortense Dufresnoy. When I did at last encounter her upon the stairs one dusk autumnal evening, she wore a thick black veil, and, darting past me like a bird on the wing, disappeared down the staircase in fewer moments than I take to write it. I scarcely observed her at the time. I had no more curiosity to learn whether the face under that veil was pretty or plain than I cared to know whether the veil itself was Shetland or Chantilly. At that time Paris was yet new to me: Madame de Marignan's evil influence was about me; and, occupied as my time and thoughts were with unprofitable matters, I took no heed of my fellow-lodgers. Save, indeed, when the groans of that much-tortured violoncello woke me in the morning to an unwelcome consciousness of the vicinity of Signor Milanesi, I should scarcely have remembered that I was not the only inhabitant of the third story.

Now, however, that I spent all my evenings in my own quiet room, I became, by imperceptible degrees, interested in the unseen inhabitant of the adjoining apartment. Sometimes, when the house was so still that the very turning of the page sounded unnaturally loud, and the mere falling of a cinder startled me, I heard her in her chamber, singing softly to herself. Every night I saw the light from her window streaming out over the balcony and touching the evergreens with a midnight glow. Often and often, when it was so late that even I had given up study and gone to bed, I heard her reading aloud, or pacing to and fro to the measure of her own recitations. Listen as I would, I could only make out that these recitations were poetical fragments--I could only distinguish a certain chanted metre, the chiming of an occasional rhyme, the rising and falling of a voice more than commonly melodious.

This vague interest gave place by-and-by to active curiosity. I resolved to question Madame Bouisse, the **concierge**; and as she, good soul! loved gossip not wisely, but too well, I soon knew all the little she had to tell.

Mademoiselle Hortense, it appeared, was the enigma of the third story. She had resided in the house for more than two years. She earned her living by her labor;

went out teaching all the day; sat up at night, studying and writing; had no friends; received no visitors; was as industrious as a bee, and as proud as a princess. Books and flowers were her only friends, and her only luxuries. Poor as she was, she was continually filling her shelves with the former, and supplying her balcony with the latter. She lived frugally, drank no wine, was singularly silent and reserved, and "like a real lady," said the fat *concierge*, "paid her rent to the minute."

This, and no more, had Madame Bouisse to tell. I had sought her in her own little retreat at the foot of the public staircase. It was a very wet afternoon, and under pretext of drying my boots by the fire, I stayed to make conversation and elicit what information I could. Now Madame Bouisse's sanctuary was a queer, dark, stuffy little cupboard devoted to many heterogeneous uses, and it "served her for parlor, kitchen, and all." In one corner stood that famous article of furniture which became "a bed by night, a chest of drawers by day." Adjoining the bed was the fireplace; near the fireplace stood a corner cupboard filled with crockery and surmounted by a grand ormolu clock, singularly at variance with the rest of the articles. A table, a warming-pan, and a couple of chairs completed the furniture of the room, which, with all its contents, could scarcely have measured more than eight feet square. On a shelf inside the door stood thirty flat candlesticks; and on a row of nails just beneath them, hung two and twenty bright brass chamber-door keys--whereby an apt arithmetician might have divined that exactly two-and-twenty lodgers were out in the rain, and only eight housed comfortably within doors.

"And how old should you suppose this lady to be?" I asked, leaning idly against the table whereon Madame Bouisse was preparing an unsavory dish of veal and garlic.

The *concierge* shrugged her ponderous shoulders.

"Ah, bah, M'sieur, I am no judge of age," said she.

"Well--is she pretty?"

"I am no judge of beauty, either," grinned Madame Bouisse.

"But, my dear soul," I expostulated, "you have eyes!"

"Yours are younger than mine, *mon enfant*," retorted the fat *concierge*; "and, as I see Mam'selle Hortense coming up to the door, I'd advise you to make use of them for yourself."

And there, sure enough, was a tall and slender girl, dressed all in black, pausing to close up her umbrella at the threshold of the outer doorway. A porter followed her, carrying a heavy parcel. Having deposited this in the passage, he touched his cap and stated his charge. The young lady took out her purse, turned over the coins, shook her head, and finally came up to Madame's little sanctuary.

"Will you be so obliging, Madame Bouisse," she said, "as to lend me a piece of ten sous? I have no small change left in my purse."

How shall I describe her? If I say that she was not particularly beautiful, I do her less than justice; for she was beautiful, with a pale, grave, serious beauty, unlike the ordinary beauty of woman. But even this, her beauty of feature, and color, and form, was eclipsed and overborne by that "true beauty of the soul" which outshines all other, as the sun puts out the stars.

There was in her face--or, perhaps, rather in her expression--an indefinable something that came upon me almost like a memory. Had I seen that face in some forgotten dream of long ago? Brown-haired was she, and pale, with a brow "as chaste ice, as pure as snow," and eyes--

"In whose orb a shadow lies,
Like the dusk in evening skies!"

Eyes lit from within, large, clear, lustrous, with a meaning in them so profound and serious that it was almost sorrowful,--like the eyes of Giotto's saints and Cimabue's Madonnas.

But I cannot describe her--

"For oh, her looks had something excellent That wants a name!"

I can only look back upon her with "my mind's eye," trying to see her as I saw her then for the first time, and striving to recall my first impressions.

Madame Bouisse, meanwhile, searched in all the corners of her ample pockets, turned out her table-drawer, dived into the recesses of her husband's empty garments, and peeped into every ornament upon the chimney-piece; but in vain. There was no such thing as a ten-sous piece to be found.

"Pray, M'sieur Basil," said she, "have you one?"

"One what?" I ejaculated, startled out of my reverie.

"Why, a ten-sous piece, to be sure. Don't you see that Mam'selle Hortense is waiting in her wet shoes, and that I have been hunting for the last five minutes, and can't find one anywhere?"

Blushing like a school-boy, and stammering some unintelligible excuse, I pulled out a handful of francs and half-francs, and produced the coin required.

"*Dame*!" said the *concierge*. "This comes of using one's eyes too well, my young Monsieur. Hem! I'm not so blind but that I can see as far as my neighbors."

Mademoiselle Hortense had fortunately gone back to settle with the porter, so this observation passed unheard. The man being dismissed, she came back, carrying the parcel. It was evidently heavy, and she put it down on the nearest chair.

"I fear, Madame Bouisse," she said, "that I must ask you to help me with this. I am not strong enough to carry it upstairs."

More alert this time, I took a step in advance, and offered my services.

"Will Mademoiselle permit me to take it?" I said. "I am going upstairs."

She hesitated.

"Many thanks," she said, reluctantly, "but...."

"But Madame Bouisse is busy," I urged, "and the *pot au feu* will spoil if she leaves it on the fire."

The fat *concierge* nodded, and patted me on the shoulder.

"Let him carry the parcel, Mam'selle Hortense," she chuckled. "Let him carry it. M'sieur is your neighbor, and neighbors should be neighborly. Besides," she added, in an audible aside, "he is a *bon garcon*--an Englishman--and a book-student like yourself."

The young lady bent her head, civilly, but proudly. Compelled, as it seemed, to accept my help, she evidently wished to show me that I must nevertheless put forward no claim to further intercourse--not even on the plea of neighborhood. I understood her, and taking up the parcel, followed her in silence to her door on the third story. Here she paused and thanked me.

"Pray let me carry it in for you," I said.

Again she hesitated; but only for an instant. Too well-bred not to see that a refusal would now be a discourtesy, she unlocked the door, and held it open.

The first room was an ante-chamber; the second a *salon* somewhat larger than my own, with a door to the right, leading into what I supposed would be her bedroom. At a glance, I took in all the details of her home. There was her writing-table laden with books and papers, her desk, and her pile of manuscripts. At one end of the room stood a piano doing duty as a side-board, and looking as if it were seldom opened. Some water-color drawings were pinned against the walls, and a well-filled bookcase stood in a recess beside the fireplace. Nothing escaped me --not even the shaded reading-lamp, nor the plain ebony time-piece, nor the bronze Apollo on the bracket above the piano, nor the sword over the mantelpiece, which seemed a strange ornament in the study of a gentle lady. Besides all this, there were books everywhere, heaped upon the tables, ranged on shelves, piled in corners, and scattered hither and thither in most admired disorder. It was, however, the only disorder there.

I longed to linger, but dared not. Having laid the parcel down upon the nearest chair, there was nothing left for me to do but to take my leave. Mademoiselle Dufresnoy still kept her hand upon the door.

"Accept my best thanks, sir," she said in English, with a pretty foreign accent, that seemed to give new music to the dear familiar tongue.

"You have nothing to thank me for, Mademoiselle," I replied.

She smiled, proudly still, but very sweetly, and closed the door upon me.

I went back to my room; it had become suddenly dark and desolate. I tried to read; but all subjects seemed alike tedious and unprofitable. I could fix my attention to nothing; and so, becoming restless, I went out again, and wandered about the dusky streets till evening fairly set in, and the shops were lighted, and the tide of passers-by began to flow faster in the direction of boulevard and theatre.

The soft light of her shaded lamp streamed from her window when I came back, nor faded thence till two hours after midnight. I watched it all the long evening, stealing out from time to time upon my balcony, which adjoined her own, and welcoming the cool night air upon my brow. For I was fevered and disquieted, I knew not why, and my heart was stirred within me, strangely and sweetly.

Such was my first meeting with Hortense Dufresnoy. No incident of it has since faded from my memory. Brief as it was, it had already turned all the current of my life. I had fallen in love at first sight. Yes--in love; for love it was--real, passionate, earnest; a love destined to be the master-passion of all my future years.

CHAPTER XLI.
A CHRONICLE ABOUT FROISSART.

See, Lucius, here's the book I sought for so!
JULIUS CAESAR.

But all be that he was a philosophre,
Yet hadde he but litel gold in cofre,
But all that he might of his frends hente,
On bokes and on lerning he is spente.
CHAUCER. &/

"L OVE-IN-IDLENESS" has passed into a proverb, and lovers, somehow, are not generally supposed to be industrious. I, however, worked none the less zealously for being in love. I applied only the more closely to my studies, both medical and literary, and made better progress in both than I had made before. I was not ambitious; but I had many incentives to work. I was anxious to satisfy my father. I earnestly desired to efface every unfavorable impression from the mind of Dr. Cheron, and to gain, if possible, his esteem. I was proud of the friendship of Madame de Courcelles, and wished to prove the value that I placed upon her good opinion. Above all, I had a true and passionate love of learning--not that love which leadeth on to fame; but rather that self-abandoning devotion which exchangeth willingly the world of action for the world of books, and, for an uninterrupted communion with the "souls of all that men held wise," bartereth away the society of the living.

Little gregarious by nature, Paris had already ceased to delight me in the same way that it had delighted me at first. A "retired leisure," and the society of the woman whom I loved, grew to be the day-dream of my solitary life. And still, ever more and more plainly, it became evident to me that for the career of the student I was designed by nature. Bayle, Magliabecchi of Florence, Isaac Reed, Sir Thomas Brown, Montaigne--those were the men whose lot in life I envied--those the literary anchorites in whose steps I would fain have followed.

But this was not to be; so I worked on, rose early, studied late, gained experience, took out my second inscription with credit, and had the satisfaction of knowing that I was fast acquiring the good opinion of Dr. Cheron. Thus Christmas passed by, and January with its bitter winds; and February set in, bright but frosty. And still, without encouragement or nope, I went on loving Hortense Dufresnoy.

My opportunities of seeing her were few and brief. A passing bow in the hall, or a distant "good-evening" as we passed upon the stairs, for some time made up the sum of our intercourse. Gradually, however, a kind of formal acquaintance sprang up between us; an acquaintance fostered by trifles and dependent on the idlest, or what seemed the idlest, casualties. I say "seemed," for often that which to her appeared the work of chance was the result of elaborate contrivance on my part. She little knew, when I met her on the staircase, how I had been listening for the last hour to catch the echo of her step. She little dreamed when I encountered her at the corner of the street, how I had been concealed, till that moment, in the *cafe* over the way, ready to dart out as soon as she appeared in sight. I would then affect either a polite unconcern, or an air of judicious surprise, or pretend not to lift my eyes at all till she was nearly past; and I think I must have been a very fair actor, for it all succeeded capitally, and I am not aware that she ever had the least suspicion of the truth. Let me, however, recall one incident over which I had no control, and which did more towards promoting our intercourse than all the rest.

It is a cold, bright morning in February. There is a brisk exhilaration in the air. The windows and gilded balconies sparkle in the sun, and it is pleasant to hear the frosty ring of one's boots upon the pavement. It is a fete to-day. Nothing is doing in the lecture-rooms, and I have the whole day before me. Meaning, therefore, to enjoy it over the fire and a book, I wisely begin it by a walk.

From the Cite Bergere, out along the right-hand side of the Boulevards, down past the front of the Madeleine, across the Place de la Concorde, and up the Champs Elysees as far as the Arc de Triomphe; this is the route I take in going. Arrived at the arch, I cross over, and come back by the same roads, but on the other side of the way. I have a motive in this. There is a certain second-hand book-shop on the opposite side of the Boulevard des Italiens, which draws me by a wholly irresistible attraction. Had I started on that side, I should have gone no further. I should have looked, lingered, purchased, and gone home to read. But I know my weakness. I have reserved the book-shop for my return journey, and now, rewarded and triumphant, compose myself for a quiet study of its treasures.

And what a book-shop it is! Not only are its windows filled--not only are its walls a very perspective of learning--but square pillars of volumes are built up on either side of the door, and an immense supplementary library is erected in the open air, down all the length of a dead-wall adjoining the house.

Here then I pause, turning over the leaves of one volume, reading the title of another, studying the personal appearance of a third, and weighing the merits of their authors against the contents of my purse. And when I say "personal appearance," I say it advisedly; for book-hunters, are skilled Lavaters in their way, and books, like men, attract or repel at first sight. Thus it happens that I love a portly book, in a sober coat of calf, but hate a thin, smart volume, in a gaudy binding. The one promises to be philosophic, learnedly witty, or solidly instructive; the other is tolerably certain to be pert and shallow, and reminds me of a coxcombical lacquey in bullion and red plush. On the same principle, I respect leaves soiled and dog's-eared, but mistrust gilt edges; love an old volume better than a new; prefer a spacious book-stall to all the unpurchased stores of Paternoster Row; and buy every book that I possess at second-hand. Nay, that it is second-hand is in itself a pass port to my favor. Somebody has read it before; therefore it is readable. Somebody has derived pleasure from it before; therefore I open it with a student's sympathy, and am disposed to be indulgent ere I have perused a single line. There are cases, however, in which I incline to luxury of binding. Just as I had rather have my historians in old calf and my chroniclers in black letter, so do I delight to see my modern poets, the Benjamins of my affections, clothed in coats of many colors. For them no moroccos are too rich, and no "toolings" too elaborate. I love to see them smiling on me from the shelves of my book-cases, as glowing and varied as the sunset through a painted oriel.

Standing here, then, to-day, dipping first into this work and then into that, I light upon a very curious and interesting edition of *Froissart*--an edition full of quaint engravings, and printed in the obsolete spelling of two hundred years ago. The book is both a treasure and a bargain, being marked up at five and twenty francs. Only those who haunt book-stalls and luxuriate in old editions can appreciate the satisfaction with which I survey

> "That weight of wood, with leathern coat overlaid,
> Those ample clasps of solid metal made,
> The close pressed leaves unclosed for many an age,
> The dull red edging of the well-filled page,
> And the broad back, with stubborn ridges roll'd,
> Where yet the title stands in tarnished gold!"

They only can sympathize in the eagerness with which I snatch up the precious volume, the haste with which I count out the five and twenty francs, the delight with which I see the dealer's hand close on the sum, and know that the book is legally and indisputably mine! Then how lovingly I embrace it under my arm, and taking advantage of my position as a purchaser, stroll leisurely round the inner warehouse, still courting that literary world which (in a library at least) always turns its back upon its worshipper!

"Pray, Monsieur," says a gentle voice at the door, "where is that old *Froissart* that I saw outside about a quarter of an hour ago?"

"Just sold, Madame," replies the bookseller, promptly.

"Oh, how unfortunate!--and I only went home for the money" exclaims the lady in a tone of real disappointment.

Selfishly exultant, I hug the book more closely, turn to steal a glance at my defeated rival, and recognise--Mademoiselle Dufresnoy.

She does not see me. I am standing in the inner gloom of the shop, and she is already turning away. I follow her at a little distance; keep her in sight all the way home; let her go into the house some few seconds in advance; and then, scaling three stairs at a time, overtake her at the door of her apartment.

Flushed and breathless, I stand beside her with *Froissart* in my hand.

"Pardon, Mademoiselle," I say, hurriedly, "for having involuntarily forestalled you just now. I had just bought the book you wished to purchase,"

She looks at me with evident surprise and some coldness; but says nothing.

"And I am rejoiced to have this opportunity of transferring it to you."

Mademoiselle Dufresnoy makes a slight but decided gesture of refusal.

"I would not deprive you of it, Monsieur," she says promptly, "upon any consideration."

"But, Mademoiselle, unless you allow me to relinquish it in your favor, I beg to assure you that I shall take the book back to the bookseller and exchange it for some other."

"I cannot conceive why you should do that, Monsieur."

"In order, Mademoiselle, that you may still have it in your power to become the purchaser."

"And yet you wished to possess the book, or you would not have bought it."

"I would not have bought it, Mademoiselle, if I had known that I should disappoint a--a lady by doing so,"

I was on the point of saying, "if I had known that I should disappoint you by so doing," but hesitated, and checked myself in time.

A half-mocking smile flitted across her lips.

"Monsieur is too self-sacrificing," she said. "Had I first bought the book, I should have kept it--being a woman. Reverse the case as you will, and show me any just reason why you should not do the same--being a man?"

"Nay, the merest by-law of courtesy..." I began, hesitatingly.

"Do not think me ungracious, Monsieur," she interrupted, "if I hold that these so-called laws of courtesy are in truth but concessions, for the most part, from the strength of your sex to the weakness of ours."

"*Eh bien*, Mademoiselle--what then?"

"Then, Monsieur, may there not be some women---myself, for instance--who do not care to be treated like children?"

"Pardon, Mademoiselle, but are you stating the case quite fairly? Is it not rather that we desire not to efface the last lingering tradition of the age of chivalry--not to reduce to prose the last faint echoes of that poetry which tempered the sword of the Crusader and inspired the song of the Trouvere?"

"Were it not better that the new age created a new code and a new poetry?" said Mademoiselle Dufresnoy.

"Perhaps; but I confess I love old forms and usages, and cling to creeds outworn. Above all, to that creed which in the age of powder and compliment, no less than in the age of chivalry, enjoined absolute devotion and courtesy towards women."

"Against mere courtesy reasonably exercised and in due season, I have nothing to say," replied Mademoiselle Dufresnoy; "but the half-barbarous homage of the Middle Ages is as little to my taste as the scarcely less barbarous refinement of the Addison and Georgian periods. Both are alike unsound, because both have a basis of insincerity. Just as there is a mock refinement more vulgar than simple vulgarity, so are there courtesies which humiliate and compliments that offend."

"Mademoiselle is pleased to talk in paradoxes," said I.

Mademoiselle unlocked her door, and turning towards me with the same half-mocking smile and the same air of raillery, said:--

"Monsieur, it is written in your English histories that when John le Bon was taken captive after the battle of Cressy, the Black Prince rode bareheaded before him through the streets of London, and served him at table as the humblest of his attendants. But for all that, was John any the less a prisoner, or the Black Prince any the less a conqueror?"

"You mean, perhaps, that you reject all courtesy based on mere ceremonial. Let me then put the case of this ***Froissart*** more plainly--as I would have done from the first, had I dared to speak the simple truth."

"And that is...?"

"That it will give me more pleasure to resign the book to you, Mademoiselle, than to possess it myself."

Mademoiselle Dufresnoy colors up, looks both haughty and amused, and ends by laughing.

"In truth, Monsieur," she says merrily, "if your politeness threatened at first to be too universal, it ends by becoming unnecessarily particular."

"Say rather, Mademoiselle, that you will not have the book on any terms!" I exclaim impatiently.

"Because you have not yet offered it to me upon any just or reasonable grounds."

"Well, then, bluntly and frankly, as student to student, I beg you to spare me the trouble of carrying this book back to the Boulevard. Yours, Mademoiselle, was the first intention. You saw the book before I saw it. You would have bought it on the spot, but had to go home for the money. In common equity, it is yours. In common civility, as student to student, I offer it to you. Say, is it yes or no?"

"Since you put it so simply and so generously, and since I believe you really wish me to accept your offer," replies Mademoiselle Dufresnoy, taking out her purse, "I suppose I must say--yes."

And with this, she puts out her hand for the hook, and offers me in return the sum of five and twenty francs.

Pained at having to accept the money, pained at being offered it, seeing no way of refusing it, and feel altogether more distress than is reasonable in a man brought up to the taking of fees; I affect not to see the coin, and, bowing, move away in the direction of my own door.

"Pardon, Monsieur," she says, "but you forget that I am in your debt."

"And--and do you really insist..."

She looks at me, half surprised and half offended.

"If you do not take the money, Monsieur, how can I take the book?"

Bowing, I receive the unwelcome francs in my unwilling palm.

Still she lingers.

"I--I have not thanked you as I ought for your generosity," she says, hesitatingly.

"Generosity!" I repeat, glancing with some bitterness at the five and twenty francs.

"True kindness, Monsieur, is neither bought nor sold," says the lady, with the loveliest smile in the world, and closes her door.

CHAPTER XLII
THE OLD, OLD STORY.

What thing is Love, which nought can countervail?
Nought save itself--even such a thing is Love.
SIR W. RALEIGH.

My acquaintance with Hortense Dufresnoy progressed slowly as, ever, and not even the Froissart incident went far towards promoting it. Absorbed in her studies, living for the intellect only, too self-contained to know the need for sympathy, she continued to be, at all events for me, the most inaccessible of God's creatures. And yet, despite her indifference, I loved her. Her pale, proud face haunted me; her voice haunted me. I thought of her sometimes till it seemed impossible she should not in some way be conscious of how my very soul was centred in her. But she knew nothing--guessed nothing--cared nothing; and the knowledge that I held no place in her life wrought in me at times till it became almost too bitter for endurance.

And this was love--real, passionate, earnest; the first and last love of my heart. Did I believe that I ever loved till now? Ah! no; for now only I felt the god in his strength, and beheld him in his beauty. Was I not blind till I had looked into her eyes and drunk of their light? Was I not deaf till I had heard the music of her voice? Had I ever truly lived, or breathed, or known delight till now?

I never stayed to ask myself how this would end, or whither it would lead me. The mere act of loving was too sweet for questioning. What cared I for the uncertainties of the future, having hope to live upon in the present? Was it not enough "to feed for aye my lamp and flames of love," and worship her till that worship became a religion and a rite?

And now, longing to achieve something which should extort at least her admiration, if not her love, I wished I were a soldier, that I might win glory for her--or a poet, that I might write verses in her praise which should be deathless--or a painter, that I might spend years of my life in copying the dear perfection of her face. Ah! and I would so copy it that all the world should be in love with it. Not a wave of her brown hair that I would not patiently follow through all its windings. Not the tender tracery of a blue vein upon her temples that I would not lovingly render through its transparent veil of skin. Not a depth of her dark eyes that I would not study, "deep drinking of the infinite." Alas! those eyes, so grave, so luminous, so steadfast:--

"Eyes not down-dropt, not over-bright, but fed
With the clear-pointed flame of chastity,"

--eyes wherein dwelt "thought folded over thought," what painter need ever hope to copy them?

And still she never dreamed how dear she had grown to me. She never knew how the very air seemed purer to me because she breathed it. She never guessed how I watched the light from her window night after night--how I listened to every murmur in her chamber--how I watched and waited for the merest glimpse of her as she passed by--how her lightest glance hurried the pulses through my heart--how her coldest word was garnered up in the treasure-house of my memory! What cared she, though to her I had dedicated all the "book and volume of my brain;" hallowed its every page with blazonings of her name; and illuminated it, for love of her, with fair images, and holy thoughts, and forms of saints and angels

"Innumerable, of stains and splendid dyes
As are the tiger-moth's deep damask'd wings?"

Ah me! her hand was never yet outstretched to undo its golden clasps--her eye had never yet deigned to rest upon its records. To her I was nothing, or less than nothing--a fellow-student, a fellow-lodger, a stranger.

And yet I loved her "with a love that was more than love"--with a love dearer than life and stronger than death--a love that, day after day, struck its roots deeper and farther into my very soul, never thence to be torn up here or hereafter.

CHAPTER XLIII.
ON A WINTER'S EVENING.

After a more than usually severe winter, the early spring came, crowned with rime instead of primroses. Paris was intensely cold. In March the Seine was still frozen, and snow lay thickly on the house-tops. Quiet at all times, the little nook in which I lived became monastically still, and at night, when the great gates were closed, and the footsteps of the passers-by fell noiselessly upon the trodden snow, you might have heard a whisper from one side of the street to the other. There was to me something indescribably delightful about this silent solitude in the heart of a great city.

Sitting beside the fire one evening, enjoying the profound calm of the place, attending from time to time to my little coffee-pot on the hob, and slowly turning the pages of a favorite author, I luxuriate in a state of mind half idle, half studious. Leaving off presently to listen to some sound which I hear, or fancy I hear, in the adjoining room, I wonder for the twentieth time whether Hortense has yet returned from her long day's teaching; and so rise--open my window--and look out. Yes; the light from her reading-lamp streams out at last across the snow-laden balcony. Heigho! it is something even to know that she is there so near me--divided only by a thin partition!

Trying to comfort myself with this thought, I close the window again and return to my book, more restless and absent than before. Sitting thus, with the un-turned leaf lingering between my thumb and forefinger, I hear a rapid footfall on the stairs, and a musical whistle which, growing louder as it draws nearer, breaks off at my door, and is followed by a prolonged assault and battery of the outer panels.

"Welcome, noisiest of visitors!" I exclaim, knowing it to be Mueller before I even open the door. "You are quite a stranger. You have not been near me for a fortnight."

"It will not be your fault, Signor Book-worm, if I don't become a stranger *au pied de la lettre*" replies he, cheerily. "Why, man, it is close upon three weeks since you have crossed the threshold of my door. The Quartier Latin is aggrieved by your neglect, and the fine arts t'other side of the water languish and are forlorn."

So saying, he shakes the snow from his coat like a St. Bernard mastiff, perches his cap on the head of the plaster Niobe that adorns my chimney-piece, and lays aside the folio which he had been carrying under his arm. I, in the meanwhile, have wheeled an easy-chair to the fire, brought out a bottle of Chambertin, and piled on more wood in honor of my guest.

"You can't think," said I, shaking hands with him for the second time, "how glad I am that you have come round to-night."

"I quite believe it," replied he. "You must be bored to death, if these old busts are all the society you keep. *Sacre nom d'une pipe*! how can a fellow keep up his conviviality by the perpetual contemplation of Niobe and Jupiter Tonans? What do you mean by living such a life as this? Have you turned Trappist? Shall I head a subscription to present you with a skull and an hour-glass?"

"I'll have the skull made into a drinking-cup, if you do. Take some wine."

Mueller filled his glass, tasted with the air of a connoisseur, and nodded approvingly.

"Chambertin, by the god Bacchus!" said he. "Napoleon's favorite wine, and mine--evidence of the sympathy that exists between the truly great."

And, draining the glass, he burst into a song in praise of French wines, beginning--

"Le Chambertin rend joyeux,
Le Nuits rend infatigable,
Le Volnay rend amoureux,
Le Champagne rend amiable.
Grisons-nous, mes chers amis,
L'ivresse
Vaut la richesse;
Pour moi, des que le suis gris,

Je possede tout Paris!"

"Oh hush!" said I, uneasily; "not so loud, pray!"
"Why not?"
"The--the neighbors, you know. We cannot do as we would in the Quartier Latin."
"Nonsense, my dear fellow. You don't swear yourself to silence when you take apartments in a ***hotel meuble***! You might as well live in a penitentiary!--

'De bouchons faisons un tas,
Et s'il faut avoir la goutte,
Au moins que ce ne soit pas
Pour n'avoir bu qu'une goutte!'"

"Nay, I implore you!" I interposed again. "The landlord ..."
"Hang the landlord!

'Grisons-nous--'"
"Well, but--but there is a lady in the next room ..."

Mueller laughed till the tears ran down his cheeks.
"***Allons done***!" said he, "why not have told the truth at first? Oh, you sly rogue! You ***gaillard***! This is your seclusion, is it? This is your love of learning--this the secret of your researches into science and art! What art, pray? Ovid's 'Art of Love,' I'll be sworn!"
"Laugh on, pray," I said, feeling my face and my temper growing hot; "but that lady, who is a stranger to me"....
"Oh--oh--oh!" cried Mueller.
"Who is a stranger to me," I repeated, "and who passes her evenings in study, must not be annoyed by noises in my room. Surely, my dear fellow, you know me well enough to understand whether I am in jest or in earnest."
Mueller laid his hand upon my sleeve.
"Enough--enough," he said, smiling good-naturedly. "You are right, and I will

be as dumb as Plato. What is the lady's name."

"Dufresnoy," I answered, somewhat reluctantly. "Mademoiselle Dufresnoy."

"Ay, but her Christian name!"

"Her Christian name," I faltered, more reluctant still. "I--I--"

"Don't say you don't know," said Mueller, maliciously. "It isn't worth while. After all, what does it matter? Here's to her health, all the same--*a votre sante*, Mademoiselle Dufresnoy! What! not drink her health, though I have filled your glass on purpose?"

There was no help for it, so I took the glass and drank the toast with the best grace I could.

"And now, tell me," continued my companion, drawing nearer to the fire and settling himself with a confidential air that was peculiarly provoking, "what is she like? Young or old? Dark or fair? Plain or pretty?"

"Old," said I, desperately. "Old and ugly. Fifty at the least. Squints horribly."

Then, thinking that I had been a little too emphatic, I added:--

"But a very ladylike person, and exceedingly well-informed,"

Mueller looked at me gravely, and filled his glass again.

"I think I know the lady," said he.

"Indeed?"

"Yes--by your description. You forgot to add, however, that she is gray."

"To be sure--as a badger."

"To say nothing of a club foot, an impediment in her speech, a voice like a raven's, and a hump like a dromedary's! Ah! my dear friend, what an amazingly comic fellow you are!"

And the student burst again into a peal of laughter so hearty and infectious that I could not have helped joining in it to save my life.

"And now," said he, when we had laughed ourselves out of breath, "now to the object of my visit. Do you remember asking me, months ago, to make you a copy of an old portrait that you had taken a fancy to in some tumble-down chateau near Montlhery!"

"To be sure; and I have intended, over and over again, to remind you of it. Did you ever take the trouble to go over there and look at it?"

"Look at it, indeed! I should rather think so--and here is the proof. What does your connoisseurship say to it?"

Say to it! Good heavens! what could I say, what could I do, but flush up all suddenly with pleasure, and stare at it without power at first to utter a single word?

For it was like *her*--so like that it might have been her very portrait. The features were cast in the same mould--the brow, perhaps, was a little less lofty--the smile a little less cold; but the eyes, the beautiful, lustrous, soul-lighted eyes were the same--the very same!

If she were to wear an old-fashioned dress, and deck her fair neck and arms with pearls, and put powder on her hair, and stand just so, with her hand upon one of the old stone urns in the garden of that deserted chateau, she would seem to be standing for the portrait.

Well might I feel, when I first saw her, that the beauty of her face was not wholly unfamiliar to me! Well might I fancy I had seen her in some dream of long ago!

So this was the secret of it--and this picture was mine. Mine to hang before my desk when I was at work--mine to place at my bed's foot, where I might see it on first waking--mine to worship and adore, to weave fancies and build hopes upon, and "burn out the day in idle phantasies" of passionate devotion!

"Well," said Mueller impatiently, "what do you think of it?"

I looked up, like one dreaming.

"Think of it!" I repeated.

"Yes--do you think it like?"

"So like that it might be her por ... I mean that it might be the original."

"Oh, that's satisfactory. I was afraid you were disappointed."

"I was only silent from surprise and pleasure."

"Well, however faithful the copy maybe, you know, in these things one always misses the tone of age."

"I would not have it look a day older!" I exclaimed, never lifting my eyes from the canvas.

Mueller came and looked down at it over my shoulder.

"It is an interesting head," said he. "I have a great mind to introduce it into my next year's competition picture."

I started as if he had struck me. The thought was sacrilege!

"For Heaven's sake do no such thing!" I ejaculated.

"Why not?" said he, opening his eyes in astonishment.

"I cannot tell you why--at least not yet; but to--to confer a very particular obligation upon me, will you waive this point?" Mueller rubbed his head all over with both hands, and sat down in the utmost perplexity.

"Upon my soul and conscience," said he, "you are the most incomprehensible fellow I ever knew in my life!"

"I am. I grant it. What then? Let us see, I am to give you a hundred and fifty francs for this copy ..."

"I won't take it," said Mueller. "I mean you to accept it as a pledge of friendship and good-will."

"Nay, I insist on paying for it. I shall be proud to pay for it; but a hundred and fifty are not enough. Let me give you three hundred, and promise me that you will not put the head into your picture!"

Mueller laughed, and shook his own head resolutely. "I will give you both the portrait and the promise," said he; "but I won't take your money, if I know it."

"But ..."

"But I won't--and so, if you don't like me well enough to accept such a trifle from me, I'll e'en carry the thing home again!"

And, snatching up his cap and cloak, he made a feint of putting the portrait back into the folio.

"Not for the world!" I exclaimed, taking possession of it without further remonstrance. "I would sooner part from all I possess. How can I ever thank you enough?"

"By never thanking me at all! What little time the thing has cost me is overpaid, not only by the sight of your pleasure, but by my own satisfaction in copying it. To copy a good work is to have a lesson from the painter, though he were dead a hundred years before; and the man who painted that portrait, be he who he might, has taught me a trick or two that I never knew before. *Sapristi*! see if I don't dazzle you some day with an effect of white satin and pearls against a fair skin!"

"An ingenious argument; but it leaves me unconvinced, all the same. How! you are not going to run away already? Here's another bottle of Chambertin waiting to be opened; and it is yet quite early."

"Impossible! I have promised to meet a couple of men up at the Prado, and have, besides, invited them afterwards to supper."

"What is the Prado?"

"The Prado! Why, is it possible that I have never yet introduced you to the Prado? It's one of the joiliest places in all the Quartier Latin--it's close to the Palais de Justice. You can dance there, or practise pistol-shooting, or play billiards, or sup--or anything you please. Everybody smokes--ladies not excepted."

"How very delightful!"

"Oh, magnificent! Won't you come with me? I know a dozen pretty girls who will be delighted to be introduced to you."

"Not to-night, thank you," said I, laughing.

"Well, another time?"

"Yes, to be sure--another time."

"Well, good-night."

"Good-night, and thank you again, a thousand times over."

But he would not stay to hear me thank him, and was half way down the first flight before my sentence was finished. Just as I was going back into my room, and about to close the door, he called after me from the landing.

"*Hola, amigo*! When my picture is done, I mean to give a bachelor's supper-party--chiefly students and *chicards*. Will you come?"

"Gladly."

"Adieu, then. I will let you know in time."

And with this, he broke out into a fragment of Beranger, gave a cheerful good-night to Madame Bouisse in the hall, and was gone.

And now to enjoy my picture. Now to lock the door, and trim the lamp, and place it up against a pile of books, and sit down before it in silent rapture, like a devotee before the portrait of his patron saint. Now I can gaze, unreproved, into those eyes, and fancy they are hers. Now press my lips, unforbidden, upon that exquisite mouth, and believe it warm. Ah, will her eyes ever so give back the look of love in mine? Will her lips ever suffer mine to come so near? Would she, if she knew the treasure I possessed, be displeased that I so worshipped it?

Hanging over it thus, and suffering my thoughts to stray on at their own will and pleasure, I am startled by the fall of some heavy object in the adjoining chamber. The fall is followed by a stifled cry, and then all is again silent.

To unlock my door and rush to hers--to try vainly to open it--to cry "Hortense! Hortense! what has happened? For Heaven's sake, what has happened?" is the work of but an instant.

The antechamber lay between, and I remembered that she could not hear me. I ran back, knocked against the wall, and repeated:--

"What has happened? Tell me what has happened?"

Again I listened, and in that interval of suspense heard her garments rustle along the ground, then a deep sigh, and then the words:--

"Nothing serious. I have hurt my hand."

"Can you open the door?"

There was another long silence.

"I cannot," she said at length, but more faintly.

"In God's name, try!"

No answer.

"Shall I get over the balcony?"

I waited another instant, heard nothing, and then, without, further hesitation, opened my own window and climbed the iron rail that separated her balcony from mine, leaving my footsteps trampled in the snow.

I found her sitting on the floor, with her body bent forward and her head resting against the corner of a fallen bookcase. The scattered volumes lay all about. A half-filled portmanteau stood close by on a chair. A travelling-cloak and a passport-case lay on the table.

Seeing, yet scarcely noting all this, I flung myself on my knees beside her, and found that one hand and arm lay imprisoned under the bookcase. She was not insensible, but pain had deprived her of the power of speech. I raised her head tenderly, and supported it against a chair; then lifted the heavy bookcase, and, one by one, removed the volumes that had fallen upon her.

Alas! the white little hand all crushed and bleeding--the powerless arm--the brave mouth striving to be firm!

I took the poor maimed arm, made a temporary sling for it with my cravat, and, taking her up in my arms as if she had been an infant, carried her to the sofa. Then I closed the window; ran back to my own room for hot water; tore up some old handkerchiefs for bandages; and so dressed and bound her wounds--blessing (for the first time in my life) the destiny that had made me a surgeon.

"Are you in much pain?" I asked, when all was done.

"Not now--but I feel very faint,"

I remembered my coffee in the next room, and brought it to her. I lifted her head, and supported her with my arm while she drank it.

"You are much better now," I said, when she had again lain down. "Tell me how it happened."

She smiled languidly.

"It was not my fault," she said, "but Froissart's. Do you remember that Froissart?"

Remember it! I should think so.

"Froissart!" I exclaimed. "Why, what had he to do with it?"

"Only this. I usually kept him on the top of the bookcase that fell down this evening. Just now, while preparing for a journey upon which I must start to-morrow morning, I thought to remove the book to a safer place; and so, instead of standing on a chair, I tried to reach up, and, reaching up, disturbed the balance of the bookcase, and brought it down."

"Could you not have got out of the way when you saw it falling?"

"Yes--but I tried to prevent it, and so was knocked down and imprisoned as you found me."

"Merciful Heaven! it might have killed you."

"That was what flashed across my mind when I saw it coming," she replied, with a faint smile.

"You spoke of a journey," I said presently, turning my face away lest she should read its story too plainly; "but now, of course, you must not move for a few days."

"I must travel to-morrow," she said, with quiet decision.

"Impossible!"

"I have no alternative."

"But think of the danger--the imprudence--the suffering."

"Danger there cannot be," she replied, with a touch of impatience in her voice. "Imprudent it may possibly be; but of that I have no time to think. And as for the suffering, that concerns myself alone. There are mental pains harder to bear than the pains of the body, and the consciousness of a duty unfulfilled is one of the keenest of them. You urge in vain; I must go. And now, since it is time you bade me good-night, let me thank you for your ready help and say good-bye."

"But may I do no more for you?"

"Nothing--unless you will have the goodness to bid Madame Bouisse to come up-stairs, and finish packing my portmanteau for me."

"At what hour do you start?"

"At eight."

"May I not go with you to the station, and see that you get a comfortable seat?"

"Many thanks," she replied, coldly; "but I do not go by rail, and my seat in the diligence is already taken."

"You will want some one to see to your luggage--to carry your cloaks."

"Madame Bouisse has promised to go with me to the Messageries."

Silenced, and perhaps a little hurt, I rose to take my leave.

"I wish you a safe journey, mademoiselle," I said, "and a safe return,"

"And think me, at the same time, an ungrateful patient."

"I did not say that."

"No--but you thought so. After all, it is possible that I seem so. I am undemonstrative--unused to the amenities of life--in short, I am only half-civilized. Pray, forgive me."

"Mademoiselle," I said, "your apology pains me. I have nothing to forgive. I will send Madame Bouisse to you immediately."

And with this I had almost left the room, but paused upon the threshold.

"Shall you be long away?" I asked, with assumed indifference.

"Shall I be long away?" she repeated, dreamily. "How can I tell?" Then, correcting herself, "Oh, not long," she added. "Not long. Perhaps a fortnight--perhaps a week."

"Once more, then, good-night."

"Good-night," she answered, absently; and I withdrew.

I then went down, sent Madame Bouisse to wait upon her, and sat up anxiously listening more than half the night. Next morning, at seven, I heard Madame Bouisse go in again. I dared not even go to her door to inquire how she had slept, lest I should seem too persistent; but when they left the room and went downstairs together, I flew to my window.

I saw her cross the street in the gray morning. She walked feebly, and wore a large cloak, that hid the disabled arm and covered her to the feet. Madame Bouisse trotted beside her with a bundle of cloaks and umbrellas; a porter followed with her little portmanteau on his shoulder.

And so they passed under the archway across the trampled snow, and vanished out of sight.

CHAPTER XLIV.
A PRESCRIPTION.

A week went by--a fortnight went by--and still Hortense prolonged her mysterious absence. Where could she be gone? Was she ill? Had any accident befallen her on the road? What if the wounded hand had failed to heal? What if inflammation had set in, and she were lying, even now, sick and helpless, among strangers? These terrors came back upon me at every moment, and drove me almost to despair. In vain I interrogated Madame Bouisse. The good-natured *concierge* knew no more than myself, and the little she had to tell only increased my uneasiness.

Hortense, it appeared, had taken two such journeys before, and had, on both occasions, started apparently at a moment's notice, and with every indication of anxiety and haste. From the first she returned after an interval of more than three weeks; from the second after about four or five days. Each absence had been followed by a long season of despondency and lassitude, during which, said the *concierge*, Mademoiselle scarcely spoke, or ate, or slept, but, silent and pale as a ghost, sat up later than ever with her books and papers. As for this last journey, all she knew about it was that Mam'selle had had her passport regulated for foreign parts the afternoon of the day before she started.

"But can you not remember in what direction the diligence was going?" I asked, again and again.

"No, M'sieur--not in the least,"

"Nor the name of the town to which her place was taken?"

"I don't know that I ever heard it, M'sieur."

"But at least you must have seen the address on the portmanteau?"

"Not I, M'sieur--I never thought of looking at it."

"Did she say nothing to account for the suddenness of her departure?"

"Nothing at all."

"Nor about her return either. Madame Bouisse? Just think a moment--surely she said something about when you might expect her back again?"

"Nothing, M'sieur, except, by the way--"

"Except what?"

"*Dame*! only this--as she was just going to step into the diligence, she turned back and shook hands with me--Mam'selle Hortense, proud as she is, is never above shaking hands with me, I can tell you, M'sieur."

"No, no--I can well believe it. Pray, go on!"

"Well, M'sieur," she shakes hands with me, and she says, "Thank you, good Madame Bouisse, for all your kindness to me.... Hear that, M'sieur, 'good Madame Bouisse,'--the dear child!"

"And then--?"

"Bah! how impatient you are! Well, then, she says (after thanking me, you observe)--'I have paid you my rent, Madame Bouisse, up to the end of the present month, and if, when the time has expired, I have neither written nor returned, consider me still as your tenant. If, however, I do not come back at all, I will let you know further respecting the care of my books and other property."

If she did not come back at all! Oh, Heaven! I had never contemplated such a possibility. I left Madame Bouisse without another word, and going up to my own rooms, flung myself upon my bed, as if I were stupefied.

All that night, all the next day, those words haunted me. They seemed to have burned themselves into my brain in letters of fire. Dreaming, I woke up with them upon my lips; reading, they started out upon me from the page. "If I never come back at all!"

At last, when the fifth day came round--the fifth day of the third week of her absence--I became so languid and desponding that I lost all power of application.

Even Dr. Cheron noticed it, and calling me in the afternoon to his private room, said:--

"Basil Arbuthnot, you look ill. Are you working too hard?"

"I don't think so, sir."

"Humph! Are you out much at night?"

"Out, sir?"

"Yes--don't echo my words--do you go into society: frequent balls, theatres, and so forth?"

"I have not done so, sir, for several months past."

"What is it, then? Do you read late?"

"Really, sir, I hardly know--up to about one or two o'clock; on the average, I believe."

"Let me feel your pulse."

I put out my wrist, and he held it for some seconds, looking keenly at me all the time.

"Got anything on your mind?" he asked, after he had dropped it again. "Want money, eh?"

"No, sir, thank you."

"Home-sick?"

"Not in the least."

"Hah! want amusement. Can't work perpetually--not reasonable to suppose it. There, ***mon garcon***," (taking a folded paper from his pocket-book) "there's a prescription for you. Make the most of it."

It was a stall-ticket for the opera. Too restless and unhappy to reject any chance of relief, however temporary, I accepted it, and went.

I had not been to a theatre since that night with Josephine, nor to the Italian Opera since I used to go with Madame de Marignan. As I went in listlessly and took my place, the lights, the noise, the multitude of faces, confused and dazzled me. Presently the curtain rose, and the piece began. The opera was *I Capuletti*. I do not remember who the singers were, I am not sure that I ever knew. To me they were Romeo and Juliet, and I was a dweller in Verona. The story, the music, the scenery, took a vivid hold upon my imagination. From the moment the curtain rose, I saw only the stage, and, except that I in some sort established a dim comparison between Romeo's sorrows and my own disquietude of mind, I seemed to lose all recollection of time and place, and almost of my own identity.

It seemed quite natural that that ill-fated pair of lovers should go through life, love, wed, and die singing. And why not? Are they not airy nothings, "born of romance, cradled in poetry, thinking other thoughts, and doing other deeds than ours?" As they live in poetry, so may they not with perfect fitness speak in song?

I went home in a dream, with the melodies ringing in my ears and the story ly-ing heavy at my heart. I passed upstairs in the dark, went over to the window, and saw, oh joy! the light--the dear, familiar, welcome, blessed light, streaming forth, as of old, from Hortense's chamber window!

To thank Heaven that she was safe was my first impulse--to step out on the balcony, and watch the light as though it were a part of herself, was the second. I had not been there many moments when it was obscured by a passing shadow. The window opened and she came out.

"Good-evening," she said, in her calm, clear voice. "I heard you out here, and thought you might like to know that, thanks to your treatment in the first instance, and such care as I have been able since to give it, my hand is once more in working order."

"You are kind to come out and tell me so," I said. "I had no hope of seeing you to-night. How long is it since you arrived?"

"About two hours," she replied, carelessly.

"And you have been nearly three weeks away!"

"Have I?" said she, leaning her cheek upon her hand, and looking up dreamily into the night. "I did not count the days."

"That proves you passed them happily," I said; not without some secret bitter-ness.

"Happily!" she echoed. "What is happiness?"

"A word that we all translate differently," I replied.

"And your own reading of it?" she said, interrogatively.

I hesitated.

"Do you inquire what is my need, individually?" I asked, "or do you want my general definition?"

"The latter."

"I think, then, that the first requirement of happiness is work; the second, suc-cess."

She sighed.

"I accept your definition," she said, "and hope that you may realize it to the full in your own experience. For myself, I have toiled and failed--sought, and found not.

Judge, then, how I came to leave the days uncounted."

The sadness of her attitude, the melancholy import of her words, the abstraction of her manner, filled me with a vague uneasiness.

"Failure is often the forerunner of success," I replied, for want, perhaps, of something better to say.

She shook her head drearily, and stood looking up at the sky, where, every now and then, the moon shone out fitfully between the flying clouds.

"It is not the first time," she murmured, "nor will it be the last--and yet they say that God is merciful."

She had forgotten my presence. These words were not spoken to me, but in answer to her own thoughts. I said nothing, but watched her upturned face. It was pale as the wan moon overhead; thinner than before she went away; and sadder--oh, how much sadder!

She roused herself presently, and turning to me, said:--"I beg your pardon. I am very absent; but I am greatly fatigued. I have been travelling incessantly for two days and nights."

"Then I will wish you good-night at once," I said.

"Good-night," she replied; and went back into her room.

The next morning Dr. Cheron smiled one of his cold smiles, and said:--

"You look better to-day, my young friend. I knew how it was with you--no worse malady, after all, than *ennui*. I shall take care to repeat the medicine from time to time."

CHAPTER XLV.
UNDER THE STARS.

Hoping, yet scarcely expecting to see her, I went out upon my balcony the next night at the same hour; but the light of her lamp was bright within, no shadow obscured it, and no window opened. So, after waiting for more than an hour, I gave her up, and returned to my work. I did this for six nights in succession. On the seventh she came.

"You are fond of your balcony, fellow-student," said she. "I often hear you out here."

"My room gets heated," I replied, "and my eyes weary, after several hours of hard reading; and this keen, clear air puts new life into one's brains."

"Yes, it is delicious," said she, looking up into the night. "How dark the space of heaven is, and, how bright are the stars! What a night for the Alps! What a night to be upon some Alpine height, watching the moon through a good telescope, and waiting for the sunrise!"

"Defer that wish for a few months," I replied smiling. "You would scarcely like Switzerland in her winter robes."

"Nay, I prefer Switzerland in winter," she said. "I passed through part of the Jura about ten days ago, and saw nothing but snow. It was magnificent--like a paradise of pure marble awaiting the souls of all the sculptors of all the ages."

"A fantastic idea," said I, "and spoken like an artist."

"Like an artist!" she repeated, musingly. "Well, are not all students artists?"

"Not those who study the exact sciences--not the student of law or divinity--nor he who, like myself, is a student of medicine. He is the slave of Fact, and Art is the Eden of his banishment. His imagination is for ever captive. His horizon is for ever bounded. He is fettered by routine, and paralyzed by tradition. His very ideas must put on the livery of his predecessors; for in a profession where originality of thought stands for the blackest shade of original sin, skill--mere skill--must be the end of his ambition."

She looked at me, and the moonlight showed me that sad smile which her lips so often wore.

"You do not love your profession," she said.

"I do not, indeed."

"And yet you labor zealously to acquire it--how is that?"

"How is it with hundreds of others? My profession was chosen for me. I am not my own master."

"But are you sure you would be happier in some other pursuit? Supposing, for instance, that you were free to begin again, what career do you think you would prefer?"

"I scarcely know, and I should scarcely care, so long as there was freedom of thought and speculation in it."

"Geology, perhaps--or astronomy," she suggested, laughingly.

"Merci! The bowels of the earth are too profound, and the heavens too lofty for me. I should choose some pursuit that would set the Ariel of the imagination free. That is to say, I could be very happy if my life were devoted to Science, but my soul echoes to the name of Art."

"'The artist creates--the man of science discovers," said Hortense. "Beware lest you fancy you would prefer the work of creation only because you lack patience to pursue the work of discovery. Pardon me, if I suggest that you may, perhaps, be fitted for neither. Your sphere, I fancy, is reflection--comparison--criticism. You are not made for action, or work. Your taste is higher than your ambition, and you love learning better than fame. Am I right?"

"So right that I regret I can be read so easily."

"And therefore, it may be that you would find yourself no happier with Art than with Science. You might even fall into deeper discouragement; for in Science every onward step is at least certain gain, but in Art every step is groping, and success is only another form of effort. Art, in so far as it is more divine, is more unattainable, more evanescent, more unsubstantial. It needs as much patience as Science, and the passionate devotion of an entire life is as nothing in comparison with the magnitude of the work. Self-sacrifice, self-distrust, infinite patience, infinite disappointment--such is the lot of the artist, such the law of aspiration."

"A melancholy creed."

"But a true one. The divine is doomed to suffering, and under the hays of the poet lurk ever the thorns of the self-immolator."

"But, amid all this record of his pains, do you render no account of his pleasures?" I asked. "You forget that he has moments of enjoyment lofty as his aims, and deep as his devotion.

"I do not forget it," she said. "I know it but too well. Alas! is not the catalogue of his pleasures the more melancholy record of the two? Hopes which sharpen disappointment; visions which cheat while they enrapture; dreams that embitter his waking hours--fellow-student, do you envy him these?"

"I do; believing that he would not forego them for a life of common-place annoyances and placid pleasures."

"Forego them! Never. Who that had once been the guest of the gods would forego the Divine for the Human? No--it is better to suffer than to stagnate. The artist and poet is overpaid in his brief snatches of joy. While they last, his soul sings 'at heaven's gate,' and his forehead strikes the stars."

She spoke with a rare and passionate enthusiasm; sometimes pacing to and fro; sometimes pausing with upturned face--

"A dauntless muse who eyes a dreadful fate!"

There was a long, long silence--she looking at the stars, I upon her face.

By-and-by she came over to where I stood, and leaned upon the railing that divided our separate territories.

"Friend," said she, gravely, "be content. Art is the Sphinx, and to question her is destruction. Enjoy books, pictures, music, statues--rifle the world of beauty to satiety, if satiety be possible--but there pause Drink the wine; seek not to crush the grape. Be happy, be useful, labor honestly upon the task that is thine, and be assured that the work will itself achieve its reward. Is it nothing to relieve pain--to prolong the days of the sickly--to restore health to the suffering--to soothe the last pangs of the dying? Is it nothing to be followed by the prayers and blessing of those whom you have restored to love, to fame, to the world's service? To my thinking, the physician's trade hath something god-like in it. Be content. Harvey's discovery was as sublime as Newton's, and it were hard to say which did God's work best--Shakespeare or Jenner."

"And you," I said, the passion that I could not conceal trembling in my voice; "and you--what are you, poet, or painter, or musician, that you know and reason of all these things?"

She laughed with a sudden change of mood, and shook her head.

"I am a woman," said she. "Simply a woman--no more. One of the inferior sex; and, as I told you long ago, only half civilized."

"You are unlike every other woman!"

"Possibly, because I am more useless. Strange as it may seem, do you know I love art better than sewing, or gossip, or dress; and hold my liberty to be a dower more precious than either beauty or riches? And yet--I am a woman!"

"The wisest, virtuousest, discreetest, best!"

"By no means. You are comparing me with Eve; but I am not in the least like Eve, I assure you. She was an excellent housewife, and, if we may believe Milton, knew how to prepare 'dulcet creams,' and all sorts of Paradisaical dainties for her husband's dinner. I, on the contrary, could not make a cream if Adam's life depended on it."

"*Eh bien!* of the theology of creams I know nothing. I only know that Eve was the first and fairest of her sex, and that you are as wise as you are beautiful."

"Nay, that is what Titania said to the ass," laughed Hortense. "Your compliments become equivocal, fellow-student. But hush! what hour is that?"

She stood with uplifted finger. The air was keen, and over the silence of the house-tops chimed the church-clocks--Two.

"It is late, and cold," said she, drawing her cloak more closely round her.

"Not later than you usually sit up," I replied. "Don't go yet. 'Tis now the very witching hour of night, when churchyards yawn--"

"I beg your pardon," she interrupted. "The churchyards have done yawning by this time, and, like other respectable citizens, are sound asleep. Let us follow their example. Good-night."

"Good-night," I replied, reluctantly; but almost before I had said it, she was gone.

After this, as the winter wore away, and spring drew on, Hortense's balcony became once more a garden, and she used to attend to her flowers every evening. She always found me on my balcony when she came out, and soon our open-air meetings became such an established fact that, instead of parting with "good-night," we said "*au revoir*--till to-morrow." At these times we talked of many things; sometimes of subjects abstract and mystical--of futurity, of death, of the spiritual life-- but oftenest of Art in its manifold developments. And sometimes our speculations wandered on into the late hours of the night.

And yet, for all our talking and all our community of tastes, we became not one jot more intimate. I still loved in silence--she still lived in a world apart.

CHAPTER XLVI.
THERMOPYLAE.

How dreary 'tis for women to sit still
On winter nights by solitary fires,
And hear the nations praising them far off.
                    AURORA LEIGH.

A bolished by the National Convention of 1793, re-established in 1795, reformed by the first Napoleon in 1803, and remodelled in 1816 on the restoration of the Bourbons, the Academie Francaise, despite its changes of fortune, name, and government, is a liberal and splendid institution. It consists of forty members, whose office it is to compile the great dictionary, and to enrich, purify, and preserve the language. It assists authors in distress. It awards prizes for poetry, eloquence, and virtue; and it bestows those honors with a noble impartiality that observes no distinction of sex, rank, or party. To fill one of the forty fauteuils of the Academie Francaise is the darling ambition of every eminent Frenchman of letters. There the poet, the philosopher, the historian, the man of science, sit side by side, and meet on equal ground. When a seat falls vacant, when a prize is to be awarded, when an anniversary is to be celebrated, the interest and excitement become intense. To the political, the fashionable, or the commercial world, these events are perhaps of little moment. They affect neither the Bourse nor the Budget. They exercise no perceptible influence on the Longchamps toilettes. But to the striving author, to the rising orator, to all earnest workers in the broad fields of literature, they are serious and significant circumstances.

Living out of society as I now did, I knew little and cared less for these academic crises. The success of one candidate was as unimportant to me as the failure of another; and I had more than once read the crowned poem of the prize essay without even glancing at the name or the fortunate author.

Now it happened that, pacing to and fro under the budding acacias of the Palais Royal garden one sunny spring-like morning, some three or four weeks after the conversation last recorded, I was pursued by a persecuting newsvender with a hungry eye, mittened fingers, and a shrill voice, who persisted in reiterating close against my ear:--

"News of the day, M'sieur!--news of the day. Frightful murder in the Rue du Faubourg St. Antoine--state of the Bourse--latest despatches from the seat of war--prize poem crowned by the Academie Francaise--news of the day, M'sieur! Only forty centimes! News of the day!"

I refused, however, to be interested in any of those topics, turned a deaf ear to his allurements, and peremptorily dismissed him. I then continued my walk in solitary silence.

At the further extremity of the square, near the **Galerie Vitree** and close beside the little newspaper kiosk, stood a large tree since cut down, which at that time served as an advertising medium, and was daily decorated with a written placard, descriptive of the contents of the **Moniteur**, the **Presse**, and other leading papers. This placard was generally surrounded by a crowd of readers, and to-day the crowd of readers was more than usually dense.

I seldom cared in these days for what was going on in the busy outside world; but this morning, my attention having been drawn to the subject, I amused myself, as I paced to and fro, by watching the eager faces of the little throng of idlers. Presently I fell in with the rest, and found myself conning the placard on the tree.

The name that met my astonished eyes on that placard was the name of Hortense Dufresnoy.

The sentence ran thus:--

"Grand Biennial Prize for Poetry--Subject: **The Pass of Thermopylae**,--Successful Candidate, **Mademoiselle Hortense Dufresnoy**."

Breathless, I read the passage twice; then, hearing at a little distance the shrill voice of the importunate newsvender, I plunged after him and stopped him, just as he came to the--

"Frightful murder in the Rue du Faubourg Saint ..."

"Here," said I, tapping him on the shoulder; "give me one of your papers."
The man's eyes glittered.

"Only forty centimes, M'sieur," said he. "'Tis the first I've sold to-day."

He looked poor and wretched. I dropped into his hand a coin that would have purchased all his little sheaf of journals, and hurried away, not to take the change or hear his thanks. He was silent for some moments; then took up his cry at the point where he had broken off, and started away with:--

--"Antoine!--state of the Bourse--latest despatches from the seat of war--news of the day--only forty centimes!"

I took my paper to a quiet bench near the fountain, and read the whole account. There had been eighteen anonymous poems submitted to the Academy. Three out of the eighteen had come under discussion; one out of the three had been warmly advocated by Beranger, one by Lebrun, and the third by some other academician. The poem selected by Beranger was at length chosen; the sealed enclosure opened; and the name of the successful competitor found to be Hortense Dufresnoy. To Hortense Dufresnoy, therefore, the prize and crown were awarded.

I read the article through, and then went home, hoping to be the first to congratulate her. Timidly, and with a fast-beating heart, I rang the bell at her outer door; for we all had our bells at Madame Bouisse's, and lived in our rooms as if they were little private houses.

She opened the door, and, seeing me, looked surprised; for I had never before ventured to pay her a visit in her apartment.

"I have come to wish you joy," said I, not venturing to cross the threshold.

"To wish me joy?"

"You have not seen a morning paper?"

"A morning paper!"

And, echoing me thus, her color changed, and a strange vague look--it might be of hope, it might be of fear--came into her face.

"There is something in the *Moniteur*" I went on, smiling, 'that concerns you nearly."

"That concerns me?" she exclaimed. "*Me*? For Heaven's sake, speak plainly. I do not understand you. Has--has anything been discovered?"

"Yes--it has been discovered at the Academie Francaise that Mademoiselle

Hortense Dufresnoy has written the best poem on Thermopylae."

She drew a deep breath, pressed her hands tightly together, and murmured:--

"Alas! is that all?"

"All! Nay--is it not enough to step at once into fame--to have been advocated by Beranger--to have the poem crowned in the Theatre of the Academie Francaise?"

She stood silent, with drooping head and listless hands, all disappointment and despondency. Presently she looked up.

"Where did you learn this?" she asked.

I handed her the journal.

"Come in, fellow-student," said she, and held the door wide for me to enter.

For the second time I found myself in her little *salon*, and found everything in the self-same order.

"Well," I said, "are you not happy?"

She shook her head.

"Success is not happiness," she replied, smiling mournfully. "That Beranger should have advocated my poem is an honor beyond price; but--but I need more than this to make me happy."

And her eyes wandered, with a strange, yearning look, to the sword over the chimney-piece.

Seeing that look, my heart sank, and the tears sprang unbidden to my eyes. Whose was the sword? For whose sake was her life so lonely and secluded? For whom was she waiting? Surely here, if one could but read it aright, lay the secret of her strange and sudden journeys--here I touched unawares upon the mystery of her life!

I did not speak. I shaded my face with my hand, and sat looking on the ground. Then, the silence remaining unbroken, I rose, and examined the drawings on the walls.

They were water-colors for the most part, and treated in a masterly but quite peculiar style. The skies were sombre, the foregrounds singularly elaborate, the color stern and forcible. Angry sunsets barred by lines of purple cirrus stratus; sweeps of desolate heath bounded by jagged peaks; steep mountain passes crimson with faded ferns and half-obscured by rain-clouds; strange studies of weeds, and rivers, and lonely reaches of desolate sea-shore ... these were some of the subjects, and all were evidently by the same hand.

"Ah," said Hortense, "you are criticizing my sketches!"

"Your sketches!" I exclaimed. "Are these your work?"

"Certainly," she replied, smiling. "Why not? What do you think of them?"

"What do I think of them! Well, I think that if you had not been a poet you ought to have been a painter. How fortunate you are in being able to express yourself so variously! Are these compositions, or studies from Nature?"

"All studies from Nature--mere records of fact. I do not presume to create--I am content humbly and from a distance to copy the changing moods of Nature."

"Pray be your own catalogue, then, and tell me where these places are."

"Willingly. This coast-line with the run of breaking surf was taken on the shores of Normandy, some few miles from Dieppe. This sunset is a recollection of a glorious evening near Frankfort, and those purple mountains in the distance are part of the Taunus range. Here is an old mediaeval gateway at Solothurn, in Switzerland. This wild heath near the sea is in the neighborhood of Biscay. This quaint knot of ruinous houses in a weed-grown Court was sketched at Bruges. Do you see that milk-girl with her scarlet petticoat and Flemish *faille?* She supplied us with milk, and her dairy was up that dark archway. She stood for me several times, when I wanted a foreground figure."

"You have travelled a great deal," I said. "Were you long in Belgium?"

"Yes; I lived there for some years. I was first pupil, then teacher, in a large school in Brussels. I was afterwards governess in a private family in Bruges. Of late, however, I have preferred to live in Paris, and give morning lessons. I have more liberty thus, and more leisure."

"And these two little quaint bronze figures?"

"Hans Sachs and Peter Vischer. I brought them from Nuremberg. Hans Sachs, you see, wears a furred robe, and presses a book to his breast. He does not look in the least like a cobbler. Peter Vischer, on the contrary, wears his leather apron and carries his mallet in his hand. Artist and iron-smith, he glories in his trade, and looks as sturdy a little burgher as one would wish to see."

"And this statuette in green marble?"

"A copy of the celebrated 'Pensiero' of Michel Angelo--in other words, the famous sitting statue of Lorenzo de Medici, in the Medicean chapel in Florence. I had it executed for me on the spot by Bazzanti."

"A noble figure!"

"Indeed it is--a noble figure, instinct with life, and strength, and meditation. My first thought on seeing the original was that I would not for worlds be condemned to pass a night alone with it. I should every moment expect the musing hand to drop away from the stern mouth, and the eyes to turn upon me!"

"These," said I, pausing at the chimney-piece, "are *souvenirs* of Switzerland. How delicately those chamois are carved out of the hard wood! They almost seem to snuff the mountain air! But here is a rapier with a hilt of ornamented steel--where did this come from?"

I had purposely led up the conversation to this point. I had patiently questioned and examined for the sake of this one inquiry, and I waited her reply as if my life hung on it.

Her whole countenance changed. She took it down, and her eyes filled with tears.

"It was my father's," she said, tenderly.

"Your father's!" I exclaimed, joyfully. "Heaven be thanked! Did you say your father's?"

She looked up surprised, then smiled, and faintly blushed.

"I did," she replied.

"And was your father a soldier?" I asked; for the sword looked more like a sword of ceremony than a sword for service.

But to this question she gave no direct reply.

"It was his sword," she said, "and he had the best of all rights to wear it."

With this she kissed the weapon reverently, and restored it to its place.

I kissed her hand quite as reverently that day at parting, and she did not withdraw it.

CHAPTER XLVII.
ALL ABOUT ART.

Art's a service.
AURORA LEIGH.

G od sent art, and the devil sent critics," said Mueller, dismally paraphrasing a popular proverb. "My picture is rejected!"

"Rejected!" I echoed, surprised to find him sitting on the floor, like a tailor, in front of an acre of canvas. "By whom?"

"By the Hanging Committee."

"Hang the Hanging Committee!"

"A pious prayer, my friend. Would that it could be carried into execution!"

"What cause do they assign?"

"Cause! Do you suppose they trouble themselves to find one? Not a bit of it. They simply scrawl a great R in chalk on the back of it, and send you a printed notice to carry it home again. What is it to them, if a poor devil has been painting his very heart and hopes out, day after day, for a whole year, upon that piece of canvas? Nothing, and less than nothing--confound them!"

I drew a chair before the picture, and set myself to a patient study of the details. He had chosen a difficult subject--the death of Louis XI. The scene represented a spacious chamber in the Castle of Plessisles-Tours. To the left, in a great oak chair beside the bed from which he had just risen, sat the dying king, with a rich, furred mantle loosely thrown around him. At his feet, his face buried in his hands, kneeled the Dauphin. Behind his chair, holding up the crucifix to enjoin silence, stood the king's confessor. A physician, a couple of councillors in scarlet robes, and a captain of archers, stood somewhat back, whispering together and watching the countenance of the dying man; while through the outer door was seen a crowd of courtiers and pages, waiting to congratulate King Charles VIII. It was an ambitious subject, and Mueller had conceived it in a grand spirit. The heads were expressive; and the textures of the velvets, tapestries, oak carvings, and so forth, had been executed with more than ordinary finish and fidelity. For all this, however, there was more of promise than of achievement in the work. The lights were scattered; the attitudes were stiff; there was too evident an attempt at effect. One could see that it was the work of a young painter, who had yet much to learn, and something of the Academy to forget.

"Well," said Mueller, still sitting ruefully on the floor, "what do you think of it? Am I rightly served? Shall I send for a big pail of whitewash, and blot it all out?"

"Not for the world!"

"What shall I do, then?"

"Do better."

"But, if I have done my best already?"

"Still do better; and when you have done that, do better again. So genius toils higher and ever higher, and like the climber of the glacier, plants his foot where only his hand clung the moment before."

"Humph! but what of my picture?"

"Well," I said, hesitatingly, "I am no critic--"

"Thank Heaven!" muttered Mueller, parenthetically.

"But there is something noble in the disposition of the figures. I should say, however, that you had set to work upon too large a scale."

"A question of focus," said the painter, hastily. "A mere question of focus."

"How can that be, when you have finished some parts laboriously, and in others seem scarcely to have troubled yourself to cover the canvas?"

"I don't know. I'm impatient, you see, and--and I think I got tired of it towards the last."

"Would that have been the case if you had allowed yourself but half the space?"

"I'll take to enamel," exclaimed Mueller, with a grin of hyperbolical despair. "I'll immortalize myself in miniature. I'll paint henceforward with the aid of a microscope, and never again look at nature unless through the wrong end of a telescope!"

"Pshaw!--be in earnest, man, and talk sensibly! Do you conceive that for every failure you are to change your style? Give yourself, heart and soul, to the school in which you have begun, and make up your mind to succeed."

"Do you believe, then, that a man may succeed by force of will alone?" said Mueller, musingly.

"Yes, because force of will proceeds from force of character, and the two together, warp and woof, make the stuff out of which Nature clothes her heroes."

"Oh, but I am not talking of heroes," said Mueller.

"By heroes, I do not mean only soldiers. Captain Pen is as good a hero as Captain Sword, any day; and Captain Brush, to my thinking, is as fine a fellow as either."

"Ay; but do they come, as you would seem to imply, of the same stock?" said Mueller. "Force of will and force of character are famous clays in which to mould a Wellington or a Columbus; but is not something more--at all events, something different--necessary to the modelling of a Raffaelle?"

"I don't fancy so. Power is the first requisite of genius. Give power in equal quantity to your Columbus and your Raffaelle, and circumstance shall decide which will achieve the New World, and which the Transfiguration."

"Circumstance!" cried the painter, impatiently. "Good heavens! do you make no account of the spontaneous tendencies of genius? Is Nature a mere vulgar cook, turning out men, like soups, from one common stock, with only a dash of flavoring here and there to give them variety? No--Nature is a subtle chemist, and her workshop, depend on it, is stored with delicate elixirs, volatile spirits, and precious fires of genius. Certain of these are kneaded with the clay of the poet, others with the clay of the painter, the astronomer, the mathematician, the legislator, the soldier. Raffaelle had in him some of 'the stuff that dreams are made of.' Never tell me that that same stuff, differently treated, would equally well have furnished forth an Archimedes or a Napoleon!"

"Men are what their age calls upon them to be," I replied, after a moment's consideration. "Be that demand what it may, the supply is ever equal to it. Centre of the most pompous and fascinating of religions, Rome demanded Madonnas and Transfigurations, and straightway Raffaelle answered to the call. The Old World, overstocked with men, gold, and aristocracies, asked wider fields of enterprise, and Columbus added America to the map. What is this but circumstance? Had Italy needed colonies, would not her men of genius have turned sailors and discoverers? Had Madrid been the residence of the Popes, might not Columbus have painted altar-pieces or designed churches?"

Mueller, still sitting on the floor, shook his head despondingly.

"I don't think it," he replied; "and I don't wish to think it. It is too material a view of genius to satisfy my imagination. I love to believe that gifts are special. I love to believe that the poet is born a poet, and the artist an artist."

"Hold! I believe that the poet is born a poet, and the artist an artist; but I also believe the poetry of the one and the art of the other to be only diverse manifestations of a power that is universal in its application. The artist whose lot in life it is to be a builder is none the less an artist. The poet, though engineer or soldier, is none the less a poet. There is the poetry of language, and there is also the poetry of action. So also there is the art which expresses itself by means of marble or canvas, and the art which designs a capitol, tapers a spire, or plants a pleasure-ground. Nay, is not this very interfusion of gifts, this universality of uses, in itself the bond of beauty which girdles the world like a cestus? If poetry were only rhyme, and art only painting, to what an outer darkness of matter-of-fact should we be condemning nine-tenths of the creation!"

Mueller yawned, as if he would have swallowed me and my argument together.

"You are getting transcendental," said he. "I dare say your theories are all very fine and all very true; but I confess that I don't understand them. I never could find out all this poetry of bricks and mortar, railroads and cotton-factories, that people talk about so fluently now-a-days. We Germans take the dreamy side of life, and are seldom at home in the practical, be it ever so highly colored and highly flavored. In our parlance, an artist is an artist, and neither a bagman nor an engine-driver."

His professional pride was touched, and he said this with somewhat less than his usual *bonhomie*--almost with a shade of irritability.

"Come," said I, smiling, "we will not discuss a topic which we can never see from the same point of view. Doing art is better than talking art; and your business now is to find a fresh subject and prepare another canvas. Meanwhile cheer up, and forget all about Louis XI. and the Hanging Committee. What say you to dining with me at the Trois Freres? It will do you good."

"Good!" cried he, springing to his feet and shaking his fist at the picture. "More good, by Jupiter, than all the paint and megilp that ever was wasted! Not all the fine arts of Europe are worth a ***poulet a la Marengo*** and a bottle of old ***Romanee***!"

So saying, he turned his picture to the wall, seized his cap, locked his door, scrawled outside with a piece of chalk,--"***Summoned to the Tuileries on state affairs***," and followed me, whistling, down the six flights of gloomy, ricketty, Quartier-Latin lodging-house stairs up which he lived and had his being.

CHAPTER XLVIII.
I MAKE MYSELF ACQUAINTED WITH THE IMPOLITE WORLD AND ITS PLACES OP UNFASHIONABLE RESORT.

Mueller and I dined merrily at the Cafe of the Trois Freres Provencaux, discussed our coffee and cigars outside the Rotonde in the Palais Royal, and then started off in search of adventures. Striking up in a north-easterly direction through a labyrinth of narrow streets, we emerged at the Rue des Fontaines, just in front of that famous second-hand market yclept the Temple. It was Saturday night, and the business of the place was at its height. We went in, and turning aside from the broad thoroughfares which intersect the market at right angles, plunged at once into a net-work of crowded side-alleys, noisy and populous as a cluster of beehives. Here were bargainings, hagglings, quarrel-lings, elbowings, slang, low wit, laughter, abuse, cheating, and chattering enough to turn the head of a neophyte like myself. Mueller, however, was in his element. He took me up one row and down another, pointed out all that was curious, had a nod for every grisette, and an answer for every touter, and enjoyed the Babel like one to the manner born.

"Buy, messieurs, buy! What will you buy?" was the question that assailed us on both sides, wherever we went.

"What do you sell, *mon ami ?*" was Mueller's invariable reply.

"What do you want, m'sieur?"

"Twenty thousand francs per annum, and the prettiest wife in Paris," says my friend; a reply which is sure to evoke something *spirituel*, after the manner of the locality.

"This is the most amusing place in Paris," observes he. "Like the Alsatia of old London, it has its own peculiar **argot,** and its own peculiar privileges. The activity of its commerce is amazing. If you buy a pocket-handkerchief at the first stall you come to, and leave it unprotected in your coat-pocket for five minutes, you may purchase it again at the other end of the alley before you leave. As for the resources of the market, they are inexhaustible. You may buy anything you please here, from a Court suit to a cargo of old rags. In this alley (which is the aristocratic quarter), are sold old jewelry, old china, old furniture, silks that have rustled at the Tuileries; fans that may have fluttered at the opera; gloves once fitted to tiny hands, and yet bearing a light soil where the rings were worn beneath; laces that may have been the property of Countesses or Cardinals; masquerade suits, epaulets, uniforms, furs, perfumes, artificial flowers, and all sorts of elegant superfluities, most of which have descended to the merchants of the Temple through the hands of ladies-maids and valets. Yonder lies the district called the 'Foret Noire'--a land of unpleasing atmosphere inhabited by cobblers and clothes-menders. Down to the left you see nothing but rag and bottle-shops, old iron stores, and lumber of every kind. Here you find chiefly household articles, bedding, upholstery, crockery, and so forth."

"What will you buy, Messieurs?" continued to be the cry, as we moved along arm-in-arm, elbowing our way through the crowd, and exploring this singular scene in all directions.

"What will you buy, messieurs?" shouts one salesman. "A carpet? A capital carpet, neither too large nor too small. Just the size you want!"

"A hat, m'sieur, better than new," cries another; "just aired by the last owner."

"A coat that will fit you better than if it had been made for you?"

"A pair of boots? Dress-boots, dancing-boots, walking-boots, morning-boots, evening-boots, riding-boots, fishing-boots, hunting-boots. All sorts, m'sieur--all sorts!"

"A cloak, m'sieur?"

"A lace shawl to take home to Madame?"

"An umbrella, m'sieur?"

"A reading lamp?"

"A warming-pan?"

"A pair of gloves?"

"A shower bath?"

"A hand organ?"

"What! m'sieurs, do you buy nothing this evening? Hola, Antoine! monsieur keeps his hands in his pockets, for fear his money should fall out!"

"Bah! They've not a centime between them!"

"Go down the next turning and have the hole in your coat mended!"

"Make way there for monsieur the millionaire!"

"They are ambassadors on their way to the Court of Persia."

"*Ohé! Pane! pane! pane!*"

Thus we run the gauntlet of all the tongues in the Temple, sometimes retorting, sometimes laughing and passing on, sometimes stopping to watch the issue of a dispute or the clinching of a bargain.

"*Dame*, now! if it were only ten francs cheaper," says a voice that strikes my ear with a sudden sense of familiarity. Turning, I discover that the voice belongs to a young woman close at my elbow, and that the remark is addressed to a good-looking workman upon whose arm she is leaning.

"What, Josephine!" I exclaim.

"*Comment*! Monsieur Basil!"

And I find myself kissed on both cheeks before I even guess what is going to happen to me.

"Have I not also the honor of being remembered by Mademoiselle?" says Mueller, taking off his hat with all the politeness possible; whereupon Josephine, in an ecstasy of recognition, embraces him likewise.

"*Mais, quel bonheur*!" cries she. "And to meet in the Temple, above all places! Emile, you heard me speak of Monsieur Basil--the gentleman who gave me that lovely shawl that I wore last Sunday to the Chateau des Fleurs--*eh bien*! this is he--and here is Monsieur Mueller, his friend. Gentlemen, this is Emile, my *fiance*. We are to be married next Friday week, and we are buying our furniture."

The good-looking workman pulled off his cap and made his bow, and we proffered the customary congratulations.

"We have bought such sweet, pretty things," continued she, rattling on with all her old volubility, "and we have hired the dearest little *appartement* on the fourth story, in a street near the Jardin des Plantes. See--this looking-glass is ours;

we have just bought it. And those maple chairs, and that chest of drawers with the marble top. It isn't real marble, you know; but it's ever so much better than real:-- not nearly so heavy, and so beautifully carved that it's quite a work of art. Then we have bought a carpet--the sweetest carpet! Is it not, Emile?"

Emile smiled, and confessed that the carpet was "*fort bien*."

"And the time-piece, Madame?" suggested the furniture-dealer, at whose door we were standing. "Madame should really not refuse herself the time-piece."

Josephine shook her head.

"It is too dear," said she.

"Pardon, madame. I am giving it away,--absolutely giving it away at the price!"

Josephine looked at it wistfully, and weighed her little purse. It was a very little purse, and very light.

"It is so pretty!" said she.

The clock was of ormolu upon a painted stand, that was surmounted by a stout little gilt Cupid in a triumphal chariot, drawn by a pair of hard-working doves.

"What is the price of it?" I asked.

"Thirty-five francs, m'sieur," replied the dealer, briskly.

"Say twenty-five," urged Josephine.

The dealer shook his head.

"What if we did without the looking-glass?" whispered Josephine to her *fi- ance*. "After all, you know, one can live without a looking-glass; but how shall I have your dinners ready, if I don't know what o'clock it is?"

"I don't really see how we are to do without a clock," admitted Emile.

"And that darling little Cupid!"

Emile conceded that the Cupid was irresistible.

"Then we decide to have the clock, and do without the looking-glass?"

"Yes, we decide."

In the meantime I had slipped the thirty-five francs into the dealer's hand.

"You must do me the favor to accept the clock as a wedding-present, Made- moiselle Josephine," I said. "And I hope you will favor me with an invitation to the wedding."

"And me also," said Mueller; "and I shall hope to be allowed to offer a little sketch to adorn the walls of your new home."

Their delight and gratitude were almost too great. We shook hands again all round. I am not sure, indeed, that Josephine did not then and there embrace us both for the second time.

"And you will both come to our wedding!" cried she. "And we will spend the day at St. Cloud, and have a dance in the evening; and we will invite Monsieur Gustave, and Monsieur Jules, and Monsieur Adrien. Oh, dear! how delightful it will be!"

"And you promise me the first quadrille?" said I.

"And me the second?" added Mueller.

"Yes, yes--as many as you please."

"Then you must let us know at what time to come, and all about it; so, till Friday week, adieu!"

And thus, with more shaking of hands, and thanks, and good wishes, we parted company, leaving them still occupied with the gilt Cupid and the furniture-broker.

After the dense atmosphere of the clothes-market, it is a relief to emerge upon the Boulevart du Temple--the noisy, feverish, crowded Boulevart du Temple, with its half dozen theatres, its glare of gas, its cake-sellers, bill-sellers, lemonade-sellers, cabs, cafes, gendarmes, tumblers, grisettes, and pleasure-seekers of both sexes.

Here we pause awhile to applaud the performances of a company of dancing-dogs, whence we are presently drawn away by the sight of a gentleman in a ***moyen-age*** costume, who is swallowing penknives and bringing them out at his ears to the immense gratification of a large circle of bystanders.

A little farther on lies the Jardin Turc; and here we drop in for half an hour, to restore ourselves with coffee-ices, and look on at the dancers. This done, we presently issue forth again, still in search of amusement.

"Have you ever been to the Petit Lazary?" asks my friend, as we stand at the gate of the Jardin Turc, hesitating which way to turn.

"Never; what is it?"

"The most inexpensive of theatrical luxuries--an evening's entertainment of the mildest intellectual calibre, and at the lowest possible cost. Here we are at the doors. Come in, and complete your experience of Paris life!"

The Petit Lazary occupies the lowest round of the theatrical ladder. We pay something like sixpence half-penny or sevenpence apiece, and are inducted into the dress-circle. Our appearance is greeted with a round of applause. The curtain has just fallen, and the audience have nothing better to do. Mueller lays his hand upon his heart, and bows profoundly, first to the gallery and next to the pit; whereupon they laugh, and leave us in peace. Had we looked dignified or indignant we should probably have been hissed till the curtain rose.

It is an audience in shirt-sleeves, consisting for the most part of workmen, maid-servants, soldiers, and street-urchins, with a plentiful sprinkling of pickpock-ets--the latter in a strictly private capacity, being present for entertainment only, without any ulterior professional views.

It is a noisy *entr'acte* enough. Three vaudevilles have already been played, and while the fourth is in preparation the public amuses itself according to its own riotous will and pleasure. Nuts and apple parings fly hither and thither; oranges describe perilous parabolas between the pit and the gallery; adventurous *gamins* make daring excursions round the upper rails; dialogues maintained across the house, and quarrels supported by means of an incredible copiousness of invective, mingle in discordant chorus with all sorts of howlings, groanings, whistlings, crow-ings, and yelpings, above which, in shrillest treble, rise the voices of cake and apple-sellers, and the piercing cry of the hump-back who distributes "vaudevilles at five centimes apiece." In the meantime, almost distracted by the patronage that assails him in every direction, the lemonade-vendor strides hither and thither, supplying floods of nectar at two centimes the glass; while the audience, skilled in the combi-nation of enjoyments, eats, drinks, and vociferates to its heart's content. Fabulous meats, and pies of mysterious origin, are brought out from baskets and hats. Pocket-handkerchiefs spread upon benches do duty as table-cloths. Clasp-knives, galette, and sucre d'orge pass from hand to hand--nay, from mouth to mouth--and, in the midst of the tumult, the curtain rises.

All is, in one moment, profoundly silent. The viands disappear; the lemonade-seller vanishes; the boys outside the gallery-rails clamber back to their places. The drama, in the eyes of the Parisians, is almost a sacred rite, and not even the noisi-est *gamin* would raise his voice above a whisper when the curtain is up.

The vaudeville that follows is, to say the least of it, a perplexing performance. It has no plot in particular. The scene is laid in a lodging-house, and the discom-forts of one Monsieur Choufleur, an elderly gentleman in a flowered dressing-gown and a gigantic nightcap, furnish forth all the humor of the piece. What Monsieur Choufleur has done to deserve his discomforts, and why a certain student named Charles should devote all the powers of his mind to the devising and inflicting of those discomforts, is a mystery which we, the audience, are never permitted to penetrate. Enough that Charles, being a youth of mischievous tastes and extensive wardrobe, assumes a series of disguises for the express purpose of tormenting Monsieur Choufleur, and is unaccountably rewarded in the end with the hand of Monsieur Choufleur's daughter; a consummation which brings down the curtain amid loud applause, and affords entire satisfaction to everybody.

It is by this time close upon midnight, and, leaving the theatre with the rest of the audience, we find a light rain falling. The noisy thoroughfare is hushed to comparative quiet. The carriages that roll by are homeward bound. The waiters yawn at the doors of the cafes and survey pedestrians with a threatening aspect. The theatres are closing fast, and a row of flickering gas-lamps in front of a faded transparency which proclaims that the juvenile *Tableaux Vivants* are to be seen within, denotes the only place of public amusement yet open to the curious along the whole length of the Boulevart du Temple.

"And now, *amigo*, where shall we go?" says Mueller. "Are you for a billiard-room or a lobster supper? Or shall we beat up the quarters of some of the fellows in the Quartier Latin, and see what fun is afoot on the other side of the water?"

"Whichever you please. You are my guest to-night, and I am at your disposal."

"Or what say you to dropping in for an hour among the Chicards?"

"A capital idea--especially if you again entertain the society with a true story of events that never happened."

"*Allons donc*!--

'C'etait de mon temps
Que brillait Madame Gregoire.
J'allais a vingt ans
Dans son cabaret rire et boire.'

--confound this drizzle! It soaks one through and through, like a sponge. If you are no fonder of getting wet through than I am, I vote we both run for it!"

With this he set off running at full speed, and I followed.

The rain soon fell faster and thicker. We had no umbrellas; and being by this time in a region of back-streets, an empty fiacre was a prize not to be hoped for. Coming presently to a dark archway, we took shelter and waited till the shower should pass over. It lasted longer than we had expected, and threatened to settle into a night's steady rain. Mueller kept his blood warm by practicing extravagant quadrille steps and singing scraps of Beranger's ballads; whilst I, watching impatiently for a cab, kept peering up and down the street, and listening to every sound.

Presently a quick footfall echoed along the wet pavement, and the figure of a man, dimly seen by the blurred light of the street-lamps, came hurrying along the other side of the way. Something in the firm free step, in the upright carriage, in the height and build of the passer-by, arrested my attention. He drew nearer. He passed under the lamp just opposite, and, as he passed, flung away the end of his cigar, which fell, hissing, into the little rain-torrent running down the middle of the street. He carried no umbrella; but his hat was pulled low, and his collar drawn up, and I could see nothing of his face. But the gesture was enough.

For a moment I stood still and looked after him; then, calling to Mueller that I should be back presently, I darted off in pursuit.

CHAPTER XLIX.
THE KING OF DIAMONDS.

The rain beat in my face and almost blinded me, the wind hustled me; the gendarme at the corner of the street looked at me suspiciously; and still I followed, and still the tall stranger strode on ahead. Up one street he led me and down another, across a market-place, through an arcade, past the Bourse, and into that labyrinth of small streets that lies behind the Italian Opera-house, and is bounded on the East by the Rue de Richelieu, and on the West by the Rue Louis le Grand. Here he slackened his pace, and I found myself gaming upon him for the first time. Presently he came to a dead stop, and as I continued to draw nearer, I saw him take out his watch and look at it by the light of a street-lamp. This done, he began sauntering slowly backwards and forwards, as if waiting for some second person.

For a moment I also paused, hesitating. What should I do?--pass him under the lamp, and try to see his face? Go boldly up to him, and invent some pretence to address him, or wait in this angle of deep shade, and see what would happen next? I was deceived, of course--deceived by a merely accidental resemblance. Well, then, I should have had my run for my pains, and have taken cold, most likely, into the bargain. At all events, I would speak to him.

Seeing me emerge from the darkness, and cross over towards the spot where he was standing, he drew aside with the air of a man upon his guard, and put his hand quickly into his breast.

"I beg your pardon, Monsieur," I began.

"What! my dear Damon!--is it you?" he interrupted, and held out both hands.

I grasped them joyously.

"Dalrymple, is it you?"

"Myself, Damon--*faute de mieux*."

"And I have been running after you for the last two miles! What brings you to Paris? Why did you not let me know you were here? How long have you been back? Has anything gone wrong? Are you well?"

"One question at a time, my Arcadian, for mercy's sake!" said he. "Which am I to answer?"

"The last."

"Oh, I am well--well enough. But let us walk on a little farther while we talk."

"Are you waiting for any one?" I asked, seeing him look round uneasily.

"Yes--no--that is, I expect to see some one come past here presently. Step into this doorway, and I will tell you all about it."

His manner was restless, and his hand, as it pressed mine, felt hot and feverish.

"I am sure you are not well," I said, following him into the gloom of a deep, old-fashioned doorway.

"Am I not? Well, I don't know--perhaps I am not. My blood burns in my veins to-night like fire. Nay, thou wilt learn nothing from my pulse, thou sucking AEsculapius! Mine is a sickness not to be cured by drugs. I must let blood for it."

The short, hard laugh with which he said this troubled me still more.

"Speak out," I said--"for Heaven's sake, speak out! You have something on your mind--what is it?"

"I have something on my hands," he replied, gloomily. "Work. Work that must be done quickly, or there will be no peace for any of us. Look here, Damon--if you had a wife, and another man stood before the world as her betrothed husband--if you had a wife, and another man spoke of her as his--boasted of her--behaved in the house as if it were already his own--treated her servants as though he were their master--possessed himself of her papers--extorted money from her--brought his friends, on one pretext or another, about her house--tormented her, day after day, to marry him ... what would you do to such a man as this?"

"Make my own marriage public at once, and set him at defiance," I replied.

"Ay, but...."

"But what?"

"That alone will not content me. I must punish him with my own hand."

"He would be punished enough in the loss of the lady and her fortune."

"Not he! He has entangled her affairs sufficiently by this time to indemnify himself for her fortune, depend on it. And as for herself--pshaw! he does not know what love is!"

"But his pride----"

"But *my* pride!" interrupted Dalrymple, passionately. "What of my pride?--my wounded honor?--my outraged love? No, no, I tell you, it is not such a paltry vengeance that will satisfy me! Would to Heaven I had trusted only my own arm from the first! Would to Heaven that, instead of having anything to say to the cursed brood of the law, I had taken the viper by the throat, and brought him to my own terms, after my own fashion!"

"But you have not yet told me what you are doing here?"

"I am waiting to see Monsieur de Simoncourt."

"Monsieur de Simoncourt!"

"Yes. That white house at the corner is one of his haunts,--a private gaming-house, never open till after midnight. I want to meet him accidentally, as he is going in."

"What for?"

"That he may take me with him. You can't get into one of these places without an introduction, you know. Those who keep them are too much afraid of the police."

"But do you play?"

"Come with me, and see. Hark! do you hear nothing?"

"Yes, I hear a footstep. And here comes a man."

"Let us walk to meet him, accidentally, and seem to be talking."

I took Dalrymple's arm, and we strolled in the direction of the new comer. It was not De Simoncourt, however, but a tall man with a grizzled beard, who crossed over, apprehensively, at our approach, but recrossed and went into the white house at the corner as soon as he thought us out of sight.

"One of the gang," said Dalrymple, with a shrug of his broad shoulders. "We had better go back to our doorway, and wait till the right man comes."

We had not long to wait. The next arrival was he whom we sought. We strolled on, as before, and came upon him face to face.

"De Simoncourt, by all that's propitious!" cried Dalrymple.

"What--Major Dalrymple returned to Paris!"

"Ay, just returned. Bored to death with Berlin and Vienna--no place like Paris, De Simoncourt, go where one will!"

"None, indeed. There is but one Paris, and pleasure is the true profit of all who visit it."

"My dear De Simoncourt, I am appalled to hear you perpetrate a pun! By the way, you have met Mr. Basil Arbuthnot at my rooms?"

M. de Simoncourt lifted his hat, and was graciously pleased to remember the circumstance.

"And now," pursued Dalrymple, "having met, what shall, we do next? Have you any engagement for the small hours, De Simoncourt?"

"I am quite at your disposal. Where were your bound for?"

"Anywhere--everywhere. I want excitement."

"Would a hand at *ecarte*, or a green table, have any attraction for you?" suggested De Simoncourt, falling into the trap as readily as one could have desired.

"The very thing, if you know where they are to be found!"

"Nay, I need not take you far to find both. There is in this very street a house where money may be lost and won as easily as at the Bourse. Follow me."

He took us to the white house at the corner, and, pressing a spring concealed in the wood-work of the lintel, rung a bell of shrill and peculiar *timbre*. The door opened immediately, and, after we had passed in, closed behind us without any visible agency. Still following at the heels of M. de Simoncourt, we then went up a spacious staircase dimly lighted, and, leaving our hats in an ante-room, entered unannounced into an elegant *salon*, where some twenty or thirty *habitues* of both sexes had already commenced the business of the evening. The ladies, of whom there were not more than half-a-dozen, were all more or less painted, *passees*, and showily dressed. Among the men were military stocks, ribbons, crosses, stars, and fine titles in abundance. We were evidently supposed to be in very brilliant society--brilliant, however, with a fictitious lustre that betrayed the tinsel beneath, and reminded one of a fashionable reception on the boards of the Haymarket or the Porte St. Martin. The mistress of the house, an abundant and somewhat elderly Juno in green velvet, with a profusion of jewelry on her arms and bosom, came forward to receive us.

"Madame de Sainte Amaranthe, permit me to present my friends, Major Dal-rymple and Mr. Arbuthnot," said De Simoncourt, imprinting a gallant kiss on the plump hand of the hostess.

Madame de Ste. Amaranthe professed herself charmed to receive any friends of M. de Simoncourt; whereupon M. de Simoncourt's friends were enchanted to be admitted to the privilege of Madame de Ste. Amaranthe's acquaintance. Madame de Ste. Amaranthe then informed us that she was the widow of a general officer who fell at Austerlitz, and the daughter of a rich West India planter whom she called her *pere adore*, and to whose supposititious memory she wiped away an imaginary tear with an embroidered pocket-handkerchief. She then begged that we would make ourselves at home, and, gliding away, whispered something in De Simoncourt's ear, to which he replied by a nod of intelligence.

"That harpy hopes to fleece us," said Dalrymple, slipping his arm through mine and drawing me towards the roulette table. "She has just told De Simoncourt to take us in hand. I always suspected the fellow was a Greek."

"A Greek?"

"Ay, in the figurative sense--a gentleman who lives by dexterity at cards."

"And shall you play?"

"By-and-by. Not yet, because--"

He checked himself, and looked anxiously round the room.

"Because what?"

"Tell me, Arbuthnot," said he, paying no attention to my question; "do *you* mind playing?"

"I? My dear fellow, I hardly know one card from another."

"But have you any objection?"

"None whatever to the game; but a good deal to the penalty. I don't mind confessing to you that I ran into debt some months back, and that...."

"Nonsense, boy!" interrupted Dalrymple, with a kindly smile. "Do you suppose I want you to gamble away your money? No, no--the fact is, that I am here for a purpose, and it will not do to let my purpose be suspected. These Greeks want a pigeon. Will you oblige me by being that pigeon, and by allowing me to pay for your plucking?"

I still hesitated.

"But you will be helping me," urged he. "If you don't sit down, I must."

"You would not lose so much," I expostulated.

"Perhaps not, if I were cool and kept my eyes open; but to-night I am *distrait*, and should be as defenceless as yourself."

"In that case I will play for you with pleasure."

He slipped a little pocket-book into my hand.

"Never stake more than five francs at a time," said he, "and you cannot ruin me. The book contains a thousand. You shall have more, if necessary; but I think that sum will last as long as I shall want you to keep playing."

"A thousand francs!" I exclaimed. "Why, that is forty pounds!"

"If it were four hundred, and it answered my purpose," said Dalrymple, between his teeth, "I should hold it money well spent!"

At this moment De Simoncourt came up, and apologized for having left us so long.

"If you want mere amusement, Major Dalrymple," said he, "I suppose you will prefer *roulette* to *ecarte*!"

"I will stake a few pieces presently on the green cloth," replied Dalrymple, carelessly; "but, first of all, I want to initiate my young friend here. As to double *ecarte*, Monsieur de Simoncourt, I need hardly tell you, as a man of the world, that I never play it with strangers."

De Simoncourt smiled, and shrugged his shoulders.

"Quite right," said he. "I believe that here everything is really *de bonne foi*; but where there are cards there will always be danger. For my part, I always shuffle the pack after my adversary!"

With this he strolled off again, and I took a vacant chair at the long table, next to a lady, who made way for me with the most gracious smile imaginable. Only the players sat; so Dalrymple stood behind me and looked on. It was a green board, somewhat larger than an ordinary billiard-table, with mysterious boundaries traced here and there in yellow and red, and a cabalistic table of figures towards each end. A couple of well-dressed men sat in the centre; one to deal out the cards, and the other to pay and receive the money. The one who had the management of the cash wore a superb diamond ring, and a red and green ribbon at his button-hole. Dalrymple informed me in a whisper that this noble seigneur was Madame de Ste.

Amaranthe's brother.

As for the players, they all looked serious and polite enough, as ladies and gentlemen should, at their amusement. Some had pieces of card, which they pricked occasionally with a pin, according to the progress of the game. Some had little piles of silver, or sealed ***rouleaux***, lying beside them. As for myself, I took out Dalrymple's pocket-book, and laid it beside me, as if I were an experienced player and meant to break the bank. For a few minutes he stood by, and then, having given me some idea of the leading principles of the game, wandered away to observe the other players.

Left to myself, I played on--timidly at first; soon with more confidence; and, of course, with the novice's invariable good-fortune. My amiable neighbor drew me presently into conversation. She had a theory of chances relating to averages of color, and based upon a bewildering calculation of all the black and red cards in the pack, which she was so kind as to explain to me. I could not understand a word of it, but politeness compelled me to listen. Politeness also compelled me to follow her advice when she was so obliging as to offer it, and I lost, as a matter of course. From this moment my good-luck deserted me.

"Courage, Monsieur," said my amiable neighbour; "you have only to play long enough, and you are sure to win."

In the meantime, I kept following Dalrymple with my eyes, for there was something in his manner that filled me with vague uneasiness. Sometimes he drew near the table and threw down a Napoleon, but without heeding the game, or caring whether he won or lost. He was always looking to the door, or wandering restlessly from table to table. Watching him thus, I thought how haggard he looked, and what deep channels were furrowed in his brow since that day when we lay together on the autumnal grass under the trees in the forest of St. Germain.

Thus a long time went by, and I found by my watch that it was nearly four o'clock in the morning--also that I had lost six hundred francs out of the thousand. It seemed incredible. I could hardly believe that the time and the money had flown so fast. I rose in my seat and looked round for Dalrymple; but in vain. Could he be gone, leaving me here? Impossible! Apprehensive of I knew not what, I pushed back my chair, and left the table. The rooms were now much fuller--more stars and moustachios; more velvets and laces, and Paris diamonds. Fresh tables, too, had been opened for ***lansquenet, baccarat***, and ***ecarte***. At one of these I saw M. de Simoncourt. When he laid down his cards for the deal, I seized the opportunity to inquire for my friend.

He pointed to a small inner room divided by a rich hanging from the farther end of the ***salon***.

"You will find Major Dalrymple in Madame de Ste. Amaranthe's boudoir, playing with M. le Vicomte de Caylus," said he, courteously, and resumed his game.

Playing with De Caylus! Sitting down amicably with De Caylus! I could not understand it.

Crowded as the rooms now were, it took me some time to thread my way across, and longer still, when I had done so, to pass the threshold of the boudoir, and obtain sight of the players. The room was very small, and filled with lookers-on. At a table under a chandelier sat De Caylus and Dalrymple. I could not see Dalrymple's face, for his back was turned towards me; but the Vicomte I recognised at once--pale, slight, refined, with the old look of dissipation and irritability, and the same restlessness of eye and hand that I had observed on first seeing him. They were evidently playing high, and each had a pile of notes and gold lying at his left hand. De Caylus kept nervously crumbling a note in his fingers. Dalrymple sat motionless as a man of bronze, and, except to throw down a card when it came to his turn, never stirred a finger. There was, to my thinking, something ominous in his exceeding calmness.

"At what game are they, playing?" I asked a gentleman near whom I was standing.

"At ***ecarte***," replied he, without removing his eyes from the players.

Knowing nothing of the game, I could only judge of its progress by the faces of those around me. A breathless silence prevailed, except when some particular subtlety in the play sent a murmur of admiration round the room. Even this was hushed almost as soon as uttered. Gradually the interest grew more intense, and the bystanders pressed closer. De Caylus sighed impatiently, and passed his hand across his brow. It was his turn to deal. Dalrymple shuffled the pack. De Caylus shuffled them after him, and dealt. The falling of a pin might have been heard in the pause that followed. They had but five cards each. Dalrymple played first--a queen of diamonds. De Caylus played the king, and both threw down their cards. A loud murmur broke out instantaneously in every direction, and De Caylus, looking excited and weary, leaned back in his chair, and called for wine. His expression was so unlike that of a victor that I thought at first he must have lost the game.

"Which is the winner?" I asked, eagerly. "Which is the winner?"

The gentleman who had replied to me before looked round with a smile of contemptuous wonder.

"Why, Monsieur de Caylus, of course," said he. "Did you not see him play the king?"

"I beg your pardon," I said, somewhat nettled; "but, as I said before, I do not understand the game."

"*Eh bien*! the Englishman is counting out his money."

What a changed scene it was! The circle of intent faces broken and shifting-- the silence succeeded by a hundred conversations--De Caylus leaning back, sipping his wine and chatting over his shoulder--the cards pushed aside, and Dalrymple gravely sorting out little shining columns of Napoleons, and rolls of crisp bank pa- per! Having ranged all these before him in a row, he took out his check-book, filled in a page, tore it out and laid it with the rest. Then, replacing the book in his breast- pocket, he pushed back his chair, and, looking up for the first time since the close of the game, said aloud:--

"Monsieur le Vicomte de Caylus, I have this evening had the honor of losing the sum of twelve thousand francs to you; will you do me the favor to count this money?"

M. de Caylus bowed, emptied his glass, and languidly touching each little col- umn with one dainty finger, told over his winnings as though they were scarcely worth even that amount of trouble.

"Six rouleaux of four hundred each," said he, "making two thousand four hun- dred--six notes of five hundred each, making three thousand--and an order upon Rothschild for six thousand six hundred; in all, twelve thousand. Thanks, Monsieur ... Monsieur ... forgive me for not remembering your name."

Dalrymple looked up with a dangerous light in his eyes, and took no notice of the apology.

"It appears to me, Monsieur le Vicomte Caylus," said he, giving the other his full title and speaking with singular distinctness, "that you hold the king very often at *ecarte*."

De Caylus looked up with every vein on his forehead suddenly swollen and throbbing.

"Monsieur!" he exclaimed, hoarsely.

"Especially when you deal," added Dalrymple, smoothing his moustache with utter *sang-froid*, and keeping his eyes still riveted upon his adversary.

With an inarticulate cry like the cry of a wild beast, De Caylus sprung at him, foaming with rage, and was instantly flung back against the wall, dragging with him not only the table-cloth, but all the wine, money, and cards upon it.

"I will have blood for this!" he shrieked, struggling with those who rushed in between. "I will have blood! Blood! Blood!"

Stained and streaming with red wine, he looked, in his ghastly rage, as if he was already bathed in the blood he thirsted for.

Dalrymple drew himself to his full height, and stood looking on with folded arms and a cold smile.

"I am quite ready," he said, "to give Monsieur le Vicomte full satisfaction."

The room was by this time crowded to suffocation. I forced my way through, and laid my hand on Dalrymple's arm.

"You have provoked this quarrel," I said, reproachfully.

"That, my dear fellow, is precisely what I came here to do," he replied. "You will have to be my second in this affair."

Here De Simoncourt came up, and hearing the last words, drew me aside.

"I act for De Caylus," he whispered. "Pistols, of course?"

I nodded, still all bewilderment at my novel position.

"Your man received the first blow, so is entitled to the first shot."

I nodded again.

"I don't know a better place," he went on, "than Bellevue. There's a famous little bit of plantation, and it is just far enough from Paris to be secure. The Bois is hackneyed, and the police are too much about it.

"Just so," I replied, vaguely.

"And when shall we say? The sooner the better, it always seems to me, in these cases."

"Oh, certainly--the sooner the better."

He looked at his watch.

"It is now ten minutes to five," he said. "Suppose we allow them five hours to put their papers in order, and meet at Bellevue, on the terrace, at ten?"

"So soon!" I exclaimed.

"Soon!" echoed De Simoncourt. "Why, under circumstances of such exceeding aggravation, most men would send for pistols and settle it across the table!"

I shuddered. These niceties of honor were new to me, and I had been brought up to make little distinction between duelling and murder.

"Be it so, then, Monsieur De Simoncourt," I said. "We will meet you at Bellevue, at ten."

"On the terrace?"

"On the terrace."

We bowed and parted. Dalrymple was already gone, and De Caylus, still white and trembling with rage, was wiping the wine from his face and shirt. The crowd opened for me right and left as I went through the *salon*, and more than one voice whispered:--

"He is the Englishman's second."

I took my hat and cloak mechanically, and let myself out. It was broad daylight, and the blinding sun poured full upon my eyes as I passed into the street.

"Come, Damon," said Dalrymple, crossing over to me from the opposite side of the way. "I have just caught a cab--there it is, waiting round the corner! We've no time to lose, I'll be bound."

"We are to meet them at Bellevue at ten," I replied.

"At ten? Hurrah! then I've still five certain hours of life before me! Long enough, Damon, to do a world of mischief, if one were so disposed!"

CHAPTER L.
THE DUEL AT BELLEVUE.

We drove straight to Dalrymple's rooms, and, going in with a pass-key, went up without disturbing the *concierge*. Arrived at home, my friend's first act was to open his buffetier and take out a loaf, a *pate de foie gras*, and a bottle of wine. I could not eat a morsel; but he supped (or breakfasted) with a capital appetite; insisted that I should lie down on his bed for two or three hours; and slipping into his dressing-gown, took out his desk and cash-box, and settled himself to a regular morning's work.

"I hope to get a nap myself before starting," said he. "I have not many debts, and I made my will the day after I married--so I have but little to transact in the way of business. A few letters to write--a few to burn--a trifle or two to seal up and direct to one or two fellows who may like a *souvenir*,--that is the extent of my task! Meanwhile, my dear boy, get what rest you can. It will never do to be shaky and pale on the field, you know."

I went, believing that I should be less in his way; and, lying down in my clothes, fell into a heavy sleep, from which, after what seemed a long time, I woke suddenly with the conviction that it was just ten o'clock. To start up, look at my watch, find that it was only a quarter to seven and fall profoundly asleep again, was the work of only a few minutes. At the end of another half-hour I woke with the same dread, and with the same result; and so on twice or thrice after, till at a quarter to nine I jumped up, plunged my head into a basin of cold water, and went back to the sitting-room.

I found him lying forward upon the table, fast asleep, with his head resting on his hands. Some half-dozen letters lay folded and addressed beside him--one direct-ed to his wife. A little pile of burnt paper fluttered on the hearth. His pistols were lying close by in their mahogany case, the blue and white steel relieved against the crimson-velvet lining. He slept so soundly, poor fellow, that I could with difficulty make up my mind to wake him. Once roused, however, he was alert and ready in a moment, changed his coat, took out a new pair of lavender gloves, hailed a cab from the window, and bade the driver name his own fare if he got us to the terrace at Bellevue by five minutes before ten.

"I always like to be before my time in a matter of this kind, Damon," said he. "It's shabby to be merely punctual when one has, perhaps, not more than a quarter of an hour to live. By-the-by, here are my keys. Take them, in case of accident. You will find a copy of my will in my desk---the original is with my lawyer. The letters you will forward, according to the addresses; and in my cash-box you will find a paper directed to yourself."

I bent my head. I would not trust myself to speak. "As for the letter to Helene--to my wife," he said, turning his face away, "will you--will you deliver that with your own hands?"

"I will."

"I--I have had but little time to write it," he faltered, "and I trust to you to supply the details. Tell her how I made the quarrel, and how it ended. No one suspects it to be other than a *fracas* over a game at *ecarte*. No one supposes that I had any other motive, or any deeper vengeance--not even De Caylus! I have not compromised her by word or deed. If I shoot him, I free her without a breath of scandal. If I fall--"

His voice failed, and we were both silent for some moments

We were now past the Barrier, and speeding on rapidly towards the open country. High white houses with jalousies closed against the sun, and pretty maisonnettes in formal gardens, succeeded the streets and shops of suburban Paris. Then came a long country road bordered by poplars--by-and-by, glimpses of the Seine, and scattered farms and villages far away--then Sevres and the leafy heights of Bellevue overhanging the river.

We crossed the bridge, and the driver, mindful of his fare, urged on his tired horse. Some country folks met us presently, and a wagoner with a load of fresh hay. They all smiled and gave us "good-day" as we passed--they going to their work in the fields, and we to our work of bloodshed!

Shortly after this, the road began winding upwards, past the porcelain factories and through the village of Sevres; after which, having but a short distance of very steep road to climb, we desired the cabman to wait, and went up on foot. Arrived at the top, where a peep of blue daylight came streaming down upon us through a green tunnel of acacias, we emerged all at once upon the terrace, and found ourselves first on the field. Behind us rose a hillside of woods--before us, glassy and glittering, as if traced upon the transparent air, lay the city of palaces. Domes and spires, arches and columns of triumph, softened by distance, looked as if built of the sunshine. Far away on one side stretched the Bois de Boulogne, undulating like a sea of tender green. Still farther away on the other, lay Pere-la-Chaise--a dark hill specked with white; cypresses and tombs. At our feet, winding round a "lawny islet" and through a valley luxuriant in corn-fields and meadows, flowed the broad river, bluer than the sky.

"A fine sight, Damon!" said Dalrymple, leaning on the parapet, and coolly lighting a cigar. "If my eyes are never to open on the day again, I am glad they should have rested for the last time on a scene of so much beauty! Where is the painter who could paint it? Not Claude himself, though he should come back to life on purpose, and mix his colors with liquid sunlight!"

"You are a queer fellow," said I, "to talk of scenery and painters at such a moment!"

"Not at all. Things are precious according to the tenure by which we hold them. For my part, I do not know when I appreciated earth and sky so heartily as this morning. *Tiens!* here comes a carriage--our men, no doubt."

"Are you a good shot?" I asked anxiously.

"Pretty well. I can write my initials in bullet-holes on a sheet of notepaper at forty paces, or toss up half-a-crown as I ride at full gallop, and let the daylight through it as it comes down."

"Thank Heaven!"

"Not so fast, my boy. De Caylus is just as fine a shot, and one of the most skilful swordsmen in the French service."

"Ay, but the first fire is yours!"

"Is it? Well, I suppose it is. He struck the first blow, and so--here they come."

"One more word, Dalrymple--did he really cheat you at *ecarte?*"

"Upon my soul, I don't know. He did hold the king very often, and there are some queer stories told of him in Vienna by the officers of the Emperor's Guard. At all events, this is not the first duel he has had to fight in defence of his good-fortune!"

De Simoncourt now coming forward, we adjourned at once to the wood behind the village. A little open glade was soon found; the ground was soon measured; the pistols were soon loaded. De Caylus looked horribly pale, but it was the pallor of concentrated rage, with nothing of the craven hue in it. Dalrymple, on the contrary, had neither more nor less color than usual, and puffed away at his cigar with as much indifference as if he were waiting his turn at the pit of the Comedie Francaise. Both were clothed in black from head to foot, with their coats buttoned to the chin.

"All is ready," said De Simoncourt. "Gentlemen, choose your weapons."

De Caylus took his pistols one by one, weighed and poised them, examined the priming, and finally, after much hesitation, decided.

Dalrymple took the first that came to hand.

The combatants then took their places--De Caylus with his hat pulled low over his eyes; Dalrymple still smoking carelessly.

They exchanged bows.

"Major Dalrymple," said De Simoncourt, "it is for you to fire first."

"God bless you, Damon!" said my friend, shaking me warmly by the hand.

He then half turned aside, flung away the end of his cigar, lifted his right arm suddenly, and fired.

I heard the dull thud of the ball--I saw De Caylus fling up his arms and fall forward on the grass. I saw Dalrymple running to his assistance. The next instant, however, the wounded man was on his knees, ghastly and bleeding, and crying for his pistol.

"Give it me!" he gasped--"hold me up! I--I will have his life yet! So, steady--steady!"

Shuddering, but not for his own danger, Dalrymple stepped calmly back to his place; while De Caylus, supported by his second, struggled to his feet and grasped his weapon. For a moment he once more stood upright. His eye burned; his lips contracted; he seemed to gather up all his strength for one last effort. Slowly, steadily, surely, he raised his pistol--then swaying heavily back, fired, and fell again.

"Dead this time, sure enough," said De Simoncourt, bending over him.

"Indeed, I fear so," replied Dalrymple, in a low, grave voice. "Can we do nothing to help you, Monsieur de Simoncourt?"

"Nothing, thank you. I have a carriage down the road, and must get further assistance from the village. You had better lose no time in leaving Paris."

"I suppose not. Good-morning."

"Good-morning,"

So we lifted our hats; gathered up the pistols; hurried out of the wood and across a field, so avoiding the village; found our cab waiting where we had left it; and in less than five minutes, were rattling down the dusty hill again and hurrying towards Paris.

Once in the cab, Dalrymple began hastily pulling off his coat and waistcoat. I was startled to see his shirt-front stained with blood.

"Heavens!" I exclaimed, "you are not wounded?"

"Very slightly. De Caylus was too good a shot to miss me altogether. Pshaw! 'tis nothing--a mere graze--not even the bullet left in it!"

"If it had been a little more to the left...." I faltered.

"If he had fired one second sooner, or lived one second longer, he would have had me through the heart, as sure as there's a heaven above us!" said Dalrymple.

Then, suddenly changing his tone, he added, laughingly--

"Nonsense, Damon! cheer up, and help me to tear this handkerchief into bandages. Now's the time to show off your surgery, my little AEsculapius. By Jupiter, life's a capital thing, after all!"

CHAPTER LI
THE PORTRAIT.

Having seen Dalrymple to his lodgings and dressed his wound, which was, in truth, but a very slight one, I left him and went home, promising to return in a few hours, and help him with his packing; for we both agreed that he must leave Paris that evening, come what might.

It was now close upon two o'clock, and I had been out since between three and four the previous afternoon--not quite twenty-four hours, in point of actual time; but a week, a month, a year, in point of sensation! Had I not seen a man die since that hour yesterday?

Walking homewards through the garish streets in the hot afternoon, all the strange scenes in which I had just been an actor thronged fantastically upon my memory. The joyous dinner with Franz Mueller; the busy Temple; the noisy theatre; the long chase through the wet streets at midnight; the crowded gaming-house; the sweet country drive at early morning; the quiet wood, and the dead man lying on his back, with the shadows of the leaves upon his face,--all this, in strange distinctness, came between me and the living tide of the Boulevards.

And now, over-tired and over-excited as I was, I remembered for the first time that I had eaten nothing since half-past five that morning. And then I also remembered that I had left Mueller waiting for me under the archway, without a word of explanation. I promised myself that I would write to him as soon as I got home, and in the meantime turned in at the first Cafe to which I came and called for breakfast. But when the breakfast was brought, I could not eat it. The coffee tasted bitter to me. The meat stuck in my throat. I wanted rest more than food--rest of body and mind, and the forgetfulness of sleep! So I paid my bill, and, leaving the untasted meal, went home like a man in a dream.

Madame Bouisse was not in her little lodge as I passed it--neither was my key on its accustomed hook. I concluded that she was cleaning my rooms, and so, going upstairs, found my door open. Hearing my own name, however, I paused involuntarily upon the threshold.

"And so, as I was saying," pursued a husky voice, which I knew at once to be the property of Madame Bouisse, "M'sieur Basil's friend painted it on purpose for him; and I am sure if he was as good a Catholic as the Holy Father himself, and that picture was a true portrait of our Blessed Lady, he could not worship it more devoutly. I believe he says his prayers to it, mam'selle! I often find it in the morning stuck up by the foot of his bed; and when he comes home of an evening to study his books and papers, it always stands on a chair just in front of his table, so that he can see it without turning his head, every time he lifts his eyes from the writing!"

In the murmured reply that followed, almost inaudible though it was, my ear distinguished a tone that set my heart beating.

"Well, I can't tell, of course," said Madame Bouisse, in answer, evidently, to the remark just made; "but if mam'selle will only take the trouble to look in the glass, and then look at the picture, she will see how like it is. For my part, I believe it to be that, and nothing else. Do you suppose I don't know the symptoms? *Dame!* I have eyes, as well as my neighbors; and you may take my word for it, mam'selle, that poor young gentleman is just as much in love as ever a man was in this world!"

"No more of this, if you please, Madame Bouisse," said Hortense, so distinctly that I could no longer be in doubt as to the speaker.

I stayed to hear no more; but retreating softly down the first flight of stairs, came noisily up again, and went straight into my rooms, saying:--

"Madame Bouisse, are you here?"

"Not only Madame Bouisse, but an intruder who implores forgiveness," said Hortense, with a frank smile, but a heightened color.

I bowed profoundly. No need to tell her she was welcome--my face spoke for me.

"It was Madame Bouisse who lured me in," continued she, "to look at that painting."

"*Mais, oui!* I told mam'selle you had her portrait in your sitting-room," laughed the fat *concierge,* leaning on her broom. "I'm sure it's quite like enough to be hers, bless her sweet face!"

I felt myself turn scarlet. To hide my confusion I took the picture down, and carried it to the window.

"You will see it better by this light," I said, pretending to dust it with my handkerchief. "It is worth a close examination."

Hortense knelt down, and studied it for some moments in silence.

"It must be a copy," she said, presently, more to herself than me--"it must be a copy."

"It *is* a copy," I replied. "The original is at the Chateau de Sainte Aulaire, near Montlhery."

"May I ask how you came by it?"

"A friend of mine, who is an artist, copied it."

"Then it was done especially for you?"

"Just so."

"And, no doubt, you value it?"

"More than anything I possess!"

Then, fearing I had said too much, I added:--

"If I had not admired the original very much, I should not have wished for a copy."

She shifted the position of the picture in such a manner that, standing where I did, I could no longer see her face.

"Then you have seen the original," she said, in a low tone.

"Undoubtedly--and you?"

"Yes, I have seen it; but not lately."

There was a brief pause.

"Madame Bouisse thinks it so like yourself, mademoiselle," I said, timidly, "that it might almost be your portrait."

"I can believe it," she answered. "It is very like my mother."

Her voice faltered; and, still kneeling, she dropped her face in her hands, and wept silently.

Madame Bouisse, in the meantime, had gone into my bedchamber, where she was sweeping and singing to herself with the door three parts closed, believing, no doubt, that she was affording me the opportunity to make a formal declaration.

"Alas! mademoiselle," I said, hesitatingly, "I little thought..."

She rose, dashed the tears aside, and, holding out her hand to me, said, kindly--

"It is no fault of yours, fellow-student, if I remind you of the portrait, or if the portrait reminds me of one whom it resembles still more nearly. I am sorry to have troubled your kind heart with my griefs. It is not often that they rise to the surface."

I raised her hand reverently to my lips.

"But you are looking worn and ill yourself," she added. "Is anything the matter?"

"Not now," I replied. "But I have been up all night, and--and I am very tired."

"Was this in your professional capacity?"

"Not exactly--and yet partly so. I have been more a looker-on than an active agent--and I have witnessed a frightful death-scene."

She sighed, and shook her head.

"You are not of the stuff that surgeons are made of, fellow-student," she said, kindly. "Instead of prescribing for others, you need some one to prescribe for you. Why, your hand is quite feverish. You should go to bed, and keep quiet for the next twelve hours."

"I will lie down for a couple of hours when Madame Bouisse is gone; but I must be up and out again at six."

"Nay, that is in three hours."

"I cannot help it. It is my duty."

"Then I have no more to say. Would you drink some lemonade, if I made it for you?"

"I would drink poison, if you made it for me!"

"A decidedly misplaced enthusiasm!" laughed she, and left the room.

CHAPTER LII.
NEWS FROM ENGLAND.

I t was a glorious morning--first morning of the first week in the merry month of June--as I took my customary way to Dr. Cheron's house in the Faubourg St. Germain. I had seen Dalrymple off by the night train the evening previous, and, refreshed by a good night's rest, had started somewhat earlier than usual, for the purpose of taking a turn in the Luxembourg Gardens before beginning my day's work.

There the blossoming parterres, the lavish perfume from geranium-bed and acacia-blossom, and the mad singing of the little birds up among the boughs, set me longing for a holiday. I thought of Saxonholme, and the sweet English woodlands round about. I thought how pleasant it would be to go home to dear Old England, if only for ten days, and surprise my father in his quiet study. What if I asked Dr. Cheron to spare me for a fortnight?

Turning these things over in my mind, I left the gardens, and, arriving presently at the well-known Porte Cochere in the Rue de Mont Parnasse, rang the great bell, crossed the dull courtyard, and took my usual seat at my usual desk, not nearly so well disposed for work as usual.

"If you please, Monsieur," said the solemn servant, making his appearance at the door, "Monsieur le Docteur requests your presence in his private room."

I went. Dr. Cheron was standing on the hearth-rug, with his back to the fire, and his arms folded over his breast. An open letter, bordered broadly with black, lay upon his desk. Although distant some two yards from the table, his eyes were fixed upon this paper. When I came in he looked up, pointed to a seat, but himself remained standing and silent.

"Basil Arbuthnot," he said, after a pause of some minutes, "I have this morning received a letter from England, by the early post."

"From my father, sir?"

"No. From a stranger,"

He looked straight at me as he said this, and hesitated.

"But it contains news," he added, "that--that much concerns you."

There was a fixed gravity about the lines of his handsome mouth, and an unwonted embarrassment in his manner, that struck me with apprehension.

"Good news, I--I hope, sir," I faltered.

"Bad news, my young friend," said he, compassionately. "News that you must meet like a man, with fortitude--with resignation. Your father--your excellent father--my honored friend--"

He pointed to the letter and turned away.

I rose up, sat down, rose up again, reached out a trembling hand for the letter, and read the loss that my heart had already presaged.

My father was dead.

Well as ever in the morning, he had been struck with apoplexy in the afternoon, and died in a few hours, apparently without pain.

The letter was written by our old family lawyer, and concluded with the request that Dr. Cheron would "break the melancholy news to Mr. Basil Arbuthnot, who would doubtless return to England for the funeral."

My tears fell one by one upon the open letter. I had loved my father tenderly in my heart. His very roughnesses and eccentricities were dear to me. I could not believe that he was gone. I could not believe that I should never hear his voice again!

Dr. Cheron came over, and laid his hand upon my shoulder.

"Come," he said, "you have much to do, and must soon be on your way. The express leaves at midday. It is now ten, you have only two hours left."

"My poor father!"

"Brunet," continued the Doctor, "shall go back with you to your lodgings and help you to pack. As for money--"

He took out his pocket-book and offered me a couple of notes; but I shook my head and put them from me.

"I have enough money, thank you," I said. "Good-bye."

"Good-bye," he replied, and, for the first time in all these months, shook me by the hand. "You will write to me?"

I bowed my head in silence, and we parted. I found a cab at the door, and Brunet on the box. I was soon at home again. Home! I felt as if I had no home now, either in France or England--as if all my Paris life were a brief, bright dream, and this the dreary waking. Hortense was out. It was one of her busy mornings, and she would not be back till the afternoon. It was very bitter to leave without one last look--one last word. I seized pen and paper, and yielding for the first time to all the impulses of my love, wrote, without weighing my words, these few brief sentences:--

"I have had a heavy loss, Hortense, and by the time you open this letter I shall be far away. My father--my dear, good father--is no more. My mother died when I was a little child. I have no brothers--no sisters--no close family ties. I am alone in the world now--quite alone. My last thought here is of you. If it seems strange to speak of love at such a moment, forgive me, for that love is now my only hope. Oh, that you were here, that I might kiss your hand at parting, and know that some of your thoughts went with me! I cannot believe that you are quite indifferent to me. It seems impossible that, loving you as I love, so deeply, so earnestly, I should love in vain. When I come back I shall seek you here, where I have loved you so long. I shall look into your eyes for my answer, and read in them all the joy, or all the despair, of the life that lies before me. I had intended to get that portrait copied again for you, because you saw in it some likeness to your mother; but there has been no time, and ere you receive this letter I shall be gone. I therefore send the picture to you by the *concierge*. It is my parting gift to you. I can offer no greater proof of my love. Farewell."

Once written, I dared not read the letter over. I thrust it under her door, and in less than five minutes was on my way to the station.

CHAPTER LIII.
THE FADING OF THE RAINBOW.

I loved a love once, fairest among women;
Closed are her doors on me, I must not see her--
All, all are gone, the old familiar faces.
LAMB.

Beautifully and truly, in the fourth book of the most poetical of stories, has a New World romancist described the state of a sorrowing lover. "All around him," saith he, "seemed dreamy and vague; all within him, as in a sun's eclipse. As the moon, whether visible or invisible, has power over the tides of the ocean, so the face of that lady, whether present or absent, had power over the tides of his soul, both by day and night, both waking and sleeping. In every pale face and dark eye he saw a resemblance to her; and what the day denied him in reality, the night gave him in dreams."

Such was, very faithfully, my own condition of mind during the interval which succeeded my departure from Paris--the only difference being that Longfellow's hero was rejected by the woman he loved, and sorrowing for that rejection; whilst I, neither rejected nor accepted, mourned another grief, and through the tears of that trouble, looked forward anxiously to my uncertain future.

I reached Saxonholme the night before my father's funeral, and remained there for ten days. I found myself, to my surprise, almost a rich man--that is to say, sufficiently independent to follow the bent of my inclinations as regarded the future.

My first impulse, on learning the extent of my means, was to relinquish a career that had been from the first distasteful to me--my second was to leave the decision to Hortense. To please her, to be worthy of her, to prove my devotion to her, was what I most desired upon earth. If she wished to see me useful and active in my generation, I would do my best to be so for her sake--if, on the contrary, she only cared to see me content, I would devote myself henceforth to that life of "retired leisure" that I had always coveted. Could man love more honestly and heartily?

One year of foreign life had wrought a marked difference in me. I had not observed it so much in Paris; but here, amid old scenes and old reminiscences, I seemed to meet the image of my former self, and wondered at the change 'twixt now and then. I left home, timid, ignorant of the world and its ways, reserved, silent, almost misanthropic. I came back strengthened mentally and physically. Studious as ever, I could yet contemplate an active career without positive repugnance; I knew how to meet and treat my fellow-men; I was acquainted with society in its most refined and most homely phases. I had tasted of pleasure, of disappointment, of love--of all that makes life earnest.

As the time drew near when I should return to Paris, grief, and hope, and that strange reluctance which would fain defer the thing it most desires, perplexed and troubled me by day and night. Once again on the road, the past seemed more than ever dream-like, and Paris and Saxonholme became confused together in my mind, like the mingling outlines of two dissolving views.

I crossed the channel this time in a thick, misting rain; pushed on straight for Paris, and reached the Cite Bergere in the midst of a warm and glowing afternoon. The great streets were crowded with carriages and foot-passengers. The trees were in their fullest leaf. The sun poured down on pavement and awning with almost tropical intensity. I dismissed my cab at the top of the Rue du Faubourg Montmatre, and went up to the house on foot. A flower-girl sat in the shade of the archway, tying up her flowers for the evening-sale, and I bought a cluster of white roses for Hortense as I went by.

Madame Bouisse was sound asleep in her little sanctum; but my key hung in its old place, so I took it without disturbing her, and went up as if I had been away only a few hours. Arrived at the third story, I stopped outside Hortense's door and listened. All was very silent within. She was out, perhaps; or writing quietly in the farther chamber. I thought I would leave my travelling-bag in my own room, and then ring boldly for admittance. I turned the key, and found myself once again in my own familiar, pleasant student home. The books and busts were there in their accustomed places; everything was as I had left it. Everything, except the picture! The picture was gone; so Hortense had accepted it.

Three letters awaited me on the table; one from Dr. Cheron, written in a bold hand--a mere note of condolence: one from Dalrymple, dated Chamounix: the third from Hortense. I knew it was from her. I knew that that small, clear, upright writing, so singularly distinct and regular, could be only hers. I had never seen it before; but my heart identified it.

That letter contained my fate. I took it up, laid it down, paced backwards and forwards, and for several minutes dared not break the seal. At length I opened it. It ran thus:--

"FRIEND AND FELLOW-STUDENT.

"I had hoped that a man such as you and a woman such as I might become true friends, discuss books and projects, give and take the lesser services of life, and yet not end by loving. In this belief, despite occasional misgivings, I have suffered our intercourse to become intimacy--our acquaintance, friendship. I see now that I was mistaken, and now, when it is, alas! too late, I reproach myself for the consequences of that mistake.

"I can be nothing to you, friend. I have duties in life more sacred than marriage. I have a task to fulfil which is sterner than love, and imperative as fate. I do not say that to answer you thus costs me no pain. Were there even hope, I would bid you hope; but my labor presses heavily upon me, and repeated failure has left me weary and heart-sick.

"You tell me in your letter that, by the time I read it, you will be far away. It is now my turn to repeat the same words. When you come back to your rooms, mine will be empty. I shall be gone; all I ask is, that you will not attempt to seek me.

"Farewell. I accept your gift. Perhaps I act selfishly in taking it, but a day may come when I shall justify that selfishness to you. In the meantime, once again farewell. You are my only friend, and these are the saddest words I have ever written--forget me!

"HORTENSE."

I scarcely know how I felt, or what I did, on first reading this letter. I believe that I stood for a long time stone still, incapable of realizing the extent of my misfortune. By-and-by it seemed to rush upon me suddenly. I threw open my window, scaled the balcony rails, and forced my way into her rooms.

Her rooms! Ah, by that window she used to sit--at that table she read and wrote--in that bed she slept! All around and about were scattered evidences of her presence. Upon the chimney-piece lay an envelope addressed to her name--upon the floor, some fragments of torn paper and some ends of cordage! The very flowers were yet fresh upon her balcony! The sight of these things, while they confirmed my despair, thawed the ice at my heart. I kissed the envelope that she had touched, the flowers she had tended, the pillow on which her head had been wont to rest. I called wildly on her name. I threw myself on the floor in my great agony, and wept aloud.

I cannot tell how long I may have lain there; but it seemed like a lifetime. Long enough, at all events, to drink the bitter draught to the last drop--long enough to learn that life had now no grief in store for which I should weep again.

CHAPTER LIV.
TREATETH OF MANY THINGS; BUT CHIEFLY OF BOOKS AND POETS.

Dreams, books, are each a world; and books, we know,
Are a substantial world, both pure and good.
                    WORDSWORTH.

There are times when this beautiful world seems to put on a mourning garb, as if sympathizing, like a gentle mother, with the grief that consumes us; when the trees shake their arms in mute sorrow, and scatter their faded leaves like ashes on our heads; when the slow rains weep down upon us, and the very clouds look cold above. Then, like Hamlet the Dane, we take no pleasure in the life that weighs so wearily upon us, and deem "this goodly frame, the earth, a sterile promonotory; this most excellent canopy, the air, this brave, overhanging firmament, this majestical roof fretted with golden fire, a foul and pestilent congregation of vapors."

So it was with me, in the heavy time that followed my return to Paris. I had lost everything in losing her I loved. I had no aim in life. No occupation. No hope. No rest. The clouds had rolled between me and the sun, and wrapped me in their cold shadows, and all was dark about me. I felt that I could say with an old writer--"For the world, I count it, not an inn, but an hospital; and a place, not to live, but to die in."

Week after week I lingered in Paris, hoping against hope, and always seeking her. I had a haunting conviction that she was not far off, and that, if I only had strength to persevere, I must find her. Possessed by this fixed idea, I paced the sultry streets day after day throughout the burning months of June and July; lingered at dusk and early morning about the gardens of the Luxembourg, and such other quiet places as she might frequent; and, heedless alike of fatigue, or heat, or tempest, traversed the dusty city over and over again from barrier to barrier, in every direction.

Could I but see her once more--once only! Could I but listen to her sweet voice, even though it bade me an eternal farewell! Could I but lay my lips for the last, last time upon her hand, and see the tender pity in her eyes, and be comforted!

Seeking, waiting, sorrowing thus, I grew daily weaker and paler, scarcely conscious of my own failing strength, and indifferent to all things save one. In vain Dr. Cheron urged me to resume my studies. In vain Mueller, ever cheerful and active, came continually to my lodgings, seeking to divert my thoughts into healthier channels. In vain I received letter after letter from Oscar Dalrymple, imploring me to follow him to Switzerland, where his wife had already joined him. I shut my eyes to all alike. Study had grown hateful to me; Mueller's cheerfulness jarred upon me; Dalrymple was too happy for my companionship. Liberty to pursue my weary search, peace to brood over my sorrow, were all that I now asked. I had not yet arrived at that stage when sympathy grows precious.

So weeks went by, and August came, and a slow conviction of the utter hopelessness of my efforts dawned gradually upon me. She was really gone. If she had been in Paris all this time pursuing her daily avocations, I must surely have found her. Where should I seek her next? What should I do with life, with time, with the future?

I resolved, at all events, to relinquish medicine at once, and for ever. So I wrote a brief farewell to Dr. Cheron and another to Mueller, and without seeing either again, returned abruptly to England.

I will not dwell on this part of my story; enough that I settled my affairs as quickly as might be, left an old servant in care of the solitary house that had been my birthplace, and turned my back once more on Saxonholme, perhaps for years--perhaps for ever; and in less than three weeks was again on my way to the Continent.

The spirit of restlessness was now upon me. I had no home; I had no peace; and in place of the sun there was darkness. So I went with the thorns around my brow, and the shadow of the cross upon my breast. I went to suffer--to endure,--if possible, to forget. Oh, the grief of the soul which lives on in the night, and looks for no dawning! Oh, the weary weight that presses down the tired eyelids, and yet leaves them sleepless! Oh, the tide of alien faces, and the sickening remembrance of one, too dear, which may never be looked upon again! I carried with me the antidote to every pleasure. In the midst of crowds, I was alone. In the midst of novelty, the one thought came, and made all stale to me. Like Dr. Donne, I dwelt with the image of my dead self at my side.

Thus for many, many months we journeyed together---I and my sorrow--and passed through fair and famous places, and saw the seasons change under new skies. To the quaint old Flemish cities and the Gothic Rhine--to the plains and passes of Spain--to the unfrequented valleys of the Tyrol and the glacier-lands of Switzerland I went, but still found not the forgetfulness I sought. As in Holbein's fresco the skeleton plays his part in every scene, so my trouble stalked beside me, drank of my cup, and sat grimly at my table. It was with me in Naples and among the orange groves of Sorrento. It met me amid the ruins of the Roman Forum. It travelled with me over the blue Mediterranean, and landed beside me on the shores of the Cyclades. Go where I would, it possessed and followed me, and brooded over my head, like the cloud that rested on the ark.

Thinking over this period of my life, I seem to be turning the leaves of a rich album, or wandering through a gallery of glowing landscapes, and yet all the time to be dreaming. Faces grown familiar for a few days and never seen after--pictures photographed upon the memory in all their vividness--glimpses of cathedrals, of palaces, of ruins, of sunset and storm, sea and shore, flit before me for a moment, and are gone like phantasmagoria.

And like phantasmagoria they impressed me at the time. Nothing seemed real to me. Startled, now and then, into admiration or wonder, my apathy fell from me like a garment, and my heart throbbed again as of old. But this was seldom--so seldom that I could almost count the times when it befell me.

Thus it was that travelling did me no permanent good. It enlarged my experience; it undoubtedly cultivated my taste; but it brought me neither rest, nor sympathy, nor consolation. On the contrary, it widened the gulf between me and my fellow-men. I formed no friendships. I kept up no correspondence. A sojourner in hotels, I became more and more withdrawn from all tender and social impulses, and almost forgot the very name of home. So strong a hold did this morbid love of self-isolation take upon me, that I left Florence on one occasion, after a stay of only three days, because I had seen the names of a Saxonholme family among the list of arrivals in the Giornale Toscano.

Three years went by thus--three springs--three vintages--three winters--till, weary of wandering, I began to ask myself "what next?" My old passion for books had, in the meantime, re-asserted itself, and I longed once more for quiet. I knew not that my pilgrimage was hopeless. I know that I loved her ever; that I could never forget her; that although the first pangs were past, I yet must bear

"All the aching of heart, the restless, unsatisfied longing,
All the dull, deep pain, and constant anguish of patience!"

I reasoned with myself. I resolved to be stronger--at all events, to be calmer. Exhausted and world-worn, I turned in thought to my native village among the green hills, to my deserted home, and the great solitary study with its busts and bookshelves, and its vista of neglected garden. The rooms where my mother died; where my father wrote; where, as a boy, I dreamed and studied, would at least have memories for me.

Perhaps, silently underlying all these motives, I may at this time already have begun to entertain one other project which was not so much a motive as a hope-- not so much a hope as a half-seen possibility. I had written verses from time to time all my life long, and of late they had come to me more abundantly than ever. They flowed in upon me at times like an irresistible tide; at others they ebbed away for weeks, and seemed as if gone for ever. It was a power over which I had no control, and sought to have none. I never tried to make verses; but, when the inspiration was upon me, I made them, as it were, in spite of myself. My desk was full of them in time--sonnets, scraps of songs, fragments of blank verse, attempts in all sorts of queer and rugged metres--hexameters, pentameters, alcaics, and the like; with, here and there, a dialogue out of an imaginary tragedy, or a translation from some Italian or German poet. This taste grew by degrees, to be a rare and subtle pleasure to me. My rhymes became my companions, and when the interval of stagnation came, I was restless and lonely till it passed away.

At length there came an hour (I was lying, I remember, on a ledge of turf on a mountain-side, overlooking one of the Italian valleys of the Alps), when I asked myself for the first time--

"Am I also a poet?"

I had never dreamed of it, never thought of it, never even hoped it, till that moment. I had scribbled on, idly, carelessly, out of what seemed a mere facile impulse, correcting nothing; seldom even reading what I had written, after it was committed to paper. I had sometimes been pleased with a melodious cadence or a happy image--sometimes amused with my own flow of thought and readiness of versification; but that I, simple Basil Arbuthnot, should be, after all, enriched with this splendid gift of song--was it mad presumption, or were these things proof? I knew not; but lying on the parched grass of the mountain-side, I tried the question over in my mind, this way and that, till "my heart beat in my brain," How should I come at the truth? How should I test whether this opening Paradise was indeed Eden, or only the mirage of my fancy--mere sunshine upon sand? We all write verses at some moment or other in our lives, even the most prosaic amongst us--some because they are happy; some because they are sad; some because the living fire of youth impels them, and they must be up and doing, let the work be what it may.

> "Many fervent souls,
> Strike rhyme on rhyme, who would strike steel on steel,
> If steel had offer'd."

Was this case mine? Was I fancying myself a poet, only because I was an idle man, and had lost the woman I loved? To answer these questions myself was impossible. They could only be answered by the public voice, and before I dared question that oracle I had much to do. I resolved to discipline myself to the harness of rhythm. I resolved to go back to the fathers of poetry--to graduate once again in Homer and Dante, Chaucer and Shakespeare. I promised myself that, before I tried my wings in the sun, I would be my own severest critic. Nay, more--that I would never try them so long as it seemed possible a fall might come of it. Once come to this determination, I felt happier and more hopeful than I had felt for the last three years. I looked across the blue mists of the valley below, and up to the aerial peaks which rose, faint, and far, and glittering--mountain beyond mountain, range above range, as if painted on the thin, transparent air--and it seemed to me that they stood by, steadfast and silent, the witnesses of my resolve.

"I will be strong," I said. "I will be an idler and a dreamer no longer. Books have been my world. I have taken all, and given nothing. Now I too will work, and work to prove that I was not unworthy of her love."

Going down, by-and-by, into the valley as the shadows were lengthening, I met a traveller with an open book in his hand. He was an Englishman--small, sallow, wiry, and wore a gray, loose coat, with two large pockets full of books. I had met him once before at Milan, and again in a steamer on Lago Maggiore. He was always reading. He read in the diligence--he read when he was walking--he read all through dinner at the *tables-d'-hote*. He had a mania for reading; and, might, in fact, be said to be bound up in his own library.

Meeting thus on the mountain, we fell into conversation. He told me that he was on his way to Geneva, that he detested continental life, and that he was only waiting the arrival of certain letters before starting for England.

"But," said I, "you do not, perhaps, give continental life a trial. You are always absorbed in the pages of a book; and, as for the scenery, you appear not to observe it."

"Deuce take the scenery!" he exclaimed, pettishly. "I never look at it. All scenery's alike. Trees, mountains, water--water, mountains, trees; the same thing over and over again, like the bits of colored glass in a kaleidoscope. I read about the scenery, and that is quite enough for me."

"But no book can paint an Italian lake or an Alpine sunset; and when one is on the spot...."

"I beg your pardon," interrupted the traveller in gray. "Everything is much pleasanter and more picturesque in books than in reality--travelling especially. There are no bad smells in books. There are no long bills in books. Above all, there are no mosquitoes. Travelling is the greatest mistake in the world, and I am going home as fast as I can."

"And henceforth, I suppose, your travels will be confined to your library," I said, smiling.

"Exactly so. I may say, with Hazlitt, that 'food, warmth, sleep, and a book,' are all I require. With those I may make the tour of the world, and incur neither expense nor fatigue."

"Books, after all, are friends," I said, with a sigh.

"Sir," replied the traveller, waving his hand somewhat theatrically, "books are our first real friends, and our last. I have no others. I wish for no others. I rely upon no others. They are the only associates upon whom a sensible man may depend. They are always wise, and they are always witty. They never intrude upon us when we desire to be alone. They never speak ill of us behind our backs. They are never capricious, and never surly; neither are they, like some clever folks, pertinaciously silent when we most wish them to shine. Did Shakespeare ever refuse his best thoughts to us, or Montaigne decline to be companionable? Did you ever find Moliere dull? or Lamb prosy? or Scott unentertaining?"

"You remind me," said I, laughing, "of the student in Chaucer, who desired for his only pleasure and society,

"'---at his bedde's head
A'twenty bokes clothed in black and red,
Of Aristotle and his philosophy!'"

"Ay," replied my new acquaintance, "but he preferred them expressly to 'robes riche, or fidel or sautrie,' whereas, I prefer them to men and women, and to Aristotle and his philosophy, into the bargain!"

"Your own philosophy, at least, is admirable," said I. "For many a year--I might almost say for most years of my life--I have been a disciple in the same school."

"Sir, you cannot belong to a better. Think of the convenience of always carrying half a dozen intimate friends in your pocket! Good-afternoon."

We had now come to a point where two paths diverged, and the reading traveller, always economical of time, opened his book where he had last turned down the leaf, and disappeared round the corner.

I never saw him again; but his theory amused me, and, as trifles will sometimes do even in the gravest matters, decided me. So the result of all my hopes and reflections was, that I went back to England and to the student life that had been the dream of my youth.

CHAPTER LV.
MY BIRTHDAY.

Three years of foreign travel, and five of retirement at home, brought my twenty-ninth birthday. I was still young, it is true; but how changed from that prime of early manhood when I used to play Romeo at midnight to Hortense upon her balcony! I looked at myself in the glass that morning, and contemplated the wearied, bronzed, and bearded face which

"...seared by toil and something touched by time,"

now gave me back glance for glance. I looked older than my age by many years. My eyes had grown grave with a steadfast melancholy, and streaks of premature silver gleamed here and there in the still abundant hair which had been the solitary vanity of my youth.

"Is she also thus changed and faded?" I asked myself, as I turned away. And then I sighed to think that if we met she might not know me.

For I loved her still; worshipped her; raised altars to her in the dusky chambers of my memory. My whole life was dedicated to her. My best thoughts were hers. My poems, my ambition, my hours of labor, all were hers only! I knew now that no time could change the love which had so changed me, or dim the sweet remembrance of that face which I carried for ever at my heart like an amulet. Other women might be fair, but my eyes never sought them; other voices might be sweet, but my ear never listened to them; other hands might be soft, but my lips never pressed them. She was the only woman in all my world--the only star in all my night--the one Eve of my ruined Paradise. In a word, I loved her--loved her, I think, more dearly than before I lost her.

"Love is not love
Which alters when it alteration finds,
Or bends with the remover to remove:
O no! it is an ever-fixed mark,
That looks on tempests and is never shaken."

I had that morning received by post a parcel of London papers and magazines, which, for a foolish reason of my own, I almost dreaded to open; so, putting off the evil hour, I thrust the ominous parcel into my pocket and went out to read it in some green solitude, far away among the lonely hills and tracts of furzy common that extend for miles and miles around my native place. It was a delicious autumn morning, bright and fresh and joyous as spring. The purple heather was all abloom along the slopes of the hill-sides. The golden sandcliffs glittered in the sun. The great firwoods reached away over heights and through valleys--"grand and spiritual trees," pointing ever upward with warning finger, like the Apostles in the old Italian pictures. Now I passed a solitary farm-yard where busy laborers were piling the latest stacks; now met a group of happy children gathering wild nuts and blackberries. By-and-by, I came upon a great common, with a picturesque mill standing high against the sky. All around and about stretched a vast prospect of woodland and tufted heath, bounded far off by a range of chalk-hills speckled with farmhouses and villages, and melting towards the west into a distance faint and far, and mystic as the horizon of a Turner.

Here I threw myself on the green turf and rested. Truly, Nature is a great "physician of souls." The peace of the place descended into my heart, and hushed for a while the voice of its repinings. The delicious air, the living silence of the woods, the dreamy influences of the autumnal sunshine, all alike served to lull me into a pleasant mood, neither gay nor sad, but very calm--calm enough for the purpose for which I had come. So I brought out my packet of papers, summoned all my philosophy to my aid, and met my own name upon the second page. For here was, as I had anticipated, a critique on my first volume of poems.

Indifference to criticism, if based upon a simple consciousness of moral right, is a noble thing. But indifference to criticism, taken in its ordinary, and especially its literary sense, is generally a very small thing, and resolves itself, for the most part, into a halting and one-sided kind of stoicism, meaning indifference to blame and ridicule, and never indifference to praise. It is very convenient to the disappointed authorling; very effective, in the established writer; but it is mere vanity at the root, and equally contemptible in both. For my part, I confess that I came to my trial as tremblingly as any poor caitiff to the fiery ordeal, and finding myself miraculously clear of the burning ploughshares, was quite as full of wonder and thankfulness at my good fortune. For I found my purposes appreciated, and my best thoughts understood; not, it is true, without some censure, but it was censure tempered so largely with encouragement that I drew hope from it, and not despondency. And then I thought of Hortense, and, picturing to myself all the joy it would have been to lay these things at her feet, I turned my face to the grass, and wept like a child.

Then, one by one, the ghosts of my dead hopes rose out of the grave of the past and vanished "into thin air" before me; and in their place came earnest aspirations, born of the man's strong will. I resolved to use wisely the gifts that were mine--to sing well the song that had risen to my lips--to "seize the spirit of my time," and turn to noble uses the God-given weapons of the poet. So should I be worthier of her remembrance, if she yet remembered me--worthier, at all events, to remember her.

Thus the hours ebbed, and when I at length rose and turned my face home-ward, the golden day was already bending westward. Lower and lower sank the sun as the miles shortened; stiller and sweeter grew the evening air; and ever my lengthening shadow travelled before me along the dusty road--wherein I was more fortunate than the man in the German story who sold his to the devil.

It was quite dusk by the time I gained the outskirts of the town, and I reflected with much contentment upon the prospect of a cosy bachelor dinner, and, after dinner, lamplight and a book.

"If you please, sir," said Collins, "a lady has been here."

Collins--the same Collins who had been my father's servant when I was a boy at home--was now a grave married man, with hair fast whitening.

"A lady?" I echoed. "One of my cousins, I suppose, from Effingham."

"No, sir," said Collins. "A strange lady--a foreigner."

A stranger! a foreigner! I felt myself change color.

"She left her name?" I asked.

"Her card, sir," said Collins, and handed it to me.

I took it up with fingers that shook in spite of me and read:--

MADLLE DE SAINTE AULAIRE.

I dropped the card, with a sigh of profound disappointment.

"At what time did this lady call, Collins?"

"Not very long after you left the house, sir. She said she would call again. She is at the White Horse."

"She shall not have the trouble of coming here," I said, drawing my chair to the table. "Send James up to the White Horse with my compliments, and say that I will wait upon the lady in about an hour's time."

Collins darted away to despatch the message, and returning presently with the pale ale, uncorked it dexterously, and stood at the side-board, serenely indifferent.

"And what kind of person was this--this Mademoiselle de Sainte Aulaire, Collins?" I asked, leisurely bisecting a partridge.

"Can't say, sir, indeed. Lady kept her veil down."

"Humph! Tall or short, Collins?"

"Rather tall, sir."

"Young?"

"Haven't an idea, sir. Voice very pleasant, though."

A pleasant voice has always a certain attraction for me. Hortense's voice was exquisite--rich and low, and somewhat deeper than the voices of most women.

I took up the card again. Mademoiselle de Sainte Aulaire! Where had I heard that name?

"She said nothing of the nature of her business, I suppose, Collins?"

"Nothing at all, sir. Dear me, sir, I beg pardon for not mentioning it before; but there's been a messenger over from the White Horse, since the lady left, to know if you were yet home."

"Then she is in haste?"

"Very uncommon haste, I should say, sir," replied Collins, deliberately.

I pushed back the untasted dish, and rose directly.

"You should have told me this before," I said, hastily.

"But--but surely, sir, you will dine--"

"I will wait for nothing," I interrupted. "I'll go at once. Had I known the lady's business was urgent, I would not have delayed a moment."

Collins cast a mournful glance at the table, and sighed respect fully. Before he had recovered from his amazement, I was half way to the inn.

The White Horse was now the leading hostelry of Saxonholme. The old Red Lion was no more. Its former host and hostess were dead; a brewery occupied its site; and the White Horse was kept by a portly Boniface, who had been head-waiter under the extinct dynasty. But there had been many changes in Saxonholme since my boyish days, and this was one of the least among them.

I was shown into the best sitting-room, preceded by a smart waiter in a white neckcloth. At a glance I took in all the bearings of the scene--the table with its un-tasted dessert; the shaded lamp; the closed curtains of red damask; the thoughtful figure in the easy chair. Although the weather was yet warm, a fire blazed in the grate; but the windows were open behind the crimson curtains, and the evening air stole gently in. It was like stepping into a picture by Gerard Dow, so closed, so glowing, so rich in color.

"Mr. Arbuthnot," said the smart waiter, flinging the door very wide open, and lingering to see what might follow.

The lady rose slowly, bowed, waved her hand towards a chair at some distance from her own, and resumed her seat. The waiter reluctantly left the room.

"I had not intended, sir, to give you the trouble of coming here," said Made-moiselle de Sainte Aulaire, using her fan as a handscreen, and speaking in a low, and, as it seemed to me, a somewhat constrained voice. I could not see her face, but something in the accent made my heart leap.

"Pray do not name it, madam," I said. "It is nothing."

She bent her head, as if thanking me, and went on:--

"I have come to this place," she said, "in order to prosecute certain inquiries which are of great importance to myself. May I ask if you are a native of Saxon-holme?"

"I am."

"Were you here in the year 18--?"

"I was."

"Will you give me leave to test your memory respecting some events that took place about that time?"

"By all means."

Mademoiselle de Sainte Aulaire thanked me with a gesture, withdrew her chair still farther from the radius of the lamp and the tire, and said:--

"I must entreat your patience if I first weary you with one or two particulars of my family history,"

"Madam, I listen."

During the brief pause that ensued, I tried vainly to distinguish something more of her features. I could only trace the outline of a slight and graceful figure, the contour of a very slender hand, and the ample folds of a dark silk dress.

At length, in a low, sweet voice, she began:--

"Not to impose upon you any dull genealogical details," she said, "I will begin by telling you that the Sainte Aulaires are an ancient French family of Bearnais extraction, and that my grandfather was the last Marquis who bore the title. Holding large possessions in the *comtat* of Venaissin (a district which now forms part of the department of Vaucluse) and other demesnes at Montlhery, in the province of the Ile de France---"

"At Montlhery!" I exclaimed, suddenly recovering the lost link in my memory.

"The Sainte Aulaires," continued the lady, without pausing to notice my interruption, "were sufficiently wealthy to keep up their social position, and to contract alliances with many of the best families in the south of France. Towards the early part of the reign of Louis XIII. they began to be conspicuous at court, and continued to reside in and near Paris up to the period of the Revolution. Marshals of France, Envoys, and Ministers of State during a period of nearly a century and a half, the Sainte Aulaires had enjoyed too many honors not to be among the first of those who fell in the Reign of Terror. My grandfather, who, as I have already said, was the last Marquis bearing the title, was seized with his wife and daughter at his Chateau near Montlhery in the spring-time of 1793, and carried to La Force. Thence, after a mock trial, they were all three conveyed to execution, and publicly guillotined on the sixth of June in the same year. Do you follow me?"

"Perfectly."

"One survivor, however, remained in the person of Charles Armand, Prevot de Sainte Aulaire, only son of the Marquis, then a youth of seventeen years of age, and pursuing his studies in the seclusion of an old family seat in Vaucluse. He fled into

Italy. In the meantime, his inheritance was confiscated; and the last representative of the race, reduced to exile and beggary, assumed another name. It were idle to attempt to map out his life through the years that followed. He wandered from land to land; lived none knew how; became a tutor, a miniature-painter, a volunteer at Naples under General Pepe, a teacher of languages in London, corrector of the press to a publishing house in Brussels--everything or anything, in short, by which he could honorably earn his bread. During these years of toil and poverty, he married. The lady was an orphan, of Scotch extraction, poor and proud as himself, and governess in a school near Brussels. She died in the third year of their union, and left him with one little daughter. This child became henceforth his only care and happiness. While she was yet a mere infant, he placed her in the school where her mother had been teacher. There she remained, first as pupil, by-and-by as governess, for more than sixteen years. The child was called by an old family name that had been her grandmother's and her great-grandmother's in the high and palmy days of the Sainte Aulaires--Hortense."

"Hortense!" I cried, rising from my chair.

"It is not an uncommon name," said the lady. "Does it surprise you?"

"I--I beg your pardon, madam," I stammered, resuming my seat. "I once had a dear friend of that name. Pray, go on."

"For ten years the refugee contrived to keep his little Hortense in the safe and pleasant shelter of her Flemish home. He led a wandering life, no one knew where; and earned his money, no one knew how. Travel-worn and careworn, he was prematurely aged, and at fifty might well have been mistaken for a man of sixty-five or seventy. Poor and broken as he was, however, Monsieur de Sainte Aulaire was every inch a gentleman of the old school; and his little girl was proud of him, when he came to the school to see her. This, however, was very seldom--never oftener than twice or three times in the year. When she saw him for the last time, Hortense was about thirteen years of age. He looked paler, and thinner, and poorer than ever; and when he bade her farewell, it was as if under the presentiment that they might meet no more. He then told her, for the first time, something of his story, and left with her at parting a small coffer containing his decorations, a few trinkets that had been his mother's, and his sword--the badge of his nobility."

The lady's voice faltered. I neither spoke nor stirred, but sat like a man of stone.

Then she went on again:--

"The father never came again. The child, finding herself after a certain length of time thrown upon the charity of her former instructors, was glad to become under-teacher in their school. The rest of her history may be told in a few words. From under-teacher she became head-teacher, and at eighteen passed as governess into a private family. At twenty she removed to Paris, and set foot for the first time in the land of her fathers. All was now changed in France. The Bourbons reigned again, and her father, had he reappeared, might have reclaimed his lost estates. She sought him far and near. She employed agents to discover him. She could not believe that he was dead. To be once again clasped in his arms--to bring him back to his native country---to see him resume his name and station--this was the bright dream of her life. To accomplish these things she labored in many ways, teaching and writing; for Hortense also was proud--too proud to put forward an unsupported claim. For with her father were lost the title-deeds and papers that might have made the daughter wealthy, and she had no means of proving her identity. Still she labored heartily, lived poorly, and earned enough to push her inquiries far and wide--even to journey hither and thither, whenever she fancied, alas! that a clue had been found. Twice she travelled into Switzerland, and once into Italy, but always in vain. The exile had too well concealed, even from her, his *sobriquet* and his calling, and Hortense at last grew weary of failure. One fact, however, she succeeded in discovering, and only one--namely, that her father had, many years before, made some attempt to establish his claims to the estates, but that he had failed for want either of sufficient proof, or of means to carry on the *proces*. Of even this circumstance only a meagre law-record remained, and she could succeed in learning no more. Since then, a claim has been advanced by a remote branch of the Sainte Aulaire family, and the cause is, even now, in course of litigation."

She paused, as if fatigued by so long talking; but, seeing me about to speak, prevented me with a gesture of the hand, and resumed:--

"Hortense de Ste. Aulaire continued to live in Paris for nearly five years, at the end of which time she left it to seek out the members of her mother's family. Finding them kindly disposed towards her, she took up her abode amongst them in the calm seclusion of a remote Scotch town. There, even there, she still hoped, still employed agents; still yearned to discover, if not her father, at least her father's grave. Several years passed thus. She continued to earn a modest subsistence by her pen, till at length the death of one of those Scotch relatives left her mistress of a small inheritance. Money was welcome, since it enabled her to pursue her task with renewed vigor. She searched farther and deeper. A trivial circumstance eagerly followed up brought a train of other circumstances to light. She discovered that her father had assumed a certain name; she found that the bearer of this name was a wandering man, a conjuror by trade; she pursued the vague traces of his progress from town to town, from county to county, sometimes losing, sometimes regaining the scattered links. Sir, he was my father--I am that Hortense. I have spent my life seeking him--I have lived for this one hope. I have traced his footsteps here to Saxonholme, and here the last clue fails. If you know anything--if you can remember anything---"

Calm and collected as she had been at first, she was trembling now, and her voice died away in sobs. The firelight fell upon her face--upon the face of my lost love!

I also was profoundly agitated.

"Hortense," I said, "do you not know, that he who stood beside your father in his last hour, and he who so loved you years ago, are one and the same? Alas! why did you not tell me these things long since?"

"Did *you* stand beside my father's deathbed?" she asked brokenly.

"I did."

She clasped her hands over her eyes and shuddered, as if beneath the pressure of a great physical pain.

"O God!" she murmured, "so many years of denial and suffering! so many years of darkness that might have been dispelled by a word!"

We were both silent for a long time. Then I told her all that I remembered of her father; how he came to Saxonholme--how he fell ill--how he died, and was buried. It was a melancholy recital; painful for me to relate--painful for her to hear--and interrupted over and over again by questions and tears, and bursts of unavailing sorrow.

"We will visit his grave to-morrow," I said, when all was told.

She bent her head.

"To-morrow, then," said she, "I end the pilgrimage of years."

"And--and afterwards?" I faltered.

"Afterwards? Alas! friend, when the hopes of years fall suddenly to dust and ashes, one feels as if there were no future to follow?"

"It is true," I said gloomily. "I know it too well."

"You know it?" she exclaimed, looking up.

"I know it, Hortense. There was a moment in which all the hope, and the fulness, and the glory of my life went down at a blow. Have you not heard of ships that have gone to the bottom in fair weather, suddenly, with all sail set, and every hand on board?"

She looked at me with a strange earnestness in her eyes, and sighed heavily.

"What have you been doing all this time, fellow-student?" she asked, after a pause.

The old name sounded very sweet upon her lips!

"I? Alas!--nothing."

"But you are a surgeon, are you not?"

"No. I never even went up for examination. I gave up all idea of medicine as a profession when my father died."

"What are you, then?"

"An idler upon the great highway--a book-dreamer--a library fixture."

Hortense looked at me thoughtfully, with her cheek resting on her hand.

"Have you done nothing but read and dream?"

"Not quite. I have travelled."

"With what object?"

"A purely personal one. I was alone and unhappy, and--"

"And fancied that purposeless wandering was better for you than healthy labor. Well, you have travelled, and you have read books. What more?"

"Nothing more, except--"

"Except what?"

I chanced to have one of the papers in my pocket, and so drew it out, and placed it before her.

"I have been a rhymer as well as a dreamer," I said, shyly. "Perhaps the rhymes grew out of the dreams, as the dreams themselves grew out of something else which has been underlying my life this many a year. At all events I have hewn a few of them into shape, and trusted them to paper and type--and here is a critique which came to me this morning with some three or four others."

She took the paper with a smile half of wonder, half of kindness, and, glancing quickly through it, said:--

"This is well. This is very well. I must read the book. Will you lend it to me?"

"I will give it to you," I replied; "if I can give you that which is already yours."

"Already mine?"

"Yes, as the poet in me, however worthless, is all and only yours! Do you suppose, Hortense, that I have ever ceased to love you? As my songs are born of my sorrow, so my sorrow was born of my love; and love, and sorrow, and song, such as they are, are of your making."

"Hush!" she said, with something of her old gay indifference. "Your literary sins must not be charged upon me, fellow-student! I have enough of my own to answer for. Besides, I am not going to acquit you so easily. Granted that you have written a little book of poetry--what then? Have you done nothing else? Nothing active? Nothing manly? Nothing useful?"

"If by usefulness and activity you mean manual labor, I certainly have neither felled a tree, nor ploughed a field, nor hammered a horse-shoe. I have lived by thought alone."

"Then I fear you have lived a very idle life," said Hortense, smiling. "Are you married?"

"Married!" I echoed, indignantly. "How can you ask the question?"

"You are not a magistrate?"

"Certainly not."

"In short, then, you are perfectly useless. You play no part, domestic or public. You serve neither the state nor the community. You are a mere cypher--a makeweight in the social scale--an article of no value to any one except the owner."

"Not even the latter, mademoiselle," I replied, bitterly. "It is long since I have ceased to value my own life."

She smiled again, but her eyes this time were full of tears.

"Nay," said she, softly, "am I not the owner?"

*   *   *   *   *

Great joys at first affect us like great griefs. We are stunned by them, and know not how deep they are till the night comes with its solemn stillness, and we are alone with our own hearts. Then comes the season of thankfulness, and wonder and joy. Then our souls rise up within us, and chant a hymn of praise; and the great vault of Heaven is as the roof of a mighty cathedral studded with mosaics of golden stars, and the night winds join in with the bass of their mighty organ-pipes; and the poplars rustle, like the leaves of the hymn-books in the hands of the congregation.

So it was with me that evening when I went forth into the quiet fields where the summer moon was shining, and knew that Hortense was mine at last--mine now and for ever. Overjoyed and restless, I wandered about for hours. I could not go home. I felt I must breathe the open air of the hills, and tread the dewy grass, and sing my hymn of praise and thanksgiving after my own fashion. At length, as the dawning light came widening up the east, I turned my steps homewards, and before the sun had risen above the farthest pine-ridge, I was sleeping the sweetest sleep that had been mine for years.

The conjuror's grave was green with grass and purple with wild thyme when Hortense knelt beside it, and there consummated the weary pilgrimage of half a life. The sapling willow had spread its arms above him in a pleasant canopy, leaning farther and reaching higher, year by year,

"And lo! the twig to which they laid his head had now become a tree!"

Hortense found nothing of her father but this grave. Papers and title-deeds there were none.

I well remembered the anxious search made thirteen years ago, when not even a card was found to indicate the whereabouts of his friends or family. Not to lose the vestige of a chance, we pushed inquiry farther; but in vain. Our rector, now a very old man, remembered nothing of the wandering lecturer. Mine host and hostess of the Red Lion were both dead. The Red Lion itself had disappeared, and become a thing of tradition. All was lost and forgotten; and of all her hereditary wealth, station, and honors, Hortense de Sainte Aulaire retained nothing but her father's sword and her ancestral name.

--Not even the latter for many weeks, O discerning reader! for before the golden harvest was gathered in, we two were wedded.

CHAPTER LVI.
BRINGETH THIS TRUE STORY TO AN END.

Ye who have traced the pilgrim to the scene
Which is his last, if in your memories dwell
A thought that once was his, if on ye swell
A single recollection, not in vain
He wore his sandal shoon and scallop-shell.
                              BYRON.

Having related the story of my life as it happened, incident by incident, and brought it down to that point at which stories are wont to end, I find that I have little to add respecting others. My narrative from first to last has been purely personal. The one love of my life was Hortense--the one friend of my life, Oscar Dalrymple. The catalogue of my acquaintances would scarcely number so many names as I have fingers on one hand. The two first are still mine; the latter, having been brought forward only in so far as they re-acted upon my feelings or modified my experiences, have become, for the most part, mere memories, and so vanish, ghost-like, from the page. Franz Mueller is studying in Rome, having carried off a prize at the Ecole des Beaux Arts, which entitles him to three years at the Villa Medici, that Ultima Thule of the French art-student's ambition. I hear that he is as full of whim and jest as ever, and the very life of the Cafe Greco. May I some day hear his pleasant laugh again! Dr. Cheron, I believe, is still practising in Paris; and Monsieur de Simoncourt, I have no doubt, continues to exercise the profession of Chevalier d'Industrie, with such failures and successes as are incidental to that career.

As for my early *amourettes*, they have disappeared from my path as utterly as though they had never crossed it. Of Madame de Marignan, I have neither heard, nor desired to hear, more. Even Josephine's pretty face is fast fading from my memory. It is ever thus with the transient passions of *our premiere jeunesse.* We believe in them for the moment, and waste laughter and tears, chaplets and sackcloth, upon them. Presently the delusion passes; the earnest heart within us is awakened; and we know that till now we have been mere actors in "a masquerade of dreams." The chaplets were woven of artificial flowers. The funeral was a mock funeral--the banquet a stage feast of painted fruits and empty goblets! Alas! we cannot undo that foolish past. We may only hope to blot it out with after records of high, and wise, and tender things. Thus it is that the young man's heart is like the precious palimpsest of old. He first of all defiles it with idle anacreontics in praise of love and wine; but, erasing these by-and-by with his own pious hand, he writes it over afresh with chronicles of a pure and holy passion, and dedicates it to the fair saint of all his orisons.

Dalrymple and his wife are now settled in Italy, having purchased a villa in the neighborhood of Spezzia, where they live in great retirement. In their choice of such retirement they are influenced by more than one good reason. In the first place, the death of the Vicomte de Caylus was an event likely to be productive of many unpleasant consequences to one who had deprived the French government of so distinguished an officer. In the next, Dalrymple is a poor man, and his wife is no longer rich; so that Italy agrees with their means as well as with their tastes. Lastly, they love each other so well that they never weary of their solitude, nor care to barter away their blue Italian skies and solemn pine-woods for the glittering unrest of society.

Fascinated by Dalrymple's description of his villa and the life he led in it, Hortense and I made up our minds some few weeks after our marriage, to visit that part of Italy--perhaps, in case we were much pleased with it, to settle there, for at least a few years. So I prepared once more to leave my father's house; this time to let it, for I knew that I should never live in it again.

It took some weeks to clear the old place out. The thing was necessary; yet I felt as if it were a kind of sacrilege. To disturb the old dust upon the library-shelves and select such books as I cared to keep; to sort and destroy all kinds of hoarded papers; to ransack desks that had never been unlocked since the hands that last closed them were laid to rest for ever, constituted my share of the work. Hortense superintended the rest. As for the household goods, we resolved to keep nothing, save a few old family portraits and my father's plate, some of which had descended to us through two or three centuries.

While yet in this unsettled state, with the house all in confusion and the time appointed for our journey drawing nearer and nearer day by day, a strange thing happened.

At the end of the garden, encroaching partly upon a corner of it, and opening into the lane that bounded it on the other side of the hedge, stood the stable belonging to the house.

It had been put to no use since my father's time, and was now so thoroughly out of repair that I resolved to have it pulled down and rebuilt before letting it to strangers. In the meantime, I went down there one morning with a workman before the work of demolition was begun.

We had some difficulty to get in, for the lock and hinges were rusted, and the floor within was choked with fallen rubbish. At length we forced an entrance. I thought I had never seen a more dreary interior. My father's old chaise was yet standing there, with both wheels off. The mouldy harness was dropping to pieces on the walls. The beams were festooned with cobwebs. The very ladder leading to the loft above was so rotten that I scarcely dared trust to it for a footing.

Having trusted to it, however, I found myself in a still more ruinous and dreary hole. The posts supporting the roof were insecure; the tiles were all displaced overhead; and the rafters showed black and bare against the sky in many places. In one corner lay a heap of mouldy straw, and at the farther end, seen dimly through the darkness, a pile of old lumber, and--by Heaven! the pagoda-canopy of many colors, and the little Chevalier's Conjuring Table!

I could scarcely believe my eyes. My poor Hortense! Here, at last, were some relics of her father; but found in how strange a place, and by how strange a chance!

I had them dragged out into the light, all mildewed and cob-webbed as they were; whereupon an army of spiders rushed out in every direction, a bat rose up, shrieking, and whirled in blind circles overhead. In a corner of the pagoda we found an empty bird's-nest. The table was small, and could be got out without much difficulty; so I helped the workman to carry it down the ladder, and sending it on before me to the house, sauntered back through the glancing shadows of the acacia-leaves, musing upon the way in which these long-forgotten things had been brought to light, and wondering how they came to be stored away in my own stable.

"Do you know anything about it, Collins?" I said, coming up suddenly behind him in the hall.

"About what, sir?" asked that respectable servant, looking round with some perplexity, as if in search of the nominative.

I pointed to the table, now being carried into the dismantled dining-room.

Collins smiled--he had a remarkably civil, apologetic way of smiling behind his hand, as if it were a yawn or a liberty.

"Oh, sir," said he, "don't you remember? To be sure, you were quite a young gentleman at that time--but---"

"But what?" I interrupted, impatiently.

"Why, sir, that table once belonged to a poor little conjuring chap who called himself Almond Pudding, and died...."

I checked him with a gesture.

"I know all that," I said, hastily. "I remember it perfectly; but how came the things into my stable?"

"Your respected father and my honored master, sir, had them conveyed there when the Red Lion was sold off," said Collins, with a sidelong glance at the dining-room door. "He was of opinion, sir, that they might some day identify the poor man to his relatives, in case of inquiry."

I heard the sound of a suppressed sob, and, brushing past him without another word, went in and closed the door.

"My own Hortense!" I said, taking her into my arms. "My wife!"

Pale and tearful, she lifted her face from my shoulder, and pointed to the table.

"I know what it is," she faltered. "You need not tell me. My heart tells me!"

I led her to a chair, and explained how and where it had been found. I even told her of the little empty nest from which the young birds had long since flown away. In this tiny incident there was something pathetic that soothed her; so, presently, when she left off weeping, we examined the table together.

It was a quaint, fragile, ricketty thing, with slender twisted legs of black wood, and a cloth-covered top that had once been green, but now retained no vestige of its original color. This cloth top was covered with slender slits of various shapes and sizes, round, square, sexagonal, and so forth, which, being pressed with the finger, fell inwards and disclosed little hiding-places sunk in the well of the table; but which, as soon as the pressure was removed, flew up again by means of concealed springs, and closed as neatly as before.

"This is strange," said Hortense, peering into one of the recesses. "I have found something in the table! Look--it is a watch!"

I snatched it from her, and carried it to the window. Blackened and discolored as it was, I recognised it instantly.

It was my own watch--my own watch of which I was so boyishly vain years and years ago, and which I had lost so unaccountably on the night of the Chevalier's performance! There were my initials engraved on the back, amid a forest of flourishes, and there on the dial was that identical little Cupid with the cornucopia of flowers, which I once thought such a miracle of workmanship! Alas! what a mighty march old Time had stolen upon me, while that little watch was standing still!

"Oh, Heaven!--oh, husband!"

Startled from my reverie more by the tone than the words, I turned and saw Hortense with a packet of papers in her hand--old, yellow, dusty papers, tied together with a piece of black ribbon.

"I found them there--there--there!" she faltered, pointing to a drawer in the table which I now saw for the first time. "I chanced to press that little knob, and the drawer flew out. Oh, my dear father!--see, Basil, here are his patents of nobility-- here is the certificate of my birth--here are the title-deeds of the manor of Sainte Aulaire! This alone was wanted to complete our happiness!"

"We will keep the table, Hortense, all our lives!" I explained, when the first agitation was past.

"As sacredly," replied she, "as it kept this precious secret!"

*   *   *   *   *

My task is done. Here on my desk lies the piled-up manuscript which has been my companion through so many pleasant hours. Those hours are over now. I may lay down my pen, and put aside the whispering vine-leaves from my casement, and lean out into the sweet Italian afternoon, as idly as though I wore to the climate and the manner born.

The world to-day is only half awake. The little white town, crouched down by the "beached margent" of the bay, winks with its glittering windows and dozes in the sunshine. The very cicalas are silent. The fishermen's barques, with their wing-like sails all folded to rest, rock lazily at anchor, like sea-birds asleep. The cork-trees nod languidly to each other; and not even yonder far-away marble peaks are more motionless than that cloud which hangs like a white banner in the sky. Hush! I can almost believe that I hear the drowsy washing of the tide against the ruined tower on the beach.

And this is the bay of Spezzia--the lovely, treacherous bay of Spezzia, where our English Shelley lost his gentle life! How blue those cruel waters are to-day! Bluer, by Heaven! than the sky, with scarce a ripple setting to the shore.

We are very happy in our remote Italian home. It stands high upon a hill-side, and looks down over a slope of silvery olives to the sea. Vineyard and orange grove, white town, blue bay, and amber sands lie mapped out beneath our feet. Not a fe-lucca "to Spezzia bound from Cape Circella" can sail past without our observation.

"Not a sun can die, nor yet be born, unseen
By dwellers at my villa."

Nay, from this very window, one might almost pitch an orange into the empty vettura standing in the courtyard of the Croce di Malta!

Then we have a garden--a wild, uncultured place, where figs and lemons, ol-ives "blackening sullen ripe," and prickly aloes flourish in rank profusion, side by side; and a loggia, where we sit at twilight drinking our Chianti wine and listening to the nightingales; and a study looking out on the bay through a trellis of vine-leaves, where we read and write together, surrounded by our books. Here, also, just opposite my desk, hangs Mueller's copy of that portrait of the Marquise de Sainte Aulaire, which I once gave to Hortense, and which is now my own again. How of-ten I pause upon the unturned page, how often lay my pen aside, to look from the painting to the dear, living face beneath it! For there she sits, day after day, my wife! my poet! with the side-light falling on her hair, and the warm sea-breezes stirring the soft folds of her dress. Sometimes she lifts her eyes, those wondrous eyes, luminous from within "with the light of the rising soul"--and then we talk awhile of our work, or of our love, believing ever that

"Our work shall still be better for our love,
And still our love be sweeter for our work."

Perhaps the original of that same painting in the study may yet be ours some day, with the old chateau in which it hangs, and all the broad lands belonging thereunto. Our claim has been put forward some time now, and our lawyers are confident of success. Shall we be happier, if that success is ours? Can rank add one grace, or wealth one pleasure, to a life which is already so perfect? I think not, and there are moments when I almost wish that we may never have it in our power to test the question.

But stay! the hours fly past. The sun is low, and the tender Italian twilight will soon close in. Then, when the moon rises, we shall sail out upon the bay in our own tiny felucca; or perhaps go down through the town to that white villa gleaming out above the dark tops of yonder cypresses, and spend some pleasant hours with Dalrymple and his wife. They, too, are very happy; but their happiness is of an older date than ours, and tends to other ends. They have bought lands in the neighborhood, which they cultivate; and they have children whom they adore. To educate these little ones for the wide world lying beyond that blue bay and the far-off mountains, is the one joy, the one care of their lives. Truly has it been said that

"A happy family
Is but an earlier heaven."